REFORGED

REFORGED

SETH HADDON

BLIND
EYE
BOOKS

blindeyebooks.com

Reforged
by Seth Haddon

Published by Blind Eye Books
315 Prospect Street #5393, Bellingham WA 98227
blindeyebooks.com

Edited by Nicole Kimberling
Copyedit by Megan Gendell
Cover Art by Julie Dillon
Book Design & Map by Dawn Kimberling
Page Proof by Zita Porter
Ebook design by Michael DeLuca

Print ISBN: 978-1-956422-00-9
ebook ISBN: 978-1-956422-01-6

Printed in the United States of America

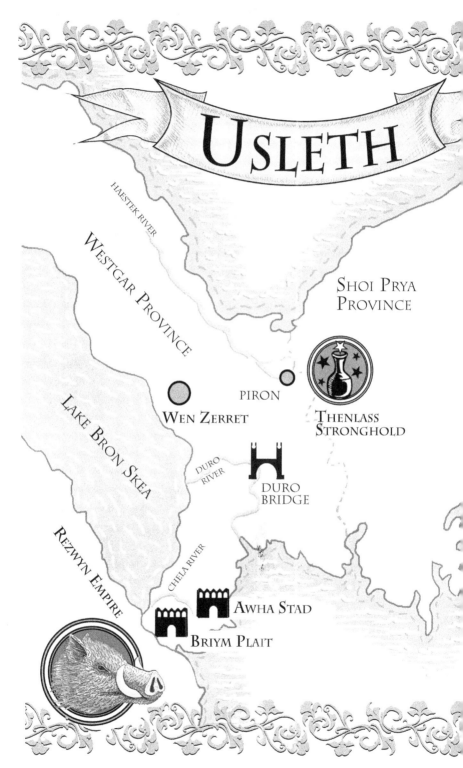

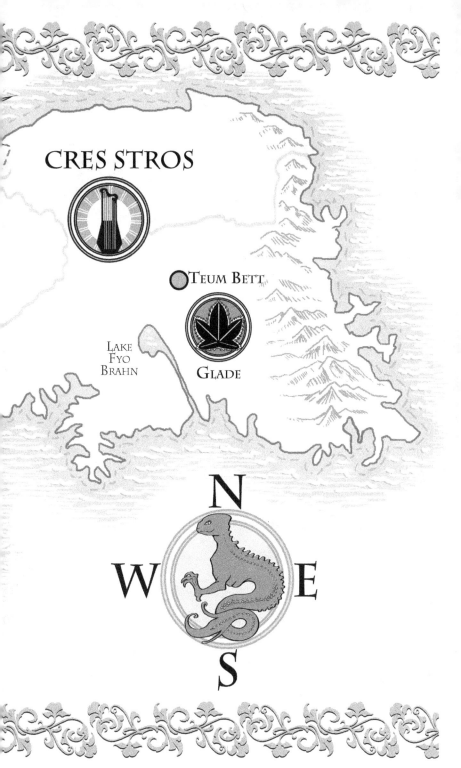

CRES STROS

TEUM BETT

LAKE
FYO
BRAHN

GLADE

N

W

E

S

CHAPTER
ONE

The moon was full and already at its zenith.

He was late.

Paladin Balen cursed under his breath. The conspicuous lack of music made his stomach twist. King Zavrius should have been playing that damned lute-harp by now. Running in full armor through a forest at night, Balen would be lucky if he didn't catch his foot on a root, fall, and break his neck. That would be his luck, dying, stupidly, just before he claimed the most prestigious role in Cres Stros. He needed to focus on the uneven path before him. But how could he?

King Zavrius, and everyone else, was waiting.

Balen's foot slipped in the mulch. He staggered forward in the dark, only righting himself by some miracle. He resolved to push the king from his mind. Always easier in theory. He failed.

Focus. You show up smeared in mud, and Zavrius will be offended.

And Zavrius knew how to hold a grudge.

The winding path straightened. It became a sudden arrow-sharp road cutting through an archway of evergreen trees. The path was lit by torches, their bare flames licking at the balmy air. Balen took a breath and slowed.

The primordial majesty of the Gedrok's Glade opened before him. A massive, ancient and long-dead creature lay slumped in a semicircle at the perimeter of the clearing, forming the northern barrier. These massive beings had been named gedrok after the ancient king who had first harnessed their magical properties. This gedrok possessed a strange, composite quality. The top half resembled a giant, bulky panther, but its lower half tapered away into a lean serpent tail. Its head looked like an earless cat's skull with a fine layer of skin laid over the bone. The rounded head sat tall; at four men high, the creature's glazed, sunken eye could watch the whole glade. Skin covered in off-white and aquamarine scales enfolded long, blood-red tendons and sheathed near-transparent bones. It smelled faintly of brine and oakmoss. Parts of it had been carved away over the years, to create both magical instruments and armor, including Balen's own. Now the creature's rib cage looked brittle and weak. Fat, wild vines wove through places where harvesting the skin had exposed the ribs. The light glinted along Balen's gedrokbone armor as he passed. Flickers of prismatic color split through the darkness.

Balen raised his head proudly to the ancient creature. This was the source of his power. He couldn't help but feel a kinship with it.

On a wooden dais beneath the gedrok's open rib cage, King Zavrius waited.

King Zavrius, fifth heir to the Dued Vuuthrik Dynasty, was a languid vision in the moonlight. He sat sprawled back in a carved wooden throne, tall, lean body stretched out with one leg softly bouncing. At twenty-two, Zavrius somehow managed to have the demeanor of a child and an old man at once. The moonlight turned the shadows on his tawny skin the color of wine. His deep-brown hair had been pulled up away from his face, so Balen had a moment to clock the king's expression. Slight knot in his brow, quirk to his lip. He was making a show of inspecting his fingernails. Balen had known Zavrius for years, and still couldn't be sure what sort of mood he was in.

Not a single soul in the dynasty had ever expected Zavrius to be king, and the tension of their uncertainty about him filled the night air.

Zavrius sat alone on the dais, facing rows and rows of seated nobility and other dignitaries. All of them were dressed in exquisite regalia, but many avoided including the deep mauves and purples Zavrius favored.

As Balen stepped forward into the clearing, a hundred faces turned to glare at him. The nobility wasn't used to waiting. The Paladin grimaced, raising his chin high as he walked. He raked over painted faces and bored expressions, looking for nobles he recognized, eyes hovering on those he didn't.

He spotted three delegates from the Rezwyn Empire in the front and felt his hand twitch instinctively toward his sword. Balen had to suppress a sneer. Two pale men sat either side of a bearlike woman. The men were dressed in cream-colored ceremonial robes. The loose garments fell like sacks over their bodies, but Balen could tell they were brawny beneath them. Fringed head covers obscured their richly beaded hair and faces. Balen suspected these two were priests. Pulled by the severity of the central figure, Balen noted her oddly pale skin and thick, black hair before his eyes caught on the sash that signified her as the Rezwyn ambassador. Balen spotted the strange symbol of the empire's war god emblazoned on her cuirass—the twisted, open maw of a human-boar crossbreed roaring at the sky. It was provocative, but not as provocative as their faces; all of them sported different derivations of the wartime paint the Rezwyns wore on the field. For a group of diplomats, it was jarring. But that was the empire for you. And with how tense things were now, it was to be expected.

At the foot of the dais, between the nobles and the king, stood a line of Balen's fellow Paladins. The newest recruits stood stiffly at the center, strikingly unarmored, as they had yet to be confirmed into the order. Balen's peers were positioned alongside them. His senior, Duart, gave him a wink as he went by, but Balen knew not many others enjoyed losing this honor to him. The hard-set jaw of Alick, another senior, made Balen feel his youth like a stone in his belly. Alick's armor was exquisite. Heavy plate crafted from anything else looked bulky, but the gedrok's body made hulking pauldrons and greaves appear sleek and fitted.

Once Balen passed through the line of his fellow Paladins, he could ignore his king no longer.

Zavrius sat with his lute-harp over his lap, watching Balen's every move. It was a stunning, magical instrument. Made from gedrokbone with tendon string, its bowled back was bone white and pearlescent. Streaks of red shot through the ribs like veins.

"Lovely of you to join us." Zavrius pitched his voice just loud enough to reach a few of Balen's Paladin brethren. Balen bristled at that.

Of course. Zavrius would make him a fool just for a laugh. But since he'd managed to arrive late for the event he'd dreamed of for years, Balen thought maybe he deserved it.

When he took his place at Zavrius's right hand, the anger turned to nerves.

"I'll make this up to you," Balen said.

Voice lower now, a private whisper from Zavrius: "Does that mean you've had a change of heart?"

Balen's breath stopped short. He glanced over at Zavrius, who was now fixing him with a cold stare. His fidgeting had stopped. The torchlight flickered around them, making Zavrius's eyes glint gold. In them, Balen saw himself with his heart in his throat at seventeen, leaning in for a kiss—a year Zavrius's senior, and three times the bumbling mess he still found himself to be. He blanched. Balen opened his mouth but found no words.

Zavrius raised a dismissive hand, his frown dissolving into a satisfied smirk as his leg resumed its playful bounce.

"Don't make promises you know you won't keep," Zavrius whispered.

Zavrius always managed to throw him off. Balen bristled, momentarily angry at how easily Zavrius got to him. Getting himself involved with the king he was sworn to protect—any half-brained dolt could tell how resuming their old love affair would end.

"Shall I begin?" Zavrius asked, though he didn't wait for anyone to answer.

There was an entire retinue of court musicians that could've opened this ceremony, but the king had insisted it be him alone. Zavrius had said something about the dull, sluggish way they performed—a long rant. Balen suspected the truth was much simpler. Zavrius loved to play. When Sirellius had been king, he rarely got the chance.

Now, he could perform.

The first lilting notes of a lute-harp glided through the glade. Balen, who knew little about music, knew at least this much: Zavrius played beautifully. There was none of the timidness he'd heard from other musicians, where the first notes lurch out of instruments and crawl their way forward. Zavrius's music rose. Balen took in a slow breath and closed his eyes.

At first, Balen thought he'd never heard this song before; that all this was Zavrius gloating, showing off a new composition. But then Zavrius peeled back on the flourish and the melody slipped through. Balen's mouth twitched with a smile. He heard the rhythmic beat of the dynastic anthem, a consistent, marchlike sound that had his new authority pounded into every note. Then, when Zavrius added some musical flourishes, he heard the influence of Zavrius's late mother, Arasne, in the notes. It wasn't that the music was sweet or gentle. Zavrius had stitched one of Arasne's arcane arrangements to the anthem. And since this lute-harp belonged to the late queen, the Paladin felt certain there was some arcane power behind Zavrius's playing now. How else could he explain the wash of calmness and awe that had come over him? A similar, comforted expression appeared on the faces of the nobility. Everyone watched with a shared awe as Zavrius's music urged flame from the torches to break free and float around him. Wisps of fire were shaped into arcane fireflies that fluttered up and illuminated the gedrok's translucent bones.

The sound swelled, swaying between the gedrok's ribs, a mournful elegy, yet triumphant in places. Zavrius was the fifth heir, newly appointed, playing in the miasma following the deaths of the whole royal line. All of that and somehow the music never sounded morose. Always, somehow, slightly reserved.

It took seconds for Balen to register that Zavrius had finished playing. The fireflies flickered out one by one. The music lingered in the glade like it was clutching to life, and the spell behind it faded slowly. Balen struggled to tell when it had vanished completely, which said much about Zavrius's power. He wondered if that should frighten him. But then Balen looked over at the king, saw him tilt his head with a satisfied sigh, and found him . . . beautiful.

Compulsively beautiful. Compelling in a way that being drawn to him was necessary and stopped feeling like it was somehow Balen's choice. This—Zavrius—wasn't something he missed, he told himself. Not the playful snark, nor the private smiles. He had trained too hard for too long to miss someone like him.

"So?" Zavrius whispered.

The Paladin looked down, suddenly interested in his sabatons. Hundreds of eyes were on them. "You know you always play well."

"Sure," Zavrius said, placing the lute-harp delicately on the stage. "But I like to hear you say it."

Zavrius stood and stepped forward, body swaying like a dancer's, and as he opened his arms the glade filled with applause. Balen was vaguely aware that since his ascension, Zavrius's formal appearances as king had been sparse. After the coronation, he'd only made the briefest appearance at the tournament that had won Balen the honor of becoming Prime Paladin. And then . . . nothing. Balen wondered if the nobility took offense to that, or if they liked the mystery. The Paladin looked out into the dark, trying to parse the expressions of their softly lit convocation. Then one man stepped from the line of Paladins and approached the dais—head of the Gifted Paladins, Balen's direct master, Lestr.

Zavrius nodded and the portly man stepped up, walking in a self-assured way that evoked the late Queen Arasne's grace. He looked every inch her brother. Since he was cut off from the royal line by default, Lestr had devoted his energies to making the Paladin order essential.

He stopped before Zavrius, a flat smile on his thin lips.

"Well." Lestr pitched his voice as loud as he could manage. He gestured with one hand toward Zavrius, who, upon realizing this would be the extent of the praise his uncle would offer him, opened his arms to another smattering of applause from the nobility. Zavrius spun on his heels to face Balen, rolling his eyes as he returned to his throne.

"Not even a smile," Zavrius said, sounding pressed. "Your master is impossible to entertain."

Balen suppressed a snort.

"I welcome you all," Lestr began, taking center stage. He cleared his throat, mumbling something incoherent under his breath. At heart, Lestr was a soldier. His speeches never involved much beyond clipped praise and urging the junior Paladins to be glad that they could hold their own in training. At Lestr's signal, four more Paladins began a procession toward the dais, carrying an intricate wooden chest between them.

Lestr continued. "When my sister, our late Queen Arasne, accepted her Prime, it was on the back of her husband's murder at the hands of the Rezwyn Empire."

Bold words. Bold tone to be setting.

Balen glanced sideways at Zavrius. The king shook his head imperceptibly, though Balen caught a twitch at the mention of his mother's name. In the periphery of his vision, the Paladin noted the Rezwyn delegates shifting in affronted discomfort.

But that was Lestr through and through—not a warmonger, not like his brother-in-law, King Sirellius, or most of the royal children, yet angry. Driven. And if the rumors Balen had been hearing were true, Lestr was smart to invoke the name of their dynasty's enemy—even if it upset all attempts at diplomacy. With so much uncertainty around Zavrius, Lestr was angling to rally the aristocracy. What better way than uniting them against a common enemy?

Zavrius clearly felt otherwise. Through a tight smile he sang, "What is your master doing?"

"Give him a chance."

"There are voices in both the dynasty and the empire who call for war between our nations," Lestr said, and Zavrius swore.

Balen steadied himself with a deep breath, suddenly aware of how on edge the nobility was. How divided. He glanced toward his fellow Paladins and wondered, if it came down to it, who would stand where. By the nature of their order, there should have been no doubt about their support of the new king. But such things were easy to promise when the battle wasn't happening.

In the weeks since his coronation, Zavrius had been dubbed everything from listless to uncaring. Balen had had those thoughts himself, had been having them for years. The Paladins were made for glory. He had to remind himself that war wasn't what he wanted. Not when they were weak. He looked once more to the Rezwyn ambassador, a clear paragon of the empire's religious zealotry. The Rezwyns were geared for expansion; the Dued Vuuthriks had prioritized defense. There was no doubt the Rezwyn Empire would crush them.

"It has been a . . . difficult few months. Expectations have, uh . . ." Lestr sighed, clearly struggling to speak around the truth. "Expectations have shifted. The tragedy that befell our great royal line has shocked us. But we still have our king, our dynasty's future."

In the low light, Balen saw many of the assembled nobles turn to whisper to one another.

Lestr pressed on with an awkward cough. He spoke of the Gifted Paladins and their role in protecting the king, briefly thanked the Rezwyn diplomats for their attendance. He then called upon the seven new Paladins to accept their pledges. When he was done, he gestured for the four Paladins who stood by the chest to come forward.

Zavrius' usual catlike smile reemerged on his face as he rose to his feet. "That's our cue as well, I believe."

Balen felt like he was either coming out of, or going into, a great delirium. He flexed his bare hands, palms clammy as he stood face-to-face with Zavrius. When they'd been together as boys, Zavrius had been taller than him. Now the situation was reversed; the new king had to look slightly upward to meet the Paladin's eyes.

Zavrius turned to face him. Balen could have sworn he winked as he said, "On your knees, then."

Balen flashed him a look, frowning at his tone, but he lowered himself to his knees and offered up his bare hands. Zavrius reached for them without hesitation, as if this wasn't the most intimate they'd been in years. Balen exhaled and looked away.

The new king's hands were soft but his fingertips were calloused, as much a mark of his training as Balen's were. They waited as the handlers bumbled around them, placing the chest beside them. Zavrius thumbed at a callous on Balen's forefinger, this strange back and forth that made his mind lurch, but whatever look was on the Paladin's face stopped the motion.

"Balen of the Gifted Paladins," Lestr began. With his name invoked, Balen tried to straighten his spine. "Do you swear to uphold your duty, to protect the king and defend the dynasty even at the cost of your life?"

"I do," Balen said, without really hearing the words. Something swelled in him, made his heart creak and stretch. Then suddenly it was racing, pumping dreamlike ecstasy through him. This was the culmination of his life. This had been brewing since his childhood, since he'd sat on his father's shoulders blinking back the sun. He must have looked elated or . . . exalted. Zavrius squeezed his hand. "I do," he said again, forcefully, this time hearing the words for their true meaning.

"King Zavrius of the Dued Vuuthrik Dynasty, Protector of Cres Stros, do you accept Balen of the Gifted Paladins to be your Prime?"

Zavrius's eyes glinted. "Without question."

"Then it is so." Lestr reached down and opened the chest. The latches sprang up with a loud pop.

Zavrius released Balen's hands slowly, then from the chest, he withdrew a set of gauntlets.

The Paladin's hands twitched involuntarily, betraying his obvious eagerness. Out of the corner of his eye he spotted the same hungry look reflected in his fellow Paladins. They'd all been trained in the same way. Using ichor harvested from the gedroks, Paladins could generate arcane power that they could channel through their weapons. It gave them an edge: more power in a swing, more bite when a blow landed. But if they attempted to use the ichor unprotected, all that magic would burn right through them, hence the development of the Paladins' trademark armor, each piece of which had to be crafted individually from the bones of the gedroks.

Among all armor, these gauntlets were special in that they served as both pieces of armor and weapons.

Unique to the Prime, they were a symbol of rank as well. In truth, none of them knew the true extent of what they could do. But Balen knew he wanted them, had always wanted them. They were beautiful, articulated, and shimmered like pearl.

And when Zavrius slipped one onto each of Balen's hands, he noted they were warm like pearl as well. Balen made a fist, feeling each polished knuckle click and curl. Something arcane flickered at the edge of his vision, like sparks. He startled out of impulse and sat back against his calves.

Zavrius let out a deep, quiet laugh. "Won't you show them off?"

Balen glanced up. Zavrius stooped over him, stray strands of slicked-back hair curling over his forehead.

"More your purview than mine." Balen smiled and turned his hands over to inspect them. "I don't think they're meant for performance."

"Shame." Then, a beat later. "Not even for me?"

Balen paused and met Zavrius's eyes. "Are you asking?"

"I wouldn't ask," Zavrius said slowly, "I would order."

A retort sat on the edge of Balen's tongue, stubborn and weighted, and refused to be spoken. A tight, indignant smile was offered up in its place. Zavrius straightened, looking disappointed.

"Go on." Zavrius gestured to the side, an odd hardness in his eyes. "This is your moment, after all."

Balen wasn't quite sure what he meant until he turned to face those assembled in the glade. Some nobles stood to applaud him, which no doubt upset a few of the others. If it wasn't for the Paladin title, he'd be no one—a pauper.

He flexed his hand again, this time feeling the arcane force unfurling inside him. Odd. Somehow strong. He pushed himself to his feet with a slight smile and walked forward. Zavrius had resumed his sprawl, lute-harp cradled in his lap. He stroked it, eyes locked on Balen with a sudden, intense interest. His left hand was balled into a fist on his thigh, knuckles white.

Nervous for him? Or something else?

Balen dragged his eyes away from Zavrius and refocused.

The gauntlets weren't meant for performance, but they were meant to protect the king, and in this case that meant a show of power. That was what Zavrius wanted him to do, Balen realized, staring down at the expectant congregation. They were fearful. Hungry for assurances. As much as he wanted to believe these people would support Zavrius, Balen knew how many had loved his deceased brother, Theo. These were the nobility who held lands and titles across the dynasty—who had personal armies, and who could turn whole regions against the king.

And for the Rezwyns, this was something else: not a threat, but a promise of arcane strength.

Maybe all that was a stretch. He told himself he was doing this for Zavrius, but he'd craved this display for years. He was Prime Paladin. He caught a few jealous gazes from his brethren and suppressed a smile. Balen raised his arms. Dim light caught the edges of the gauntlets, sending the light spinning. Then he took a breath. His lungs opened and small pockets of arcane energy began to widen, stretch, come to life. Where previously the magic he'd had access to was always capped by the filter of his armor, Balen now felt the full reach of his arcane ability. Power rushed through his forearms, unfettered. Nerves twinged and sparked.

Lightning crackled in the palms of his hands and shot out in snaking waves. A stark white light lit up the glade.

Balen caught the sight of a dozen wide-eyed people staring up at him in awe, and pride swelled in him. He took a knee and slammed a gauntlet to his chest. It sizzled with the contact, sparks glancing off his cuirass as he spoke.

"As Prime Paladin," he said, voice reverberating through the glade, "I will defend this dynasty with my body. I will defend our king to my death. With the power in my blood, the ichor of the gedrok, no empire will fell us. The dynasty will live!"

The oath seemed to buzz through him. His heart thrummed; he meant every word.

Though the diplomats stayed silent, the rest of the convocation responded in turn with applause; a sudden coming together, a rallying under tradition: the king and his Prime.

And when Balen turned, Zavrius was wearing a splitting grin, sparkle in his eyes.

An hour later, Balen found himself backed against the gedrok's thigh, eavesdropping.

He leaned against the gleaming scaled mass that protected the hard muscle beneath it. Warmth radiated from within. The magic was incubated in a way that made the dead thing seem alive. He had his eyes on Zavrius, who was an odd eight or ten paces away on the stage, surrounded by a variety of nobles who all vied for his very limited attention while Zavrius's paternal aunt, Petra, glad-handed them. She was seventy-something and stout, with her thick gray hair pulled up into a beehive bun. She had the same big nose Zavrius had gotten from Sirellius, making her look as severe as Balen knew she could be, even though she was trying to appear sweet and docile to this noble horde. Over and over again, she promised that the king would hold court as soon as he returned to the palace and that he would hear their various woes, complaints and disputes at that time. Zavrius smiled, nodded and remained silent.

Balen kept an eye on them but listened to the group closest to him—his fellow Paladins.

"All I'm saying is no one knows who he is. Not in the way we knew the previous Heir Ascendant or any of his brothers or his sister. We knew Theo and Lysio—we knew Avidia better than Zavrius. And this is—I mean, this is it, isn't it? This is the time you get up and speak to the men and women who will be defending your life, but he's up there with that bloody harp mistaking himself for the entertainment."

Balen shifted his gaze from Zavrius.

Another Paladin spoke. "No need to convince us. He may have been dedicated to war, but at least when Theo was Heir Ascendant he had some direction."

"Zavrius is the king now. We shouldn't be—" a woman hissed nervously.

"He's not our king." A tight silence followed.

"By the gedrok's bones, have some sympathy, Alick," a voice said. Balen thought it might be Duart. "What was I like at twenty-two? What am I like now? He was fifth in line. You can't blame him for not knowing what he's doing. No one thought—"

"It's not good enough," Alick said. A few others murmured their agreement. Then, as if remembering where he was, who he was, "But I'll defend him with my life."

"Of course."

Balen shivered. A cool breeze cut through the warm night.

The conversation shifted to rumors after that: the Rezwyn army milling in the isthmus, seeking to seize control of the gedroks that were unique to their lands. Then came new rumors.

"There's folk missing, too," some newer recruit was saying, hoping to be included in the Paladin camaraderie. "Nobility. Our elites. You can be sure he won't do a thing about that."

People going missing, so-and-so's fifth son or third daughter, aristocrats, trading class, monied elites. Bogus stories, Balen presumed—the Rezwyns darting over enemy lines and stealing people in the night. It's what he expected to hear from nobility, who seemed to fear having nothing to say and believed everyone was out to get them, but now the Paladins were shifting course too.

"They're not missing." It was Frenyur, Balen deduced, by the gruff sound of his voice. He was older than Balen by nearly two decades and well jaded. Definitely bearing a grudge after Balen had put him on his back in the tournament. "People aren't happy. The Dued Vuuthriks are finished after this. You know he's . . ." Frenyur clicked his tongue. "King Zavrius won't have a natural heir. Nothing stable about his rule. We have to be ready . . ."

Balen caught the suggestion, that subtle hitch in Frenyur's breath as he lost his gall to admit that he'd be willing to oppose Zavrius.

Balen narrowed his eyes, feeling torn between a misguided sympathy for the Paladin's complaints and his recently sworn oath to defend the king against any threat. Zavrius was a pain, and when you didn't know him, he was a lazy sod with an attitude problem. He only became tolerable once you learned the language of his humor. But to betray him? To defect? These were Paladins, by the gedroks' sake. Paladins. Protecting the king under any circumstance was in the oath they had all taken.

There was a long silence.

A voice Balen didn't recognize said, "No."

Balen thanked them silently for their loyalty. A few others said the same, a few others said nothing. Either way, Balen wasn't happy about it.

Righteous anger swelled in him. A proper indignation. He pushed himself off the gedrok's thigh to spin around.

Someone grabbed him by the arm.

Balen went stiff. He felt all that brewing anger lose its footing and slip, hurtling into his fingers. The gauntlets crackled.

"Enough of that." It was Lestr, voice low. A full head shorter than Balen, his master stared up at him with a stern gaze. Lestr was stout and had none of his nephew's grace, save for the steadiness in his hands. Balen's eyes shifted to Lestr's grip on his arm. He dragged his eyes to meet Lestr's gaze, cheeks hot, and felt his anger buckle in the face of Lestr's authority.

"Come on." He tugged Balen away. "Let them have their griping and gossip. Trust me. It'll help you with your sanity."

Balen folded his arms against his chest. "Mm."

Lestr blinked. "Listen. You're only twenty-three. It shows."

Balen bristled. Lestr put up a hand to stay him.

"Let them gossip and whine," he said. "And when they're ready, they'll be what they promised. Right now, they're just being people."

Balen wet his lips to speak, and then said nothing. Lestr was right, but it was too hard to say as much. He made a noise instead, a soft grunt of agreement. Lestr slapped him on the back twice, grip tight on his shoulder.

"Good." He squeezed, directing his gaze to Zavrius. "His highness is getting restless. You bundle him up to go and I'll rally a party of Paladins to protect you." Lestr stared at him for a moment too long, then nodded once. He turned and clanked away toward the gedrok's tail at the edge of the clearing.

Balen looked over his shoulder. Zavrius sat strumming his lute-harp so softly the sound didn't carry over the voices of the nobles surrounding him. He looked absolutely miserable. Balen strode up the dais and knelt beside him.

"Are you sad that I was the one to get the standing ovation?"

"Positively vexed." Zavrius smiled slightly, eyes hooded. He glanced over to the retreating figure of Lestr, nodding toward him. "What did he do to you? Scold you for being late?"

"That's your job now, I think."

"Well." Zavrius leaned forward to rest his chin in his palm. "I'm sure you had your reasons."

"Nothing interesting," Balen said flatly. Zavrius raised a brow, and Balen laughed, shaking his head. "Lost track of time."

"Lost track of time," Zavrius repeated. "Load of crap. Your obsession with those gauntlets wouldn't let you do something like 'lose track of time.'"

Balen felt himself tense. He should've known Zavrius would see through him. Still, the lie was out there now. He tried to sound sincere. "It's the truth."

Zavrius's jovial demeanor vanished. "Had your cock in a stable hand, then? Or somewhere even less savory?"

Balen opened his mouth, genuinely shocked. "Here? In the glade?"

"No?" Zavrius crossed his arms. "If you say. But I can't think of any other reason you'd want to lie to me."

Balen was smart enough to know when he was being goaded. He wasn't quite smart enough to avoid taking the bait.

"My cock's whereabouts have nothing to do with you anymore." There was heat in his cheeks now, and with Balen's pale skin, there was no chance he could hide his embarrassment at the vulgar language.

"On the contrary, now that you're my Prime its location could be said to be a matter of dynastic importance," Zavrius said. Balen looked at Zavrius a long while. A snide smirk crept back along his face.

Balen leaned toward him, forgetting for a moment Zavrius was king and that at least a dozen people were watching. "What is your problem? Why do you do that?"

"Why do I—" Zavrius began, just as angry, half out of his throne. Then he collapsed back into it and held up a hand. "I don't know."

This movement seemed to trigger a resurgence in Zavrius's waiting crowd. Before any eager noble stepped onto the dais, Petra intervened. She walked with purpose, shawl held tightly around her shoulders, as she approached the milling crowd.

"Oh, I do apologize, but that's quite enough, I think," Petra said cheerily. A grumble of protest went up, and Petra met it with the same happy expression. "Yes, yes. It's tradition, you know? Once the king and his Prime speak, they must be left alone. It's a private and eons-old ritual. I'm sure I can scrounge up the tome for you, if you'd like to read further on—no? Well. Your loss."

"She's brilliant," Zavrius said quietly, trying to hold back a smile. The nobles moved away, and Petra went with them without another glance back.

Balen wondered in horror if she'd overheard their banter. The number of times they'd uttered the word "cock" in the last few moments made him want to implode.

Zavrius rubbed his forehead and looked up at Balen from underneath his hand. "I'm sorry. So where were you really?"

Balen considered lying again, but only because he felt duped. He missed Zavrius—missed how he'd been when they were younger and sharing a bed, when their form of intimacy was more than cutting quips. What he had been doing wasn't exactly criminal, but he wondered how

Zavrius would take it. He was still reeling from Zavrius's line of questioning.

He sighed. "I really did lose track of time."

"Doing what?"

"Shadowboxing," Balen admitted.

Zavrius couldn't stop his smile. "So you still do that when you're nervous." The idea seemed to please Zavrius. Balen remembered boxing out his anxiety in the courtyard years ago, trying to work up the courage to speak to Zavrius for the first time. The memory made him feel small. How little he'd changed. "And what about Lestr? Why were you speaking with him just now? What does he want?"

Balen cleared his throat. "He told me he's organizing defenders for your traveling party."

Zavrius raised a brow. "My what?"

"For the road."

Zavrius scoffed. "The terribly long two-hour journey to the palace? On an internal royal road? What terrifying creatures have sprouted from the ground since we've been in the glade?"

"Oh, haven't you heard?" Balen said with a grin. "There are insurrections, invasions—all manner of death traps for a king. And I'm only one man after all."

Zavrius's smile turned sour.

"King," Zavrius said, like it was something stuck on his tongue. "Yes. Well. Another kingly joy. Spending all my time surrounded by my late brother's greatest admirers."

"They're not—" Balen began, then stopped himself. A moment earlier he was ready to round on his brethren, and now he was here, defending them before the king they were openly questioning. Still, he was reminded of what he'd walked away from with Zavrius, and decided he was glad for it. How little did he think of the Paladins, of the life Balen had chosen? Did Zavrius think he worshipped Theo? Balen closed his eyes.

"Come on," Zavrius said. Suddenly he was on his feet, loping down the stairs to the side of the dais and shouldering his way through the surrounding nobles.

Balen darted after him. They ran until Zavrius disappeared in the tall grass at the edge of the glade. Balen slowed, scanning the night for the shape of him. Somewhere ahead he heard the lute-harp strum, a little signal in the dark. When he caught up, he saw a gleaming white carriage was hung with four lanterns. The driver sat ready and gave an awkward bow to Zavrius as he approached.

This carriage had belonged to the late Queen Arasne—it oozed her personality, from the gold inlaid doors to the carved flowers poking out between the spokes. Even the luggage rack hadn't escaped Arasne's decorative urges. The iron railing twisted to resemble vines and had been painted with gold leaf, though that detailing was chipped in places. Zavrius had brought nothing with him, it seemed: the rack sat empty, which only emphasized the gaudiness of the entire carriage. He wondered what the carriages Zavrius would commission for himself would look like. Not this . . . he hoped.

As he had that thought, Balen heard the approach of hooves on the path. Two armored Paladins rode abreast: Alick and Duart.

They looked starkly different alongside one another. Balen found himself blinking at the comedy of it: Duart, broad shouldered and stout with a kind, round face, next to Alick's sharp-angled jaw and hard eyes. They were both from the province of Cres Stros, center of the dynastic lands, their skin a rich taupe like Zavrius. Balen always envied that—Westgar was a colder region, closer to the Rezwyn Empire, and his pale skin betrayed every thought or emotion he ever dared to have.

Balen smiled up at Duart. He was Balen's senior by twelve years and had always been kind to him. Duart grinned wide and winked at Balen, nodding down at the gauntlets in a silent congratulations. Alick didn't even look his way, eyes distant and uncaring even when the clenched jaw and puckered lips gave away his resentment. Balen didn't mind that; discomfort looked good on Alick. They'd never gotten along. Alick had always been full of quips about his attraction to Zavrius, and when that was done, he made the same quips about Balen's supposed crush on Theo, though these were harsher and more cutting, less about making Balen blush and more about ensuring he never cheapened the Heir Ascendant with lustful thoughts.

Never mind that Balen felt nothing toward Theo— he was attractive, but only physically. He'd become near unhinged after Arasne's death. Alick was just the type of man to tease people for the fun of it.

So now that Alick was sitting like he had a stick up his ass, Balen thought it suited him.

Balen called up at him. "You here on Lestr's orders?"

"The others'll be here soon." Alick clearly wished he was anywhere else. His roan gelding snorted beneath him.

"They'll find us gone," Zavrius said.

Duart frowned at Balen before turning to the king. "Your Highness?"

Zavrius approached his carriage. "You two and Balen are quite sufficient. I want to go."

He opened the door, stepped inside and placed the lute-harp delicately down on the only clear spot on the floor. Balen caught a glimpse of the carriage interior and realized with a start there was no room for him. Or anyone else, for that matter. It was packed full of Zavrius's instrument cases.

Alick and Duart exchanged a nervous glance. Balen shrugged at them, making his way toward the carriage. He peered inside, not bothering to comment on the lack of space for him. How many bloody instruments had Zavrius brought for just one ceremony?

Zavrius turned his face away as Balen approached. Balen took the snub in stride. It looked like he would be the luggage for this ride.

"You heard the king," Balen told the carriage driver. Then he climbed onto the roof. "We ride out."

CHAPTER
TWO

The kingdom of Usleth lay east of the Rezwyn Empire on a peninsula surrounded by the dark Prauv Ocean. The king's residence at Cres Stros was situated just east of the peninsula's center, deep in the Khef Ro forest. East of Cres Stros the Ashmon Range rose up before the land fell back into the water. The Royal Highway cut through the kingdom's main provinces. It stretched from Cres Stros all the way to the Province of Westgar at the border between Usleth and the Rezwyn Empire.

Westgar was Balen's home. The cold province stretched across the northern portion of Usleth around Lake Bron Skea, making it the major point of trade between the Rezwyn Empire and Usleth. It was a rocky, rolling region of hilly outcrops and long, flat plains.

Though still covered by forests, swaths of lowlands had been cleared for towns and cities. Balen often missed it, but he had rarely returned.

Here in the Khef Ro forest, only two hours from Cres Stros, the density of the trees and loose cobblestones meant slow going. The carriage jolted beneath Balen, sending his armor clanking.

He lay on his back atop the carriage roof with his hands tucked behind his head, staring up at the stars. He'd thought he might sleep—had felt the fatigue the moment he lay down—but his body was uncooperative. There was, as always, a beat at the back of his mind urging him to pay attention. He wished it'd shut up. During his training he'd had the sheer pleasure of committing the entirety of the Royal Highway to memory.

The whole map of this road was etched in his mind, so that Balen knew where each offshoot led: from the large towns like Karthosk, well positioned near the expanse of Fyo Brahn Lake, to the unnamed hamlets to the east that bordered the Khef Ro forest. In boring detail, he knew which settlements had mayors, which had pledged themselves to the various lords, which towns were the best to visit for inns, fresh horses or with the aim of getting blind drunk.

His mind never stopped, only now he needed it to stop so he could center himself. He'd only ever known the power of the gauntlets in theory. Having immense arcane power at his fingertips was overwhelming—especially when Paladin training had been about control and moderation, lest you go mad from overuse. He needed a quiet moment to unify with them.

It didn't help that Zavrius kept strumming at his lute-harp. Part of Balen wanted to shout for quiet, but that would at best only earn him a sarcastic rejoinder. Zavrius had always been like this, since Balen had first seen him during his training days in the palace. Then he'd been hungry to earn this title and longing for the honor of protecting Zavrius's older brother Theo, the Heir Ascendant. Zavrius never quite fitted well into Balen's dreams of glory, but somehow always edged his way into them—as a harmless and amusing distraction in the entourage of his older brother Theo.

Balen rolled onto his side. That wasn't exactly fair. His interest in Zavrius had never been trivial and apparently Zavrius's ambitions had never been harmless either.

Zavrius's mother, Queen Arasne, had been ill a long time. Her death was sad, though expected. But then a mysterious disaster in the province of Westgar had killed all four of Zavrius's siblings, leaving him the sole heir and the subject of much suspicion.

None of the heirs had been meant to go close to the border. Before heading into Westgar, they'd spent a few days with Huez Thenlass, the ex-Paladin who had led an assault against the Rezwyns in the war and thus had earned his title as the provincial lord of Shoi Prya. Afterward, Zavrius had gone off to give a private recital for an enterprising—and famously handsome—merchant who had an estate in the southern isthmus of Westgar. And after he'd left, the rest of his siblings had gone their separate ways.

It was reported that before their deaths, Zavrius's sister, Avidia, was foraging in a remote hilly outcrop for ingredients to concoct her poisons. Brothers Lysio and Gideonus had gone to inspect the border fortifications and hound the Paladins stationed there. Theo had been meant to meet with Thenlass to further discuss defense strategies. Thenlass claimed he had spent days riding into Westgar, only to find no one waiting for him.

No one knew what had happened then. But the bodies of all four heirs had been discovered the next morning on the far shore of Lake Bron Skea in Rezwyn territory, presumably slain by Rezwyn soldiers guarding the border.

Zavrius had ridden back from his performance the next morning to learn he was now the Heir Ascendant.

The scarcity of the details frustrated Balen. The Rezwyns returned the four bodies immediately but declined to give up the soldiers responsible—denied any damn part in the whole thing. They, in turn, demanded an explanation as to why the entire royal family had breached the treaty and crossed the border into Rezwyn lands.

No one had a good explanation.

When news of Heir Ascendant Theo's death had reached Cres Stros, the whole region had mourned. Balen remembered wails—not professional mourners, but genuine cries: the dynasty's great heir gone. He'd had his own shocked cry, but it'd been tainted, not wholly selfless. He'd imagined being Prime so many times, and Theo was always part of that dream.

Balen didn't know how Zavrius felt about any of it. He could imagine it, could assume the sudden death of his family would upset him, but Zavrius was always . . . reserved in that way. The Dued Vuuthriks had never been close. In fact, they'd always been separate. Their father, Sirellius, had trained his children to be little soldiers, but Zavrius had never excelled in anything beyond music. Even Avidia, who excelled in poison, had been of more use to Sirellius's dynasty than Zavrius would ever be. Balen remembered overhearing something as a young boy: Sirellius, frustrated, bemoaning the use of gedrok ichor on a boy like Zavrius. With gedrok ichor being such a finite resource, the king had opposed using it on a child of no value. He had been overruled by Zavrius's mother, Arasne, and Zavrius had received his birthright.

Even imbued with ichor, Zavrius was thought too soft for the rest of them. A dove in a nest of hawks. He was never going to be a soldier, so Arasne had plucked him up and turned him toward her own specialty: music.

The tune Zavrius played now was mellow and sweet. A fitting match to the moonlit summer night.

The more Balen, the more his earlier frustration ebbed away. Under the stars after claiming his prize for being the best of the Paladins—it wasn't a bad spot to be in. Zavrius really did play beautifully. The notes seemed to resonate through him like a physical caress, but perhaps that was because he was sitting in Paladin armor made from gedrok scales, serenaded by music conjured from a gedrokbone lute-harp, notes strummed on strings made from gedrok tendons. Was this feeling the old body calling to itself? Could this calmness he was feeling be familiarity? Synchronicity?

Or was it just magic? Zavrius's lute-harp was an arcane instrument. Without intention behind his music, Zavrius could play whatever pretty tune he wanted to, and affect nothing. But if he wanted to, as he had that very night performing in the glade, Zavrius could direct the magic in whatever way suited him. Tonight, the music had seemed to soothe everyone, including him. Who was he playing for now? Had the sensation Balen had just felt been a deliberate use of magic or an unconscious wish? If there really was hidden force and intention behind the king's playing now, would Balen even recognize what it was? Could this sensation be Zavrius reaching out to him?

Listen to yourself. As if he cares that much.

The horses suddenly whinnied and the carriage lurched to a halt. Balen sat up, staring out into the darkness.

From beneath him, Balen heard the muffled sound of a crash as a stack of Zavrius's instruments collapsed. The lute-harp twanged.

Balen crawled to the edge of the luggage rack and peered down at the driver. The man caught the movement and looked up at him with a nod.

"Tree's fallen," he said. "Big one, too. Might need all three of you boys to move it."

Balen made a noise of acknowledgment and squinted into the dark.

Duart and Alick had been taking the rear and came up on Balen's right. They said nothing to him, but they didn't have to; the shared furrow in all their brows said enough about what they were feeling.

Nothing felt good about this.

Zavrius stuck his head out of the carriage window and called up to Balen. "What's going on?"

"Tree's down. Blocking the road," he said. Even in the dark, Balen could see his expression. A tremble went through him, a spark of dawning fear that he quickly shuttered, that impassive, kingly face covering Zavrius like a mask.

Duart clicked his tongue and brought his mare back toward the carriage.

Balen shifted himself to the ladder, preparing to descend. Something itched in his mind, a little gnawing guilt, a sudden fear that his pride had walked them all into a trap. He squinted into the darkness.

A keening wail sounded. It devolved into a strange jabbering and echoed in the forest.

Balen tensed. If it was an animal, he'd never encountered it before. But the echo came in multitudes before them and behind.

Balen's grip tightened on the rungs of the ladder.

"Get your head back inside," he hissed to Zavrius.

"What?"

"Just do it."

Zavrius's eyes were wide. He set his jaw but retreated.

"How many?" he asked Duart.

"I don't—"

A figure darted out from the darkness.

Duart's horse reared up in screaming panic, legs kicking the air. The sharp smell of blood hit Balen full force. By the glow of the lanterns, he could see the horse's entire steaming flank split open, oozing blood and intestine.

Duart fell with a grunt, rolling twice before he found his feet.

The gauntlets buzzed and crackled. Balen jerked his hand back, disrupting the magic. He barely had any grasp on their power. He glanced at the carriage. Staying where he was would only draw attention to Zavrius, who was sitting inside. Balen dragged his sword from the scabbard.

With a frenzied speed, Balen launched himself off the carriage. He landed in a crouch, spent the half moment there to draw from the ichor in his blood. Arcane power pooled in his belly. Balen shot to his feet and pivoted, searching for their assailants.

From within the darkness, a man threw himself toward him. Balen wrenched the blade up to block. The force reverberated through his arm; he went sliding, back slamming against the carriage. The lanterns jostled, sending the light spinning. The haphazard glow revealed his enemy: a man with light brown curls, skin the same washed-out tone of Balen's. His skin had an eerie, translucent quality to it. He was not right.

Balen shoved him back and slammed the hilt of his blade into the man's jaw. The attacker shrieked and stumbled backward and Balen finished him with a single thrust through the chest. He scanned the darkness, trying to spot Duart. He heard the clank of blades to his left, labored breathing—Duart, fighting how many? Then, to Balen's shock, the man he'd just stabbed stood back up and lurched forward.

"Damn it," Zavrius hissed from the window above him.

Balen shoved off the carriage, releasing a bolt of arcane power through his blade. The bolt of magic was bright and glowing, a dart of iridescent light that spun through the air with a hiss.

It struck the pale man's chest. He went wheeling backward with a high keening scream. Balen drew his blade up defensively just as another blade scythed down to his left. He caught a glimpse of thick hair and deep-brown skin. The attacker kicked him back against the carriage.

Duart came up beside him, frantic, and slammed a dagger deep into the assailant's back and shoved her away. The woman roared but astonishingly didn't fall. She spun and brought her sword down hard on Duart's shoulder. Balen watched with horror as the blade, which should have bounced off the gedrokbone armor, cut right through and went deep into Duart's shoulder.

With Duart's cries ringing in his ears, Balen stood. He swung at the attacker, who hissed at him and darted back, strangely nimble. Duart grunted, glinting Paladin blood dripping from his shoulder. Balen nodded back. In the darkness he could hear Alick clashing with the enemy.

The man closest to him grinned. The expression was horrifying, too broad. Then a sizzle, a blinding flash of light. The force of a massive pulse hit Balen in the chest and punched the breath out of him. It sent him hurtling backward until his back slammed against the carriage.

Whoever they were, they were using ichor.

Alick rode toward them with his blade drawn. A stream of arcane energy jolted out from the pale attacker's finger, striking Alick in the chest. Balen watched aghast as Alick fell from his horse. Now was the time to make his move. With his sword, he sent a bolt of energy straight into the pale man's head, blasting three-quarters of it away. Finally, the attacker stilled and fell.

The carriage door swung open. Three notes sounded: a tuning scale on a lute-harp.

Balen was halfway through turning around to yell at Zavrius, to tell him, for the gedrok's sake, to stop—had to stay inside, stay safe, stay alive.

Zavrius peered through the edge of the carriage door and flicked his fingers forward. An arc of energy sliced through the air, crescent-moon shaped and faintly blue. Balen watched as it struck the woman and Duart both. The arcane sickle bounced off Duart's armor, but their assailant was not so lucky. An incision appeared on her neck and the skin peeled back, flayed from an invisible source. Her head toppled to the ground. Her body followed shortly thereafter.

Duart clutched his ear. Infused by ichor, his bright-specked Paladin blood pooled between his fingers.

Balen looked back at Zavrius, eyes wide. "Watch what you're doing!"

But Zavrius said nothing. He jumped out of the carriage and strummed again. Another hooked blast cut through the air. Duart slammed himself into the ground, desperate to avoid the attack. Alick swore. Balen grabbed Zavrius's hand.

"I told you to stop!" Balen scanned the moonlit path. Where were the men Alick had been fighting?

He saw a slight movement behind them and Balen's stomach dropped. Balen rushed forward with the speed of reflex, punching wide through the air. Power moved through him at a startling speed, igniting his gauntlets. He felt tendons strain, a pressure behind his eyes, the sudden warm tingle as his nose began to bleed. The gauntlet met the man's flesh and crushed it.

The man staggered back. He pulled in a sickening gasp. Balen expected him to fall. Instead, the man looked up at him, chittered angrily under his breath, and Balen understood from the look in his eyes that whatever drove this man, whatever arcane power burned inside him, was nothing close to human. A foreign, arcane will had taken over.

"Don't you bloody dare!" Zavrius yelled behind him, but Balen kept his eyes ahead as he rushed forward. Balen raised the gauntlets again this time, aiming to crush the man's throat.

Suddenly, Zavrius's music became frantic. He sent a barrage of arcane sickles into the darkness, seeking attackers that may not have even been there. Balen grabbed his attacker by the neck and hurled him to the ground. An unnatural growl spiraled out of him as he hit the earth. He squirmed and kicked.

Balen shoved his palm into the man, held him steady and still just long enough to look up.

By the carriage, Balen caught sight of Duart on his knees. A blade was buried in Duart's chest.

Alick had his sword locked with Duart's attacker, hilt grinding against the blade.

Balen felt a moment of uncomprehending fury, and then nothing. Balen looked down at the man beneath him. His hands quivered. He saw the gauntlets pressed flat against the man's chest, felt something at the edge of his vision—an unbridled force growing in the pit of his belly, burning and furious. Balen let it out. The force surged through the gauntlets. His mind felt raw, felt empty: outside of his body, Balen watched his opponent spasm and scream. The flesh of his torso melted, collapsing as it crisped. Balen peeled his hand away. The gauntlet sizzled.

He launched off the corpse and took a step toward Duart. The man was on his knees, slumped over the blade, staring down at it protruding from his chest. Duart said nothing. He was dead. Dead—punctured like a fucking animal. The rest of them would be dead soon enough, picked off one by one by overwhelming odds. Zavrius would be dead, and Balen would go down as the most incompetent Paladin in history. Rage and shame swirled through him. He drew his hands together and dragged every lick of arcane energy in his body out. The gauntlets sparked.

"Alick!" Balen screamed. "Get down!"

Alick dove out of the way, falling prone near Balen's feet. Duart's murderer was exposed. Balen launched a ball of blinding energy forward, watched it come together into a thick bolt. It skewered Duart's murderer. The man stumbled back, an odd smile curling on his face. The sight made Balen's stomach open. Rage seeped into him, this growing force of unfettered anger he couldn't contain. It wanted out of his body. Balen yelled and cast again. Arcane missiles spun out of the gauntlets toward the man, into the carriage, and farther out into the dark forest. Damn it. Damn it all.

"Balen!"

It was Zavrius's voice. Balen lurched forward, blinking away the dark focus his anger had lent him. The carriage was vibrating. One of Balen's bolts had lodged itself into the carriage's side and was sparking and flashing as it burrowed into the wood. Balen braced himself, expecting an explosion. The bolt was swallowed by the carriage. But there was no blazing flash, only a high-pitched keening. Balen squinted, watched as Zavrius's instrument cases popped open. A dozen instruments twanged and sounded, sparked to life by arcane power, a cacophony of a dying orchestra. The discord came together suddenly in a rich, mournful howl, like the gedrok they were made from was reliving its death. Then, all at once, a blinding-white blast of power.

The shock wave spun toward them, shaking the walls of the carriage and causing the horses to bolt.

Zavrius rushed forward. "Get back!" He grabbed the lute-harp and played three desperate chords. The rolling blast was subdued, hovering unnaturally in the air before Zavrius sent it spinning into the last standing attacker and out into the forest. The neck of Duart's murderer suddenly split apart.

The instruments stopped abruptly. The silence was loud.

Balen crumpled forward like a doll, falling heavily into the dust.

He lay panting for a time. The gauntlets felt as heavy as manacles chaining him down to the earth.

Alick appeared above him.

"Get up." Alick's voice was strained. Balen felt his face flush as he rolled onto his side and got to his knees. He looked up at Duart's body, looked away, face hot.

"Get up," Alick said again. He felt the man's hands reach under his torso and heave. Balen shook him off and stood, staggering forward to his friend's corpse. He wanted to drop, to dislodge Duart from the blade he'd been impaled on, but instead he stood still, unable to move.

He felt—

But in truth there was a numbness in him, an empty buzz in his mind where no thoughts came.

Zavrius struggled up from the dusty cobblestones hugging the lute-harp against his chest, hands slightly trembling. Blood gathered beneath his fingernails from the force of his playing. Balen looked up at him, but Zavrius didn't meet his gaze.

"Well," Balen heard Zavrius say, "that could have gone better."

Alick shook his head in open disgust. "I'll check on the driver."

Balen could tell Zavrius was posturing and gave no response.

Zavrius grimaced, shoulders deflating. He was all nerves: adrenaline and shock bubbling beneath the skin. Balen felt the same, though he had an added dose of shame. He knew he was flushed from more than the fight. Zavrius knew it too—said nothing aloud, but was thinking it. What sort of Prime would walk them into this?

He looked down at Duart's mangled body. The blade jutted out from his chest. His mouth was open. Balen felt his chest tighten and got to his knees. He closed Duart's eyes and dislodged the sword. Then he wiped his hands in the dirt.

"Lestr should know about this," he said as he stood. "Not just Duart's death. Them. They were . . ."

Suddenly, Balen wasn't sure whether or not to say it. He rubbed at his forehead and looked away.

"Arcanists," said Zavrius. "Somehow they've drunk the ichor of a gedrok—and not just one of them. All of them. Someone is trying to usurp the throne, and someone in the Paladins is helping them."

Balen must have stared too long at him—Zavrius flinched and looked down at the lute-harp, starting to polish specks of blood from it. He looked at Balen from under his brows, still polishing.

"I'm not wrong," he said. "Am I?"

"No," Balen said quickly. He opened his mouth, apology almost spilling out before he stopped himself. He could feel the bruise forming beneath his cuirass. He couldn't afford to look any weaker than he already did.

The remains of Duart's murderer lay before him on the road. He felt heavy, stupid: a child after a tantrum. How idiotic could one man be? Thinking he could protect Zavrius alone, having his ass handed back to him, bruised and beaten . . . He'd been humiliated. A surge of shame fell on him as he remembered what it took to get here. What it took to be Prime. After all those years of training, he was a useless mess in battle. How was he meant to face Zavrius now?

Then Balen's gaze fell back on the still body of the man whom he'd beheaded. He'd given a clean death to someone who deserved much less. His first kill. The sight of his mangled body sickened him.

But on the other hand, he felt proud.

Which wasn't right either—he wasn't supposed to feel anything close to pleasure after taking a man's life. That was perverted and unnatural. There were enough mental hurdles he had to overcome to keep himself a Paladin, not a murderer—genuine satisfaction only blurred the distinction. So he focused on the task at hand: protecting Zavrius.

"We need to get out of here," he said. "Now."

CHAPTER
THREE

Once Alick found the driver, he jogged back over to them. "Found the carriage driven off the side of the road. It's got a broken axle. The driver's unhurt, but it will take a while to calm the horses."

"What about the instruments?" Zavrius asked.

"They're . . . shattered. Beyond repair," Alick answered. He looked ashen-faced and uncomfortable. He wouldn't look Balen in the eye. "Just broken pieces of wood and gedrokbone lying in the road."

Balen looked down at his hands, as if the power of the gauntlets was something he could see. He peered around Alick and squinted into the dark, trying to make out the shapes in the road. The king's instruments were obliterated. He'd done that.

Zavrius said nothing for a while. But he was tense, holding himself with his fists balled at his side. He started forward, walking stiffly until the debris of the destroyed carriage was at his feet. Then he dropped to his knees, soft hands running over the jagged pieces of bone and wood that were once his instruments.

Balen let him sit there. He was surprised the king didn't cry out—he'd collected these instruments for years. Instead, Zavrius slowly stood and wiped himself off. He slipped the lute-harp from off his back and hugged it close.

Then his low, smooth voice broke into Balen's ruminations. "All right. So, Prime Paladin, what's the plan?"

"Are you really asking me this, just like that?" Balen turned with a frown. Zavrius stared at him defiantly, no sign of sadness on his face. Balen grimaced and made himself think. Did he even have a plan? It would be foolish to go forward in the direction their attackers had come from. But retreating would be just as dangerous. One of the Paladins who would be following their trail was a traitor. His brethren's clandestine meeting in the glade that night confirmed that some of them were on the verge of sedition. It all seemed too much. He put a hand up for Zavrius to see. "Give me a minute."

Zavrius crossed his arms. "Aren't well-thought-out plans designed to protect my life your purview?"

Balen smiled flatly. "And what do you think I'm doing now?"

Coming from anyone else, Zavrius would've scowled. But now he grinned wide, leaning back on his heels. "Oh, are you thinking? I suppose it makes sense. Pulling a cunning plan directly out of your ass would be too grueling for you."

Balen conceded that with a noisy exhale.

"Please do take your time then," Zavrius continued. "There's absolutely no rush."

"Do you mind?" Balen's voice took on a frustrated edge. He stamped it out before he said, "If you were quieter, this would go faster."

Zavrius's lips compressed into a sarcastic, but silent, smirk that could best be described as a mockery of compliance. Alick remained motionless, eyes darting between the two of them. He was clearly uncomfortable with their interaction. His strange look made Balen regret the lapse in formality with Zavrius. He'd been plenty negligent in his duties that night, and even if he didn't care about Alick's approval, he needed to maintain it, if Balen hoped to keep the other Paladins loyal.

Balen straightened and puffed his chest. "Right," he said, walking farther into the center of the road. He stared up at the pitch-black past the fallen tree, where the palace waited. The glint from its highest towers could be seen over the trees. They had another hour of travel. It was so close—but the night stretched dark and long. How could he have them ride on without knowing what lay ahead?

Balen cleared his throat. "We aren't making it to Cres Stros tonight."

He'd expected some dissention and blinked a moment too long when none came. Alick averted his gaze and went to the driver, coaxing both him and the horses out of the brush. With Alick's horse spooked and Duart's horse gutted, only the four horses from the carriage remained.

"Our options are what, exactly?" Zavrius said unprompted. He gestured down the dark path to the palace. "You think there's more of them?"

"Of course," Balen said quickly. He paused, hating how anxious he sounded. Balen slowed his breathing. "Our enemy knew we'd be here. If they had an ounce of an idea of your movements, they'd know the size of the entourage you were supposed to travel with."

"Assuming this is planned," Zavrius countered, apparently just for the sake of argument.

Balen tried not to roll his eyes. "You're not that naive to think it's not."

Zavrius pressed his lips together firmly.

"No," he said. Then, with his usual energy, "Well, forward is death, then. And likely humiliation before it. Hardly an option."

"Lestr would've sent the others after us," Alick said. "No way he wouldn't have. Duart and I . . . we were just ready first. If we head back, we should meet the Paladins on the road."

But that was too presumptive, Balen thought, especially when they'd walked into one ambush already. If it were him laying this trap, he would have prioritized cutting off his target's ability to retreat toward reinforcements. Balen turned his attention toward Zavrius, dirtied, fingers bleeding. His belly twisted again—a king wasn't supposed to look like that. Zavrius only looked like that because of him, because Balen knew the royal road so well he'd been cocky. Now, surrounded by black trees, vision obscured both ways, he could feel a twinge of humility creeping up his spine.

Balen rubbed his forehead. "We don't know if we're surrounded. We don't know anything about the enemy, except they're . . . they are arcanists." He turned to Zavrius. "And I won't—"

I won't put you in danger, he almost said, but in that moment the promise felt empty. He gestured vaguely down the path. Zavrius blinked and looked away.

"Then we go off-road," Zavrius said.

Balen snapped his head toward him, halfway through rolling his eyes before he met Zavrius's gaze. "And what? Galivant about in the forest in the dark?"

Under his breath, slight smiling creeping onto his face, "Alone with me? Would that be so bad?" Zavrius's eyes dropped over Balen's armor before he cleared his throat and spoke loud enough for Alick to hear. "You've convinced me the road is unsafe. There doesn't seem to be another option you're happy with. We can't go forward or backward and we can't go up. That leaves sideways." He waved a hand at the dense bush alongside the road.

Balen gave Zavrius a long, appraising stare. He still wore his king's tunic: long, embroidered, made from oknum and rare silk. The tunic was bright purple, dyed first in the secretions of forest-dwelling snails from Khef Ro and then, as if the garment wasn't dripping enough wealth, the hem had been coated in a thin layer of gedrok's ichor—just enough for it to shine. Even in the dark, Balen could see the glimmer of it. He looked down at his own grand armor. If anyone spotted the pair of them, there'd be no doubt who they were. Whoever they encountered, arcanists or not— well, there was enough tension in the dynasty for every random encounter to be dangerous. But staying here was as much of a risk. At least in the forest, their movements would be more unpredictable than stalking back along the road.

"I could take the horses," Alick said as he patted the flank of the big gelding. The carriage horses were a Khef Ro breed, used to harsh climates and strong. Alick nodded over at Duart. "I could take the bodies to the forge."

"You'd be alone," Balen said, like Alick wasn't already aware. "Save for the driver, who—and don't take offense—is not a fighter."

The driver looked up sheepishly, both hands clamped over his stomach. He leaned against the horse's flank, foot slipping in the dust. He looked weak. Balen flashed a look to Alick, his point proven. "Besides, you'd have to make two trips."

"Why?"

"Because I'm taking one of those horses to carry my armor," Balen replied.

Alick's face twisted, struggling to understand.

"By the bloody gedroks," Alick said, gesturing at the pair of them, "what are you doing?"

"Ensuring the king's safety. If we walk anywhere dressed as we are, we'll be discovered instantly." Balen turned to Zavrius. "Find yourself some other clothes to wear."

Balen risked a look at Zavrius and jolted at his expression. There was a dangerous glint in the king's eyes. Oddly amused. Zavrius immediately began to undress. Balen looked away.

He deftly unfastened his cuirass. The Paladin armor was nothing like a set made from plate or chain mail. Lestr's design was ingenious and fairly easy to put on alone. The plates slotted together and fused with an arcane binding, and when Balen wanted out of it he merely stopped the flow of magic around the armor's joints. The cuirass popped open. Balen peeled it off. The shirt he wore beneath was so slick with sweat it stuck to his body. He made a disgusted noise as he pulled it from his skin. Halfway through the movement of taking it off he groaned as all at once he felt a radiating bite of pain pulsing around his back. The armor had taken the brunt of his multiple impacts, but he knew the bruise would be large and mottled.

Alick hissed at the sight of it and came over to pick up his cuirass. "Are you sure about this?"

"I don't trust the road." Balen stripped off more of his armor.

Last, he looked down at his gauntleted hands. He didn't fully understand the surge of panic at the thought of taking them off—he only had them a few hours—but the power in them made him feel safe and in control, even when the results of his magical tantrum still burned around them. With or without them, he'd still be the Prime. Wouldn't he? If he kept them, surely anyone with half a brain would know who they belonged to. He tugged them off—he couldn't use them without the rest of his armor, not without letting arcane power rip through every tendon in his body. But he didn't set them aside. Instead, he wrapped them in a silk curtain from the carriage and secured them to his sword belt. Keeping them with him felt good regardless.

Alick said nothing, jaw twitching with restraint. Balen knew what he was thinking: the king would've been safe if you'd waited. As much as he wanted to ignore that, Balen couldn't. He gestured to the flaming chaos around them. "I fucked it up. I won't risk—"

Alick frowned. "Heading into the forest at night alone, without your armor, is a bloody big risk."

"Not as much of one as walking around drawing attention to myself by wearing it. The longer we stand here talking, the more time we give the enemy," Balen replied. "And I'll still have my sword." Channeling arcane energy through the sword without the buffer of his armor would destroy his mind, but he could still wield it as a simple blade.

"Without your armor . . ." Alick trailed off. Balen knew what he meant. They both had ichor in their bodies, a corrosive magic that wasn't meant for humans. Gedrok plate kept the effects at bay, but Balen had been trained to handle them.

"It's a few hours," he said. "A few days at the worst. I'm the Prime. I can handle it."

Balen shoved his greaves and sabatons into Alick's waiting arms. The man bobbed a little with the new weight.

Balen looked down at himself, then glanced to Alick and nodded. The two of them began loading the armor onto one of the horses, using the remains of the traces from the carriage.

"Are you sure—" Alick began.

"I know this countryside well. We can find a place to lie low for the time being. Then if you're right and the rest of our entourage is just behind us, we can rejoin them when they catch up. And if you're wrong and you don't return for us, he and I can keep traveling in the morning as just two ordinary men," Balen said. Alick frowned. And then, because Alick was about to open his mouth again, Balen continued, "This isn't a debate, Paladin. It's my decision."

Alick scanned his face, lip curling up in defiant disgust. All he said was, "Fine."

Balen nodded once, then turned to the bodies. Zavrius was squatting over one of them, shirtless, tugging off the corpse's tunic. His own raiment was crumpled on the ground. Balen picked up the costly garment and handed it to Alick.

"Throw it over one of the bodies." Balen didn't think this would fool their opponents, but they'd at least have to check if the body belonged to Zavrius.

Alick exhaled and finished securing Balen's armor onto the horse, hidden beneath a blanket. "I'll take Duart and the driver. We can pick up the assassins' fallen bodies on the way back."

"And the gedrokbone," he murmured. "It'll need to be reforged."

He patted Alick on the arm, took the horse's reins and began to lead it away. Balen looked down at his hands. In the dark, the blood on them looked like deep shadows. There was a shake to them. He didn't like that. Balen shook his hands out and walked toward the king.

Zavrius rolled on his heels to look up at Balen's approach. The moonlight seemed to climb over him: light curling over his cheekbone, the hard arch of his back, brown skin glowing blue. It arrested Zavrius's motion, made him a momentary statue, carved and posed.

Beautiful, Balen thought, as he always did when he looked at the king.

Zavrius smiled and stood slowly. He dropped his gaze over Balen, eyebrow raised. "Have you increased your training? You look bigger."

"Fuck off," Balen said, suddenly aware of his own half nakedness. He clamped his mouth shut—again, that informality—but Zavrius only laughed and shook out the blood-spattered tunic. It was bright green, with brass buttons that ran down to the waist. From there it split open into two tails just long enough to skim Zavrius's knees. There was some perfunctory embroidery at the hem, but all in all it was nothing to get excited about. Though he suspected that Zavrius loved the novelty of it.

Balen sighed at him. "You're enjoying this entirely too much."

"Maybe." Zavrius began to put the bloodied tunic on. He kept on his boots and trousers. Balen saw he had a belt strapped to him, two daggers tucked snugly against his back. He had a thin stiletto, and another, a swordbreaker Balen had gifted him many years ago. Balen flushed and refocused. The tunic was enough to distract from the fine make of the rest of his clothes. "But there's been very little to enjoy this evening. I'm merely making the most of what you've given me."

Balen tried to ignore the teasing. He snatched up a jerkin that Zavrius had discarded and dressed quickly.

Zavrius spun once in his new tunic and took a bow.

It was odd, but Zavrius looked regal, more a king tonight than he ever had. He was specked with blood, had a slight sheen to his skin, and Balen's breath caught on the glint in Zavrius's eye. Balen met the stare, lips parting to speak.

Zavrius refocused his gaze somewhere in the gloomy dark. "Shall we?"

Balen nodded stiffly. He turned to see Duart slung over one of the horses' backs. Balen stamped down a momentary panic; there wasn't time to feel what he wanted to. Alick sat ready, right palm splayed against his injured leg. The carriage driver slumped forward into his own horse's mane. He was breathing heavily—he was still bleeding. The horses fidgeted, clearly unused to being saddled or ridden.

"Go," Balen said, nodding back toward the glade. "We'll head east."

"You better not die," Alick said. "Lestr will be pissed enough as it is."

Then he nudged the horse's flank and set out.

Balen spent a moment watching them retreat before getting off the road began to feel urgent.

"Come on." Zavrius tilted his head toward the forest. They walked forward together into the dark.

Balen grabbed Zavrius's hand and headed east.

He'd done it without thinking—muscle memory took over easily when he was alone with Zavrius. The king made a noise that sounded halfway between startled and pleased. A soft, happy sound. Balen tried to ignore it, but it kept clanging around his head: a persistent echo, catching on a memory. Looking back, he saw Zavrius's stare fixed on their clasped hands. Balen swallowed.

"It's dark," Balen said suddenly, by way of explanation. "If we get separated—"

"Of course." Zavrius sounded serious. Balen took a breath, wondered how it got away from him, and pressed on.

They edged around the Khef Ro forest and headed toward the almost inconsequential hamlets that dotted its outskirts, coaxing the horse along between the shafts of moonlight.

They walked for close to an hour in near silence, freezing at any sudden motion or sound. Though once they were deep in the forest, Balen noticed a shift in Zavrius's bearing. He'd reclaimed that comfortable feeling that only settled in Zavrius with the dark. It might have been the obscurity; thick forest trees would hide him from another attack. Or perhaps Zavrius reveled in a different kind of obscurity, Balen thought, remembering the look on the king's face when he removed the markers of his station.

When they came upon a massive fallen tree, they stopped. The gnarled roots arced, slightly elevating the trunk above the ground near its base. Balen tethered the horse, removing the heavy weight of the gedrok armor for the night. It ate a couple of mouthfuls of grass, then leaned against the tree trunk to drowse.

"We'll rest here until morning," Balen whispered. He let go of Zavrius's hand and gestured for him to sit.

"You take me to the nicest places," Zavrius said as he settled against it. Balen snorted and sat next to him. Dry leaves crunched as he sat. He put the sword by his side and patted the gauntlets. Zavrius undid the sheaths from his around his stomach and put the daggers on the ground. He kept a hand on them.

This silence felt different. Walking had occupied him, but now there was nothing but the night and Zavrius. He could feel the warmth of Zavrius's body radiating off him. Zavrius shifted. Balen saw the dark shape of Zavrius's hand edge closer to his own.

He'd held the king's hand minutes earlier, but the intimacy of it had been masked by necessity. Or the pretense of it. This felt more real, more like their past. Suddenly, the moment felt familiar. How many times had they met at night? How many times had they kissed in the forest surrounding Cres Stros?

Balen's heartbeat cleaved the silence.

You have to stop.

But his mind couldn't stop. Some part of him that hadn't quite managed to distance itself, the part that was snagged on Zavrius's thorny exterior, felt the nearness of him, that closeness, and was forgetting he was the king. Forgetting Balen had a job to do. Balen squeezed his eyes shut and readjusted.

When he opened his eyes, Zavrius was staring out into the night.

"What is it?"

"My instruments," he said.

Balen took a breath, recalling how he'd destroyed them. "You brought so many. What for?"

Zavrius said nothing. Then, as if finally registering Balen had spoken, he grunted. Balen cleared his throat, almost apologizing, and stopped himself.

For a time, they sat in silence, and Balen thought maybe they'd spend the rest of the night without saying another word. Balen figured he was good at keeping silent when he had to be—he was a Paladin, after all. A soldier. He'd learned early on speaking his mind would never get him anywhere. But Zavrius always had him breaking his own rules. Balen couldn't help himself. He ground his teeth. Tried to distract his mind. Nothing helped. He kept looking at the nape of Zavrius's neck. Tried to guess by the way he held his shoulders if he was relaxed or faking it, if he was angry, disappointed.

Balen, who was already full of disappointment in himself, thought that would be the worse one.

He started to open his mouth, stopped himself. Took another breath and tried again.

"By the bones, Balen," Zavrius said flatly, not bothering to turn around. "What is it?"

Balen swallowed. "I—" He grunted, struck his hand through the air to cut his own indecisiveness. "Back there. I wasn't . . . I should have done better."

"Yes. Probably."

It stung, even though he was expecting it. He looked toward Zavrius with hot cheeks, but the king was inspecting his fingernails again. Balen looked away. He felt embarrassed, felt like he was carrying his bruised pride in his hands and that's what Zavrius was picking at.

"Next time. I'll be better next time. You know I've trained—"

"Yes, yes," Zavrius said, turning to face him. "You've trained for this. But so have I."

Zavrius's grip on the lute-harp tightened. Balen recalled Zavrius's haphazard casting of sickle after sickle into the darkness around them.

Zavrius continued, "I wasn't going to sit around waiting for you to win the day like the useless dilettante they all think I am."

"I am here to protect you," Balen said slowly, trying to sit straighter without touching his king. "Too many people are out to get you. Your position is weak."

Zavrius leaned back. His head thumped against the trunk. "You really are too familiar with me. I'm your king. If I want to fight, then I'll fight."

Balen grunted. "I wasn't saying . . . I'm not sorry that you fought. I just . . ." Balen looked down at his hands, bare skin exposed. He'd never be good at this. It always got twisted around Zavrius.

Zavrius looked back, confused. He shrugged. "It's not really surprising, is it? It's bound to happen again."

"If I'd been better—"

Zavrius snapped. "What do you want me to say? Am I supposed to placate you, tell you what a good job you did?

Pat your head? I'm not your mother, Balen. I'm not even your lover—not anymore."

Balen clamped his mouth shut and smiled tightly. "I just had my ass handed to me. And if you'll let me finish a damn sentence, I'll tell you this: Whatever our past, I am sworn to protect you. You—not Theo, not anyone else."

A moment passed.

Zavrius looked up at him, lips parted. He leaned back but put a hand on Balen's forearm. There was a strange look in his eyes. "Well. If all goes to plan, you'll be proving that for the rest of our lives."

Zavrius scanned his face, then sat back against the trunk, repositioning the lute-harp to lay across his lap. Balen took a deep breath.

"And since that is the case, we need to train together," Balen said. "When we get back, we need to learn to fight alongside one another."

Zavrius looked up at him. "We used to train."

"We used to spar," Balen clarified.

"We trained! We trained for—"

"—all of one day, since every time we tried a joint move, we fucked it up," Balen said.

Zavrius snickered. "Oh, I don't know. I still think we were on to something."

Balen grunted and they lapsed into silence. He watched Zavrius stroke the wood. He thought of the carriage, full of instruments—overflowing with them.

"Will you at least tell me what you planned to do with all those instruments?" he said.

Zavrius grunted. Offered nothing else.

Balen tried again. "You haven't played anything but that lute-harp since it was bequeathed to you. But you crammed that carriage full anyway."

"I might've chosen something else for tonight. You don't know."

"Don't I?" Balen matched Zavrius's expression.

Zavrius shrugged. "I'm a man who likes variety. Nothing worse than having no choices. What other possible reason could I have to bring them all?"

What other reason indeed? Balen could think of a few. One that stuck out like a sore thumb was that Zavrius had wanted to ride alone, surrounded by instruments that doubled as weapons.

That made Balen's stomach sink—Zavrius felt unsafe. And Zavrius feared a conversation that might slip into something intimate. Something uncomfortable. And now they were entirely alone, trapped by their closeness.

Balen offered a tight-lipped smile. "Can't think of a single thing."

"Well, there you have it." Zavrius splayed both hands in a mock bow. "At the very least, they might've shielded me from some of those arcane attacks, had any made it past your mighty defense. Though now I'll have to start my collection all over again. Woe is me." It was too dark to pick his expression, but Balen heard his tone shift: the lightness in his voice dimmed.

Balen wanted to press him further, but what was the point? He barely understood the arcane power at his own fingertips. The gedroks were too ancient for him to really understand.

"Who do you think sent the assassins?" Zavrius asked.

It was the first time either of them had said the word aloud. Assassins. Balen took a breath and shifted his weight. He had to remind himself to get used to that word—to the whole concept of assassins. With the amount of tension in Cres Stros, Zavrius's rule would not be smooth.

"I don't know," Balen said. "Do you?"

Zavrius snapped a stick in his hand. "Oh, I have a hundred thoughts about who it could be."

"Oh?"

"Sure," Zavrius answered. "Everyone from here to the Rezwyn Empire." He turned toward Balen, the dark shape of his face bobbing with a half-hearted laugh. "I wish I did. But I don't even know who it couldn't have been. I can't eliminate anyone. Not even among your Paladin order."

"Well, at least two people are innocent: you and me," Balen said.

"How can I be sure you're not involved?"

That surprised Balen. His stomach dropped a notch. He didn't want to kill Zavrius, he wanted to kiss him—hoped it wasn't as obvious as it felt. But maybe Zavrius felt Balen's desire was just as big a threat to his rule as a plot against him would be. Just another weakness, a reason to view the king as a submissive dandy willing to bend at the urging of a Paladin's wink. So Balen said nothing of the sort. Instead, he scoffed, "Because if I had been a conspirator, you would have already been dead."

Zavrius's silence almost made him regret it.

Balen began, "You don't really believe I—"

"No." Zavrius cut him off. "I just wanted to hear you say you had nothing to do with it. Because unlike everyone else, you don't lie."

He could feel Zavrius's breath on him, uneven and short. Suddenly Zavrius turned onto his side away from Balen.

"I'm tired," Zavrius said. "We should sleep."

Balen felt tired too. His body ached. He thought his mind would be racing, trying to make sense of the night. But the thoughts came to him slow and muddled, more impressions of the fight than actual clear thoughts. Eventually even they faded.

Sleep hit him like a pommel strike to his forehead.

CHAPTER
FOUR

Zavrius was gone when he woke.

It didn't quite register at first. Balen woke empty-minded and aching, saw the space where Zavrius should have been and wasn't—but panic was a secondary emotion to the sweeping pain across his back. Balen rolled with a groan. He gingerly touched his right shoulder blade. The flesh was tender, obviously bruised. Balen pressed his fingertips against it and felt pain flare immediately. He hissed and tried to sit up. Every hit from the previous night seemed to strike him again. Balen saw a flash of white spots. He pressed a palm against his forehead. He'd been sweating. The leather jerkin clung to his skin.

The hollow where he lay felt cavernous, strangely vacant. The empty space and the meaning behind it dawned on him. He spun toward the trunk, saw the spot where Zavrius's body had rested—leaves pressed flat into the ground.

Balen's heart seized. He touched the space and found it warm but cooling fast. He looked up at the sky. Sunlight flickered through the trees, warmth washing out the blue dawn light. Had Zavrius risen with the sun? Both his daggers and the lute-harp were gone, and there were no signs of a struggle. He wanted the reason to be simple. But if Zavrius had only wandered off to shit, taking his weapons made no sense—unless he was expecting to be caught with his pants down. So Zavrius had left willingly, for whatever reason.

At least he'd left the horse and Balen's armor behind.

Zavrius knew better than to wander back to the road without him, and he should have known better than to wander off at all, but overconfidence had always been Zavrius's personal trademark. As Balen scanned the surrounding landscape, he saw something drawn in the dirt. Zavrius had left him a marker, a cursive note that read "Gone to town," along with a taunting arrow.

Balen gritted his teeth. He felt an icy clarity, one sharp flash running over his anger. He could rage—wanted to, knew if he slipped into it, he would feel inconsolable. Zavrius was selfish. Zavrius was doing something stupid and reckless. He could feel himself flushing and pushed down the shame of it. It would be a worse thing to lose the king entirely.

After packing up camp and reloading the horse, Balen followed Zavrius's trail. From what he knew of the area, there should be a slow river and a village close by. Teum Bett, the place was called. It was not one of Balen's favorites— not known for its taverns, or pretty boys, but for a sawmill. Inhabited by woodworkers, furniture makers and the like. He led the horse and tried not to wonder what Zavrius had hoped to find by going off alone. What he hoped to prove.

Teum Bett smelled of smoke. It billowed out into the Khef Ro forest, streams of it joining from a dozen private workshops. He followed the woody scent up a slope, until he heard the trickle of water. Teum Bett's river was a slow, fat stream, a branch of a lake somewhere high in the Ashmon Range. He walked parallel to it until he saw color through the trees.

Teum Bett was a collection of wattle-and-daub structures: homes and workshops. Balen walked closer. Nestled as it was in a clearing, it reminded him of the Gedrok's Glade.

The town was open and unwalled. Even though it sat on high ground, the lack of fortifications made Balen feel exposed walking into it. If there were more assassins out there—and there were, there would always be, so long as Zavrius was alive—this kind of open, friendly town might be the best place to lie low.

It was close to the Royal Highway. Just a few short hours from Cres Stros. A convenient place to rest before another attempt at thwarting regicide.

And about as convenient as you could get with Zavrius wandering the village.

Balen felt outside himself—outside the low burn of anger roiling in his belly. He let it happen. Moving from the natural quiet of the Khef Ro to this pocket of sudden life sparked his mind.

If Zavrius died here, it would be because of his own stupidity. His selfishness. Whatever slight grip Balen had had on his anger slipped at this realization. His mind showed him Duart, run through and prone; his mind saw Zavrius dead the same way. There was a twist in his stomach, not quite shame and not quite anger. Maybe it was a combination of both those forces shocking his nerves to shit.

Bloody, entitled son of a bitch.

Balen took a breath at the edge of the village. On the opposite end of town, a group of men and women hauled a large log into the clearing. Next to them, a set of hunters walked with hares slung over their shoulders. Two children ran screeching into the forest. And somewhere: music.

The sound of the lute-harp brought Balen's attention into sharp focus. He stalked toward the sound with an aggressive, singular purpose until people started looking at him. Then he made himself slow down and slouch back into his disguise—a sellsword looking to hawk himself, weary from the road.

Save for the children, everyone was working. Most had an ashy taupe tone to their skin, as expected from central Cres Stros, but there were a few southerners, a few Westgar-fair like him. He watched people greet one another as they got to work, twenty-odd people out already, just past daybreak.

At the village center stood a towering pedestal with an even taller statue rising above the rooftops. The statue depicted a helmeted Paladin, hands resting on the pommel of a sword. A glyph was marked at the statue's base, marking it as the Paladin for Teum Bett.

Centuries ago, there'd been enough Paladins to post one in every settlement off the Royal Highway regardless of its size. But as the raw material mined from the gedroks dwindled, the Paladin order became pickier with its recruits. It had been the long-ago Queen Rostaiva who'd commissioned Paladin statues for the smaller settlements—a sad, half-hearted apology for pulling any real protection back to Cres Stros. He knew of one instance where a village, Karthosk—a smaller, less-established settlement—had hauled the thing into Lake Fyo Brahn in protest. But this one was clean and well cared for. Not covered in bird shit, like some others he'd seen. A prized watcher. And for good reason, too. Balen caught the glint of something in the statue's cuirass. It had been carved to look like a gemstone embedded in the stone armor, but it had that same pearlescent shine as real Paladin armor. Part of a gedrok was in this statue. If the town was under attack, a Paladin could activate the statue, sending up an arcane signal to alert Cres Stros. Hardly the same as an active Paladin in the community, but it let the capital know when help was needed and where.

Not that the empire had ever expanded this far.

He saw something that looked like a temporary fighting pit being assembled. Wooden posts partitioned off a square of dirt. Beyond that someone was assembling the castelet for a puppet show.

He'd come on market day, apparently.

The music continued; in Zavrius's hands, the lute-harp was like a spear, seeking Balen. It was coming from the vicinity of the statue.

He found Zavrius there.

Zavrius was playing some ribald, jaunty tune Balen often heard in taverns. A few people watched him and clapped. Others threw coins into the lute-harp's open case. The king leaned back against the base of the towering statue, his head well below the Paladin's feet. Balen found that amusing enough that the surge of anger he felt was delayed. The king was still dressed in the assassin's tunic. After a night sleeping rough, the bloodied patches could easily be mistaken for average road filth.

He positioned himself between Zavrius and the fighting pit and watched the king play as the market square filled with people. The horse nuzzled his neck. Balen patted it, then folded his arms and waited. He wanted Zavrius to turn. The petty part of him hoped Zavrius would spot him and be appropriately chastised by the look on Balen's face alone. But if the other man saw him, he made no effort at a greeting.

Feeling both blindsided and frustrated, Balen took the horse's reins and led him over near the castelet stage. There was a set of four posts under an open thatched stand. It was clearly not a permanent stable, but a rest point set up for the market. He fished around for a coin to give the young stable hand—he had very few on him now—and looped the horse's reins over a post. It snorted happily at the sight of hay. Balen made sure the cases containing his armor were strapped down securely, then wandered out toward the stage.

The puppeteers had already started their first performance. The crowd was mostly older, which told Balen this early show would probably be political in nature. Comedies for the children would follow in the afternoon when the crowds were bigger.

The puppets on stage had the Dued Vuuthrik features, if grossly accentuated. Zavrius was obvious: his long, narrow nose had been twisted into a hook that swamped the puppet's face. Balen grasped the other must portray Theo by context—the two puppets were locked in a tug-of-war for a wooden crown. Balen hovered behind the laughing audience.

"My crown! My crown!" Theo's puppet howled.

"Gimme, gimme!" Zavrius's voice was gruff. Horrible sounding—nothing like the real thing. Balen set his jaw.

Theo tugged hard and dragged Zavrius with him. The puppet held the crown above its own head and screamed, victorious, "I'm the Heir Ascendant! It's my crown!"

And from behind its back, Zavrius's puppet drew a knife.

"We'll see about that!"

The crowd screamed and booed.

Balen turned with a sigh. The sounds of the lute-harp began to punctuate the cries of the puppet show audience. He couldn't help but think that Zavrius was doing it on purpose. Providing musical accompaniment to his own critics would amuse him. But it didn't delight Balen.

Sulking had done nothing to dull his anger. It was time to stop wallowing.

When Zavrius saw Balen marching forward, he closed the song with a loudly strummed chord and bowed to scattered applause.

"Ah, my companion arrives!" he called, gesturing wide toward Balen. He held the lute-harp in the air and waved. A few heads turned toward Balen, letting him through as they dispersed. Balen ignored them. Ignored everything but the feeling in him—anger, a twist in his chest he refused to name. Balen strode toward Zavrius and grabbed him by the tunic.

Zavrius laughed. "Wh—"

"What the fuck?" Balen shook him, dragged him forward to hiss it in his face. Now that he was close, he could see Zavrius's sunken eyes, dark circles underneath. There was no way he'd slept. He had a manic look about him. He was disheveled. Hardly himself.

Zavrius's smile dropped from his lips. He looked down at Balen's hand. "How dare you. Let go of me."

"Why would you wander off? Can you really be that stupid?"

"I think you'll find I can," he spat. "You said it yourself. I'm the king."

Balen knew he was pushing it, but his anger overpowered all sense in him. He looked Zavrius up and down. "When you want to be."

Zavrius pried Balen's fist from his tunic and stumbled. His back met the pedestal with a soft thud. He laughed, breathless. "Why are you being like this? I couldn't sleep. No one will recognize me, anyhow. I—"

"You almost died last night. We both did. Now you're wandering off—what is going on with you?"

Balen thought Zavrius might try his usual deflection and laugh it off again. Instead he stared, mouth settling into a hard line.

"I don't know. I don't . . . I just needed to move. I need to . . . run." He took a long, gasping breath and pushed his left palm against his eyes. Balen didn't know what this was. Nothing could touch Zavrius usually. Nothing he'd show to the world.

Someone was lingering from Zavrius's performance. An older man. Balen thought he might be waiting for another tune, but he turned to find the man staring intently at Zavrius. Balen grimaced. That curiosity was too much and too dangerous. However innocent it might have been, he couldn't risk them being discovered. He took Zavrius by the shoulders and urged him toward the other side of the statue until they were out of sight and in the shade. The man lingered for a moment more before he walked away.

Balen put his hands on his head and sighed. He considered Zavrius for a moment.

"Is this . . . just about last night?" Balen's hand twitched, halfway through the movement of reaching to comfort Zavrius before he stopped himself. Touching him out of want was different from touching him out of necessity.

Zavrius frowned at the motion and looked up at the Paladin statue behind him. Balen couldn't be sure, but

Zavrius's admission seemed to refer to something bigger, somehow, than the events of the previous night.

"Last night," Zavrius said, "I dreamed of Theo."

Balen opened his mouth to speak but found he couldn't. Zavrius looked down from the statue. His eyes were glassy, expression reserved.

As Zavrius opened his mouth, the sound of a horn blaring dominated the air. Balen expected the sight of a royal entourage come to take Zavrius home. But the sound came from the fighting pit, now cleared of its fighters. The crowd around the empty square waited in silence, all eyes on a young girl who stood in the center of the wooden partitions. She held a bone horn proudly above her head. She was no more than twelve, tawny skinned, with stringy black hair tied in a haphazard bun.

"Esteemed fighters!" she yelled. "Prepare for the next event!"

The crowd began to whoop and clap. Balen watched several people step forward and climb into the pit. Now that he was closer, he could see the pit was larger than he'd realized. It would take fifteen or so paces to stride across in any direction. That much space would make for interesting fights.

The girl spun, arms wide. "This round is a special event." She bent down, hovering over the wooden partition, arms splayed to steady herself. As she lowered herself, she brought one finger to her lips. The crowd hushed expectantly. Then she sprang back up and shouted, loudly, "Doubles!"

The villagers cheered. Several merchants stepped out from behind their stalls and moved closer.

Balen shifted his weight and bit the inside of his cheek, trying to keep his expression neutral. He was caught up on Zavrius—on this strange, newly audacious version of him. He'd dreamed of Theo, and what? Decided to risk his life?

"What you said before—"

"All right." Zavrius cut him off with a sigh. He pushed away from the statue and gathered up the lute-harp's case. All talk of last night was forgotten. "Shall we?"

Trying to get anything more out of Zavrius right now wouldn't work, not when his usual deflection was back in full force. Balen narrowed his eyes. He glanced between the fight pit and Zavrius. "What have you done now?"

Zavrius gestured behind him. "You said we'd need to train together."

"Oh, for—" Balen touched his forehead. "You know I didn't mean this."

"It'll be fun." Zavrius dragged Balen forward by his hands. "Besides, the winner gets a whole gold piece."

Balen laughed despite himself. "What's a whole gold piece to you?"

"I don't know what you're talking about," Zavrius said with a frown. He shrugged his shoulder and the lute-harp bobbed behind his back. "I'm but a humble bard."

A little more seriously now, Balen said, "That's a whole lot of money for a town like this."

"And one lucky cart driver will get the whole lot to drag us back to Cres Stros," Zavrius said. Whatever look was on Balen's face made Zavrius drop his hands. "We're stimulating the economy."

". . . you really have no coin on you?"

"Not a single one," Zavrius said with a proud nod as he stuffed the coin he'd earned by busking into his pocket. Balen ignored the obvious lie. Zavrius tugged him forward, and Balen let himself be pulled. Zavrius laughed, and Balen thought he could feel every nerve in his body, a different kind of arcane power flooding him.

Balen still had anger in him. He still had the lingering fear of waking to find the king gone, the embarrassment of the previous night. But the more he considered Zavrius's happiness now, Balen found he couldn't crush that—he would not be responsible for stripping Zavrius of that smile.

Still, at the thought of fighting, his body ached.

"I'm not in good form." Balen gestured to his back.

Zavrius lifted an eyebrow. "Oh? Show me." He lifted Balen's shirt and made a sharp noise at the sight of Balen's bruised back. Balen flinched and pulled his shirt down, moving out of Zavrius's range. Zavrius made a face like he'd been slapped. Then he shrugged and pouted, expression turning mischievous.

"The thing is," Zavrius said carefully, "I've already gone and signed us up."

"Of course you have."

"We couldn't possibly pull out now." Zavrius gestured with his head toward the swelling crowd. People were abandoning the rest of the market to join. Zavrius smiled. "Honor, and all that."

Balen sighed. "Mm."

Zavrius dragged him forward, a slight bounce in his step, and Balen resigned himself to fighting. He took a steadying breath as they walked toward the pit. The young girl had climbed off the partitions. She waited in front of the pit, chatting and directing pairs to different squares.

"Magdol!" Zavrius called the girl's name with a flourish. He was vying for her attention, but Magdol only side-eyed him, taking the time to finish her conversation.

Zavrius's hand faltered. "Rude."

Balen snorted. "Not used to being sidelined?"

"Oh, all my life. Theo and all." Zavrius's smile slipped. "Now I've had a taste of the attention, though, I can't bear to be ignored."

Magdol made an appraising nod as she came over to them. "Category?"

"Unarmored," Zavrius said. "Weapons."

Balen glanced at him, had a dizzying moment of terror as Zavrius pulled the lute-harp forward. Only the royal line and the Paladins had arcane power—if Zavrius were to use that, it would give them away instantly. This sensation filled him: the puppet show that bordered on sedition, the obvious loyalty to Theo over Zavrius. Balen nearly reached over to rip the damn instrument from Zavrius's hands. But Zavrius only held it delicately in front him. "Somewhere I can store this?"

"There." Magdol pointed to a wooden table strewn with various objects. The girl nodded to a rack lined with wooden training swords. "Put your real weapons down, too."

Balen's eyes fell to the gauntlets strapped to his side. He flexed his hands, ignored the strange fear that filled his belly, and gently unstrapped them.

At the table, Balen carefully placed his sword and the gauntlets. Zavrius pulled his daggers from his belt.

He surrendered the stiletto but held the swordbreaker aloft for Magdol to inspect. The swordbreaker, or parrying dagger, was a defensive weapon. It came to a fine point but was hardly sharp. It was a thick blade with deep, arc-like serrations along one edge of it. Those grooves could catch a blade, allowing for a more effective parry. Balen had given it to Zavrius and taught him to use it, wanting him to have another line of defense if he'd ever be disarmed of the lute-harp. Those lessons had often devolved into something more intimate. It always seemed like Zavrius wasn't paying attention. And until the previous night, Balen hadn't realized Zavrius had kept it. But here it was.

Zavrius ran his finger along the flat edge, showing Magdol it was blunt. "I can't stab anyone with it," he reasoned. "Let me spar with it?"

The girl thought for a time. Balen figured she was assessing whether Zavrius could do any real damage with it. Balen thought it might be too obscure a thing to use, but eventually she waved him on. Zavrius suppressed a wild grin and pulled a short wooden dagger from the rack. Balen followed suit, finding a training sword that felt well balanced enough to fight with.

Zavrius turned to Balen, nodding toward the pit. "Are you ready?"

Balen wasn't. He felt sore and tired, but sleep felt far away and impossible. He had a hundred questions buzzing through his mind. What had happened on the road? What had Zavrius dreamed about Theo?

Beyond that, they hadn't sparred together in years— and not ever like this. Their fight on the road had been sloppy, four individuals fighting without strategy. Balen shivered. Luck had played a larger role than it should have.

"Balen?" Zavrius turned to face him, his smile inquisitive.

What was he to say? The king wanted to fight.

Balen nodded. "You chose this fight. I'll follow your lead."

A smile burst across Zavrius's lips. "Let's begin."

The pair Zavrius and he were to fight were twins, but in face alone. Their bodies differed greatly, one with the strong form of a woodworker, the other lean and quick. They must have been locals, or at least frequented these pits enough to be popular and known. The crowd was on their side. Balen heard them chanting for Mallet and Lance, and assumed they were nicknames for the fighters' professions. They'd clearly done this before. Both had specialized wooden weapons shaped like the mallet and lance they were named for. They each held up their respective weapon, pumping them in the air to the beat of the chant. Someone wove through the crowd taking bets.

Zavrius and he were not the crowd favorites.

There was something about having the crowd against him that made Balen sweat. The last time he'd fought for an audience was the tournament that had won him the position of Prime. He'd been a dark horse then, too, but Cres Stros knew the order as one entity. There weren't favorite Paladins with their own supporters, but there had been bias and assumption. Balen, young and smooth skinned, against Alick, or Duart, or Frenyur—he looked like he would fall easily to the experience of his older brethren. But when he'd defeated Frenyur, when Olia had put a hand up in defeat, he'd felt the audience shift their support to him. The cheers of the crowd felt like ichor in his veins: invigorating, powerful. He'd felt unstoppable.

This time, he doubted the crowd would ever cheer for him.

The rules were simple: Whoever became disarmed or was pushed out of the square lost. A weapon that hit the dirt couldn't be retrieved. Any attack was game.

"They'll attack together and fast," Balen whispered to Zavrius. "They'll want to separate us."

"We are already separate," Zavrius said, a lick of venom in his voice. That felt like it came from nowhere, but Balen didn't have time to correct him. Zavrius drew his daggers, displaying the swordbreaker for the crowd. At the sight of such a specialized defensive weapon, Lance made a strangled note of surprise.

Balen grimaced a little, feeling the absolute danger of letting Zavrius do anything so careless. The hilt of his wooden sword dug into the bare skin of his palm. Without his armor, Balen had to ignore the feeling of being naked.

True to Zavrius's prediction, Mallet and Lance attacked first. They rushed Balen together, Lance straight on and Mallet from the side with a low swing. Balen could see the attack coming. He sidestepped the mallet aimed at his legs and spun left to avoid the stabbing motion from the lance. Lance staggered forward, carried by the motion of his own attack. Zavrius appeared beside him and kicked Lance in the back.

Lance crumpled forward as the crowd booed. Zavrius swung the daggers for the show as he moved to Balen's side, breathing heavily.

Zavrius plainly had no plan. He rushed at Lance, swinging both his weapons crazily. His attack was as wild as he'd been on the road—expectant of a win, overconfident that he could do this alone. Lance remained calm, stepping back to draw Zavrius away from Balen. Mallet advanced from Zavrius's flank and swung high. Preoccupied with Lance, Zavrius didn't see him. Balen lunged forward to block the incoming swing. The blow was strong, but Balen shoved it off to his right. Pulled along by his weapon, Mallet overbalanced and fell forward, almost falling face-first into the dirt. Balen brought his knee up into Mallet's jaw. The man jerked back with a low groan but did not fall.

Lance pressed his attack, thrusting forward toward Balen's face. Zavrius burst from the ground, swordbreaker aimed to catch it.

The swordbreaker caught the tip of the wooden lance in one of the grooves. Zavrius twisted his wrist slightly, locking it in place. The wooden weapon cracked slightly with the pressure. Then Lance gave a twist and yanked the swordbreaker from Zavrius's hands. Zavrius skidded back, hand flexed open like he'd touched fire. His eyes were wide with shock. Something twisted in Balen's stomach. He realized the ease with which Zavrius had been disarmed, the speed of it—felt with immediate certainty how lucky they had been on the road. Zavrius could be dead.

A shout sounded to their left. Magdol was up on the fence waving a flag toward Zavrius.

"Pretty boy!" she shouted at him. "You're out!" She pointed Zavrius out into the crowd. Mallet and Lance froze in place: sportsmanship, waiting for the defeated Zavrius to leave the field.

The side of Zavrius's mouth quirked, fractionally surprised. He seemed like he was about to laugh. Balen knew better. He could see the distance in the king's eyes. Zavrius had been so confident—so confident he was now disarmed and disqualified.

Zavrius turned his head, but he didn't meet Balen's gaze, kept the motion a half apology. He was too proud to admit his defeat. It would mean Balen had to win this fight alone.

If he even recognized that.

Balen felt an odd mix of vindication and regret—but not for long. With Zavrius out, Balen didn't have to focus on protecting him. He was glad for it. Beating these two might resolve that latent anger in him. Balen refocused on the fight. Mallet and Lance were each settling into a stance, ready for Magdol to give the signal.

When Magdol's hand came down, they moved as one. Balen stayed still, waiting, watching their approach. Balen pushed everything else from his mind. He didn't blink when they split apart to flank him. Lance jabbed forward. Balen sidestepped the long weapon, gliding easily out of range—but he was closer to Mallet now, who swung his weapon toward Balen's knees.

Balen skidded backward. The mallet whooshed through the air, just missing him. In his periphery, the lance struck forward. Balen stepped back again. He was suddenly on the defensive. He felt an angry burst of arcane power eager to rip through his tendons. That lance was a bane. He'd need to take care of it first before he took out the mallet.

A glint caught his eye—the swordbreaker, just off to his side. He rolled without thinking, left hand jutting out to snatch the swordbreaker from the ground. Balen got to his knees just as the lance jabbed forward. He struck up and caught it. Mallet came up behind him and swung. Balen spun on his knees, dust flying up around him. Balen yanked the swordbreaker and Lance stumbled forward with a curse. Mallet staggered, again carried by the force of his own swing.

But Balen expected this. He swung down on Lance's wrist with the training sword and wrenched the swordbreaker backward. Lance howled at the sudden burst of pain and let go. Balen dropped his sword and grabbed the lance, swinging it around to slam into Mallet's back and sending him across the boundary.

There was a silence. Blood pooled in Balen's ears, thrumming loudly. Adrenaline soothed every ache in his body. He forgot the blunt pain in his back and stood with a focus, muscles loose and ready to move. But no other attack came. He'd won. Relaxing, he stood to his full height.

The pounding in his ears was slowly replaced with the shouts of the crowd. It was a cacophony, a mix of outrage and gleeful, happy cheers.

Faintly over the noise he heard Magdol shout, "Disqualified."

Balen frowned. Then he remembered the swordbreaker; remembered the rules to this little match. It had hit the ground, and any weapon touching the dirt couldn't be retrieved. Not only that, but he'd dropped his own sword for the lance. Doubly quashed, then, for not following the rules.

Balen stood straight. It didn't matter to him, not really.

It was midmorning now, and the fighting pit had lured most of the town from their beds. Balen turned to seek Zavrius in the crowd, but his vision was obscured by the sheer mass of people that had gathered for the fight.

A hand came down on his shoulder.

Balen jumped, on edge. The hand was massive, the fingers stocky. Balen looked up to see Mallet staring back at him. Balen half expected the man to spit in his face, but Mallet was grinning. He patted Balen again.

"Gave 'em a fucking show," he said. "Even if you cheated."

"Yes," Balen said, stuttering. He looked around again for the swordbreaker. "I'm—"

"Better not say you're sorry." Lance walked forward with a nod toward his brother. He handed Balen the sword-breaker. Balen slipped it into his belt and acknowledged his opponents with a dip of his head, feeling awkward. It had just been another market day show, he realized. He'd taken it way too seriously.

Lance slung his arm across his brother's neck. "Really. That was the kind of fight we were after. Magdol's rules can get a bit . . ."

"Out, out!" Magdol shouted from the sidelines. "'Nother fight's 'bout to start!"

Mallet and Lance waved to the crowd. The sound changed for them; everyone cheered, Balen's transgression forgotten as the gamblers collected their winnings.

"All right," Mallet said under his breath. He lightly pushed Balen forward and the three of them walked out together. One man hooted loudly and hefted three silvers he'd clearly just won in the air toward them. The instant they left the pit, the crowd forgot about them.

Balen craned his neck for Zavrius, but Mallet pulled him back before he had a chance to peel off.

"Listen," Mallet said. "I think you've got it, kid. Some real talent there."

"My brother's right." Lance playfully choked Mallet with a light squeeze. Balen looked between them, tongue-tied in the face of such a display of fraternal affection.

"Where you headed after this?" Mallet wrestled free of his brother.

He snapped his head back toward them, blinking. "Why do you ask?"

The brothers pulled the same excited expression.

Lance said, "Cres Stros put a call out for new recruits. Not for the Paladins, but the capital always needs defenders. We're headed there after this."

Balen said nothing, gritting his jaw to keep the anxiety in his belly from showing on his face.

Mallet slapped his shoulder again. "All we're saying is, you'd be a good fit for that band, too. And it's always better to have a bigger party traveling the Royal Highway."

Balen felt like laughing. He had a moment out of his body, a feeling of inevitability: he imagined he wasn't the Prime, just a young man being pulled to Cres Stros. He wondered if he'd always be drawn there. Always drawn to Zavrius, no matter what he chose. Then he cleared his throat and broke the feeling.

"I'm headed that way, yes," Balen replied.

Mallet and Lance turned to each other, oddly playful smiles on their faces. Mallet gave Balen an assessing glance.

"We're good to leave today," he said. "That boy coming with you?"

Balen frowned deeper. "Yes. He should—why?"

Mallet made a face and shrugged at the same time Lance said, "Not upset you lost the gold?"

"Well." Balen smiled a little, eyes scanning for Zavrius but not finding him. "Money isn't really a problem for him."

"No," Lance said, laughing. "No, I imagine that's more your problem."

"What?" Balen asked, not quite understanding. Something touched his wrist. Balen spun.

Zavrius stood there beside him, staring at the ground. He had their gear bundled in his arms and gently lowered it to Balen's feet.

Mallet hushed Lance and tugged him back. "We're leaving at noon if you want to join our party. Our mother's house is by the mill. Everyone knows us." He pointed vaguely toward the river, slapping at his brother as he went.

At the sight of Zavrius's dejected expression, Balen dropped his immediate need to scold him. He grabbed Zavrius and held him. He squeezed instinctively, leaning forward to rest his chin briefly on Zavrius's shoulder—and then remembered himself, remembered who Zavrius was, and let the king go.

Zavrius took a slow breath. His grip on the lute-harp's strap tightened. Then he glanced up at Balen, eyes shadowed by his brow. His lips parted slightly.

"You did well," he said, voice soft. There was none of his usual smirk.

Balen tilted his head lower, scanning Zavrius's eyes. "What is it?"

Zavrius shook his head. "Oh, I don't know. That fight gave me a headache."

Balen smiled. "Are you sure that's a headache?"

"What?" Zavrius's head snapped up, all shame whisked off his face.

"You're embarrassed."

"Me? Well—all right, a tad." Finger waving like he was trying to get rid of Balen's smirk. "But not for myself. How melodramatic you were! Breaking the rules to keep the honor of a win."

Balen smiled. There was no point saying it aloud, airing whatever ugly feeling he was sure Zavrius had welling up in him. The angry part of Balen hoped the king had learned something. But you could never be sure with Zavrius.

And Balen found, really, he couldn't let it go. Not all of it. Not waking up to find him missing, not realizing Zavrius would prefer overconfident independence to admitting he needed help. He gave Zavrius a push so weak it made Zavrius smile.

"What?" he said with a laugh.

"I'm your damn Prime," Balen said. Zavrius's smile became a thin, firm line. "I'm your . . ."

He wanted to say "partner," wondered if "tool" would be more appropriate. Neither word was right. Balen cleared his throat, tried again. "Don't think it's a mistake to trust me. It's not a mistake."

"I'm sorry. Truly, I—" Zavrius swallowed. A true apology was a rare thing from a king, and slippery. Hard to hang on to. Balen straightened at the words. "I trust you."

Balen pulled the swordbreaker out of his belt and handed it over. "Do you see now why we need to train together?"

"Perhaps." Zavrius laughed. His smile slipped as he turned the swordbreaker over in his hands. Balen wondered what he was thinking, if any particular memory of the swordbreaker came to mind. Zavrius slipped the weapon into his belt and nudged the stiletto toward Balen with his foot. "In the meantime, you can keep that dagger. I'll stick to my instrument."

They collected their effects from the table. Balen, buzzing with adrenaline, found his hands jittered as his picked up the gauntlets. He grimaced. Ichor was a harsh substance. Without his armor, the unnatural magic coursed through his body unchecked. Someone like Zavrius, who had been born of a woman with ichor in her blood, would feel the effects a little less. But Balen's body had only been exposed to it when he was initiated into the order. For now, it was nothing more than a slight feeling of nausea. He had the experience and the training to ride through it. But it would only grow in unpleasantness the longer he was without his full gedrok plate.

"What is it?" Zavrius asked as they collected the horse. He bought a flake of hay from the stable hand with his busking money.

"Headache," Balen replied, shooting Zavrius' weak excuse back at him.

Zavrius didn't seem to notice. "Nothing a drink won't fix, I'm sure." He grinned broadly at Balen and then they were off, headed toward the mill.

The mill was an old, raised structure. Several stacked tree trunks lay waiting to be processed, but the water wheel sat unmoving in the placid river. Without the sound of churning water, the mill was calm. Birds chittered quietly in the surrounding trees. It was a far cry from the boisterous market, but a good place for a quiet drink. There were a few houses nearby, but they didn't have to venture far. They found Mallet and Lance camped outside the mill, drinking with some of the woodcutters. Lance raised an arm to wave at their approach, which made the others snap around to look at them. When they were close, Mallet stood and stretched.

"Good to see you found your way."

"Fairly easy to find," Zavrius said with a smile. "Your biceps are like a beacon, sir, I could spot them from down the hill."

"My—" Mallet slapped his chest like he'd never before had cause to notice the state of his body. "Oh. Hopefully not the only reason you ventured up here."

Balen thought he sounded embarrassed. If he ever found out it was the king who was flirting with him, he'd probably lose his mind.

"Not the only reason," Zavrius said, grinning. "I'm also partial to strong hands."

"Ah, well." Mallet nodded at Balen, completely unflustered. "I can see that."

Balen, flushing, opened his mouth just as Zavrius bowed, the lute-harp sweeping low in one hand. "I am the bard Zircus, and this is, uh, Balo. My food taster."

"Food taster?" Balen and Mallet said at the same time.

"Oh, he hates it when I downplay it," Zavrius said to Mallet, before spinning toward Balen. "You're my bodyguard, too, Balo, I haven't forgotten. But food tasting is his main role."

Mallet crossed his arms. "People want to poison you?"

"I'm thinking about it right now," Balen said under his breath.

Zavrius hit him without taking his eyes off Mallet. "Far too many. I know I'm rather good," he said with a flourish, spinning the lute-harp around to hold it in his arms. "But it turns out not every nobleman can handle the truth in my songs."

"Ha!" Mallet said with a nod. "You dare tell the truth to a nobleman? No wonder they want to get rid of you."

Zavrius gave another little bow, as if it were natural.

Mallet turned to Balen. "And you don't mind the thought of being done in?"

"Zircus plays beautifully." Balen leaned into it and shrugged. "I'm happy to stick around."

Mallet considered that for a moment. His eyebrows quirked suggestively. "I'm sure you are." The big man cleared his throat and gestured with his head to the side of the road. He led them over to their ride: a wagon carrying a polished wooden chair for some patrician in the city.

Two horses sat saddled and ready. It was a four-wheeled wagon, with an axle at the front for the sharp turns necessary in a place so full of trees. The wagon itself was made of a plain, light wood, and it was covered by a white canvas top.

Balen ran his hands over the chair. He knew little about woodwork but could see it was finely made. "Did you make this?"

Mallet shook his head. "Not us. Just delivering it to a family in the city. Szargrid!" He pointed over toward the makeshift table and their drinking circle. A dark-skinned young woman raised her hand. "It's her work. Fancy a drink before the road? She's buying for us all."

Zavrius went first with a skip in his step, still too pleased with being unrecognized out in the world. He accepted a flagon—Balen imagined him being poisoned, briefly, until he saw them all drinking from the same barrel—and pointed a flagon in Balen's direction. It was a dry ale. Balen sipped it slowly.

"That chair is a marvelous beauty crafted by an equally marvelous beauty. Who commissioned it?" Zavrius leaned toward Szargrid.

Balen turned his focus toward inspecting their horse's bridle.

"The Polvercs," she said proudly. Another person, a carpenter from the look of his work apron, patted her on the back, congratulating her again for the commission. The Polvercs were a prominent Westgar family.

"For Adzura Polverc?" Zavrius said, incredulous. The king gave Balen a sideways look; surprise and disbelief, Balen figured, given the Polverc family's rumored obsession with imported empire goods. Balen wondered if this was an attempt to reclaim some face, commissioning a wooden chair from a small dynasty town.

"For her sister, I'm told," Szargrid said with a shrug. "I think it was a condolence gift. Whatever. Polverc was a bitch to work for."

Zavrius stifled a laugh—no one would speak so candidly in front of him about anything, but especially not the nobility. "I've always thought the same."

"You've met that bitch?" Szargrid asked. Balen thought she might ask how, but she only tilted her own flagon toward Zavrius. "I'm sorry. She must be hell to play for."

Zavrius laughed loud that time. "Oh, she was. Thank you."

"A condolence gift?" Balen asked as the king recovered himself.

"Mm. For the loss of her sister's niece," Szargrid said.

"What happened to the niece?"

"Missing." Szargrid turned to Balen, gave him a serious look. "From Westgar, too. Might give credence to some of them rumors going around."

Zavrius's laugh died. He threw his head back and drained his flagon.

Balen was sure the conversation would turn to politics—even the Paladins hadn't been quiet about tying the rumors of missing nobles to Zavrius's incompetence. But the concerns of the patrician class really didn't matter to these artisans. The conversation turned to a discussion of dovetail joinery and Balen was glad for it.

He had another drink and a few pieces of smoked meat someone bought from the market, which subdued the nausea in his belly. He watched the king grow tipsier and tipsier with every passing minute. Someone finally demanded he play a song and Zavrius complied. He plucked a few bars, his face serious and serene to start, like he was about to serenade them all with something classical. Then that raunchy tune from earlier started up and made Lance whoop with surprised excitement. Zavrius knew his audience.

For a time, they listened to Mallet and Lance talk about their fighting experience. They'd grown up in Teum Bett, learned the craft of the town, but wanted more. Balen could respect that.

"Those aren't your real names, though, are they?" Balen asked at one point. He couldn't imagine how they could be, not unless coincidence had a sense of humor.

Mallet and Lance looked at each other, shrugging. Lance said, "Not if you mean what our mama called us."

"But we figured those names weren't really ours. Didn't fit right." Mallet stretched his legs.

"So you chose?" Balen asked. He could hear the hint of awe in his own voice, and couldn't quite understand why.

"Well, a mace fits my hand well. Figured it's a good tool. Lots of uses. And I like to be useful. Lance is just a show pony."

Lance scoffed, affronted. "A show pony?"

"Only reason you learned to fight with one's 'cause of how it looks," Mallet pronounced. At this revelation, Lance stared at him, open mouthed. Mallet raised a brow. "Not wrong, am I?"

"No," Lance said after a moment, smile creeping back onto his lips. "But you could've found a nicer way to say it."

They laughed at that, and Balen realized the awe he'd felt was a tinge of jealousy. They had chosen their own names—he imagined himself or Zavrius having the luxury of choosing what to call themselves. He imagined the power in the name Dued Vuuthrik, the life that went with it. That made him turn to Zavrius, made him consider him as more than the king. He watched the king strum chords and drink and laugh like he was a simple bard. Was this life something Zavrius would've chosen if he'd been given a choice?

And by then it was time to leave. They decided that they'd ride in the wagon, rather than walking, and took a moment to unburden their horse of Balen's heavy armor.

"That's a lot of instruments," Mallet commented.

"You don't know the half of it," Balen returned. He tied the horse's lead rope to a ring at the back of the wagon. It would still have to walk, but at least it wouldn't be carrying so much weight.

They said their farewells. Balen dragged Zavrius to the back of wagon to sit behind the crafted chair. Zavrius gazed around at the wagon's interior as though it were strange and wondrous. Mallet grabbed the reins and climbed up onto the driver's seat.

"Oh, there he goes again," Mallet muttered.

Balen turned in time to see Lance kissing Szargrid's hand.

"Gedrok's balls, you flirt as much as Zircus," Mallet called. "You coming or what?"

Lance waved and skipped over to them, smiling as he climbed up next to his brother.

"Don't look at me like that," he said, hitting Mallet lightly in the arm. "Go on, then, if you're in such a rush."

They sat in silence for a minute. Balen watched Teum Bett fall away behind the forest trees, and suddenly they were on the highway again, bright afternoon sun bearing down at them. After a few minutes, the revelry of their morning slipped. The attack on the road kept flashing in his mind.

Zavrius was staring at the road too. Balen knocked him lightly with his shoulder. "Daydreaming?"

Zavrius blinked rapidly and breathed deep.

"Contemplating sleep," he said. He pulled the lute-harp to his chest, strummed it once, then stopped.

"Why don't you?"

The king scrunched up his face and frowned like Balen was stupid, but didn't elaborate. The frown dissolved into something more pained and he sighed, leaning back on his elbows.

"I don't want to dream anymore," he said. "I dream they're back from the dead—Gideonus and—" He gestured to suggest the rest of his siblings. "Theo. Not Sirellius, but my mother. I just wish they'd leave me alone."

Balen wasn't sure what to say to that. They were dead. And Zavrius was more alone than he should have been—politically, physically. Balen assumed this was the closest he'd been to someone emotionally in a long while, though that was presumptive. There were plenty of rumors about Zavrius and that handsome merchant in the south of Westgar. Rumors Balen routinely tried to avoid. Spontaneously, Balen had a jealous vision of Zavrius waking in some faceless man's bed, loved and happy, and riding back to the dynasty camp to learn of his siblings' deaths.

But Zavrius was not in Westgar. He was sitting beside Balen now.

He patted the king's arm. "Sleep. I'll keep the ghosts from your dreams."

Zavrius regarded him, brittle and exhausted, and did not try to fight. He nodded once and scooted back into the cart, curling up around his lute-harp.

Balen watched him until his uneven breathing became slow and steady. Zavrius fell into sleep quickly, and Balen risked a touch: one palm over his calf, one stroke of his thumb over the trousers.

"All right back there?" Lance asked.

The question triggered an awareness of Balen's own body: the nausea muted by drink, the jitters he was ignoring. Even if the pain in his temples wasn't acute, his whole mind felt heavy. Soon enough, his thoughts would be stunted and erratic. Lestr had made them go days without their gedrok plate to understand its importance, but it wasn't an experience he wished to repeat.

It was times like these he envied the Dued Vuuthrik resistance. The king had generations worth of exposure to ichor in his blood at birth, years before he was dosed himself. These kinds of side effects wouldn't happen to him, unless he cast some arcane attack without channeling it through his lute-harp.

Balen sighed. If he'd had more ale in Teum Bett, he might've been able to lie to himself that this was drunkenness. But he knew what it was. He'd need his armor soon. Balen let go of Zavrius and crawled his way past the chair to the front of the wagon. Mallet and Lance were passing a pipe between themselves. Balen could smell it. Ogir moss. When dried out and smoked, it gave a euphoric effect. Lance breathed deep with a happy sigh and leaned back, pipe hovering over his shoulder for Balen to take.

"I'm fine." Balen waved it back. It didn't matter that Teum Bett's road had spat them out well past the scene of the previous night's attack. The last time he'd been incautious, a man had died.

"Suit yourself," Lance said, taking another drag. "Helps pass the time."

Balen imagined it would.

"My brother gets sick of conversation," Mallet said with a quick glance over his shoulder. "Ends up passing out most trips just to avoid speaking to me."

"Not my fault you've nothing interesting to say." Lance folded his arms and settled back into his seat.

"Don't be rude in front of our guests."

"At least with guests we might have something decent to talk about." Lance shot Balen a happy look. "You two are some of the more interesting folk to wander into Teum Bett."

Balen sat back on his haunches. "In what way?"

The brothers shared a look. Mallet nodded his head to the back of the wagon. "Well, for one thing, he's covered in blood."

"Mm," Lance choked on his inhale with a short laugh. "That he is. But not a blemish on that skin."

"And he can fight—but maybe not well enough to have another man's blood on him," Mallet added.

"Very intriguing," Lance said.

Balen exhaled noisily, not sure what to say. He found himself wanting to trust them—knew that impulse was misplaced. These past few weeks had changed so many of his friendships. Becoming Prime had made him untouchable: still a Paladin, but something more than one. These men didn't know him at all. They weren't prying for gain, but for curiosity. Something about that comforted Balen.

"Very intriguing indeed," Balen agreed.

"Don't think we haven't noticed that horse of yours bearing the brand of the house of Dued Vuuthrik," Mallet said in a stage whisper.

Lance snorted and waved his arms. "Might be better you don't tell us."

"I can assure you we have every intention of returning the horse," Balen said.

"That's your business. We don't need to know it. But you could tell us where you learned to fight like that." Mallet turned again to smile at him. "Really. You're well skilled. City guard will take you in a heartbeat. Could try for the Paladins, even."

Balen slowly closed his eyes, smiling. "Oh, maybe."

"Well, whatever you pick better pay well," Lance said.

Mallet whacked Lance again. "Stop it. You'll have to excuse my brother."

"Will I now?" Balen raised a brow.

The brothers looked at each other again. Mallet turned back to the road with a heavy sigh. Lance took that as a sign he could say whatever he'd wanted to.

"I only meant," Lance said, smile growing on his lips, "that your skinny bard looks expensive."

Balen flushed immediately.

Mallet didn't turn around. "Very expensive. But he's got class."

"Oh, sure, in buckets. But that kind of class needs coin to keep it," Lance pointed out.

"Well, I'm sure he's worth the coin," Mallet said.

Lance looked at Balen, giving Balen a wry smile. "If you have the coin."

Mallet reached out to hit Lance again. "Our guest has managed it so far."

Lance dropped his gaze over Balen. "Mm. I'm sure he has his ways . . . strong hands."

"All right." Balen laughed, embarrassed. He put both his hands up and shifted, crossing his legs. "Your imagination goes too far."

Mallet clicked his tongue. "Uh-huh."

"I mean it," Balen said, over the sound of another of Lance's giggles. Balen found himself laughing too. He turned to the sleeping Zavrius, lowering his voice to say, "It hasn't been like that for some time."

When he turned back around Lance was looking at him. With pity. Balen felt something in his chest—an awkward kind of guilt, a giddy self-consciousness filling him up. Lance reached out to pat his arm. "That's why you need the coin."

Everything in his chest dissolved: Balen laughed, still flushing, and pressed his palms against his eyes.

"But in all seriousness," Mallet said over the two of them, "you'll be a good fit for the guard if you can't find another line of work."

"All right," Balen said, still laughing. "If nothing works out, I'll come find you."

Lance seemed satisfied with this and slapped Balen heartily on the arm. He turned around and started smoking again, all with a pleased sigh.

They sat like that for a time, Balen feeling oddly friendly, oddly at ease with the two of them, watching the road.

For a moment, it felt like he was living a different life. Perhaps the life he would have lived if he'd never joined the Paladins. He had a few good memories of his early child-hood: fishing with his father, listening to his mother sing as she stared out at the ocean at night. Everything to do with Westgar was always tinged by the ocean and the smell of fish. A dampness in his very heart.

He'd lived in Wen Zerret, an inland port town built flush against Lake Bron Skea. His family had never been rich. He'd been the son of a reasonably well-off tailor. But with three children, that hardly mattered. They always struggled with food. His two brothers had been many years older, and his mother fawned over them a lot more than she ever did him. It wasn't her fault. They were struggling. Balen's birth had been unexpected and a strain.

So it had never quite felt like his life. Not until he saw the armor.

It was a parade for the Heir Ascendant's sixteenth birth-day. Theo Dued Vuuthrik had traveled across two provinces with King Sirellius, Queen Arasne, the rest of his siblings and an entourage of Paladins. Balen was maybe half his age, a year older than Zavrius, who at that point was the most unremarkable thing to Balen. Just another little boy clutch-ing his mother's hand. Balen's father had hoisted him up to sit on his neck, and he was hit with the image of Theo on horseback framed by two lines of Paladins. His heart had lit up. When the sun hit the armor, when the planes of gedrokbone went glinting off in a dozen fractal streams, technicolor splitting the pale morning—he'd lost his breath.

He remembered imagining it was him out there, sworn to something bigger than himself. He'd loved it. And at the age of ten, when it came down to it and joining the Paladin order meant forswearing his blood family entirely, Balen honestly hadn't hesitated. His father barely reacted. His mother had cried, but deep down, he knew she felt relief. One less mouth to feed was an unimaginable solace.

Besides, the life of a tailor wasn't for him. It would have never satisfied him.

Balen shook off the memory. This was his life now.

Eventually he took a deep breath and settled himself. Balen stared at the road, trance-focused, and let his hundred racing thoughts grow quiet.

CHAPTER
FIVE

It was early evening by the time they arrived in Cres Stros.

The city came into view gradually; it appeared on the horizon through the trees and filled up Balen's view. But this perspective was limited. From the cart, he could see only the rise of the russet-brown stone wall that encompassed the city. Though it towered high, the tips of needle-sharp pinnacles shot above the wall.

Balen crawled to the other side of the cart and reached over to Zavrius, intent on brushing back a rope of hair that had fallen over his face. But the king was awake, staring blankly at the lute-harp in his hands.

"We're home," Balen said softly.

Zavrius grunted and sat up. "And without incident. Such a feat deserves a song, don't you think?"

He seemed to put away the apathy, dragged the hint of a sparkle from somewhere deep in his body. Zavrius started strumming random chords until he settled on a song: "The Happiest Pauper," a light jaunt about a patrician-class man falling into poverty and finding renewed joy in life. Balen side-eyed the king with a smirk and took a deep breath as Cres Stros grew above them.

Within minutes, the gates swallowed them up. Balen shivered. He had the strange sense of an ax hovering over his neck, like there was some finality in coming home. Balen turned his attention to the heavy wooden doors that lay open on either side of the stucco-covered archway. They'd been open for a decade following the end of the war and the trade agreements made between Usleth and the empire, but their hinges were polished, well oiled. Ready to slam shut at a moment's notice. The everlasting expectation of Rezwyn incursion governed most decisions in

Cres Stros. A line of city guards stood on the ramparts and watched their entry impassively, themselves tiny dots compared to the gate guards—two towering Paladins chiseled from stone pillars in front of the gate itself. They were similar to the statues in Teum Bett. Each had part of a gedrok embedded deep within it. Balen couldn't stop himself from admiring them. He craned his neck as he'd done since he was a child, hoping to feel like he was a part of something bigger. But the feeling of coming home—bruised, beaten, on the back of a common wagon—sank into Balen's bones, giving him the anxious sensation of falling.

Still, once the wagon passed through the gates, once Balen caught sight of the vast mass of buildings and streets and life, a rush of exhilaration passed through him. It was a brief respite from the worry that had filled him up.

Balen gazed back at the city. The decades-long empire threat had made Cres Stros incredibly inward facing. There were dozens of narrow streets with high walls and archways. Not only were they useful for ambush and an effective maze against foreign invaders, several of the walls throughout the city doubled as aqueducts. In these alleys, midrise blocks of rooms were built against the longer, flat homes of the middle class. Greenery grew everywhere—not the lush, thick shrubs of the glade, but trailing vines and hanging plants laden with fruit.

Balen directed Mallet and Lance down the main thoroughfare. The narrow streets grew wider. The central part of the city was massive and old, shaped like a five-sided star, each point another thoroughfare leading to another district of the city. There were fewer homes here, all patrician class: wide, tall, some with their own walled gardens.

And then there was the palace.

Abruptly, Zavrius stopped playing. The palace was raised, built into a small hill. It was a tall, domed column surrounded by a sprawl of open colonnaded halls. Steep steps ran from the road to the high entrance. It was made of sandstone and lavishly decorated with stucco, gold-accented in places, shining. At its highest point, a flock of birds circled in the air above, specks in Balen's vision.

"This is where we part ways, my friends," Zavrius said.

Lance made an incredulous noise. His brother pulled the wagon to a halt.

"Here?" Mallet asked, skeptical.

"Here." Zavrius grinned wide as he shambled off the wagon. "Thank you again for the ride. After you deliver the chair to that Polverc bitch, please return here and ask to see a woman named Petra. She can supervise your induction into the palace guard—if that's what you want. Otherwise, she'll send you to the city."

With that, Zavrius turned on his heel and left. There was a skip in the king's step—or an anxiety that made him quick. He started up the stairs, taking the steps in twos.

A few Paladins moved to block him as if he was an unwanted beggar, then stopped in their tracks, returning awkwardly to their posts. The doors flung open. Within moments it was chaos: people darting everywhere, the sounds of an entire palace on edge returning to function.

The brothers had turned their eyes on Zavrius, brows furrowed. Balen wondered how long they'd sit there, if the realization would ever dawn.

"Not a bad outcome. Are you displeased?" Balen asked with a smile. "The palace pays more and you don't have to stand in the sun all day."

"What? Who the hell is he really?" Mallet's voice curled up. He waved toward Zavrius's back. "Who are you?"

"My name is Balen, Prime Paladin of Cres Stros." Balen patted the big man's shoulder. "I'd appreciate your discretion about everything that happened today in Teum Bett."

Lance looked him up and down again, reassessing, an excited smile spreading across his face. "Why, you sneaky—"

"Bloody . . . ," Mallet said, swallowing. Lance stopped speaking to look at him. "If you're Prime, then he must be . . . what we said before . . . we didn't offend His Royal Highness, did we?"

Lance's smile slipped. He looked to Balen, eyes ever so slightly widening.

"He's harder to offend than you might think," Balen said. Then, for a chance at keeping their fleeting camaraderie, he leaned forward to whisper, "And even harder to please."

Lance hooted, surprised. Mallet went to whack him again, but now that he had some idea who he was talking to, the big man seemed sheepish. He moved to untie the palace horse from the wagon.

"Paladin!" Zavrius's booming shout broke the moment. Balen turned to see the king waiting at the top of the steps. "Are you coming?"

Balen smiled at the brothers and waved his goodbyes. "You have my gratitude. If you have trouble, you can leave word for me at the Paladins' Forge."

He made it to the top just as Zavrius's aunt Petra arrived on the scene. Her gray curls were cowled with a blue linen shawl—and she was angry. But overwhelmingly, she just looked tired. No doubt she hadn't slept with the king missing. Zavrius tried to slip her a smile, but she cut her hand through the air to silence him. Balen knew what she was feeling: relief mixed with fury.

Balen barely had a chance to say anything—the king winked at him as he was dragged off to be cleaned up. And there was no rest for him, either.

A Paladin Balen didn't recognize materialized in front of him, face hidden behind her helmet.

"Prime," she barked. "You're wanted in the forge."

Something about her tone sounded like Lestr, like his master had managed to infuse her with a hint of his anger.

Balen gave a stiff nod. Once he'd changed back into his armor, he reported to the forge.

The forge's ceiling vaulted high into a dome. It should have made the space feel large and open, but something about how Lestr had filled it always made Balen feel small. Suffocated. Cool blue stone layered the walls and floor. The hearth burst from the center. It was decorated with great, thick chains that ran to the ceiling. The massive stone structure was fashioned to resemble the open maw of a gedrok. The fire lit up its eyes, flew out its nose. Balen found himself lulled as he watched it and had to pull himself away. The forge always looked different when Lestr was at work.

There was always the warmth and the deep-orange gleam, but now the furnace was alive. It roared and hissed, sparks spitting through the air. The way the light moved reminded him of watching sunsets at Wen Zerret, the ocean tide coming and going. He tried to find some comfort in that, knowing he was about to be so severely disciplined he might as well throw himself on his sword now.

Alick was already there, crammed into a corner amid the clutter and half-finished armor. He gave Balen a perfunctory wave.

"Lestr," Alick began, walking forward toward their master. He was still limping, leg not fully healed.

Lestr frowned at him. "You sit down. I'm not finished." Then, to Balen: "Duart is over there."

They'd laid Duart on a workbench, covered him with a tarp. Balen crossed his arms and stared down at the shape of his friend. Part of him wanted to peel it back and look at Duart, but another, more overwhelming part of him was a coward. Balen flexed his hand at his side.

"I'm sorry," he said quietly. Then, having said it aloud near his master, the finality of what had happened struck him again. Balen's chest seized. He grabbed Duart's hand through the tarp. "I'm sorry," he said again. But it wasn't good enough. How could it be? Duart was dead, and all for a chance to prove Lestr wrong.

Lestr pulled a molten gedrok scale from the furnace and went to cool it.

Alick stood standing for a valiant moment longer before he sank onto a stool, wheezing relief the moment the weight was taken off the leg. Balen settled himself farther against the wall and crossed his arms. His heart raced, but he tried to look collected.

The Paladin looked down at himself, white shirt dirtied and sweat-stained. He looked odd, embarrassing.

A clang. Hammer met scale met anvil. The forge echoed with beat after beat of Lestr's hammering, the sound reverberating off the stone. Balen closed his eyes, but his mind made him imagine he was that piece of armor, being beaten back into obedience. He grimaced and opened his eyes, stepping off the wall.

"Shit, Balen," Alick said under his breath. "You really pissed him off."

Balen glared at him. How quick Alick was to distance himself. He wanted to say, You followed Zavrius's orders too—but it was clear Alick had decided he was hardly at fault. Balen didn't have time to waste arguing with him on that point.

Moving away from the forge, Balen exhaled noisily while gazing at the stone dome. He turned to look at Lestr, who ignored the two of them, hammering away at the spurs on a piece of gedrokbone. He felt ridiculous, dressed as he was. But whatever Lestr had to say to him—or shout at him—he'd accept it.

The sturdy piece of gedrok scale Lestr was working on now resembled a doughy greatsword, but its original shape still remained. The sword had once belonged to Zavrius's brother Theo. The siblings' other weapons were laid carefully in the forge. Balen had inspected them weeks ago, when they were first recovered. They'd all been damaged in some way.

Gedrok was rare and precious. Carving from a gedrok was a sacred act, requiring a reverence and a ritual to take from the preserved remains. The gedroks weren't gods—but they held a power that deserved respect. There had never been any doubt these weapons would one day be repurposed.

Balen watched his master work. Where Paladin armor was made from the bone, gedrok scales were a sharp, metal-like material perfect for royal weapons.

The monotonous banging echoed through the hall, the beat consistent and strong.

Lestr's hammer jolted off the anvil, one final scrape of metal against scale, and then silence. Balen closed his mouth and swallowed hard. Lestr splayed both hands on either side of the anvil. He didn't turn around. He didn't need to.

Balen stalked forward, stopping a few paces from his master.

Lestr looked over his shoulder. "Who put it in your head? That confidence?"

Balen hadn't been feeling any such thing after the attack, but Lestr's tone helped him recapture some. He squared his shoulders, found some indignation to paint his face with. "It's gotten me this far."

"It'll get the king killed if you keep up with it," Lestr said. "Maybe not you, maybe not the Paladins, but Zavrius for sure." Lestr turned. He seemed to mirror Balen's stance on instinct. Looking at him standing tall and stiff, Balen understood why Lestr was his master. Lestr was sturdy. Balen's confidence had the decency to waver. "You want to know why? He trusts you. He always has. And he wasn't built for this, Balen, not like us. Not like the other heirs."

The Paladin swayed, tilting his head. He knew Zavrius could hold his own with an arcane weapon—he and Alick had just seen him do it firsthand.

"He's been trained in magic, just not the sword. He's good. The late queen—"

"Arasne, bless her, taught him enough," Lestr cut him off. "He has enough know-how to defend. That's a necessity when you're king. But I'm talking warfare. Sirellius was brutal with the rest of them. Really made them fighters. Zavrius can't compete with that. Why did you allow him to leave unprotected?"

He's never unprotected, Balen thought. Not when I'm by his side.

But Balen kept that to himself. He knew what Lestr was saying. Sirellius had been king of war and had raised his children at a distance. To him, they'd live and die defending the dynasty from incursions. With that kind of childhood, it wasn't any wonder the lot of them hungered for war long after it was over. It had shaped them all. Even Balen had spent the first three years of his training waving a wooden stick around imagining he was defending Theo from the savage Rezwyns. By the time he'd progressed to a sword of steel, any real threat from the empire had vanished. But he also knew why the royal heirs had craved the glory of proving themselves in battle.

Lestr looked at the king and, like everyone, thought he was weaker than his brothers and sister. Balen knew this, and knew something else, too.

Lestr didn't know Zavrius. He didn't know what Zavrius was capable of. Maybe all he heard when Zavrius played was a pretty tune, or maybe Zavrius played so well Lestr was unaware what kind of effect his magic could have. Either way, Balen knew he was wrong and so did Alick. They'd both witnessed the immense power of Zavrius's attack. Hadn't Alick reported that?

Balen shrugged. "He defended himself well enough on the road."

"He fought those assassins?" Lestr cut his finger through the air. Balen went stiff, said nothing. "Your king shouldn't have had to fight on his own road. He shouldn't have even been aware there was a threat at all. Not if you were any good at defending him. Not if you were doing the bare fucking minimum."

Balen closed his eyes. He felt the flush coming on, was sure Alick was staring at him, enjoying this far too much. If he groveled before Lestr now, if he waxed lyrical about how sorry and stupid he was, would Lestr rip those gauntlets from his belt and call him unfit to be Prime? But what if he was unapologetic and brazen? Lestr would also take exception to that. This wasn't about what he or Zavrius had done during the battle, but before.

"Don't pretend to care so much about the king's abilities. You're not upset that he fought. You're upset I disobeyed your orders," Balen stated.

Lestr's face twitched. His whole body seemed to expand with a slow breath in. "How dare you—"

"I know I'm right." Balen stepped forward. His mind was buzzing. "I'm not your obedient little pet."

"Maybe not." Lestr's words scraped through gritted teeth. "But you are his."

Balen narrowed his eyes. He ignored the strange drop of his belly and got ready for another dig. It wouldn't be hard. The Paladin had plenty to say. But he made himself speak slowly, his chin raised.

"No, I'm his humble servant," Balen said. "As you should be."

Lestr said nothing, but his eyes were fierce. Balen knew he was overstepping, but when he saw the hint of defiance in Lestr's eyes, he pressed his palm flat against his master's chest.

"I know this is your realm." Balen opened his arms to encompass the forge. "But it falls very much into his kingdom."

Lestr looked like he might yell. Balen braced himself for his master's wrath, but instead Lestr spoke quietly, enunciation crisp and sharp. "I am going to overlook this, Prime. Usually, I would not let this insubordination go unchecked. But under the circumstances, it makes sense. Alick told me you went days without your armor. It's obvious the time without it has affected your rational mind."

Balen bit down on his tongue. It didn't matter that he was wearing it now. He felt baited and ready to snap, which would only prove Lestr right.

His master held his gaze for a moment longer. When it was clear Balen wasn't going to counter, he nodded.

"Give your report, Prime," Lestr said as he turned back to his machines. "Start with where your armor is."

Balen sneered and opened his mouth. Before he could speak, the forge echoed with the sound of clacking footfalls. He turned around.

A young woman dressed in the trousers and closely fitted white blouse of a palace servant came toward them. She gave Lestr the slightest of bows, hinged at the hip. Then her small eyes peered over at Balen. He nodded back at her.

"I bring a summons," she said. "King Zavrius requests your presence in his hearing room. And Paladin Lestr as well. The king wishes to see the bodies of his attackers."

Lestr leaned back against the anvil, arms crossed. He was still and staring. Abruptly, he pushed himself off and went to quench Theo's blade: an angry stab into the water, the action short and punch-like. Lestr kept his back turned as the soft hiss of steam sounded. He was unhappy. The forge was his territory—a safe, familiar pocket in Zavrius's kingdom. Calling Lestr to his hearing room was not a subtle move from the king. It was a reminder of Lestr's exact station. Balen smiled with all his teeth, not bothering to hide his enjoyment.

"Lead the way," Balen said to the servant. She turned on her heel with a nod and clacked her way out of the forge. Balen didn't wait for Lestr to get over his pride. He left his brooding master staring into the tank, Theo's blade loosely drooping from his hand. He'd have to follow eventually.

Alick tried to stand as Balen approached. "I can—"

"You can't." Balen waved him back down. "You really can't. Not with that leg."

Alick looked pained, like he was biting back something snide. Balen doubted it would ever be easy for the older man to take orders from him. But Alick said nothing in the end. He slipped back against the wall, disgruntled.

"Do you plan to keep the king waiting?" The young servant had half turned to stare at them.

"Of course not," Balen managed with a smile. He gestured to the edge of the forge. "Lead on."

Zavrius's hearing room was a fairly small study tucked into the Royal Apartments in the palace's eastern wing. The walls were a light blue-green with decorative geometric stuccoes on the ceiling. A large half-circle window sat behind the desk. One wall was lined with books. From previous visits Balen recalled there used to be weapons mounted on the wall behind Zavrius—a marker of Sirellius. Those had gone, replaced by Arasne's decorations: instruments too old to be played nicely. Zavrius had left these up.

Zavrius was sitting in an emerald-green wingback chair, reading one of the letters piled on the desk. Balen's king was dressed in bone-white with gold powder over his eyelids, kohl lining his eyes.

The last time he'd seen the king, he'd been bloodstained and messy. Dressed in the clothes of his attackers, he'd looked like a king, but Balen had meant duty-bound. Committed.

Now Zavrius wore a boned mantle, a rigid attachment that clasped at his neck and curved over his chest, flaring wide at the shoulders. It was far too formal a look for a simple summons, but perhaps that was deliberate. Beneath the mantle was a many-layered tunic made from a stiff material. It was so formfitting it looked like he'd been sewn into it. His legs disappeared behind a grand wooden desk. It was covered with paper and trinkets that made Balen sure it had also belonged to Queen Arasne—golden floral paperweights, a golden letter knife cast to one side. What looked to be a handheld chest filled with gifts and food sat open, its goods strewn over the desk's surface. The Paladin spotted a large pink fruit, some purple roots. Nothing that was native to Usleth. Had the Rezwyn diplomatic entourage sent this pleasant gift to Zavrius's desk, while at the same time sending arcanists to murder him on the road?

He abandoned that line of thinking instantly, focusing his emotions into neutrality. Jumping to conclusions did no good.

"Your Highness," the servant girl said, introducing them. This time she bowed so deeply Balen was surprised she didn't topple forward.

Zavrius nodded at the servant girl. "Thank you, Illia. And has my uncle declined to accompany you?"

"He's straggling," Balen supplied. "Brooding. I'm sure he'll come."

Zavrius smirked and nodded at Illia to leave the room. Once she'd gone, he tossed the letter he held aside with a sigh.

He tapped it with one hand. "From Huez Thenlass."

Balen made a face. Thenlass made him feel conflicted. As a Paladin of legend, Balen had always looked up to him. But everyone knew he had been one of Theo's supporters, even if the provincial lord of Shoi Prya hadn't been too vocal about it. The royal siblings had spent a few days with

Thenlass for Theo's preemptive succession tour. But after they'd entered Westgar, the Heir Ascendant had planned to meet with Thenlass again, supposedly to discuss reestablishing the dynasty's defenses. Balen wouldn't be surprised if their negotiations would have strayed from defense to offense. Thenlass had been a soldier, after all. And Shoi Prya had little in the way of resources. Balen only said, "How much of that letter is for you?"

Zavrius blinked at him, uncomprehending for a good few seconds before his face twisted in a smile.

"Ah. Less than half." He held up two pages of the letter. "Clearly two different stationery sets—that's pathetic, isn't it? First page is all vague congratulations for the 'Exalted One'— not a single pronoun in the whole thing, in case Avidia claimed the title instead of Theo—and then the second page is an inch more customized. Uses my name, at least. Lazy bastard."

The Paladin raised a brow and stepped farther into the room. He clasped his hands behind his back and looked down at a round carpet spread over the deep-brown hardwood floor. The carpet was old and faded, handwoven silk. For some reason it made Balen think of the dynasty—of the Dued Vuuthriks, generations ago, setting the decor of the palace. How little had changed since then. Balen frowned and looked up at Zavrius. "I wonder what he would've written to Theo."

"I know what he would've written," Zavrius said with a sigh. "He's never been subtle about his hopes for the dynasty's future."

"I'm sure he never had to be."

"Of course not. My velvety voice has long been the only dissenting one in any room. Everyone else wanted war." Zavrius drew out the last word into a long, triumphant note.

They said nothing else for a time. Balen might have been on the border right now, if Theo were king. If any of Zavrius's crazed siblings were on the throne.

"It must have been hard to listen to."

Zavrius laughed in agreement. "Well, why do you think I went to perform for the merchant Oren Radek in Westgar?"

Balen had a suspicion—really, there was endless talk about what Zavrius had gotten up to while his siblings were being slaughtered. If the rumors weren't about Zavrius murdering them himself, they were about the handsome aristocratic merchant he was "performing" for. Balen gritted his teeth.

"I have a few ideas," he said.

Zavrius's smile slipped. Then, suddenly, he straightened in his chair. Balen turned.

Lestr stood in the doorway.

"Uncle," Zavrius said. "Good of you to join us."

Lestr walked into the room without a word and folded his arms. Then he clicked his fingers twice and four Paladins entered the room. They each carried a tarp-covered body between them. Balen glanced over in Lestr's direction, but his master was staring at his nephew, blank and angry.

Zavrius waved the other Paladins from the room. He waited a moment before he clasped his hands together. To Lestr he said, "These people were arcanists. Can you explain it?"

Immediate, spitting reaction: "Impossible."

Zavrius scoffed. "But is it?"

"Yes," Lestr said, fist shaking at his side. "Gedrok ichor is finite. It's not like everyone who wishes can wander into the glade and sip on it. So if what you're suggesting is true, then you're also suggesting that I've let someone take something reserved for the royal family and the Paladin Order."

"I'm not suggesting anything," Zavrius said. His voice was airy, full of disbelief. "I'm telling you what I saw. What we fought. Three Paladins and a trained arcanist struggled to vanquish a handful of ordinary assailants? That's the narrative you'd prefer?"

Lestr's top lip curled.

Zavrius dropped his hands to the desk. "Please, Uncle, at least look at their bodies."

Then, when Lestr didn't move, Balen stepped forward and tried another angle. "Sir, you have expert knowledge on ichor and the arcane."

Lestr cut his eyes upward. He had the grace to pretend for a few moments that he was unaffected, but when Lestr's shoulders softened, Balen knew it'd worked. Lestr wanted to know he still had their respect.

"All right," he said. Lestr knelt and pulled back the tarp.

Balen sucked in a breath. Of the four assassins who had attacked them on the road, two lay before them now, bloody and shirtless.

They looked different in the daylight. Younger, much younger, than he'd expected. Part of him assumed if they were attacking Zavrius, they were part of Sirellius's generation—war lovers, people concerned with the direction of the dynasty. Not that Zavrius had set a direction for them. People concerned by uncertainty, then? Or insurrectionists, revolutionaries thriving on terror? In any case, two men from Westgar—and the others, who'd been a man and woman with the deep skin tones from the south of Shoi Prya—were not what he was expecting. Death had made them human to him. They were all clear skinned and smooth. One was decently in shape, and the other was a little soft and broad, like Balen had come to expect of monied people without the need to work. That observation made even less sense. Balen frowned and looked to his master.

Lestr was rubbing his forehead. "They just look like people."

Balen gestured to the bright arcanist blood on the attackers. "Look. You're not blind. They have ichor in their veins."

But Lestr didn't want to hear it. "Three Paladins and the king fought in that battle. Each one of you is imbued with ichor."

"Then make sure they aren't arcanists," Balen said, growing more frustrated. He offered the hilt of his sword to his commander. Lestr looked at him for a long time, almost like confirmation was what he'd been avoiding. He waved Balen's sword away and unsheathed a small knife at his belt. Balen watched Lestr bring the edge to one of the corpses' wrists. It was still soft, fresh. The blade cut into the floppy flesh with ease. Even knowing the man was dead, Balen scrunched up his nose at the sight of the open vein. A brief surge of queasiness went through him, but it all dissipated when the brightly flecked blood dripped from the wound.

Lestr's only reaction was a deep, unhappy grunt. He wiped the blood up from the ground, put the knife away and resolutely kept speaking.

"And they weren't wearing armor?" Lestr's morose acceptance of the situation was a relief.

"It'd be worse if they had been," Balen said, coming to his knees beside him. "If they were trained, that is. But they weren't. They were—"

"Wild," Zavrius whispered.

Lestr frowned. "What do you mean?"

"They weren't being careful with their power," Balen said. "I don't think they'd been careful about their usage for a long while. They weren't in their right minds."

Lestr clicked his tongue. With a broad thumb, he wiped the blood away from one of the men's cheeks. "If they even knew they were supposed to be careful."

"What do you mean?" Zavrius asked.

"Not many people appreciate the Paladin armor. Plenty of people think it's all for show. You know the type I mean. The armor is a uniform for some, a shield for others. How many people understand that it helps to regulate ichor inside of a Paladin's body?"

"Not many," Balen said. Even among the Paladins, there was talk on whether arcane madness was a fable.

"How do we know it's not the Rezwyns?" Lestr said.

"There are rumors, you know. Taking people from the dynasty, turning them—"

"How adorable," Zavrius said. "You think I'm so well loved I can't have enemies in my own country."

Lestr frowned stiffly. "There are enemies everywhere, Your Highness."

He touched one of the dead assassins' faces, turning it in his big hand. Balen heard him mumble under his breath, "Who were you?"

Balen squatted down and ran his hands over the body. There was nothing that might distinguish the man. No jewels of any kind. The clothes he was wearing were made from oknum by their texture: rough and unprocessed on the outside, but soft on the part that would meet skin. That cloth was popular in Westgar, if you could afford it. That felt important and inconsequential at the same time. Balen sighed and ran a hand over his forehead.

"They all wore these oknum shirts. There's nothing unique on any of them." But was that deliberate, or was it chance? He mulled it over. "Might be I'm overthinking it, but oknum is expensive. And see the trim at their hands? Very fine."

Lestr made a noise in the back of his throat, nodding with understanding. "So you think they're not commoners?"

Balen heard Zavrius's breath hitch.

"If I look at these bodies I can see the marks of an idle life," Balen said. "Smooth complexions, full sets of teeth, fine make of their boots. Underneath the grime and blood, there is still a sense they were all well groomed, well looked after." Balen felt a brief surge of pride when his suspicions came together, followed by a deeper sense of dread.

Lestr grunted, his earlier anger coming back in a new, righteous way. "Nobility. You've butchered nobility."

Balen shot him down quickly. "What we did was save the king's life. Protected him from assassins. These were rightful executions. No butchering involved."

Balen tried to pick apart the look on Zavrius's face. Underneath the kingly visage, Balen could see the younger version of Zavrius that was a little more vulnerable. Balen went to touch Zavrius's shoulder, a residual habit, and stopped short.

Zavrius grunted. "Rezwyns on one side, my own nobility on the other. What's one more diplomatic crisis?"

Balen wanted to lean forward and tell him he was there, always. Whatever happened. But it felt too forward, and like the comfort one would give a child. Balen refused to embarrass him like that.

He told himself to think about managing the situation. Four noble youths attempt regicide while under the influence of ichor. If it were made public, how would the rest of the nobles take it? As a threat? A warning? Would it cause more problems than it would solve?

"We'll contact their families," Zavrius said. "Discreetly. Once we figure out whose children they are, of course."

It wasn't the offensive play Balen had been expecting. For that reason alone, he respected Zavrius more than before.

Lestr seemed to approve. He took a breath and gestured over the bodies. "They aren't anyone I recognize."

Which meant they were aristocrats, but not too important.

"How do you think they got the ichor?" Zavrius asked.

"I don't know. Maybe there's a traitor. Maybe there's a gedrok that we have yet to discover." Lestr got to his feet and repositioned the tarp over their faces. Balen, staring at one of their half-opened eyelids, was shocked back to the present when the tarp cut his view. "At least you're both still alive."

That seemed to be all Lestr was going to say. He summoned the Paladins to remove the bodies and departed with them.

Balen was buzzing with a hundred other questions—they'd solved nothing, come to no real conclusion. But then he looked over at Zavrius, saw a wondering, vacant stare, and knew it could wait. The king was tired. So was he.

"All right," Balen said, "let's rest."

Zavrius pressed his lips together, then gestured to the stack of correspondence in front of him. "You go. I have a lot of reading to catch up on." Balen hesitated for a moment before bowing and leaving Zavrius alone. The Prime Paladin's chambers were directly next to the king's and shared a door in case Zavrius was attacked at night.

This chamber was for the Prime, and meant entirely for sleeping near the king. In general, Paladin quarters in the barracks were shared, so the amount of space for personal effects was limited. While this chamber had space, it seemed to actively discourage that kind of self-expression. The room was spacious, though stark, save for a four-poster bed—which Balen could admit was more lavish than he'd expected—and a stand for his armor.

The stand backed against a bright mural: purple grays, blues, reds, interwoven in a bold, structured depiction of the king and the Prime. It was strikingly beautiful. The triptych showed the figures side by side, then in battle, and finally with the Prime dead at the feet of the king. The Paladin's gauntlets glinted with a line of crystals. If Balen hadn't been so tired these past few nights, that message was so absolute he might've stayed awake thinking about it. He'd always known death was a potential. But seeing it emblazoned on a bedroom wall reduced what Balen imagined a great sacrifice to a bit of paint: a deed easily scraped away.

The Paladin settled in, but hours later, well into the night, candlelight glowed through the crack of the shared door.

When Balen woke close to dawn, it was still lit, like Zavrius hadn't slept.

CHAPTER
SIX

Three days passed in a blur.

Zavrius was caught up in his kingly duties. It was all quiet, tactful letters coming and going for days with the king pent up in his study. He wanted to identify the corpses, to match their pallid dead faces to the reports of missing nobles in the east. Zavrius found them all. He sent for the parents in letters and mentioned the circumstances under which their sons had died. Shame was a powerful thing. When pressed about their involvement in the plot, representatives of the families arrived at the palace to proclaim their fealty and expunge any suspicion. Hercig, Jurak, Zubov— they were smaller families, not nobility with deep roots, but Balen knew the king still felt the threat keenly. Even with their refreshed pledge and renouncement of their children's deeds, it didn't feel like closure. But attempted regicide left just enough of a black mark that Zavrius seemed confident there'd be nothing like revenge.

During this time, Balen felt his absence like a vague ache at the back of his head, but he'd spent years learning to ignore that. He spent his days at the training ground adjacent to the forge learning to control the gauntlets in preparation for what would inevitably be the next attack.

Once Lestr knew for certain the assassins had been nobles, he only grew more paranoid and demanding of Balen.

"It's not good," he said, which Balen thought was a massive understatement. "Nobles outright attempting to kill him is a call to insurrection."

Balen didn't know what to say to that. Four assassins trying to kill the king might just be extremists. He hoped that's all they were. Luckily, he had little time to think about it. Lestr ordered him to perform more drills designed to enhance his connection with the gauntlets. The Paladin spent those days in the glaring sun, sweating and casting drill attacks for hours until the gauntlets felt like a second skin.

"Good," Lestr told him, after he was sweaty and exhausted. That was high praise, and Balen relished it.

Lestr clapped him on the back and left him panting and recovering by the training ground. The Paladin slumped, trying to catch his breath as he watched the older man stalk back to the forge. They were at the very back of the palace, out of sight of the noble guests. He watched Alick approach in his periphery. Balen stood and stretched to his full height, nodding his greeting.

"You're glistening," Alick said, gesturing to the sweat dripping from Balen's forehead.

Balen smirked at him, clapping his gauntlet into Alick's outstretched hand. "How are you holding up?"

The smile slid from Alick's face. He shrugged and scanned the palace for something else to talk about. That was Alick all over. Any confrontation not involving steel was to be avoided.

Then Alick went still. A sneer crept over his face. "You're kidding me."

Balen turned to look with him. His own breath caught. Walking through the colonnaded square was the Rezwyn ambassador. She was big, clearly strong, and still wearing the cuirass bearing the visage of her eerie god. She looked so incongruous in the austere training ground, with her strange garb and her two priests at her heels.

Alick tutted next to him. His disdain was so palpable it was like Balen could taste it. Balen put a hand on Alick's shoulder.

"Easy, Paladin," he murmured. It had the wrong effect; Alick tensed as he spoke. Balen squeezed. "They are guests of our court."

Alick bristled, then squeezed his eyes shut. When he'd contained his temper, he stepped out from Balen's grip.

Alick turned his back to the Rezwyn entourage. "I know, it's just . . ."

He didn't finish and didn't have to. Standing there, in the very place they'd trained for a war that never happened. . . Balen glanced over to the forge, the heart of what had allowed them to survive the old confrontation with the Rezwyns.

"There's peace," Balen said aloud, as a comfort to himself.

Alick only snorted. "For now."

Balen flashed him a look, but it was pointless. Alick wasn't alone in his sentiment. Too much of the court had been gearing up for a war the moment Theo was crowned.

"Let's talk of happier things," Balen said, patting Alick on the back. They walked across the dusty flats toward the colonnade and the palace entrance that led to the barracks.

Alick grunted. "I heard they're going ahead with the ball."

Balen barely stifled his surprise. Zavrius's coronation ball had been delayed for a number of things. Lestr warned it would appear disrespectful so close to the mass funeral for his siblings. But Zavrius's aunt Petra thought the opposite.

"More than necessary," she had said. "We need to show the court is settled. And everyone loves a party."

He tried to appear aloof. Zavrius hadn't told him—or worse, had explicitly kept it from him.

"You all right?" Alick prompted.

"Glorious," Balen said. "Just dripping with excitement for a party."

Alick snorted at him. "Might want to work on your delivery, then."

Balen slapped him on the back with a grin. It was good to joke with Alick again. There'd been some definite shift in their friendship since Balen had beat him in the tournament. Balen knew it had to do with his youth—a bit of shame from the older man mixing with jealousy. But without Duart, Alick was the closest friend he had in the Gifted Paladins.

Alick grinned at him and knocked their shoulders against each other.

"Ah, we've gone and done it now, Prime." Alick bobbed his head toward the colonnade. "You're doomed."

Petra spotted them from a distance, her face scrunching with a determined zeal. As she hurried over to him, calling his name, Alick patted him on the back and departed.

"The king wishes to see you about the ball." As chancellor, Petra was diplomatic and skilled at playing the games of the court. She had plenty of servants tasked with delivering whispers to her. It made her a formidable player, and Balen had no doubt she'd helped Sirellius secure his throne. Zavrius needed her, and if she believed the coronation ball would help cement his reign, Balen couldn't say no to it.

But damned if he wasn't frustrated at being shut out of Zavrius's machinations.

"I'm wary about hiring an orchestra. Bringing in too many external parties—with this climate, that's a recipe for disaster." Petra wrapped her shawl more tightly around her, speaking delicately, like what she was saying might hurt to hear.

"Of course, it's up to your best judgment. What does he need me for?"

"This is an important night!" she said, sounding everything like a flustered aunt.

The palace was full of moving bodies. The city guard had Lestr locked in conversation. Balen spotted a few men and women in palace guard uniforms helping the servants haul long tables toward the Great Hall. He glimpsed the familiar faces of Mallet and Lance carrying large pots of flowers. They grinned at him from behind the painted ceramic, eyes vaguely bloodshot. Balen shook his head, impressed by their ridiculousness.

Petra pulled him toward the eastern wing of the palace, mainly occupied by the Royal Apartment, a sprawl of rooms for the king and queen and their children. Zavrius's private study was here, but before Balen could walk to it, Petra tugged him aside.

"What happened on the road is not a good sign," she said. All her party-related joviality had vanished, leaving Balen to wonder if it hadn't all been for show. "You cannot let anything happen at this ball, do you understand? Zavrius needs to have a night in front of the noble class to show them he is a competent king. Maybe not a warlord like his father, but sturdy. Do you understand?"

Balen did. If Zavrius could show that peace with the Rezwyns was just as attractive as a war with them, he might just live long enough to be a good king.

"He is under my protection," the Paladin said. Petra scanned his eyes and smiled at him, seemingly satisfied.

"Right. Off we go." She guided them both into Zavrius's study.

It was a shock after not seeing him for days. Zavrius was in a simple blue tunic and billowy pants. He had braided his hair and laid it over one shoulder. When Balen and Petra entered, he glanced up to look at them, the cool blue of his clothes accentuating the warm brown of his skin.

Balen realized how sweaty he was. He knew—there was no doubt—he smelled. He felt laughable standing there in front of Zavrius looking so pristine.

Zavrius put down his quill and rocked back in his chair, stretching his arms overhead. He reached for the letter he'd written and handed it across to a young woman Balen hadn't even noticed.

Zavrius picked a small cake off a silver platter next to him and bit into it. "Send this off."

The girl took the letter and left with a short bow, leaving Balen blinking, disoriented that he'd missed her presence. That was dangerous. Zavrius shouldn't have had that effect on him.

"Thank you for coming," Zavrius said after the door closed. "I need your opinion."

Balen shrugged. "On?"

"Oh, a number of things. I'm dragging Huez Thenlass's sorry ass to my coronation ball," Zavrius said over another mouthful of cake.

Petra jumped at little at his words. If Zavrius had been anyone else, she would've commented on his language.

Balen couldn't help his smirk. "You are?"

Zavrius leaned forward conspiratorially, hooded eyes sparkling over his grin. "I can take his half-assed letter, but the coronation ball?" Zavrius flicked the air with faux disgust. "That man is mourning a family that isn't even his. It doesn't matter that he wanted Theo on the throne. He's got me. And his hold is vitally placed in Shoi Prya. If he doesn't want to be friendly with me, I'm sure someone else will."

Balen held back a smile. Zavrius's surge of confidence as king felt secondhandedly good.

Zavrius licked his fingers clean with relish and propped an eyebrow up at Balen's expression. "You disagree?"

"Not in the slightest."

Zavrius gave him a small nod.

Petra, though, tutted under her breath. She didn't wait for Zavrius to question her. "Thenlass is an important man. Getting him on your side would do wonders for your image."

"I think," Zavrius laughed, "my image is unsalvageable."

"Oh, don't say that," Petra said, voice hardening. "If you want to survive at court, you must have allies. King or no, your vassals won't tolerate a leader they don't resonate with. And let's not even start on the people. Shore up your image. Get Thenlass on your side. Or Polverc. A big name."

Balen flashed Zavrius a glance, remembering Zavrius's choice words about Polverc by the sawmill. Zavrius gave him a private smile.

"Hm, well, I didn't call you here for any of this," Zavrius said. He pushed back his chair and stood. He dragged a large piece of parchment off his desk with him.

Beside Balen, Petra's shoulders slumped. "Oh dear."

Zavrius held the parchment aloft. Balen spied the Rezwyn and Dued Vuuthrik names written in bold ink at the top. Below it, most of the page was filled with a tiny, flowing script—not Zavrius's hand, but Arasne's. At the bottom, Zavrius's thin hand had amended what Balen suspected was a document that would deeply upset everyone.

"We already have a trade agreement," Petra said.

"This is more than that." Zavrius's voice had a frustrated edge to it.

"Symbolic," Balen offered, despite not knowing what was happening.

"Symbolic," Zavrius repeated with a nod.

Petra shook her head and gestured out toward the palace. "They will think it humiliating." Zavrius only cocked his head at her, so she continued. "Arasne was forced to sign that peace treaty upon Sirellius's death—"

Zavrius interrupted, "She wasn't forced—"

"—and it stripped the Paladins of their honor. They were trained to win wars, to fight for territory and for Usleth. The Rezwyns' concession was patronizing. It reduced our Paladins to little more than emblematic protectors when they could have won us the war." Petra's voice was high and sharp. The Rezwyns' concession had been a slap in the face to much of the Paladins' ideology. Honor and glory—and all material things that came with it—were to be won. Not handed over on a piece of parchment. That was the sentiment among many of the Paladins, particularly the older members, who'd been fighting in Sirellius's army and imagined themselves the magic cavalry that might have won Cres Stros's victory.

Zavrius put the parchment down and leaned against the desk, folding his arms to say, "The Rezwyns renounced claim on Briym Plait. They conceded territory they did not have to because they knew most of Cres Stros's people wouldn't take the slight. We pay no subsidy, they have no input in how the dynasty is run—and they could have. They could have given us peace after crippling us. And they haven't."

Petra's mouth became a thin line. "Good relations make theft easier."

Zavrius's face twisted, a sudden thunderclap of anger that made his eyes dark. "The ichor is protected."

An uneasy silence came between them. Petra would relent eventually. She had to. But she was holding on to that uncomfortable moment for as long as she could and imbuing it with her disdain.

Balen cleared his throat. They both snapped around to stare at him. He nodded his chin toward the parchment on Zavrius's desk. "What did Arasne try to change?"

Zavrius stood and picked it up again. "She signed a peace treaty, but it kept Usleth and the empire at a permanent distance. There's no quick way to travel, no shared resource beyond the bare minimum. She wanted an ease of restrictions."

Panic crossed Petra's face. "Not an enhanced trade agreement, then?"

"Of sorts," Zavrius said. He turned back to Balen. "If we ease restrictions, it could foster free migration. Education, even."

An exchange of ideas. Balen frowned, unsure how to feel. He'd grown up expecting to fight the Rezwyn Empire to the death, and even if he'd never craved it like many had, there was fear of them imprinted in him that he couldn't shake so easily.

He'd seen a few of the extremely pale empire faces in Westgar, but most of the trade with the empire happened at the ports there. Seeing empire folk was inevitable. But free migration? Education? If the empire brought their strange gods to Usleth, what would happen then? The Paladins were a small order now, and would grow smaller every year.

Until they unearthed another gedrok somewhere, they had to be frugal with the ichor.

"You're very quiet, Balen. What is it?" Zavrius prompted.

The Paladin considered lying and agreeing with him outright, but what good would that do?

Balen shook his head. "If you do that, you won't be able to get anyone on your side."

Zavrius stared at him for a moment, then nodded. "Thank you. I thought so too." He brought the document toward them both. "I have amended my mother's suggestions."

"Migration only with permits. Very limited reasons for travel unless you apply for an exception. Still rigid, but just open enough we could actually make progress with them in terms of trade and mutual aid." Zavrius was gushing. He believed every word he was saying. Balen opened his mouth, but he stayed silent, happy to linger in Zavrius's joy.

"You're announcing this?" Petra asked.

"Not in so many words, but yes."

"Then what? Has their emperor seen this?" she asked.

Zavrius inhaled loudly. "I reached out for his opinion before my coronation."

Petra was incredulous. Her voice went high. "You did what? Don't take anything that lying old man says seriously."

Zavrius started to reply when there was a knock on the door.

"Your Highness." An older Paladin called Frenyur was at the door. A shadowed figure stood behind him. "As you requested."

"Yes, Frenyur, please."

Frenyur stood aside. One of the Rezwyn priests walked in.

Petra barely contained her fear. She was panicked by the sight of him: broad shouldered, wearing a fringed headdress that obscured his eyes but revealed his mouth, which had been painted a deep blood red. Balen carefully walked to shield her, hoping the move wouldn't upset the priest.

The man bowed deeply.

"Your Highness," he said, voice extremely accented. "I come on behalf on Ambassador Dziove."

Zavrius nodded at him. He'd apparently been expecting this visit. "Thank you for coming. I have a message I'd like you to pass to the ambassador at your earliest convenience."

"It shall be done."

"I humbly request she attend my coronation ball in three days time. There, when I call her, I would like the ambassador to join me on the dais. It is there I will announce the new relationship I will forge with His Excellency Nio Beumeut."

Balen could tell Petra wanted to scream.

The priest bowed again. "Your Highness."

Zavrius watched him leave before he turned back to Petra.

She shook her head. Zavrius raised an eyebrow. "I know you've seen this document before. I know you would have advised Arasne. You're not worried about the empire's reaction. You're worried about Cres Stros's."

Petra pursed her lips. "What I think personally doesn't matter."

"I know what you're thinking," he said sympathetically.

"But a party is not the correct place to make this kind of announcement," she said.

He nodded. "I need to show Usleth the right direction. I need to show them I have direction. The nobles value strength. The Rezwyns need to be shown good faith, too. Especially after Lestr's little speech at the glade mentioned talk of war."

"And if it all goes wrong?"

"Then I'm here." Balen stepped forward. He put his gauntleted hand over his heart. "Always." He'd struck down

Usleth nobles already, and if it meant defending Zavrius's life, he would do it again.

Petra looked between them. Worry was carved deep on her face. She had every right to be scared. She'd lost her brother, a niece, nephews. Zavrius was all that was left. But he was also the king, and though she was an adviser, she'd have to concede eventually.

"You're here," she said, nodding at Balen. It was obvious that she was trying to convince herself. "Then protect him. Every moment from here until you die."

Balen hadn't forgotten his pledge. He looked Zavrius in the eye, saw him not as the man he'd once loved, but as king. Cres Stros's future standing tall.

Balen nodded at him, certainty in his bones.

"I will."

CHAPTER
SEVEN

Balen didn't see Zavrius for another three days, but the state of the palace in the lead-up to the coronation was an excellent distraction.

He was a man who trusted his gut, and when his gut twisted, Balen knew to listen to it. The palace was flooded with people. It didn't matter that those people had been invited, or even that some of them were there to bolster the palace's defenses. When the palace was crawling like this, Balen felt it like ants in his blood. Lestr had been right. A coronation ball was the perfect time to dispatch the king.

It was late afternoon, and with the ball due to start at sunset, it was chaos. Balen stood opposite the entrance to the Great Hall watching servants rush about, clocking the faces of every person running past. A stone Paladin statue stood sentinel on either side of the Great Hall's entrance. Balen mirrored their stance, leaning on the pommel of his sword as he watched a hundred potential threats move erratically through the palace. He wished those stone Paladins were more useful.

Two hundred city guards had been called from their posts in Cres Stros for the event. That meant there were three orders of fighters in the palace now: defenders of the city, defenders of the palace, and the battle-ready Paladins sworn to defend the king. The city guard were milling uselessly until their post assignments came through from their lieutenant, who Lestr had bundled off somewhere to go over defenses. At least some of them would be tasked with the front of the palace, ensuring the only people who entered were the ones supposed to. Balen watched them talk to each other in low whispers. He wished he could hear them. Who had selected them? How were they vetted? He made a mental note to follow up with Lestr when next he saw him.

Someone moved in his periphery. Balen stood to attention just as they said, "You don't look happy."

It was Lance, smirking at him with a lopsided grin. Mallet stood alongside him. Both were dressed in the regalia of palace guards, a high-necked maroon shirt and pants. Their sets were crisp and brand-new. Over the uniforms, they each wore a simple iron cuirass. Side by side, they were comically different. Lance's uniform hung off his lanky body, where the cloth was stretched tight over Mallet's massive frame.

It was good to see them. Balen's uptight posture crumpled a little. "Hello, Lance."

"Oh, Balo, Balo, Balo." Lance patted him gently on the shoulder, clearly forgetting his decorum in the moment.

But his brother hadn't forgotten.

"Lance," Mallet hissed, darting out from the Great Hall to yank his brother away from Balen's shoulder. "Your, uh, Your Greatness, I apologize."

Balen couldn't help but smile. "No greatness here that needs a title. I'm still a soldier, just like you. And it's Balen."

Balen pointed at them. "Enjoying the post?"

"We're in your debt." Mallet nodded seriously.

Balen considered dismissing that but thought better of it. If something did happen at the ball, he wanted to call on people whose fighting skill he could rely on. Neither Lance nor Mallet were particularly ambitious. Lance's greatest aspiration was clearly to marry a pretty girl. The two of them were as devoid of political thought as the stray dogs that slept on the kitchen stairs, and twice as loyal. He barely knew them, but he almost trusted them more than some of his own Paladins.

Balen looked them over. "So it's not a disappointment, then?"

"Well . . . wouldn't go so far as to call it fun. But you've done right by us." Lance slumped against the Paladin statue and folded his arms. He knocked his shoulder against Balen. "You sure you're all right? Something dark's happening behind your eyes."

Balen snorted. He didn't doubt it—all this chaos was making him paranoid. His shoulders were tense, so he deliberately stretched, hoping to shake the feeling in his gut.

"I think I know what you need," Lance said.

Lance's stare was almost sultry as he reached into his pocket and removed a small box that Balen knew contained his clay pipe. Lance waggled his brows. If it wasn't for his previous experience with the two, Balen would've thought it an entirely different kind of proposition.

Balen tutted. "You're not seriously suggesting I should smoke with you, are you?"

Balen watched Lance process who he was and what they were doing all over again. The smile dripped from his lips. "Right. No. No . . ."

Mallet crossed his arms and shook his head fervently. "Wouldn't dream of it, sir. Never."

Balen only smirked and rested his weight against the Paladin statue behind him. A woman went barreling forward with a pot filled with flowers, nearly spilling its contents on the tiles. She looked up in sheepish apology before she was hurried into the Great Hall by another servant behind her. He knew most of these outsiders would leave immediately after they were done with setup, and really, it was only a handful of hours before the guests would start arriving. He knew everyone here had been vetted and vetted again. But he'd made mistakes before. He'd been foolish enough to allow the king to be underprotected, because Zavrius had wanted it that way. And he'd paid for that stupidity with Duart's life. Now Balen's unshakable confidence in himself had diminished and he felt like disaster lay in every corner of the palace. Or every corner of Cres Stros.

Lance waved a hand in front of Balen's eyes. "What is it?"

Balen blinked and shook his head. He'd been staring at the gaggle of servants. "Oh, I don't know," he said, smiling sadly at the brothers. "An event this size is fraught with danger."

Mallet stepped forward. "What are you worried about? An attack?"

"Something like that." Balen was worried about it all. A full-blown attack made him feel safer than the thought of a silent arcanist assassin slipping through, noble born like the others on the road. They would be able to blend right in at the party. How would he even know until it was too late?

The brothers exchanged a look. They spoke silently to one another, just a widening of the eyes and a quirk of the head apparently enough to communicate their thoughts.

"Come on. We want to show you something." Mallet patted Balen on the back. It should have been a gentle urging, but Mallet was such a large man Balen felt he had to walk forward. The pair ushered him into the Great Hall.

Twenty-odd pots lined the walls, all filled with jasmine and other flowers. The floral scent hit him like a wave.

It was a long stretch of a room, white stucco walls and a vaulted ceiling. Stained-glass windows ran all along each wall, casting multicolored streams of light across the white and black patterned tile. Wooden tables with cream-colored tablecloths and golden candelabras had been arranged around the periphery to allow for an open space in the center for dancing. A raised wooden dais sat at the far end of the hall. It held twin thrones that sat side by side under a huge stained-glass window depicting the first Paladin, the ever-watchful eye of his order overlooking the Dued Vuuthrik line.

"Yes, it's very grand," Balen said, turning to the brothers. But they kept dragging him to the far corner of the room.

Balen glanced back to the doors of the Great Hall. Most of the servants were turning to leave, their setup complete. "What are you—"

"Just trust us," Mallet said, which was a difficult request when Balen was being coerced forward.

Up close, Balen had to crane his neck to see the shape of the Paladin outlined in the window. Iridescent light fell over the twin thrones beneath it, the same familiar sheen as his Paladin armor. Balen had approached the throne only a handful of times before. He remembered bowing low before Sirellius upon his initiation, a year before the king was killed in battle and peace with the Rezwyns drawn up. He remembered the Paladins on display before Arasne, as the Heir Ascendant Theo sat by her side. Tonight, it would be Zavrius, and from that new angle stationed behind him, Balen would be the one looking down at the crowd.

Lance climbed onto the dais. It took Balen a few quick heartbeats to comprehend what he was doing. He jumped forward, eyes wide. "What are you doing?"

Lance got to his feet. "It's fine. I'm just showing you—"

"The thrones?"

"No!"

Mallet bounded forward and offered his arm. "Would you just get up here?"

Balen felt like he was about to piss on something sacred. He flexed his hands, feeling the power in the gauntlets. "Shit . . . fine." He took Mallet's hand and let himself be dragged onto the dais.

Balen turned back to the emptying hall. "I'm not sure how this is supposed to make me feel any better."

"Balen," Mallet said in frustration. "You're worried about this ball."

Balen grimaced, shrugging at him.

"You were worried in Teum Bett, too," Lance said.

Mallet pointed to his chest. "Covered in blood, and all that."

Balen peered at them both. "What's your point?"

Lance gestured wide. "Well, if you keep on like this, you'll be a useless Prime. You need to unwind."

"Manners, Lance," Mallet hissed.

Lance balked, expression clouding. "Shit. Sorry, Your, uh . . ." He gestured in the air for Balen's title, couldn't grasp it and promptly gave up. "Ah, whatever. Just come here."

Balen knew he was supposed to be feeling wary, or at the very least, a little bruised at Lance's near indifference to his station. But he wasn't. This attitude was refreshing. He'd made mistakes before—but that was when he'd ignored his gut. If he were to trust himself now, he would trust the brothers.

Balen threw up his hands. "All right."

He walked forward across the dais. Lance guided him behind the thrones. They were whittled from a warm-colored wood and were intricately carved. Precious stones were inlayed into their decoration. There was nothing but the wall and a large pot of flowers placed between the thrones.

Balen raised a brow at them. "So?"

"We were up here last week. You know, guarding."

"He was talking to a girl who was decorating," Mallet clarified. He gestured to the pot. "She was arranging those flowers."

"And I was craving, you know? Because this place can be suffocating, Balo, with all the stress of guarding, and I—"

"Just get to the point," Balen said.

"Right." Mallet tugged his brother out of the way. "Well, Lance was leaning on this throne."

Balen shot him a look. The throne wasn't to be touched by just anyone. Let alone leaned against.

Lance grimaced at Balen's dark expression. "I'm sorry, all right? I was tired!"

"Yeah, yeah." Mallet waved him away. "He's a dolt, I know. But he came across this."

Mallet walked to the throne on the right, the throne Sirellius had sat upon. He pressed his hand against the wood. A soft pop sounded. Balen jolted, thinking the big man had cracked the wood. His stomach dropped imagining the aftermath of a broken throne. Zavrius would suffer from that symbolism. And when a panel at the back of the throne dislodged, a fearful anger erupted in Balen's belly.

"What in the gedrok's bloody name—"

"See?" Mallet calmly cut across him. Balen stuttered and shut up. The big man put his hand around the open edge of the panel and gently pulled it open. It gave a soft creak, almost making a surprised sound at its own discovery. Balen squinted. The door opened to a narrow set of stairs leading to a dark drop.

Balen gave an irritated shake of his head. He tried to contain the feeling before it got the better of him, but a secret door? Either he was an incompetent Prime, or this passageway had long ago been forgotten. He hoped for the latter. If he'd believed in the empire gods, he would've prayed.

Balen looked between the brothers carefully. "I've lived here for years and never found anything like this."

"Well, it's a secret," Lance said.

Mallet nodded. "That would be why."

A very well-guarded secret.

Lance leaned forward toward him. "Why'd you look angry?"

It was an invaluable thing to know. Balen wasn't sure what his face was doing. He shook his head and sighed. He had a feeling in him like Zavrius was holding back, keeping vital things from him. At the very least, Balen needed the information to do his job.

But maybe Zavrius didn't know about it. Maybe the brothers had stumbled upon an ancient secret of Cres Stros.

Balen looked up at Lance and shrugged. "Close it. Really. This is . . ." He gestured to the doorway. "Thank you for showing me this. I hope I never have to use it."

"Sure." Mallet shrugged. "But when you're standing up here tonight, maybe you'll feel better just knowing it's there."

Balen knew he would. He stepped back with a smile. "And where does it lead?"

The brothers exchanged a glance.

"What, uh . . . what makes you think we know?" Mallet asked.

Balen smirked and glanced between them, "Because if Petra, Lestr, or any palace guard with a lick of sense had stumbled upon the two of you smoking, you wouldn't be in uniform."

The brothers stared back.

After a long moment of silence, Mallet nodded. "Fair cop. It goes to a drainage ditch near the stables on the eastern side of the palace."

Balen looked around the hall. Though the room was clear of servants and guards, Balen wasn't willing to risk any eyes seeing them disappear into something he needed protected.

"Take me to the place—not through there. Just take me where it lets out," Balen said.

They replaced the door to the passage. Lance patted Balen on the back and led him out of the hall, in a way that was both overly familiar and strangely reverential. They moved in silence down the main corridor, which led out into the courtyard, where the warm sun baked the ground and made Balen squint. Some Paladins were training near the forge to the left, but the brothers steered him right. At first they moved toward the secluded walled garden at the end of the palace grounds, where Cres Stros's stripped gedrok skeleton lay entombed by flowers. But they headed right again, down the thoroughfare between the palace and the outer walls. A few city guards were already stationed along it and nodded at Balen as they passed. Eventually the ground sloped down. The three of them walked down the terraced hill, parallel to the massive stone steps that led to the palace entrance.

Balen looked back at the grand structure rising out of the hill. Several grassy terraces jutted out from the steep steps. The stables were positioned on a level near the bottom. Mallet brought them around. A grassy mound was built into one of the terraces. Balen spied a small grate with suspiciously well-oiled hinges and a broken lock affixed to it.

"Here," Mallet said. He patted the tumulus-like tunnel.

Lance folded his arms triumphantly like he'd carved the tunnel himself. "Useful?"

Balen smiled at him. "Very. Did you break the lock yourself?"

"No, it had rusted through already," Lance replied.

The soft whinny and snort of horses sounded from the stables. Over that came the rise of voices. Balen turned and spied them: nobles attempting the slow ascent to the palace. Their carriages left them at the bottom of the stairs to await their return. Balen glanced up at the sky and saw the sun was starting to set.

People were arriving for the ball.

"Ah," Mallet said, vaguely pointing. "That's the chair lady."

Balen knew her. Hawk-faced Lady Adzura Polverc walked solemnly up the stairs, languid like her own existence was tiresome to her. She was dressed in a long gray gown and clutched a handkerchief in her right hand. Balen doubted she was mourning in truth. But it was a good show on behalf of her sister, and Balen had no doubt Polverc's missing niece would be quite the conversation piece at the ball.

She wasn't the only one to have arrived early.

A woman with the dark brown skin of a Shoi Prya native followed a hundred paces behind Polverc. She was wearing a light-blue dress with a pattern Balen had to squint to see. He figured they were birds of some sort. A dainty metal corset slotted in neatly under her breast. No doubt she was a warrior. She moved like she was unused to being formally dressed. She wasn't anyone Balen recognized, but he'd committed the list of guests to memory and guessed she was Lady Juuls, representative of the Sorbetka family. They were a small noble house in Shoi Prya, but they'd been vocal supporters of the Dued Vuuthriks—when Theo was in line for the throne. Zavrius likely wanted to test their loyalty now.

The final early arrival was a man severely underdressed compared to the two women proceeding before him. Newly wealthy, perhaps? His tunic was slightly out of fashion, expensive but well-worn. Balen's stomach flipped at the sight of him.

Likely just to spite Balen, Zavrius had gone and invited Oren Radek, the aristocratic merchant he'd gone to play for the day his siblings died. And there were plenty of rumors about what had kept the king so busy he only returned to camp well after their demise.

What did it matter? It wasn't any of his business. Zavrius was the king, and the king could do whatever he pleased. Balen had no right to feel—

What was he even feeling?

Mallet prodded him. "What is it?"

"Nothing," Balen said, even though his voice betrayed him with a slight crack. He dragged his stare away from Radek.

Mallet gripped his shoulder. "You know him?"

Before Balen could rely, the brothers' lips quirked, like they knew something they shouldn't.

"Haven't had the pleasure," Balen said shortly, eyes cast down. He couldn't be so obvious with his disdain. But Balen felt now the same quiet horror as when his eyes had landed on Radek's name on the list.

"Stay close by and watch this exit—subtly," Balen said, looking up at Mallet and Lance. "If anyone asks you what you're doing, tell them you're under my orders."

"All right," Lance said. "You're welcome."

"Thank you," Balen said with a laugh, always surprised by how bold Lance was. "If you notice anything tonight, come find me."

Mallet frowned. "Like what?"

Balen turned serious and pointed sharply to the tunnel's exit. "Like someone trying to enter this tunnel to kill the king."

"Right," Mallet grunted. Balen thought he saw the man pale.

Lance did a sweeping bow. "You'll be the first to know."

Balen could only hope that was true.

Balen spun toward the palace. The white walls shifted to golden, reflecting the rays of the setting sun.

The change in the light threw a redder glow over the stairs, and over Radek himself. His skin was a russet brown that turned near golden in the oblique light. The sight of him like that made Balen feel pallid. Small.

This wasn't a smart thing to be doing. But it was like Radek was a lure, and Balen's body was reacting to something instinctively. He was drawn forward, but by nothing substantial. Perhaps the rumors of the man, the draw of what he and Zavrius might have done together that evening. Or perhaps it was just the ugly twist in Balen's gut that kept him walking forward.

His heart stuttered with every step he took. Far ahead, he heard Polverc speaking, but the shape of her words was muffled. Whatever she said made Juuls Sorbetka laugh roughly. Radek reacted as if stung by a bee and took the stairs in twos to reach the conversation.

There was a man who clearly craved a higher station. No doubt he'd ferociously claw his way up the ranks any chance he got.

Balen hung back for a moment on the lower steps so he'd be out of sight when Radek caught up to Polverc and Sorbetka. But he didn't linger there for long. Balen moved as quickly as the Paladin armor allowed him, cresting the final stretch of stairs just as Polverc said—now with complete clarity—"He'll never be the man we might have had."

It could have been nothing. They might have been talking about any other man. But Balen had already stumbled upon his own Paladins voicing their dissent, and they were sworn to protect the king no matter what. The nobles had no such loyalty.

Balen grimaced. He'd feared this. Love for Theo and his ardent wish to do battle was a fervor, a gangrenous limb on the body of the dynasty. If there was no cure, it would have to be severed. They hadn't spotted him, all three of them walking slowly to the grand doors that opened onto the palace. Balen kept his footfalls soft to keep in pace.

Sorbetka put her arms over her head and stretched, the ropelike muscle of her back accentuated by the motion. "As long as he is king, we must expect to play this game."

She seemed so different from the reserved, solemn Polverc, which made Radek's appearance with them even more confusing. Polverc's family was very old and very prominent. The Sorbetka family had only had two or so generations of marked nobility. Radek's merchant business had propelled him into aristocratic waters. That any of them were interacting felt like seeing the sun and moon walking hand-in-hand across the sky.

"What game? He's little more than a coddled child."

"Either that," Sorbetka said slowly, "or a kin-slayer."

Very softly, Radek said, "You don't know that. You haven't given him a chance."

Polverc and Sorbetka shot him a glance.

"Of course you're on his side," Polverc laughed. "You bedded him."

Radek said nothing to that, but Balen saw his shoulders tense. He was surprised to hear Radek speak at all, even more so that he might risk ruining a potential friendship with Polverc in favor of Zavrius.

He was surprised, too, by the near disappointment he felt to hear Radek defend the king. He almost wanted Radek to be involved in what happened on the road. There would be an easier reason to mistrust him than the messy feeling in him that was only born from hearsay and jealousy. Part of him had already given the thought of Radek's betrayal a foothold, even if he wanted to give Zavrius the benefit of the doubt. And if anything physical had happened between them, Radek's betrayal would make that reality easier for Balen to swallow. Radek was a seducer, a trickster—not a man Zavrius had legitimately fallen for.

What kind of Prime would wish that? The wish for Radek to be a traitor was beneath him.

After a heavy moment, Polverc glanced up at the tall palace walls. "You should hush now. The court is not the place to speak on this."

Balen savored that understatement, but he was almost grateful to see these three in an unguarded moment. It would keep him focused at the ball.

Balen stomped heavily on the ground. His sabatons rattled with the impact.

All three guests went rigid.

"Good evening." He pulled a smooth grin as they turned.

Polverc had the same Westgar-pink undertones as Balen, but she was near translucent with shock when she turned.

"Prime," she said. To her credit, her voice didn't shake, and Balen barely registered her resume her usual confident posture until she was in it. "It's an honor."

"The honor is mine." He dipped his head to them all. "Lady Sorbetka, thank you for attending. And you are . . . ?"

He'd thought about snubbing Radek entirely but relented when he saw a momentary lost look that passed over the other man's face.

"Oren Radek," he said, holding out his hand.

That gesture Balen did pass on. He replaced it with a tight grin. He then leaned closer and whispered, "It's considered rude for anyone to lay hands on the Paladin armor. In the future it's best for you to greet other members of my order with a bow." The pettiness felt stupid and wonderful all at once. "Have an excellent evening."

He walked off, elated with the thought that they were sweating wondering what he'd overheard. Zavrius hadn't proved what kind of king he was. For all they knew, they might well be executed over dinner.

The feeling vanished as he walked farther into the vestibule and saw that Polverc and the others had not been the first to arrive. He saw several nobles chatting, taking in the sights of the great hall. Some huddled together and talked, but in Balen's mind he saw them whispering. Conspiring. Drawing up sides against his king.

Balen composed himself and refused to let the paranoia run him in circles.

 CHAPTER EIGHT

Balen went immediately to collect Zavrius. The palace was abuzz with noise, the early excitement of the party seeming to thrum through the halls. Nobles had crowded the colonnaded garden, but some were making their way to the Great Hall to assemble for Zavrius's arrival.

Balen lurked at the edge of the Royal Apartments, watching them go. A few palace guards shepherded the nobles, with two Paladins taking up the rear. That made him feel momentarily better, but dread still hung over him. It was like he was on the carriage again, hurtling down the Royal Highway, only this time Balen felt wide awake. Ready for the assault from the shadows.

He approached the Royal Apartments slowly. It was directly next to his own, and though his personal chamber was spacious, this was a sprawling room with big oak doors. Through the walls, a sound reached Balen's ears. A lilting hum. Zavrius was singing to himself. Balen smiled as he knocked and entered.

Something behind one of the doors stopped it from opening. Balen thought nothing of it as he slipped through the other one, but his eyes dropped to the source and he froze. Zavrius had dragged a heavy chest close and abandoned it at an angle. It sat ready to be shoved against both doors. Balen grimaced at it.

If Zavrius was feeling unsafe, it could only be Balen's fault.

The suite was bright with color. The walls were a warm, muted red and the whole chamber was filled with firelight from the hearth and several scattered oil lamps.

A stained-glass triptych window spread high across the back wall. Balen's eyes dropped over a giant bed centered beneath it. A mass of pillows and throws smothered the surface. Balen spotted the lute-harp laid carefully on a pillow.

Above them sat a beautifully made ceiling, tessellated to appear almost like honeycomb: a patterned, starburst stretch of honey-gold laced with midnight blue.

The suite was not one long stretch of room. It was sectioned into three by two arches with deep-crimson curtains that could be drawn closed. Those smaller areas were a private sitting room and a walk-in wardrobe filled with Zavrius's various robes.

But Balen's attention was hardly on the room.

Zavrius was half undressed, bent over something on a desk to the left. His hair was out. Long curls hid part of his face from view. He was only wearing a long linen shirt that brushed his midthigh. The remaining length of his legs were exposed. Balen's eyes lingered. He wasn't surprised to still be moved by Zavrius, by his body, but he was surprised at his own apprehension. His heart raced like this body was new. Something in his lower belly seized.

"Stop acting like you've never had a good look at me," Zavrius murmured, not even glancing up. He was clearly distracted by his own tinkering.

Balen shut his eyes, cutting off the sight of the king and every latent feeling the sight of his body brought forward. Then Balen walked forward, dispassionate. It was just a body, and not one belonging to anyone who was his.

"You aren't ready," Balen said.

"Astute," Zavrius said. He picked up the object of his focus and turned it over in his hands. It looked like a lyre, or the cousin of a lyre. Something with a proper wooden body, not an instrument crafted from the rare gedrok. He tweaked the string at one end, gave it a strum, and sighed. "Sound's too shallow."

"What are you doing?"

"Procrastinating. Forestalling the inevitable," Zavrius said with a sigh. "And catching up on light reading."

He gestured to a few opened letters on the desk.

"From the Ashmon Range, most of them," Zavrius said with a nod. "A lot of apologies."

Balen picked a few up. "They're not attending."

Zavrius shrugged. "The distance makes it understandable. I'm not worried, though. The Ashmon nobles have always been loyal to my family."

Balen scanned the desk. He saw a Cres Strosian stamp on one of the letters and picked it up with a curious look at Zavrius.

The king shrugged. "Some delay from the Lady Mariel Kus."

Balen frowned. The Kus were a small noble family based in Cres Stros. "What could possibly delay a letter that had to travel a few hundred paces?"

Zavrius shot him a grin. "At least she sent one. Eventually. There are plenty more noble houses who have yet to congratulate me at all."

Balen put the letter down. No one would have delayed with Theo. No one would have dared.

Zavrius went back to tinkering.

Balen looked toward the door and back. "Your Highness—"

"I know, I know." Zavrius put it down and went to change. He stretched as he walked, arms overhead dragging the shirt up farther and farther. Balen forced his eyes down.

Zavrius rummaged through his wardrobe, throwing robes and tunics onto the floor.

"Should I call a chamberlain?" Balen asked.

"If I wanted one here, they would be."

Balen shut his mouth and stood in the center of the room. That Zavrius was without a servant piqued Balen's interest, but when his eyes came to rest again on Zavrius's makeshift barricade, he stopped chasing for the reason. Zavrius wanted to be alone.

Balen waited a few long minutes in silence. Part of him wanted to ask if Zavrius needed help, but he knew Zavrius would make some quip. He didn't want to hear it. More than that, Balen wanted to ask why Zavrius had invited Radek. He craved some innocent reply but couldn't say it aloud. Couldn't risk hearing Zavrius say something true. So he stood there starting to swelter in his heavy armor by the heat of the fire.

Balen thought about the ball beginning outside. He thought of Polverc and Sorbetka spreading that insidious rumor of what Zavrius had done for the throne. With Polverc's standing, it'd have more weight to it. But with a Rezwyn ambassador running around, was it better to have his countrymen think Zavrius murdered his siblings, or that he was inviting their murderers to dine with them? They all seemed to believe either the Rezwyns were involved or Zavrius was, and neither reality would do much for his standing as king. Which rumor would Balen prefer to spread?

Neither. He'd rather they all kept their mouths shut, but that seemed an impossible task for the dynasty's nobility. Gossip was their life's blood. He just wished the cruel lot of them would give Zavrius a chance. But it would never happen. Even if Zavrius was a good king, he would always be a controversial one.

"Stop pacing," Zavrius called from the wardrobe.

Balen jolted to a stop, surprised he'd been moving. He edged himself around the corner and peered into Zavrius's wardrobe.

Zavrius looked up as he appeared, brow quirking high. "Spying on me while I'm dressing, Prime? How improper."

"Deeply sordid," Balen said, matching the king's tone. The humor was there, but it was muted in Zavrius's voice. His lips twitched a little, but a true smile seemed an insurmountable task for him.

He was dressed in a heavy, ill-fitting robe over a bright maroon tunic. The robe didn't suit him. The shoulders were too wide, and it was made from a drab boiled wool that was nothing Zavrius would normally wear.

Balen couldn't keep the expression from his face. "I've seen you look better."

"Of course you have, Balen, you've seen me naked." Zavrius gave him a wink.

Balen swallowed his surprise, reeling from Zavrius's constant change in tone. It was impossible to tell if Zavrius was serious or teasing, or some conflicting combination of the two. That seemed to be how their interactions went these days. A soft familiarity undercut with something acrid.

Balen scratched his head and positioned himself to lean against the wardrobe's arch. "It's Theo's, isn't it?"

Zavrius looked away, lips pursed. "It would have been."

Balen frowned. Was this Zavrius mourning? Or was there strategy behind it? "Why wear it?"

Zavrius shrugged. "Ill-fitting clothes for an ill-fitting man."

Balen pushed himself off the wall. He'd intended to move closer, but the movement had spooked Zavrius; he shot him a warning glance, a reminder that they were barely friends and certainly weren't lovers. They were only a king and his Prime, and the intimacy of that pairing did not extend this far.

Balen folded his arms and stopped with a small, conceding nod. "You are not ill-fitting. You will be a good king. Take this off. Wear something appropriate . . . please."

Something changed Zavrius's posture, but Balen sensed it wasn't relief. Something close to regret passed over the king's face. Zavrius wound himself tighter, stood straighter and dropped the heavy robe off his shoulders. It thumped to the floor. Then he waved Balen backward and slid on a robe that was formfitting and colorful. The robe was gold and covered in a geometric design in a burgundy thread. It was also sleeveless, letting Zavrius's tunic peek through.

Zavrius gave a little bow.

"If I'm not a murderer, I'm a pansy," he said, guiding them both back into the main chamber. "Which I suppose I prefer, of the two. Though it does mean I'll have a harder time convincing them I'm competent."

"An easier task to accomplish if you keep your head."

"My thoughts exactly," Zavrius said with a nod. He tilted up his own chin with the back of his hand. "And it's such a pretty head."

Balen smiled at him and nodded toward the lute-harp on the bed. "Will you play tonight?"

Zavrius snorted. "I'm ashamed to say I thought about it. Not about playing one song, but a great many long ones back to back. Imagined them all sitting there, tight-lipped and hiding a grimace. Would have been fun."

"What stopped you?"

Zavrius gestured like it was obvious. "We just covered it, Balen. I want to keep my pretty head."

Their smiles slipped.

Balen took a breath. "You're concerned about tonight?"

Zavrius shrugged and stalked to the other end of the chamber. The robe billowed out behind him as he walked. He poured a glass of dark liquor from the mantel over the hearth.

"I'd offer, but you're on the job," he murmured, before downing it. He said nothing else for a moment before turning back to Balen with a nod, though whether he was admitting to being concerned or something else, Balen wasn't sure. "What happened on the road was no accident. There were arcanists, and they were noble born. Anyone with a lick of connection to nobility is either here tonight or represented. Anyone who isn't here, I intend to follow up on after the night's festivities are at an end."

Balen nodded, but still said, "It is not my place to question you—"

"No, it's not."

"—but I am worried." After a beat he added, "About you."

Zavrius closed the gap between them, head tilted to one side. "Canceling this event will do worse things for this dynasty than me dying. And I mean that. The empire is watching. They might overhear dissent this evening, but if I cancel out of fear—if they see me struggling . . ."

"I know."

"Do you?"

Balen closed his eyes with a sigh. He regretted saying anything. He'd meant it. Fiercely.

But that feeling didn't change what his job was.

Balen opened his eyes. "What do you need from me?"

Zavrius walked to the desk and strapped his sword-breaker under his robe. He spoke softly.

"It's just me on the dais. I don't want anyone else up there. Lestr and a few Paladins will be there, and Petra has her agents. But you were with me on the road. We don't know how many attacked. It's likely some of them got away."

"You really think any of them would be bold enough to attend in person?"

"I do." Zavrius was doing it again. Playing with information, withholding parts from Balen that he shouldn't. As a little rebellion, Balen didn't prompt him and stood there waiting until Zavrius got bored enough that he would deign to elaborate.

Zavrius rolled his eyes. "There's no better place to make noble allies than in a room full of nobles. At the very least, we must assume that some of them are here. But if I'm wrong, I'll be glad for it."

Balen would be glad for it too. He didn't ask what would happen if he found nothing when there was something to find. Thinking on that made his stomach curdle.

Balen grimaced. He hated this new doubt that had manifested after the events on the road.

He'd always associated being Prime with omniscience, felt that taking up the title would transform him into someone who understood the world and his place in it. Everything he was meant to be and everything his role entailed would make sense. Instead, his whole idea of the world had unraveled into something unimaginably complex. The more he knew, the more he understood how much more he didn't.

"Are you ready?" Balen asked him.

Zavrius turned to look at him. His long curly hair fell either side of his face, framing his cut jaw and warm eyes. The light of the hearth haloed him from behind and Balen's breath caught.

"Not yet," he said, turning back to the hearth. He nodded at a box sitting on the mantel, gesturing for Balen to walk.

Zavrius stepped aside to let Balen pass. The box was wide and flat, made from mahogany. A crown bordered by swords and flowers was painted onto the top of the box. Balen brushed his hand over it and glanced back and Zavrius.

"Crown me," Zavrius said with a purr.

Balen swallowed, swinging back to the box. Hands on either side of it, he carefully opened the lid. The Dued Vuuthrik crown sat golden and glistening inside.

It had been just over two weeks since Zavrius's coronation, days before the tournament that had named Balen his Prime. Balen remembered sitting there in the crowd, still yearning for the title of Prime that he had spent years of his life training for. And when Zavrius walked out, dressed and drowning in Sirellius's coronation clothes, Balen had wanted it more. To protect him. To protect the last remaining Dued Vuuthrik. Balen had watched Zavrius receive the crown with a silent, haunted expression: a man fighting to come to terms with his life's new direction.

He wondered if Zavrius was still fighting it.

Balen carefully took the crown out of the box. Zavrius turned fully to face him, expression blank and hard to read. Balen hovered the crown above Zavrius's head, and then pressed it gently over his curls. A shadow of something passed over Zavrius's face. A creeping horror at the reality of his life, or a reserved acceptance? Balen didn't know.

"My king," Balen murmured, returning his hands to his side.

Zavrius looked up at him. Even softer than Balen, he said, "My Prime."

They stood like that, face-to-face, breathing in time. Then Zavrius spun away with sudden vigor and walked to the door.

CHAPTER
NINE

The hall was warm with firelight: one giant hearth glowed with a roaring fire, and dozens and dozens of candles illuminated the long tables. The room bordered on uncomfortably warm. By the dais, a hidden quartet played a gentle tune.

"His Highness, king of the dynasty, the first of his name, Zavrius Dued Vuuthrik!"

"And last," Zavrius murmured cheerily to Balen as the hall erupted in applause. "Well, the last Dued Vuuthrik, anyway. You know, succession is going to be quite the problem for me to solve."

Balen said nothing. He wasn't in the mood for joking—if that's what Zavrius was doing at all.

All the nobles were seated, waiting for the king. Every head swung toward them. As they passed, people began to rise.

The dais had been set up with an ornate table for serving the king. Another empty table sat off the dais to the king's right for the Rezwyn Ambassador. As they ascended the dais to another round of cheers, Balen scanned the crowd. He searched for the people not clapping, for the half-hearted cheers and rolls of the eyes. But all the guests there had been playing politics for years. No one was so obvious with their disdain.

Balen saw Zavrius hesitate at the top of the stairs, then move decisively to take his place on the throne, facing the crowd.

"Welcome." Zavrius's voice projected easily over the applause. "Whether you have stumbled up the palace steps from Cres Stros, or spent much time traveling on my behalf, I thank you. Before the festivities commence, there is one announcement."

He made an upward gesture with his hands, signaling to the crowd that they should remain standing.

Balen stood behind him in relative silence, scouring the room as Petra made her way toward the dais.

For such a short woman, her presence was large enough to command attention from the entire room. She wore a long maroon dress with a high-necked collar, her gray hair in a high-sitting bun. When she came before the dais, she bowed deeply.

"Chancellor Petra." Zavrius gave her a nod of acknowledgment.

"Thank you, King Zavrius," she said with another dip of her head. "It is my pleasure to welcome our most honored guests from the Rezwyn empire: Ambassador Dziove and the priests Thal and Jolir."

The applause was polite but scattered. The air shifted in the hall too: a tense kind of brooding. Hardly anyone was happy about peace with the empire, but certainly no one would crack a smile at having them in their home.

All heads swung toward the great open doors, where a massive shadow stretched. Ambassador Dziove was a tall, muscular woman, flanked by two shorter men. Balen had seen them from afar at his oath ceremony, but he'd never had to confront the empire up close before. Soldiers visibly bristled as they entered.

Dziove wore a thickly woven blue tunic with a leather cuirass that was decorated to appear like fabric. Balen couldn't be sure if the armor was hidden purposefully, out of cautiousness, or if it was simply empire fashion. She had her black hair down and a silver circlet around her forehead. Her face was heavily painted with blue and black kohl—lining the eyes, big stripes down her chin—echoic of war paint, the same thing she'd worn at Balen's ceremony, lodged somewhere between ritual and threat. The priests wore the typical fringed headdresses that covered most of their faces. They also carried strange instruments; one had something like a primitive violin, the other a hollow block of wood.

Zavrius sat up straighter. The three of them walked slowly in a clear ritual procession. Dziove put her hands up and started speaking rhythmically in Doskorian. A look of horror twisted the faces of the seated nobles. Even the entourage that had visited Arasne had not spoken their natural tongue. Had this language ever been spoken in all the years of this hall?

Zavrius stood as they got closer, and when the ambassador bowed, the king responded with a slight nod to his head.

"Let's welcome our empire guests," Zavrius said loudly, arms wide. Another round of polite applause sounded.

Petra pursed her lips tightly. She clenched her hands together, her whole body seeming racked with tension at her proximity to the Rezwyn ambassador.

Balen made eye contact with Alick in the crowd, Lestr at the far end of the hall by the doors, and put a hand on the hilt of his blade.

"For years the dynasty has been locked in a bloody and angry war against the empire. For many of you, this was your life—and for a long time, it was my future. But tonight, I announce a shift in our direction: a continuation of the path my mother, Queen Arasne, put us on."

Immediately, there was talk.

Zavrius continued over the noise, "The initial thirty years of peace agreed upon by my mother has been expanded. We will enter a new era of peace, and usher in a future of continued trade and prosperity."

The chatter only grew. Balen saw a wash of panic cross Petra's face as she heard it all.

Dziove ignored the noise and turned to the crowd. "On behalf of the True Commander, His Excellency Nio Beumeut, I congratulate you on your ascension."

Lestr squared his shoulders, eyes scanning the room. Balen followed suit, scouring for any sign of movement. He was half expecting some enraged noble to throw their chair back and rush the king.

"This only expands the peace we live in," Zavrius called, trying to sound at ease and not like he was plugging holes in a sinking ship. "There will be no noticeable change to your day-to-day lives unless you are engaged in trade—and even then, it is entirely up to your individual enterprise whether or not you trade with the empire more fully. This is a happy moment."

The crowd quietened. A few lone nobles began to clap: merchants, Balen recognized. Radek was among them. There was a surge in his chest, a frustration that made no sense until he realized part of him was begrudgingly grateful for Radek's support.

Zavrius opened his hand again and Dziove and her priests took their places at the empty table.

"Lucky. But keep sharp, Prime," Petra whispered back at Balen as she, too, took her place. Balen watched Petra seat herself next to Polverc. But everyone's attention was on Zavrius as he resumed his seat.

The king continued as if he hadn't made such a grand announcement.

"This is the first celebration of my coronation not bound up in ritual and formalities. I have waited these weeks to put some distance between the tragedy that befell my family—our country—and the future this celebration represents."

The Paladin's shoulders relaxed. He saw a few nobles turn more fully to face him. Zavrius was earning their attention, gently pulling them away from the defiant few.

"I will not tarnish my parents' name," Zavrius said with a solemn tone. "Rather I will lead us to a better future. A brighter, fulfilling peace."

No recognition, no applause. Zavrius reached for his goblet and lifted it high.

"So eat and be merry!" Zavrius bellowed, and finally the hall resounded with cheers.

Zavrius brought the goblet to his lips and hesitated before setting it down again.

"Poison?" Balen whispered from behind the throne.

Zavrius gave near imperceptible shrug. "Who knows? But I must say, I'm rather sensitive to the thought."

Balen would get wine—maybe commandeer a jug from the nobles' table. No assassin would poison their allies. But before Balen could act, there was movement in the hall.

At first, Balen's eyes landed on several underdressed people that wandered into the hall. They were people from all provinces, all types. Many wore gold bands on their upper arms, while others had parts of their face painted with clay—both marks of professional entertainers. Courtesans. Balen looked to Petra, concerned, but when her impassive mask didn't slip, he let the tension fall from his shoulders. Zavrius certainly didn't seem to mind their presence: a smirk was on the king's face.

As the guests sat and ate, the entertainment encompassed the floor with a spinning group dance. Their whirling dance was so mesmerizing that even the Paladin found it hard to look away.

But he quickly refocused when another ripple of movement disrupted the stream of servants. Balen jerked his head and scoured for the source. There: a nobleman, unhurriedly approaching the dais.

Zavrius tilted forward with interest. "Well, well."

Huez Thenlass, longtime supporter of Theo Dued Vuuthrik, gave a shallow bow as he approached. He had salt-and-pepper hair that was cut short to his head and a beard that overpowered most of his face. Thenlass had been a Paladin, the man who had led the assault to retake Shoi

Prya from the empire. Seeing him was difficult for Balen. He was a living legend, lauded among the Paladins for Balen's entire childhood. He had grown up trying to model himself off Huez Thenlass. Now, standing before him, Balen noticed himself standing taller, like the straighter he could make his spine, the more impressed the other Paladin would be.

His old Paladin status showed in his stance. Years of military training kept Thenlass tall and sturdy as he walked. He wore an ankle-length kaftan made of a densely woven fabric. It fitted tightly over his shoulders. A maroon sash was slung across his body. It was embroidered with the decanter used in Paladin ceremonies and the pine trees that dominated much of the eastern provinces. The clasps at the front of the kaftan shone iridescent and gave Balen pause— the only gedrokbone Thenlass should have had access to was his own armor. Balen couldn't fathom Sirellius's favored Paladin carving that up for a costume, even if he'd long ago retired. Something that small would be useless in mitigating the effects of ichor.

"Your Highness," Thenlass said, deep voice projected loud.

Zavrius crossed his legs. "We missed you at the coronation, Lord Thenlass."

According to Petra, Thenlass had been too distressed by the news of Theo's death to travel—though more likely he was reeling from a sudden shift in his prospects. Just days before his death, Theo had met with the man, no doubt discussing what he might do as king with Thenlass's invaluable support. Thenlass had been on good terms with all of Zavrius's siblings, though he had neglected to foster any kind of relationship with the man who'd ended up on the throne.

Thenlass didn't acknowledge him. Balen gnawed at his inner cheek. Thenlass's position as the provincial lord of Shoi Prya, as well as his ties to Westgar, made him invaluable.

Zavrius didn't have the power to shake him from that position. At least not yet.

"Did you?" Thenlass said, sounding surprised. "I'm honored that you should think me significant enough to notice."

"I've a keen eye," Zavrius said.

Balen caught Thenlass stiffen momentarily and had to suppress his own conflicted satisfaction. Whether Zavrius was talking about the noticeable change in stationery sets in Thenlass's letter, or how obviously patchworked Thenlass's congratulations were, it had some effect.

Zavrius leaned back. "In any case, I'm glad you could join us today."

"How could I miss it?" Thenlass said with a smile so genuine Balen almost forgot about the official court summons.

Thenlass gave another bow and took his place. Zavrius watched him go.

When he was well out of earshot, Balen bent down to Zavrius's ear. "You don't trust him?"

"Of course not. But did he orchestrate the attack on the road?" Zavrius gave a noncommittal shrug. "Perhaps not directly. In any case, I'd be remiss to let him sit peacefully in his own hold."

"Should I keep an eye on him? Entertain him somehow?"

Zavrius glanced back at Balen and carefully shook his head. "I think he's well on his way to being entertained."

Balen turned in time to glimpse Thenlass slip an arm around one of the dancers' bare waists. He pulled her close and she went willingly.

Balen frowned. He really should've been informed about the courtesans. "Who hired that lot, anyway?"

Zavrius ignored the question. "Stay with me until the food comes. Then you may feel free to greet the nobles of Cres Stros. You wouldn't want to seem aloof."

Balen scanned the hall for someone he'd be comfortable leaving Zavrius's defense to. Lestr. Alick, maybe. In truth, he wanted to pull the whole Paladin order and station them in front of the dais.

Balen bobbed his head toward the crowd. "They won't tell me a thing."

"No," Zavrius agreed. "But they might tell someone else. Someone more charming."

Balen lingered for a few more moments until food was brought in from the kitchen. He grabbed the jug of wine on Zavrius's table and put it into the hands of the nearest servant.

"Take it back to the kitchen."

The boy nodded and departed. Balen had an unopened bottle of wine brought from the cellar for Zavrius. Once he was satisfied it hadn't been tampered with, he descended into the crowd.

He didn't like being down there. Among the revelers, it was stifling. The bulk of his armor made slipping through unnoticed completely impossible. He was seen with every step. The usual methods of a simple reconnaissance would have to be abandoned, but it was for the best. Everyone was so bunched together he saw nothing in detail. Laughter and chatter overwhelmed the lilting orchestra.

Balen skirted the edge of the crowd until he spotted the pearlescent shine of Paladin armor and swung toward it. Alick was pressed up against a wall with a goblet in his hand. He was surrounded by four nobles and kept staring out into the crowd like he wanted to be swallowed by it. Balen moved toward him. The sight of his armor made the dense crowd split apart like an overcooked pea.

"Such effort to produce a midtier armor is mind-boggling. This is before we even consider the pompous ceremony the order performs before they harvest it," a man was saying, right hand gripping the shoulder of a younger man beside him. There was no doubt they were father and son, but it took Balen a moment to place them. They were both dressed in mustard-yellow tunics with rampant hounds stitched onto the shoulders. The crest of Mordsson. Small hold in southern Westgar.

Alick's eyes widened as he approached. "Balen!"

Balen let himself be pulled into the small group, if only to relieve poor Alick, who seemed to be trapped there against his will. The circle shuffled apart with great interest to accommodate him. Ignoring the obvious disdain with which Mordsson inspected his armor, Balen greeted all but one: Sorbetka stood next to a short lady the Paladin couldn't place. She had no marker on her, no house symbol displayed anywhere, no glinting signet ring. She was in a light-blue dress and had a silver chain around her neck, though it seemed broken, like its pendant had snapped off. It took him a moment, but her light brown skin and straight hair was familiar enough to Balen. He caught the name somewhere in his mind; remembered Zavrius less than an hour earlier reading her delayed tepid letter of congratulations.

Balen had skimmed it. "The Kus House congratulates King Zavrius Dued Vuuthrik on his successful ascension. The Lady Mariel Kus offers her fealty to the crown."

Weak, bland and later than letters traveling across most of Usleth.

"Lady Mariel Kus," he said with a delayed, but low, bow. Her family lands were deep in Cres Stros, toward the east, but he knew little else about them.

She beamed up at him with genuine surprise. "Now that's a keen mind."

"She made it tricky for you, Prime." The elder Mordsson tilted of his glass toward one of the long tables where a shawl lay abandoned over a chair. Balen saw the faint lines of some embroidered symbol on it.

"I had no idea such identifiers were necessary," Kus said. She spoke softly, as if the attention overwhelmed her.

Balen thought about appeasing her, but that would cement his place in the circle. He didn't want to be trapped there for much longer. He scanned the crowd, saw Polverc slip a note into a noble's hand as he passed. He tried to track the man's movements, but he was short enough he got swallowed in the mass of bodies. When Balen's eyes darted back to Polverc, she was innocently talking to someone else. The Paladin frowned.

"Excuse me," he murmured, and made to step away.

"So soon?"

Balen turned to find Thenlass's outstretched hand in his face.

Though retired, Thenlass had been a Paladin and deserved the same respect. More than that, Balen felt a boyish glee burn brightly in his chest. Conflicted as he was about Thenlass's person, and though the other man had never made Prime, he was a legend. Balen took his hand and flashed a smile. "Lord Thenlass."

"Prime," Thenlass said, rotating the pair of them back toward the circle before he released Balen's hand. "Congratulations on your appointment."

Balen glanced over his shoulder, but his heart sang with Thenlass's praise. A grin spread across his face. "Thank you."

"What do you think about this, Huez?" The elder Mordsson spoke to Thenlass but gestured to Alick. "The fabled Paladin armor."

Thenlass raised a brow. Balen's eyes flashed once more to the clasps on Thenlass's kaftan. "What of it?"

"Always such stories about it," Sorbetka said. "The power of it. That it protects the mind from their magic."

Thenlass gave her a short smile. "You think otherwise?"

Mordsson scoffed loud enough to make his own son flinch. "She's got enough wit to not be fooled by such fiction."

Balen kept his mouth shut. His days without his armor in Teum Bett had affected him badly, and he hadn't even been using his power.

Sorbetka shrugged. If she was glad of Mordsson's defense, she didn't show it. Her face was so carefully unexpressive Balen couldn't tell how she really felt about it.

"Do you think those stories are only children's stories?" Kus asked with a laugh. She leaned close to Sorbetka, who shrugged again, struggling with her imitated nonchalance.

"Wouldn't that make the Paladins really powerful?" Mordsson the younger spoke for the first time, only to be gently whacked on the back of the head.

"Stop it, Silas," his father hissed.

Kus cocked her head toward the young man. "Oh, I doubt it, young Silas. Certainly our dear late king Sirellius always framed the Paladin order as Usleth's magical cavalry. But I imagine if their armor really was as powerful as the stories say, Queen Arasne would have let them avenge the king rather than accept his murderer's terms of peace. Perhaps that's what Lady Sorbetka is saying."

She smiled sweetly, but there was no missing the harshness of her commentary. Balen felt like one of those Paladin statues at the entrance: wildly surprised he was overhearing all this freely. He looked to Thenlass, was intrigued to find the man not hiding his discomfort. A little gladly, Balen recognized his expression. Thenlass disagreed with Kus—or at the very least, her openness.

"Oh, Lady Sorbetka wants to dream of a different world, I imagine." Thenlass said it with a slow drawl, like he was sick of the conversation already. "A world where Paladins are more magic than men, and all the nastiness of war could be avoided with their power. Isn't that right?"

Sorbetka's face was blank, devoid of any smile. Something was passing between Thenlass and her. Balen could see the edges of it. Sorbetka had already said aloud that she doubted the future of Zavrius's reign. Was Thenlass warning her to back down? Or was he actively challenging her brewing critique?

Sorbetka's face crumpled. "I only wished that it could be true. Our days appeasing that scum might come to an end." She gave a pointed glance at the Rezwyn ambassador. "That's all."

Balen bristled. He made himself breathe deep and slow, one long inhale that raked over his raised hackles until he could relax. It wasn't the sentiment that irked him—most of his own order shared it—but how willing she was to speak it aloud. What did these people think about Zavrius's expanded peace? What did they think about Zavrius's rule?

He knew.

Polverc passing notes, Sorbetka entertaining Theo's empire war in casual conversation, Kus and Thenlass both congratulating Zavrius late. Little acts of defiance. But they carried something significant in them, a real threat made all the worse when it passed so casually in front of him.

"Lord Thenlass?" It was a woman, voice curling at the edges.

Balen turned to see the courtesan Thenlass had been speaking to earlier lace her arms around Thenlass's neck.

"Won't you introduce me to your friends?" she asked.

Thenlass gave a short, dismissive laugh, but Mordsson held out his hand toward the woman.

"Might as well, Huez. It's the king's coin, after all."

Thenlass looked like he might protest for a moment until he turned to the woman and took her in. Pale brown skin, full lips, heavy swing to her hips—objectively, Balen could tell she was attractive. And for Thenlass, she clearly had some pull to her. He lifted a hand to brush a ring of curls out of her face.

"All right," he replied to Mordsson, without taking his eyes off her. "Zavrius knows how to entertain, I'll give him that."

Balen cleared his throat and gave a stiff bow. "Lords, ladies. I must complete my rounds."

He was sure Sorbetka would make some quip about the dynasty's dandy king, but as he spun into the waiting crowd, he heard nothing but laughter. The courtesans spread out and pulled guests onto the floor to dance. Men and women laced their limbs over one another. Most of the nobles were content to have a pretty face beside them, to laugh loudly at their stories, or to kiss, but a few nobles wandered out into the palace with a courtesan on their arm.

The Cres Strosian court wasn't particularly prim when it came to gratification of this nature. The empire, though, was very different. That nation was gods-driven, and that piety came with a modesty. Balen looked around for the ambassador or her priests, just to see if their pale faces had somehow blanched further. They weren't in the crowd.

Balen pushed between the mingling guests, hoping to overhear something he could take back to his king, but he was too obvious in his Paladin armor. Every time he wandered near, the conversations dwindled or quickly changed course. It was expected, but he still felt stupid wandering around aimlessly in a crowd full of courtesans—until Balen spotted the man Polverc had slipped a note to on the other side of the room. He was short and bearded, with large, bushy eyebrows hanging over his eyes. He leaned against the wall alone, swirling a glass in front of his face. As Balen approached, he downed the whole thing.

"Enjoying yourself?" Balen asked.

The man smiled tightly. "Prime Paladin." He pressed a hand to his chest. "Lord Estok of Westgar."

The Estoks were aristocratic merchants of the same standing as Radek.

"You seem to have caught the Lady Polverc's eye," Balen said, smiling. "I'd be more discreet passing notes, though, if I were you. Her husband can be very jealous."

Estok considered him for a moment. His eyes drifted out over the hall, as if hoping to confirm with Polverc. Balen kept his face blank, leveled out his breathing.

Eventually, Estok shrugged and retrieved the folded paper from his pocket and handed it to Balen. Days and times were written on it.

"It's about her damn chair." Estok sighed, not hiding his irritation. "Trying to organize moving the thing from her Cres Strosian estate to Wen Zerret in Westgar. I'm leaving Cres Stros midmorning tomorrow."

The chair. Balen grimaced, feeling stupid. Mallet and Lance had transported a chair, commissioned by Adzura Polverc for her sister in Westgar. A condolence gift. That's all this was.

Balen returned the note to him. Estok grunted and stuffed the paper back in his pocket. He seemed deeply unimpressed with Balen, still fixing him with a dark frown.

Trying to keep Estok friendly, Balen gestured out into the crowd before he stepped away. "Not a fan of the entertainment?"

Estok shrugged. "Not particularly interesting to me," he muttered. Then he raised a glass toward the dais. "Though our king seems quite amused."

Confused, Balen turned toward the king.

On the dais, a boy was in Zavrius's lap. The boy was young. Eighteen, nineteen. He had the same russet-brown skin as Radek. For a long, anguished moment, Balen thought he could see some similarity in this boy's face. Then his mind ran away with that. Zavrius's hand was on his hip.

Balen jolted. He stepped away from Estok into the middle of the hall. Balen's heart felt wrong, felt heavy, like something in his stomach was tugging it down.

Balen knew Zavrius was attractive. And attractive to more people than just him. He knew, too, that any kind of right he had to jealousy was long gone. Balen had for-feited it—him—when he'd focused so heavily on training to be Theo's Prime. When Balen had put all his focus on his order, when Zavrius had realized he was being put aside, once again, for his own brother . . . It meant Balen had no right to this feeling now. But all those thoughts were born from logic, and his logic was currently suffocating under a fervent need to skewer the boy Zavrius was touching.

Balen didn't look away as he forced his way through close-pressed bodies. He heard a few surprised sounds as nobles edged apart—wasn't sure, in the back of his mind, if he was causing a scene—but he couldn't stop himself. He saw Zavrius break into a smile as the boy in his lap laughed loudly with his head thrown back.

No one else was supposed to be on the dais. That's what Zavrius had said. No one else but him. And that smile. Balen knew it, had seen it before. Always undercut with lust.

"Prime!"

Radek stepped into his path and Balen stumbled to a stop. If fate had a mind, it was cruel. He faced Radek with as much of a smile as he could muster.

"Good evening," he said. It came out quickly, backed by the pent-up adrenaline in his blood.

Radek smiled. "I want to . . ." He gestured in the air, taking his time. The Paladin forced himself not to glance at Zavrius. "I want to apologize. For what you overheard on the steps."

Unthinking, filled with the image of Radek's hands on Zavrius, Balen hissed, "Which part?"

Radek stilled for a moment, in apparent confusion.

Balen tried to recover. "You're hardly responsible for other people's talk."

Radek's shoulders softened a little. "I suppose. But it was a careless thing to discuss anyway."

He looked nervous. Balen watched his eyes dart over to the throne. Was he affected, too? Seeing Zavrius with someone else—a right he had not only as king, but as a man bound to no one.

Balen didn't want to share a single thing with Radek. He tried to stand taller, tried to feel the unfamiliar pull in his heart a little less.

"Was that all, Lord Radek? I have duties to attend to."

"Of course." Radek jumped a little. He smiled apologetically and stepped aside. But as Balen moved, Radek grabbed his arm. "Please tell him . . . that it's good to see him."

Balen wrenched his arm free. "I'll convey your regards."

As Balen climbed the stairs, the boy in Zavrius's lap stood and descended. They crossed paths. He smelled like lemongrass and florals. Balen's nostrils flared. He swallowed to keep a sneer from his face.

Zavrius bounced his leg. He raised his glass toward Balen. "Find out anything useful?"

"Why did you let him up here?" He thought he caught the ghost of a smirk cross Zavrius's face. Heat spread across Balen's chest. He closed his fist and bristled on the spot, not trusting himself to speak.

Zavrius looked him over, eyes dropping to the ground. By the bones, he was enjoying this. "Why do you care?"

What could Balen say? He didn't know himself. Zavrius was not his. Zavrius had not been his for years. But he was king, so Balen focused on that.

"If you were not king, I doubt anyone would blink at your obvious show of affection to a courtesan. But your image could too easily be fashioned into something it isn't. In short, he shouldn't have been up here."

Zavrius turned so his back was against the arm of the throne. "Am I not allowed some entertainment?"

Balen clamped his jaw shut, his throat tight and heart heavy. After struggling to find the words, he repeated, "He shouldn't have been up here."

Zavrius seemed to lose interest. He swung back to the crowd, drank his wine, and refilled his glass. "Your jealousy is hilarious to me."

"I'm not—"

Zavrius held up a hand. Balen quietened. The king fixed him with a long, dark stare. He slowly shook his head. "I'll ignore the irony of it. I'll ignore your bluster and your audacity. But never take me for a fool who would taint my image for something so trivial as a courtesan's kiss."

Balen stared, uncomprehending.

Quietly, Zavrius said, "Anyway, he's one of Petra's. The Chancellor is the queen of intrigue." Zavrius waved him off. "What good does it do to spread that?"

Balen flushed. Zavrius evidently wanted to jeopardize him: his job, his life, the entire throne. He heard the gravelly cut of his own voice, a flare of anger barely kept at bay.

"It would do me good," Balen seethed, "to know who I can trust."

Zavrius's eyes rolled toward him. "No one, Balen. No one. Are you finally understanding that?"

"Keeping me at bay won't help you. It certainly won't save your life."

Zavrius's face twisted. He opened his mouth, but something stopped him from speaking. Zavrius breathed deep and slouched back into the chair. "Petra has eyes everywhere. In the courtesans, in the kitchen. In the palace guards. In the city guards." Zavrius shrugged. "By the bone, I'm sure she's found a way to have them in other households, too."

Balen briefly closed his eyes. "What did the boy find out?"

"We'll get to that," Zavrius said. "But first. I saw Radek intercepted you."

"He said to say that it was good to see you. Why he couldn't just tell you himself, I don't know."

"I do," Zavrius said, face scrunched. He shook his head and didn't elaborate. "But he said nothing else?"

Balen narrowed his eyes. "Were you hoping for pleasantries, or something incriminating?"

Zavrius's frown dissolved. He snorted and shook his head. "Never mind him, then."

"No, I'll—"

"Just tell me what you found out about my lovely court."

Balen sighed and told Zavrius what he could: about Sorbetka's questions, the turn of that conversation. He admitted his own misstep regarding Polverc's transport, too, in case Zavrius saw something there that he didn't. By the time he was done, Zavrius was bouncing his leg quickly and staring out into the crowd, expression dark and searching.

Something was wrong. When the anger ebbed out of him, Balen could feel it.

"Tell me," was all Balen said.

Zavrius whispered, "I was right to doubt the wine."

Balen slowly turned to stare at him.

"Thank you for humoring me, Balen. For taking it away. You saved me. Again." Zavrius stayed staring out into the crowd. "Someone's dead in the kitchen. Petra's already there. I want you there as well. But I have to stay on the throne. You'll have to leave me up here alone."

"But not unguarded," Balen said. "I'm not leaving you unguarded."

It sounded fearful, a little like he was trying to convince himself he was doing the right thing. Leaving Zavrius exposed to seek out another threat felt like a paradox that would consume the rest of his life. But it had to be done.

"Alick is there." Balen pointed to the left wall where the older Paladin was stationed.

Zavrius repositioned himself in his chair, fidgeting, unable to sit still. "Wonderful." His voice wavered. His grip on the arm of the throne was turning pale. "I feel safer already."

"He took the same oath as me," Balen said, even as a flash of that late-night congregation at his ceremony sprang to mind. "There are other Paladins, too. And Lestr. And Lok. He's newly initiated but good."

"If there's poison in the wine," Zavrius muttered under his breath, "there could be poison everywhere. Every damn surface, every—"

"Zavrius." Balen leaned so closely into him Balen could feel his shuddering breaths. "Nothing will happen to you. I won't let it."

Zavrius set his jaw, but he couldn't quite iron out the furrow in his brow. His eyes were stormy and unfocused, filled with the dizzying thoughts of a man at war with his own panic. Balen squeezed his shoulder. "Do you trust me?"

Zavrius scanned his eyes, expression stuck in that statuesque worry. He didn't say anything, but eventually he glanced away.

Balen hesitated for a moment. Then he straightened, caught Alick's attention and, with a flick of his hand, he called all three Paladins to him. They fell in one by one.

"What is it?" Lestr said under his breath.

Balen lowered his voice. "There's been a murder." He locked eyes with his master. "Most likely an attempt to assassinate the king. You, Alick and Lok must protect Zavrius."

Lestr made a gesture and the two Paladins moved ahead to flank Zavrius. Lestr and he watched them for a moment. Zavrius relaxed against the throne and happily bit into a bread roll. But beneath the table, Balen spotted the jitter of his leg.

Lestr asked, "And you?"

"I'm going to find Petra," Balen said.

Lestr leaned close. "Don't speak of this to anyone."

CHAPTER
TEN

The palace halls were full of guests.

Balen moved quickly, eyes darting over nobles and courtesans, servants and guards. He wanted obvious dissent, someone hiding the poison away right before his eyes. But that was just desperation. His mind was somewhere between paranoia and rage, and both of those feelings were too personal for the Prime. He'd told Zavrius he wouldn't let anything happen to him. That meant he had to focus. So Balen concentrated on moving, refusing to acknowledge the rising fear in him that Zavrius was, and always would be, surrounded by threats.

He found Petra outside the kitchen. Seeing the chancellor brought a rush of premature relief.

"Chancellor." He whispered it, voice tight.

"Prime." She smiled brightly. They hovered near the kitchen, not fully committing to entering it, but shielded enough from the rest of the palace that no wanderers would spot them. The courtyard was full of guests and their courtesan lovers. They'd be distracted for a few more minutes at least. "The king?"

"Eating bread," Balen said. "Watching his loyal guests dance."

He couldn't keep the agitated spite from his voice. He was angry when he needed to be composed, steady.

Petra put a hand on his forearm. Balen met her eye and knew she saw him. All of it, all of the agitation, the undisciplined fear he was supposed to be able to control. She patted him once.

"He's alive," she said, to remind him. She seemed hardened to what had almost happened. Perhaps after the deaths of so many around her, it made sense. That calm acceptance was an elixir: cool and biting, it let Balen get ahold of himself. He exhaled and nodded.

Alive. Zavrius was alive. And Balen would be the one to keep it that way.

She gestured with her head to the kitchen and pushed her way inside.

The entrance sat on an angled wall and opened onto a massive stretch of room. This single kitchen serviced the whole palace: the royal family, guards and staff. The kitchen was bright with candles. The floor and walls were a pale gray stone and the ceiling had been paneled with wood. Sausages and cured meats were strung over three large beams that ran the length of the room. Two wrought-iron chandeliers hung overhead, bushels of dried herbs tied to them. There were multiple doors, some heading to staff quarters, and another that led directly out to the side of the palace.

Most of the staff had been excused. The head chef was a lean woman in her later years. She smoothed down her apron as the king approached and gave a low bow. The dessert had been laid out on one of the three massive tables that sat end to end across the room's length. Massive amounts of sweet lemon cakes and fruit-filled rolls were stacked in pyramids on several gold platters. Balen's eyes glanced at a set of feet poking out from behind the table.

Petra nodded toward the platters. "When were those made, Zhula?"

"Just finished them, Chancellor. Made them myself."

Petra drew a circle in the air with her finger. "Did anyone else touch them?"

She shook her head. "Haven't been out of my sight. If I'd been here, then . . ." She glanced down at what was undoubtedly the poisoned corpse at her feet.

Petra nodded, seemingly satisfied. "Get the staff ready to take these out. We must keep up appearances."

Zhula nodded and clicked her fingers, summoning a few servants to carry the desserts out. Balen walked around the table. They hadn't touched the body. The boy lay with his eyes open, head jerked unnaturally to the side. Balen recognized him as the boy he'd passed the jug to and tried not to feel a stab of guilt.

"Tell me," Balen said with a nod to the corpse.

Zhula touched her face. "Oh. Just a young lad, really. Drank it and was dead a few minutes later."

The boy's mouth had frothed. Balen asked, "What kind of poison?"

Petra responded quickly. "It looks like eridahk."

Balen didn't know his poisons, but before he could ask, Petra followed with, "Which was a pointed and rather cruel decision, I think."

Balen cocked his head. "Why's that?"

"That was one of Avidia's favorites," said Petra.

Zavrius's sister had always been very good with poisons. That had been common enough knowledge.

Balen looked up at the ceiling. That potentially moved this act from strictly political to personal. He rubbed his forehead. "All right. Let's speak with the staff. See who came through here, check if anyone was bribed."

He headed for the staff quarters, but Petra held up a hand to stay him. "Zhula," she said, flashing the woman a serene smile. "You can go."

Zhula half curtsied as she left. Petra waited for the door to close before she turned back to Balen.

Balen opened his hands. "Well? Where do we start?"

"Oh, we have started, Balen. Don't you worry, dear."

Balen frowned but watched her stalk over to the far door that led to the outside of the palace. She wrenched it open with more force than was strictly necessary. Someone was shoved to their knees and forced inside. Balen squinted, trying to make out features as he edged around the table. The shadows around whoever had been thrown resolved into a bald head and Westgar-pale skin.

Behind the prone body, a well-muscled courtesan stepped into the bright kitchen. Petra closed the door as the courtesan—though Balen suspected he was more of a spy—hauled the bald man to his feet.

His hands were bound with rope. A gag had been stuffed into his mouth. A fine trickle of blood was making its way down his cheeks; a bruise had formed around the split skin near the man's eye.

Balen didn't need to ask to know, but he wanted confirmation for his anger. "This is him?"

Petra flashed him a look but didn't answer him directly. She laid a soft hand on the courtesan's arm and smiled brightly. "Do you have a name yet?"

The courtesan nodded.

Balen's heart was in his throat. Petra had seen this threat and crippled it. Balen knew she had servants whispering to her, and Zavrius had even called her the queen of intrigue, but this was . . .

Thorough. Fearless. The kind of player Balen himself would need to become.

The courtesan tugged the gag free of the bald man's mouth. Before the would-be assassin spoke, Balen spent a moment running through what he'd heard and who he'd seen. If there was anything there, it was buried. He couldn't see it. Polverc, Sorbetka, Kus, Mordsson. Radek, even. Or Thenlass. One or all of them could be behind it. Or it could be none of them.

"Speak," Petra ordered. Never once did she raise her voice, but the authority in her tone was more than enough. "Who ordered you to administer the poison to our king?"

The bald man shivered. "Kus."

Petra's face remained impassive. Her eyes rolled toward Balen. "Do you believe that, Prime?"

Balen flinched. He frowned, momentarily dumbstruck. What was she asking him to do, exactly? To prove himself—how?

"Could this man be lying?" Petra prompted.

"Are you testing me?" Balen said, growing frustrated. "This isn't the time."

Petra's face darkened. "We are about to condemn a noblewoman, Prime. We had better be sure. And though my agent Carteg is quite persuasive, people tend to lie. So tell me. Could it be someone else?"

The bald man was shaking in Balen's periphery.

Balen glanced at him. "Describe her."

The courtesan's hand pressed firmly into the bald man's neck, earning a muffled whimper. The distant sounds of the orchestra sounded as it started playing something more fast paced. Balen wondered if there was dancing, couples swirling and twisting together, while here a trial of sorts was taking place.

The bald man squeezed his eyes shut. A trickle of sweat moved down his brow. "Mousy hair. Short. Skinny. Wearing blue."

Balen set his jaw. "Why did you obey her?"

The man shook his head, but the courtesan behind him held him fast and shook. A strangled whimper edged out of the bald man's lips. "Because she's right." He seemed to gain some righteous confidence: he pulled his shoulders back and held his chin up. "Usleth needs a king. A proper leader. Not some weak pansy who—"

Balen bristled, but before he could do anything, Petra made a gesture and Carteg slapped the bald man across the face. The man grunted and spat over his shoulder.

Balen stepped forward, refusing to give him a chance to recover. "How long have you been working for Kus?"

Still feeling principled, the man said, "Not as long as I'd have liked. Kus has been there since the beginning. From the day it was clear Usleth would be driven into the ground.

The day we learned what happened to the Heir Ascendant."

From the moment they realized Zavrius would be king. Before Balen gained the title of Prime. They hadn't even given Zavrius a chance; he was Theo's successor, and that was enough to damn him.

The bald man was staring at Balen with the hint of a smile. He believed this wholeheartedly. But when Balen asked, "Who else do you know that works for her?" he seemed to shrink.

It was as if he was only now realizing the position he was in, and what he was giving his enemy. The smile vanished from his face. He tried to crane around to look at Carteg, but the courtesan's grip on his neck only tightened.

Balen stepped forward and charged his gauntlet. It sparked with arcane energy, and the air in the kitchen changed. A shadow fell over the bald man's face.

"I . . . only know a few," he said. "Teo Hercig. Uh, Dario Jurak. I think someone called Zubov, but I never spoke to her."

Balen knew those names. He'd matched them to the corpses they'd taken from the road. Zavrius had spent days contacting their families.

The man continued, "They had a . . . they had a job. A great honor, to destroy the pretender king. I was supposed to go with them, but I wouldn't have been much use."

Balen did his best to ignore the outright treason. He stepped forward and wiped a gauntleted finger over the run of blood on the man's forehead. He held it up to the light, but there were no bright flecks. It was just blood.

Balen locked eyes with the man, who flinched at whatever look was in Balen's eyes. "I met your friends on the Royal Highway. We had a good chat. Swapped some blows. All of them had ichor in their blood. Not you."

That was a sore spot: the man's nostrils flared as he tried to stand straighter. "It is the greatest honor. I have yet to earn it."

The greatest honor was something these people didn't comprehend. He thought of the conversation in the hall, where it was clear Kus had no idea of the Paladin armor's importance. These people had no idea what they were doing to their bodies. Or they didn't care.

In any case, Balen believed this man was telling the truth. He turned back to Petra and gave her a solid nod.

Petra turned back to the bald man with that same placid smile. "Such a surprise. You were telling the truth."

Without anything more, she gave a dismissive flick of the wrist. To the courtesan, that communicated a lot more than to simply leave: he hauled the bound man out of the door. There was one muffled scream and then silence.

Petra inclined her head.

Balen looked at her. "So tell me about Mariel Kus."

"Important in the war. A soldier family, like Sorbetka and Mordsson. Only Mariel is the last Kus. Mariel's mother was one of my brother's most favored soldiers, but she died in that final battle with him," Petra replied.

Balen nodded. After a beat he said, "Her congratulations to Zavrius only just arrived."

If Kus lived in Cres Stros, she could have sent anyone across town to deliver Zavrius the letter. Why would she risk ill favor when her family name was almost dead? Unless she didn't expect her impoliteness to cause a problem for very long. Zavrius was the last Dued Vuuthrik, after all. What better way to ingratiate yourself to a new dynasty than by showing no loyalty to the last one?

Slowly, Balen said, "There's no point in sending a letter if its recipient will soon be dead."

Petra smiled at him. "A fair assessment, Prime. I would have to agree."

"But that does bring up the question of why she belatedly sent the letter at all." Balen rolled his shoulders back. It was good to feel certain about something again.

"My guess is that someone else made her do it," Petra said. "I may be wrong, but to me Kus has neither the connections nor the funds to mastermind this plan. It would be impolite to not ask her directly, don't you agree?"

"I'll politely excuse the Lady Kus from the party. Where can I bring her?"

"The east wing drawing room," Petra said.

Balen nodded. It was well placed between the guest chambers and the staff quarters; close enough for Balen to call the guard and well away from Zavrius's private chambers. A quiet place to deal with a traitor without their guests noticing.

Balen launched himself out of the kitchen. The halls were nearly empty. Most of the guests had been lured back to great hall by the lively music. Balen was grateful for the emptiness. The certainty of Kus's betrayal had made him angry, and he needed a moment alone. By the time he made it back to the hall, all the blood was in his ears. A hint of arcane power sparked desperately in his stomach, but he stamped it down. Lingering by the entrance, he peered into the dancing mass and calmed his breathing.

He needed to do this quietly. Alerting the nobility and the empire to what had happened would be just as bad as regicide. It would ruin Zavrius.

So he'd need to be subtle.

Balen slipped into the room. He tried to lock eyes with Zavrius, but the king seemed to be purposefully avoiding him: he was focused on dessert or laughing at something in the crowd, looking anywhere but at his Prime. The Rezwyn ambassador sat off to the side, silent, flanked by her priests. Zavrius wouldn't be able to show a lick of worry with her so close, so he shifted his gaze to Lestr. His master was watching him sternly.

Balen nodded once and hoped that was enough to communicate that he was gaining ground. Then he turned his attention to the floor.

The dance was magic, a different kind than the arcane in his blood, but just as real. The guests were laughing, spinning, gowns flaring with every twist—in that instant, Balen could pretend the joy was real and shared by everyone in the room.

But when Mariel Kus spun into his view, the feeling shattered. Balen moved closer to the floor. This dance was Cres Strosian, and thankfully something from an older season. Everyone in Usleth knew it. Balen was no exception.

No individual danced with a single partner: people spun in pairs for a circular turn around the floor before separating and partnering with the person behind them. The dance continued until the music stopped. It required good timing and spinning in the right direction, and very little else.

Balen knew joining mid-dance would disrupt the flow, but he did it anyway. As one partnered pair split apart, Balen slipped his hand around a woman's waist and joined the dance. Her partner spun off into oblivion. Balen lost sight of him and turned to the woman with a smile. She yelped, relaxed when she recognized his armor, and tensed again when she realized she was dancing with the Prime.

"Hello," Balen said with a smile. He glanced down at the embroidered anchor on her shoulder—a Westgar family—and rummaged through his thoughts for a name. "Lady Kavran."

He craned over her shoulder; Mariel Kus threw her head back and laughed. She hadn't seen him.

"I, I . . . ," Lady Kavran stuttered, doe eyed and flushed. She didn't bother searching for her lost partner. Balen smiled flatly and pulled her closer for a better view of the dance hall. She squeaked.

The dais came into view. Above Mariel Kus's head, Zavrius sat. Balen and he locked eyes. There was one long moment of imbalance that stretched out between them. The king was on his throne and his Paladin was beneath him—as it should be—but all Balen could think of was how his arm was wrapped around the wrong waist.

Balen blinked rapidly. The rotation completed. Lady Kavran let go and Balen spun into a new partner. The motion disoriented him, and he briefly he lost his mark. Panic flooded him. He'd been distracted by Zavrius. Had she spotted him? Had she pieced it all together and fled? Another spin and he spotted her dancing with the younger Mordsson. Momentarily relieved, Balen knew he couldn't lose her again. Balen barely looked at who he was dancing with—another lady of many—and lifted her, taking them out of the defined circle to move next to Kus. The disruption caused a ripple; there were murmurs, frustrated comments. A few dancers jolted to a stop. The orchestra continued and the song picked up: a rising crescendo of speed and power. Laughter and clapping filled the hall. The dance pushed on.

As he came close, Mariel Kus looked up at him.

Balen laid on all charm and grinned for her. "Lady Kus. I was rather hoping we might dance."

"I'm flattered, Prime," she said. Silas Mordsson started to protest, but she patted his chest and broke apart. Still moving, she flashed Balen a broad smile. "But I fear this song draws to a close."

At once, the music stopped.

The hall erupted in applause and cheers. Balen skidded, and the sudden end made Balen's partner stumble. He glanced away to catch her—a moment, just half a damn moment—and snapped his head back up. But Mariel Kus was gone.

Balen untangled himself from his dance partner and stepped out from the floor. The guests had already begun to bleed out into the halls again. He scanned the heads, looked for Kus's dress or her hair, but she wasn't there. Struggling not to curse, Balen pushed forward toward the entrance.

She knew. Balen was sure of it. And if she made it out of the palace alive, they might never catch her. Worse, she would never stop trying to get her revenge. There'd be nothing else left for her to do. Her house, her titles—all of it would be stripped from her. But not her anger. Not her outrage.

He was glad when he didn't have to force his way through the mass of bodies. Guests stepped aside as he walked toward the doors. He stood tall, chest puffed; he was going to charge out of there, he realized with a growing dread. He couldn't afford to be subtle about this any longer. Mariel was missing. He had to find her.

Balen reached the doors and looked right to left. The Paladin statue's shadow shifted along the ground.

Balen spun toward it and raised a gauntlet. Adrenaline sent a rush of arcane power into his hands and the gauntlets crackled with energy. "Halt!"

The shadow went rigid. Then there was shuffling. Huez Thenlass stepped out into the light.

Balen hesitated but kept his gauntlet raised. The old general looked haggard, but fury burned in his fierce glare. Mariel Kus struggled in his arms. Thenlass had a hand clamped over her mouth. She screamed angrily, thrashing in his grip, but he held her fast. Thenlass's gaze was serious. Stern.

"Prime!" he said, sounding relieved. "You were chasing her."

Balen scanned Thenlass's face, at first unsure how to react. The old general had been so charming to Kus only an hour before. Now he seemed furious.

"There has been a small incident. We have some questions to ask her," Balen said, taking Mariel by the arm. Balen gave him a short nod. He tugged the Lady Kus toward him. He had his hand poised, ready to quieten her if she decided to scream, but it seemed all the fight had vanished. She whimpered but went willingly.

Thenlass bristled and glanced back toward the hall. "The king—"

"—is fine," Balen concluded.

Thenlass nodded, handing Kus over to Balen fully. He stood for a moment and readjusted the sash over his shoulder. "Good," he said, regaining composure.

Balen nodded back to the great hall. "I wouldn't want you to miss the rest of the party, Lord Thenlass."

Thenlass bowed deeply. "Pass my regards to the king."

Balen held Kus tightly, but she'd stopped struggling. Some morose acceptance had come over her. Balen looked up and saw a sea of faces gawking at them. He'd made a scene: Balen jolted, cursing himself for providing the noble class another thing to question Zavrius over.

"The party awaits," Balen called to them, gesturing to the waiting hall.

Thenlass slipped out from behind him and slung an arm around a nobleman's neck. "Come now," he said, with enough charm and confidence that the nobleman laugh.

Balen could swear the tension evaporated.

Thenlass led the guests in the corridor back into the hall. "The king has brought us the most excellent entertainment, and here we are being poor guests. Look how many are without dance partners! Let us drink and dance."

The crowd thinned, following the old general. Balen silently thanked him as Thenlass disappeared into the packed hall. When the corridor was clear, Balen pressed her forward.

She slumped with every step. Balen half expected her to spring around and try to stab him, so he kept her at arm's length. His one gauntleted hand sitting on her shoulder was enough threat to keep her silent. Save for the ambient chatter at either of the corridor, where guests filled the hall and the garden, there was nothing. Candles burned low here, vignetting Balen's view. It gave him a growing sense of unease. Luck had been kind to him suddenly. He wasn't about to squander it.

The east wing where he'd agreed to meet Petra was dim and cordoned off.

Balen could hear Kus's breathing; he was straining to hear it, expecting a sharp intake of breath whenever she tried to wrench herself free or attack. But he heard something else.

A whistling tone to his right. Something flew toward them.

A shocked gasp punched the air. Balen spun to Kus, ready with his gauntlets raised—but she wasn't fighting him. She was stock-still. When she moved, it was stilted, one action at a time. She looked down. She saw what had happened.

"Oh," she said.

Her hands shook over her abdomen, where something sharp and blood covered jutted through her flesh.

Balen whirled around. There was no one. The hallway was empty. He turned back to Kus, cursing. She wasn't dead yet, but she was dying fast. They were too exposed here. He quickly scanned for any guests that might have seen before he grunted and hauled her into the first room he could. It was a guest bedroom. Balen saw the basics: bed, carpet, candles. His whole attention was on Kus.

She groaned low and fell onto her side, sprawling with a cough. Even though her fingers were shaking, she started trying to edge the knife out of her guts.

"Stop it." Balen went to his knees beside her. "You'll only die more quickly."

"Seems I'll be doing everyone a favor, then," she said with a weak smile. She wrenched it free and threw it. The knife hit the floor with a clang. "Did you want to be the one to kill me, Prime?"

Balen ignored the bait and tried to stem the bleeding. After what she'd tried to do to Zavrius, he wanted her dead. But he wanted answers more.

"Who else is there? Give me a name. You clearly weren't working alone."

She blinked at him, fading.

He held her fast, imploring her. "Tell me, Kus."

Kus laughed, saliva and blood dribbling from her lips. "Oh, what does it matter? You want a single name when there's a chorus." She wheezed as she reached up to touch Balen's face. He flinched, feeling the streaks of warm blood as she dragged her fingertips down his cheek. "This nation's blood is on your hands, Prime. Yours and your false king's."

She swallowed; her breath came in shorter, shallower.

"Kus," he urged, knowing it was useless. "A name."

Her breathing slowed. Faintly, she shook her head. "A chorus, Prime. A chorus. All of us . . . everywhere."

She breathed her last and was dead.

Balen rocked back on his haunches and pressed the cool metal of the gauntlets to his forehead. His heart was racing. He reached for the bloody knife, but it was as non-descript as a knife could be. Brown wooden handle. Iron blade. There was no sigil to mark it, nothing to track where it might have come from. It wasn't arcane in the slightest, or he would have felt the thrum of recognition in his veins.

Balen clenched his jaw. That blade had moved unnaturally fast, with the kind of strength that only came from the arcane. When he'd turned in the hall, he'd expected an assassin, another unhinged arcanist ready to fight. He knew his instinct was right.

Whoever had thrown was like him. Like the arcanists on the road.

Balen yelled and hurled the knife across the room. It hit the wall with a twang, quivering with the force of the throw. He sat there panting, staring at it, a potent wrath burning through him. How did it keep happening? How was Zavrius supposed to prove his detractors wrong while fighting for his life?

Balen wanted to fall into self-pity, to have one indulgent moment where he could hold his head in his hands and feel all the frustration and upset of the last few weeks. His temples were pounding. Mariel Kus's blood was on his cheek.

But in another room, the king was waiting for Balen to make him safe.

Balen caught his breath and composed himself. He stood and pulled the knife from the wall.

When he turned, Petra was standing in the threshold. She closed the door behind her. Her eyes fell on Kus's body. She sighed, not disappointedly. "Did you dispatch her?"

"No," Balen said. He held the knife up. "There was an assassin. I couldn't get a name out of Kus. There's someone else behind her."

Petra looked at him seriously. "There will always be someone else."

Balen grimaced. He mulled that over and made himself nod, like he could force himself to accept it. That truth was becoming clearer and clearer.

Balen wiped the blood from his cheek and tossed the knife to the floor.

"Remove her without being seen, chancellor," he ordered.

Petra bowed her head. "Yes, Prime." Then, when Balen moved to the door, she added, "And well done."

Balen paused near the handle. That sentiment felt complicated. But he accepted it. After a moment, he breathed deep, wrenched the door open, and returned to the Great Hall.

It was still a party, still full of dancing and laughter. Most of the nobles had gathered in groups at the tables to drink and chat, though several dancers still filled the floor.

Balen looked over all their heads toward Zavrius. The king sat alone. The Rezwyn entourage had abandoned their right-hand table, and save for the Paladins stationed nearby, it was only Zavrius. He was like a figurehead at the bow of a ship, entirely rigid. Lestr spotted Balen's return and whispered into the king's ear. A jolt went through the king. Zavrius turned to Balen as he approached the dais.

They didn't speak. They didn't have to. They locked eyes and Balen was overcome with emotion: part relief, part a deep knowledge that this would be the rest of their lives. That he would be negotiating Zavrius's life from those who wished him dead until he could no longer do it. As Balen came close to the throne, he bowed low, lower than was strictly necessary—a veneration of sorts. When he looked up, Zavrius's stare was fierce. Balen could see the question in them.

Was it done? Could he relax?

Balen nodded, letting his eyes soften with a small smile. Zavrius blinked slowly, like he didn't quite comprehend. Then he sighed. His eyes fluttered shut. Zavrius's relief was palpable. That moment when his eyes were closed, the king was vulnerable, a man reveling in being alive. And when he opened them, he was Zavrius again, that languid prince, free of the rotting force of his paranoia—at least for tonight.

Alick and Lok peeled away as Balen stepped onto the dais.

Zavrius didn't turn as Balen approached the side of the throne. Balen stood silently for a few moments before he heard Zavrius say, "Thank you."

"It's my duty," Balen said, habitually.

Silence stretched between them. Zavrius stared unblinking into the hall.

"Of course," Zavrius said. "I thank you nonetheless."

Another few minutes passed in silence. Then Zavrius turned. "You should enjoy the rest of your night. Dance. Drink."

"I'm fine."

"It's boring up here," Zavrius said with a laugh, meeting Balen's gaze.

Balen shook his head. "I'm where I want to be."

Zavrius's smile faltered. He folded it away neatly and gave Balen a stoic, contented smile. "Of course. As you said, you're a man of duty."

Zavrius turned back around.

His duty was to the king, but that was not what Balen had meant at all. Correcting it felt too heavy. Instead, he considered debriefing him, warning him that there was someone else. But surely Zavrius knew that by now. There would always be someone else. And for now, the immediate threat was gone.

So Balen let him have the night without sharing the worry in his own heart.

 CHAPTER
ELEVEN

In the week following the ball, Balen spent most of his time training with the newer recruits, while Zavrius was once again holed up answering correspondence. But this morning, Balen had received his first summons for the week. He rose and headed toward Zavrius's study.

When he arrived, he'd obviously interrupted some conversation he wasn't meant to overhear. The muffled conversation ended abruptly with his knock. To his surprise, it was Petra who opened the door.

"Prime," she acknowledged, stepping out of the way for him to enter.

"Chancellor," he said, trying and failing to keep the curiosity from his face. He could feel his brow curl as he glanced between her and the king.

Zavrius was standing by the window, dressed in a white oknum kaftan. His hair was out of its usual braid and draped over one shoulder.

Dressed for comfort today, Balen thought, but he still looked beautiful. Zavrius glanced over his shoulder as Balen approached, half his face illuminated by the sun. He offered Balen a smile.

"Petra's brought me some interesting news," Zavrius said as he took a seat. "I'd like your opinion on it."

Balen acquiesced with a nod but kept his mouth shut, unsure what kind of weight his opinion would have before the king.

"It appears my uncle—your master—has already begun to melt down and recast the arcane weapons used by my siblings."

Balen froze. He glanced at Petra, who only nodded.

He'd seen it. The information wasn't new, but he could hear the fresh implication in Petra's tone. The weapons of

Zavrius's siblings were made from gedrok, like Zavrius's lute-harp. But where Zavrius's instruments were carved from bone, skin and tendon, like the Paladin armor, the other royal weapons used gedrok scale. It was a rare, metal-like material, and there had been no doubt those weapons would one day be recast for the needs of the order. Balen knew the order took great pains to take only what they needed from gedroks, and with ceremonial respect. But what he hadn't asked himself in the forge was why would Lestr be melting these weapons down so soon?

Balen had seen them at the forge in the days before his own ceremony. Now he recalled returning from Teum Bett, disheveled before his master, who had been repurposing a longsword made of gedrokscale—but where had he gotten it?

Balen had known in the moment it was something that had once belonged to Theo. It was only now he was realizing the weight of Lestr's actions.

He nodded at Zavrius. The king glanced over at Petra with a raised brow.

Petra gestured to Balen. "Tell us what you know, Prime."

Balen wished he didn't have to question his loyalty between his master and Zavrius. He was the king's Prime, no matter what Lestr was to him. But the more he thought about, the less he could pretend it wasn't a betrayal—a betrayal he was bound by oath to follow through on. The Paladin gritted his teeth. Lestr was his master and more a father to him than the real thing had ever been. Yet Balen was sworn to the king. That pledge overrode everything else. Guilt swamped him: immediate, churning in his stomach and making his chest heavy, like some attack he couldn't parry. He was selling out the man who had trained him. He was turning his back on the man who had made him who he was. And at the same time, he was doing his duty. The king asked, and he would answer.

Balen squeezed his eyes shut, scrambling to find the words to explain.

"Last I saw, he was melting down Theo's sword. All of your siblings' weapons were recovered shortly after their deaths. It's. . . interesting that he'd melt them down so soon."

That seemed to pique Zavrius's interest. He leaned forward, resting his chin on his fist. "What are you thinking?"

Balen shrugged, feeling foolish as he said, "All weapons have a story to tell. Especially that one."

Zavrius frowned at him but said nothing.

Petra stepped forward. "You're speaking about the rumors, aren't you?"

Balen held her gaze, then glanced away. This felt dangerous, like he was admitting to treason by association.

"We've been told that King Zavrius's siblings all crossed enemy lines and were killed there. Accidentally, or perhaps not. Either option irks me. And when the Rezwyns find out the royal line has breached the treaty, they not only claim to have nothing to do with the assassinations, they don't even retaliate for our incursion into their territory? That makes no sense. Strategically—I mean, forgive me, Your Highness, but if that were all true, what could be their reasoning? What does any of this mean?"

He knew that was a step too far. Zavrius looked up with a glint in his eye. At first Balen thought he was tearing up, or angry, but there was something calculating happening there. "And what do you think that means?"

Balen bit back his answer. When he'd first viewed the weapons at the forge, weeks before his ceremony, Balen had run his hands along the weapons, inspected them from every angle, hoping for some insight into what happened to their owners.

"I'll tell you what I saw from the weapon," he said. "Theo's brilliant greatsword was in three parts—that's not right. Not when you have the greatest arcane weapons of the dynasty somehow marred by the regular steel wielded by empire dogs. Impossible."

Petra ignored the revelation about the damage to the weapons and instead said flatly, "You think the empire should've started a war."

Balen shook his head. "No. But if they were going to start a war, they had the perfect opportunity."

"So what, then?" Zavrius raised both brows. "What do you think happened?"

Balen said nothing. He wasn't sure what Zavrius was implying—if he was implying anything at all. Was this a test?

Zavrius stared at him. "I've heard people say that I had them killed."

"People say a lot of things." Balen dismissed the accusation with a wave.

Immediately, reflexive, Zavrius's eyes widened a nearly imperceptible amount.

Balen shrugged at him. "I'm your Prime. Do you really think I listen to sedition? I don't know what happened. Maybe you don't fully understand it either. But I do know the Rezwyns don't want a war."

Zavrius turned back to the window and rested his chin on his hand. "Not an overt one, anyway."

Petra stepped up, apparently deciding that their debate was now over.

"They returned the bodies as well as the arcane weapons," Petra said. "Speculation won't get us far, my king, and I know you've rejected my suspicion before, but . . . It is entirely possible the heirs were dispatched by criminals. They stumbled into Rezwyn territory and were met with a brigand of empire vagabonds who took it upon themselves to eliminate a threat. An act that would be entirely unsanctioned by the emperor. A tragedy. But not an act of war. This is, in my opinion, what has occurred."

Balen opened his mouth with a dozen or so questions, but Zavrius redirected him.

"So what does that mean for Lestr?" Zavrius cut in. "A Rezwyn diplomat stays with us, and he melts down evidence under her nose, without consulting me. What kind of speculation does he have about the tragedy?"

But Lestr's thoughts were his own. Balen shook his head. "He has never shared those thoughts with me."

Zavrius grunted and resumed staring out of the window. "Well, there's a dozen reasons it could be. He thinks me a murderer but wants to protect the crown. Or he thinks me a murderer and wants to defend himself from said murderer by destroying the evidence. Or he's the one who murdered them. Or he's melting them down out of simple material necessity."

Zavrius was rambling, clearly put out by not knowing. He seemed to catch himself, because his jaw slammed together, teeth clattering as they collided. He stopped talking, readjusted himself and turned back to the two of them with a small smile.

"Thank you for your insight, Prime. You may leave."

Whatever Zavrius was thinking, he wasn't ready to share it with Balen. Balen tried not to take it as a slight. He bowed and left the room.

Zavrius's reticence irked him, especially since it wasn't new. To couple that with whatever Lestr was doing only made Balen's mind a mess of thoughts. Balen decided he wouldn't dwell on it that afternoon. Hitting things and training tended to help clear his head, so he resolved to focus on the new recruits. Lok was good but green, and many were still getting used to the ichor and the armor they wore to temper its effects. He headed back to his quarters to retrieve his sword and saw Alick and Frenyur drilling them outside the forge. For some reason, the sight stopped him in his tracks.

Balen's position was interesting. He didn't lead the Paladins, but he'd been marked as the best of them. His role as Prime put him aside from the others, and watching them train together now brought with it a pang of nostalgia.

Before he could pull himself away toward his quarters, a voice called for him.

"Balo!" It was Lance. His voice was high, like he was close to tears. "You came to check on me?"

Balen swung around, momentarily thrown out of his slow descent into loneliness. The brothers sat together in the courtyard. Mallet had one big arm wrapped around Lance's shoulders, the near comical size difference making it appear like Lance was being smothered against Mallet's meaty bicep. At the sight of Balen, Mallet hauled Lance to his feet. They were both out of armor, clearly on a break from their duties in more ways than one. Up close, Balen could see the red in their eyes. A carrot stuck out of Mallet's pocket. It was so out of place it caught Balen's attention, and it was then he saw a bowl had been carved near its stem. Balen froze.

"No," Balen said with a laugh. "Did you make a pipe out of a damn carrot?"

Mallet ripped it out of his pocket and flung the thing into a flowerpot. Balen half spun before he decided a carrot pipe was both desperate and ingenious enough an invention that it deserved to be ignored.

"Oh, Balo," Lance said again, louder. He looked like he was about to give Balen a hug, and he likely would have had Mallet's grip on his brother's shoulder not kept him in place.

"You must forgive my brother," Mallet said with a dip of his head and a sheepish smile. "He often forgets himself. And, uh . . . he's out of sorts, today."

"Oh?" Balen asked, staring toward the flowerpot. "What's happened?"

Lance opened his mouth, but instead of words, he gave a despondent whimper and glanced away.

Mallet grimaced and raised a hand to hide his mouth from Lance's ears. He whispered poorly, "Yulia, the kitchen girl—"

"I have been cast aside!" Lance cried with a healthy infusion of sorrow. "Your Primeness—"

Balen, snorting, cut in with, "Lance, it's just Balen."

"I thought she was the one! And now?" Lance patted his own heart. "This is a man who is bereft of all hope!"

Balen shifted his gaze to Mallet. "That's . . . quite the dramatic sentiment."

"He's been reading poetry," Mallet explained, rolling his eyes. "Thinks it'll help with the wooing."

Balen didn't have to ask to know how that was going. "Well, I'm sure it has nothing to do with you being a flirt, Lance," Balen said. "Last I heard you were doting on a girl named Inez."

"Inez?" Mallet said with a scoff. "She was weeks ago now."

"Oh, you're one to talk," Lance snapped. He spun to Balen. "Mallet's barely any better, sir. He's had his heart broken, same as mine. And now he's sworn off love altogether."

"And what about you?" Mallet said with a wide, drowsy smile.

"Yes, Balo!" Lance laughed, grabbing Balen's shoulders. "How go your attempts to woo that expensive skinny bard?"

Balen went rigid as the blood rushed to his cheeks. He opened his mouth, jaw slack. Quietly he whispered, "Are you talking about the king?"

Something clicked behind their red eyes, the realization walloping them out of their smoke-induced haze. Both their faces crumpled.

"Oh, bones," Lance whispered.

"Sir," Mallet started forward. "Sir, please, we didn't mean—"

"That never happened." Balen cut through the air with his hand, tone terse. "Let's hope you've both smoked enough to forget that whole interaction."

Balen put up his hands to be done with it and started off toward his own quarters. The brothers followed in a stunned silence. Balen stamped down the embarrassment—blood was in his cheeks and Zavrius was in his head—and asked them more questions about the kitchen girls. That got them talking again.

"Do you think it might serve you both better to focus on your duties?" Balen called over his shoulder.

"No!" Lance said.

Balen suppressed a laugh. His quarters could be accessed from the courtyard as well as the Royal Apartments, giving Balen many exits should the palace be breached by an attack. He pressed a gauntleted hand against the door and stopped the flow of arcane energy keeping it locked. The lock worked the same way as his armor did and was attuned to him.

When the magical hum stopped abruptly, Balen pushed the door to his chamber open and went to retrieve his sword and helmet. Light spilled over the sparse room. Once more, the sun illuminated that triptych outlining Balen's potential fate: Paladin dead before his king. He grimaced as he reached for his sword.

Lance gave a low whistle. Mallet grunted behind him. "Damn," the big man said, pointing right at it. "That's a little bleak, don't you think?"

Balen strapped his sword to his belt and watched them drag their eyes up and down his wall.

Lance clicked his tongue and shook his head. "I mean, what's the point of it?"

"To scare him half to death every night before he sleeps, most like," said Mallet. "Lets him know what happens when he does a poor job."

"Actually, that's a Prime who's played his part perfectly," Balen said, "The king survives. No matter what."

The brothers stayed silent, but only verbally. They always managed to convey so much with their raised brows, set jaws and pointed looks to one another.

"Come on," Balen said dismissively. He gestured up at the triptych. "It's part of what I've vowed to him. It's my duty."

"To die?" Lance asked, incredulous.

"No," Balen said, with bite. "To protect him."

"His gauntlets look fancier than yours," Mallet murmured.

Balen swung back to the triptych, eyeing the odd, crystal-lined gauntlets splayed at the depicted king's feet. He exhaled and shook his head. "That's an old tale. The crystals, I mean. This was before even Queen Rostaiva, so I doubt it was ever real. But the legend has it that a gedrok was found in a crystal cave to the east, near the Ashmon Range. The armor forged from it was different."

"Powerful?" Lance prodded.

Balen nodded. "The crystals grew over the gedrok and could refract arcane power. So its attacks were immensely powerful. Explosive. The stories say they could wipe out armies."

"Not powerful enough to stop him from dying, though," Mallet noted.

Balen shot him a dark look, flushing. It already sounded idiotic, but proclaiming the mythical power of the gauntlets next to their dead painted wearer only made Balen feel worse.

Lance pointed at his hands. "I thought the gauntlets you wear have been passed down for ages, anyway."

"There's a ceremony to taking from a gedrok," Balen said. "Only Lestr and the Prime can decide to harvest new material, and we thank the gedrok. All of us, in ceremony, thanking it for its power. That's why most things are reforged to preserve what we can."

"So are these gauntlets new, or . . . ?" Mallet wagged a finger between Balen and the painted Prime.

Balen sighed, willing the conversation to end. "I told you, it was just a story."

Lance shrugged. "All right," he said. He dusted his hands to be done with it, then opened them up to press the air back, like he was trying to keep the triptych and its depiction of death at bay. "Either way. The thing's a little off-putting."

Balen opened his mouth to retort and stopped himself. He thought about arguing, defending the very order he was sworn to, and then he turned back to the triptych. He saw his potential future: a bit of paint for him and every Prime before him. The fight left him. Off-putting was perhaps too light a term.

Balen pressed a thumb to the bridge of his nose and nodded. "Sure," he said softly. "I'll admit it's not the brightest thing to witness first thing in the morning. But—"

Lance cut over him, "No wonder you wear that armor every waking minute. I'd wear it to sleep, too, if I was reminded of my own death in my own bed."

Mallet clamped a hand on his brother's shoulder. "Sir, I'm sorry, he's an idiot."

But Balen only laughed and ushered them out of his chambers, resetting the arcane lock behind him. He led the brothers back into the courtyard, tucking his helmet under one arm to pat Lance's shoulder with the other hand.

"Listen," he said, "you have a point about the triptych. It's an ugly thing. But you're off the mark with the armor. That's not why I wear it. Do you want to learn why?"

The other man nodded fiercely. Balen glanced up at Mallet, who nodded too.

"Ichor wasn't meant for humans. Not really. It's a corrosive magic; its hard for our bodies to regulate. The king and his family have the upper hand. Their blood has been dosed with ichor for generations. But me? All the Paladins training out there?" He waved toward the forge, where the drills were continuing. "None of us have the capability of withstanding the effects of ichor without armor. We train for it, and we can go a good week or so before hitting the point of no return. But that's without casting a single attack. If the ichor is triggered in the blood without the gedrokbone to regulate it, it burns through us."

Lance paused for a moment and gave a low whistle to Balen's cuirass. "Protected from attacks inside and out."

"In a way," Balen said, smiling. The thought of the arcanists burning through their bodies hit him with a grueling, nauseous twist of his stomach. He shoved it from his mind. Exhaling, Balen knocked shoulders with the brothers and directed them toward the west wing and the guards' quarters. "Get cleaned up and back on duty. And stay away from the kitchen girls. They'll only break your heart."

Lance pouted and nodded. Mallet drew him away. Balen waved as they left and pretended not to notice Mallet digging around in the flowerpot.

As he was heading to train, Petra stepped out from behind a column.

"Oh, by the bone," Balen hissed.

She only smiled at him, hands behind her back. Had she been watching that whole interaction? To what end? Balen could think of nothing more disturbing than Petra having her eyes everywhere.

"What is it?" he said, frowning. He glanced back toward the main corridor. "Is it the king?"

Petra shook her head and walked up to Balen slowly. "You speak to those two quite often."

Balen glanced over his shoulder as the brothers entered the west wing. Then he met Petra's eyes and tried to read her. It didn't take long to know she was much better at concealing her feelings than he would ever be at reading them. He couldn't tell what she wanted so he said, "They're good conversationalists."

"I somehow doubt that," she said. Balen turned back to her. He could tell there was something she wanted to say—something delicate she was darting around. Balen raised a brow.

"They're good men," he told her. "They returned the king to the palace without injury."

Petra turned her head, exposing her profile and the sharp pursing of her lips.

"Prime," she said, eyes flickering as she watched the Paladins train, "I'm truly glad you're building a base of people upon whom you can rely. But, I must say, I don't believe those two should be relied upon."

Balen took a slow, deep breath in. He knew what she was saying, could see it spelled plainly in the scrunch of her nose. Still, he asked, "And why is that?"

But Petra wasn't taking the bait. She slashed him with a meaningful look and raised one perfectly curated brow. That was all she did to communicate her thoughts.

Balen sighed and shook his head. "Chancellor, I believe you're wrong."

That got her attention. She turned to Balen more fully and crossed her arms. "Go on."

"They have an ingenuity, a creative determination that my Paladin brethren lack," Balen said. "Their perspective is refreshing, and I admire that."

He tried not to think about the carrot as he said it.

Petra looked like she was going to question him. She considered him a very long time with her arms folded tightly against her chest. Balen readied himself to defend them. He knew they were capable men. But Petra only sighed heavily to convey her disappointment and nodded.

"As you say, Prime. You are perfectly capable of choosing your friends. I just hope for the sake of the dynasty that you choose them well."

She left him to think on that for the rest of the afternoon.

CHAPTER
TWELVE

He next saw the king when Zavrius came to him at dawn.

Balen opened the door to find the silhouette of the king haloed in the peach glow of the rising sun. Balen had slept well, but finding Zavrius outside his room with that usual playful smirk made him unsure he was awake. It felt too close to dreams he'd been having for years.

Balen turned to their shared door with a frown. That Zavrius had gone to the trouble of knocking from outside was a formality. Balen wondered if Zavrius was making a point, setting boundaries that might have been blurred, but then he glided over the threshold and came to rest his palm against Balen's chest. Warmth seeped out of it. Balen was hit with a prickly shock. He blinked, surprised at the heat behind the touch—surprised at the touch itself. It took him a moment to realize what felt so strange about it. He looked down at Zavrius's hand with a slight frown before he remembered he was unarmored. Balen's heart raced. That sudden intimacy, flesh against flesh, felt wrong somehow: a hope that could never be reality. Balen stepped back, leaving Zavrius's hand hovering in the air.

What are you doing to me? he almost asked. What do you want?

His mouth sat dry and unused. He said nothing at all.

With the sun behind him, Balen couldn't see Zavrius's expression. But from the way the king's fingers curled, one by one into the palm of his hand, Balen knew Zavrius felt slighted.

"You're not quite as useful to me like this," Zavrius said, half turning toward the door. Without looking at Balen, Zavrius gestured up and down. Balen had on only the long loose shirt worn under his armor. "Not anymore, at least. Paladin up for me, would you? I'm bored. I want to go out."

Balen briefly closed his eyes, blotting out the source of both his longing and deep annoyance.

"Are you waiting for my help?"

Balen blinked, cast a quick look back at Zavrius. "I won't be long."

Balen turned to the stand holding his armor, avoided looking at the final panel of the triptych, and started with the sabatons.

It only took Balen a handful of minutes, but Zavrius still looked impatient when he turned around.

Zavrius looked him up and down. "Leave the helmet off."

"Why?"

"You won't need it."

Balen shucked the helmet and tucked it under his arm, too tired to press Zavrius further. Zavrius nodded. "Walk with me," he said, and Balen followed him, a dog at his heels.

The king's private chambers were the central part of the palace, as protected as they could be.

Their quarters opened into the colonnaded garden at the center of the palace. Even the open colonnade was impossible to get to from the roof, and always guarded regardless.

Balen could see Paladins posted in the towers now, looking out at the royal road or at the small, private garden to the west of the palace. There, Cres Stros's gedrok skeleton sat, the garden as its tomb. The palace gedrok was much smaller than the one in the Gedrok's Glade, and mostly stripped of its scale and sinew. Its bones sat exposed. If Mariel Kus had been after ichor, she could have tapped it from there. All it was now was a well protected but rarely visited symbol.

The garden was a hedged-off rectangular space at the south-west of the palace. If one climbed up to the high window in the king's quarters, one would be able to see the gedrok skeleton peeking above the hedges to the right. Equally, one could see it stepping out of the forge, which sat directly to the east of the garden. But the garden was closest to the Paladin barracks, which sat at the bottom of the palace's west wing. Balen often wondered if its placement was deliberate. For both the Paladins and the Dued Vuuthriks, it was like a reminder of their power, an everyday visual reminder of the ichor in their blood.

They walked the length of the colonnade in silence.

Balen had spent most of his life here, but he didn't think it was possible to tire of this place. The colonnade curved around a lush but tidy garden, green burnished by the sun, and well kept in a way a public place could never be. A few Paladins sat about, reading, chatting. Those that noticed the king tried to scramble to their feet, but Zavrius waved them to be at ease.

With the lute-harp strapped over his shoulder, Zavrius strummed at it half-heartedly, never quite forming a tune. Balen didn't know what to make of that—whether he wanted Balen to remain silent, or whether he loathed that silence and was trying to fill it. After a minute Zavrius seemed to give up, tugging the strap to reposition the lute-harp on his back.

"I want to see the Gedrok's flowers," Zavrius said, without inflection. Balen couldn't pick his mood. Or at least didn't want to try. Silence was the safer option for now, but his heart rate increased all the same, imagining whatever reason Zavrius wanted to talk.

Balen cast a glance toward the forge before they started down the path to the gedrok's bones.

"Come on," Zavrius called.

The path to the garden was on a downward slant, walled on either side by a light sandstone. Bushes and hanging vines burst over the tops, so thick the sun only struck the tops of the plants. Aside from the soft glow, the path was shaded. It opened into a large walled area filled with shrubs and flowers.

This garden looked so different from the glade; this skeleton seemed a different creature from that hulking glade beast by the light of dawn. At night, it was sometimes easy to get caught up in the horror of what the massive glade creature represented. In front of them now, pink and orange dawn light cracked through the open rib cage. Each bone was accented with the sunrise. The light edged through the trees and spilled onto the ferns and grass. The dew glowed.

The gedroks had been colossal creatures. There was no record in the dynasty as to what they had looked like or what had killed them. Whatever had taken them out would've been catastrophic, natural or otherwise, but there was nothing written to suggest it.

If he thought too long about the dead gedroks, Balen always felt uneasy. This great, ancient thing, with a body that could withstand so much—dead. But death was stillness. Decay. When the bodies of gedroks were immune to rot and death, it was no wonder Paladins took from gedroks so reverently.

Zavrius walked them through the gedrok's skeleton.. As Zavrius's hands skimmed against the bones, Balen heard Zavrius humming but couldn't quite discern the tune.

Zavrius stopped between the gedrok's gullet and mouth. He turned back to Balen. The king was radiant, half his face in shadow, one eye hit with the morning sun, and glowing. As always, that smile waiting on his lips. Balen breathed so deep he felt his chest constrict against his cuirass. He looked out into the walled garden, pretending something in the trees or flowers had caught his eye more than the king.

Balen exhaled nosily. "What do you want, Zav?"

"Zav," he repeated, light giggle under his own name. "So informal. What would the court say?"

"Something about scandal," Balen said flatly, tone not quite matching Zavrius's playful inflection. "Is that what you're looking for?"

The mask of Zavrius's cynical nonchalance slid away. He cast a nervous glance farther down the path. Balen heard the crunch of footsteps on the gravel.

"What are you doing?" he said.

Zavrius laughed softly. "Well. Nothing yet."

Balen didn't like that answer. "Who are you really here to meet?"

He squinted at the path, watching the rustle of rushes and ferns as bodies pushed through.

The diplomatic entourage for the Rezwyn Empire stepped into view. The trio moved together in the same formation Balen had seen previously. Two priests flanked the ambassador, all of them still decked in the overwhelming array of beads and fur, war paint touched up and vibrant on their fair skin. The air seemed to bend around them, like they were being marked as foreign and out of place.

A swath of curses came to Balen's mind. He said none of them. They would be part of a larger conversation. "You know diplomacy isn't really my strong suit."

"Diplomacy is my job, not yours," Zavrius said under his breath. His lips twitched into a contained smile as the diplomats moved closer. "Just stand there and look intimidating and shiny."

Balen clenched his jaw. His throat filled with all the nervous energy he usually shadowboxed out. The Rezwyns walked forward into the mouth of the gedrok, all of them unfazed by the size of it, and stopped five paces from them. Balen calculated how long it would take to draw his sword and reach them, a brief flash of tactics, the potential formations they might use to trap him. If he'd had more time, if Zavrius had bloody told him—but these few seconds were all he had.

He tried to settle himself. On the one hand, he needed to trust that Zavrius knew what he was doing, and on the other, Zavrius had brought his lute-harp. Battle was always a possibility, but if it came down to battle with the empire's ambassador, Balen knew that'd be the start of a war.

So, most likely, this would be a battle of words only.

Balen had barely seen the ambassador up close. He tried not to balk, tried not to imagine meeting her on the field in battle. She matched Balen's height. She was muscular, well trained. What looked to be a massive two-handed sword was strapped to her back. Her long black hair was pulled away from her face, but it burst into curls down her back. The Rezwyns always looked unnaturally pale to Balen, and the ambassador was no exception. She took a breath and bent from the waist in a stiff bow. Her lips turned upward in a not-quite smile, half pained, like her face was untrained in the motion.

Zavrius returned the greeting with an empire gesture, fist across his heart, expression blank and vacant. He did little more than tilt his head to the left, but the two priests mirrored him. Balen stayed as still as he could manage.

"I thank you for this." The ambassador's voice was gruff and heavily accented. Her tongue struggled with the smooth, consistent tones of Uslethian.

Zavrius nodded at her, said, "Tezlackip," in a similar show of diplomacy. The welcome was a guttural sound from the chest and throat so harsh it must've hurt to say. The ambassador's expression changed. Balen knew little about the empire's expressions—it could've been she was impressed at Zavrius's attempt, but equally, she could've been amused.

"No need for that. Doskorian is a punishing tongue. We wouldn't want your royal throat to strain," she remarked.

Zavrius took the slight with his usual charming smile. "A kindness. But you must forgive me—I was not the expected heir for the Dued Vuuthriks. My education is lacking."

Zavrius must have known how he looked to them: very young, very inexperienced. Balen realized with a start he himself only added to that image: without his helmet, there was no denying his youth, either. How would that look to the empire? Weak? Or easy to manipulate? Balen scanned the three faces of the diplomats, their impassive stares as they stood in the heart of the dynasty's power.

"Odrica Dziove," the ambassador said with a bow. It wasn't the first time they'd met, but empire courtesy seemed to demand it. "It is good to finally talk."

"Dziove," Zavrius repeated. "Please give my thanks to His Excellency Nio Beumeut for the agreement we've reached. Thank him also for the swift return of my siblings' bodies."

"It shall be done." She bowed slightly, the action mirrored by the two priests. "Though if you have agreed to this meeting to pressure the Great One—"

Zavrius held up a hand. "You have asked for this meeting. I agreed to it because I wish for continued peace between our countries." Zavrius put down his hand and smoothed down his tunic. "I imagine the death of my siblings is part of why you wish to talk."

"Not the death of your siblings, Your Highness," Dziove said, "but where Usleth places the blame."

Balen glanced to Zavrius but couldn't see his reaction.

Where they placed the blame?

Were the Rezwyns denying any involvement in the deaths? Balen silently wished he'd been paying closer attention to the diplomatic party at his confirmation ceremony. Lestr's words then had been bold. It was clear his master had no qualms with blaming the empire for the heirs' deaths. And the nobles weren't quiet about their suspicions of empire involvement, either.

Then again, why would anyone take issue with that narrative? It was what they'd all been told.

Balen's gaze fixed on the back of Zavrius's head, and he stared like he could see into it.

Zavrius took a breath. "I can see how any type of admittance of involvement would be uncomfortable—"

"The empire had no involvement," Dziove snapped. Balen saw her face contort. She was ferociously angry, uncharacteristic by empire standards. By the time Balen had blinked, she had recovered. She lightly touched the emblem on her cuirass, that roaring god of war.

The priests on either side of her swayed a little. The beads on their face covering clacked together. One of them said, "Ambassador Dziove, if I may?"

Dziove looked over at the man to her right and gave him a nod. He ambled forward. The beads parted as he walked, giving Balen glimpses of a high brow, wide-set eyes balanced over broad cheekbones. As he moved closer, he clasped his hands together. A prayer, or supplication. The motion made the long sleeves of his tunic fall to his forearms and bunch there, revealing pale skin marred by multiple angry red scars. Balen blinked at them. He had a moment of nausea, head spinning as he took them in. He tilted forward with a step. Grooves in the flesh, some still fresh and healing, others thick and old like they'd been cut upon again and again. Was this the price their god demanded? Ritual bloodletting?

Zavrius must have heard the crunch of Balen's footfall. The king's head turned slightly, shadowed eye breaching over his ridged nose. More than enough to convey his aversion. Balen grimaced before he recalled his audience. He wiped the look from his face, but felt out of his depth.

"I am Thal," the man said, "priest of the Great Berserker, Borviet, Who Rides on Chaos."

Zavrius acknowledged this with a tight-lipped nod.

The priest continued. "Ambassador Dziove is devout and pious. A true believer. Her line comes from the gods, and she lives as Borviet requires. I tell you this knowing your dynasty has . . . less knowledge of our pantheon. The gods beseech us to claim new territory. But this peace between our nations satisfies our great emperor, the True Commander Nio Beumeut, and it will not be breeched. Do you understand, King Zavrius? It is not your exanimate gods that stop us"—at this, the priest gestured to the prone skeleton of the gedrok encompassing them—"but the wishes of our emperor. We did not kill your brothers and sister. We have returned their bodies. We are not involved in your problems. That is what our emperor wishes to convey."

"Emperor Nio Beumeut is both gracious and benevolent." Zavrius smiled and looked younger than he was.

Ambassador Dziove pushed past the priest, forcing him to step back in line with his companion. She had regained that impassive empire stare. Balen returned it.

"Then you understand," she said. "Commander Nio Beumeut has heard your hails, has acknowledged them, but there are no soldiers, nor murderers, to give up. None were responsible. None saw your heirs die. Why do your people spread this lie?"

Balen risked at glance at Zavrius but saw no reaction: no tensing of his shoulders, no clenching of a fist—nothing. The Paladin wasn't sure if he wanted Zavrius to have one. His gut twisted. The rumors said that Zavrius had killed his siblings, but the official story pinned their deaths on the empire. Now the Rezwyns denied involvement. Someone was lying. But what was Balen supposed to do if the liar was the king?

The ambassador continued. "A lie between commoners would mean nothing. But spread between patricians, proclaimed at your sacred ceremonies . . ." She trailed off, passion slipping through the cracks in her calm. "Such shadowy work is an insult to honor. You blemish the emperor with such claims. This is not a road to be traveled, King Zavrius. We both know where it leads."

Ambassador Dziove wasn't brazen enough to say the word, but the threat was clear.

Balen bristled at the same moment Zavrius chuckled. The sound was bright and surprised before it dissolved into a tired sigh. Something about the tone of it felt genuine. Zavrius suddenly looked exhausted, like this conversation had been dragging for hours. Or weeks.

The ugly thought came to a head: Could the Rezwyns be telling the truth?

It was easy to think it was the empire. He wanted them to be lying, to be harboring a troop of elite soldiers capable of taking down the heirs. For them to be responsible for the attack on the road. But if they weren't, if Odrica Dziove and her priests were telling the truth, then what had really happened?

Zavrius rolled his shoulders. "My father died in your territory. My brothers and sister died there too. When I die, I want it to be here in Cres Stros." Zavrius spoke slowly. "Preferably old and fat from empire sweets and wines. Of course, we'd need a treaty to make that a reality."

Odrica Dziove smiled for the first time. "Of course."

"But as for the deaths of my siblings," Zavrius said, severity cutting through his light tone, "I have nothing more I can say. And so long as their deaths remain unanswered, I am forced to consider everything, including that your people may have had a role in their demise."

The ambassador's smile dropped from her face. The diplomats stiffened in place. Everything shifted: the fading tension came back in full force. Both priests made odd gestures with their hands that Balen guessed was a supplement to prayer. He was standing beneath this immense skeleton with the pearlescent bone of the glade gedrok stretched over his body, feeling like he'd let the enemy wander into

Usleth's heart. Balen readied himself for whatever was to come.

"This is not an accusation," Zavrius added, "only a statement of fact. So long as we don't know who is responsible, it could be anyone. But I will do my best to quell the unnecessary rumor-mongering or speculation."

"Then we'll take our leave." The ambassador turned to go, then turned back. "If we come across the details of what happened to your siblings, the empire will not hesitate to inform your people. We are not the only subjects of speculation in this regard."

Balen knew what she was implying: you had them killed yourself to take the crown.

"We all look forward to uncovering the truth." Zavrius gave a little bow. "Let me see you off," he said with an outstretched hand.

Diplomatically speaking, Balen wondered if declining a foreign king's invitation was even possible, but Dziove looked like she might do it anyway. Then she relented and allowed Zavrius to walk alongside her.

Balen followed at a polite distance. It meant he was out of earshot. He saw Zavrius smile, likely trying for something amicable. The ambassador returned the smile, though hers was clipped and looked unnatural on her face. He didn't hear what they said.

But he did hear the sound of an arrow whistling through the air.

The arrow struck Thal in the neck.

For one dizzying moment, Balen felt like he was falling. His vision blurred with the sudden rush of adrenaline, head spinning as Thal fell, as the ambassador turned on her heels, screaming—and Zavrius, eyes locked on the dying priest, was exposed.

The arrow glowed once and dissipated into fractal light.

Balen slammed his helmet on and rushed forward, leaping the paces to Zavrius. Arms outstretched, he blocked

Zavrius's body from the incoming arrows. Three arcane arrows thudded into the back of his armor. Zavrius's eyes were wide. He heard Dziove give a little cry behind them. Balen spun and dragged Zavrius forward, pressing his palm into the small of the king's back. Balen shoved him toward the gedrok's skeleton. Balen watched him run, heard the strange crackle of an arcane arrow whizzing toward him, and dove to the side. He scrambled to his feet. Dziove was bent over Thal's body, crying, the other priest running frantically toward the path that would return him to the central palace—but something shot at him from the east of the garden. He fell and sprawled, twitching on the ground.

Balen opened his palms and charged the gauntlets, shooting three half-formed blasts of energy over Dziove's head for cover. He considered leaving her—Zavrius was his to safeguard—but if she died, there was no telling how the empire would react. He shot in the direction of their attacker and came up behind her, hooking his arms around her body.

There was no moving her. She was strong, had her knees planted in the ground. He turned his body to shield her. He felt another arcane arrow thud against his back. The armor reacted, absorbing not only the force of the blow, but the arcane power in the arrow itself. Balen felt it seep into the gedrok plate. It was a burst of power he could use in his attacks later—his assailants had made a mistake.

But he took little comfort in that. Dziove wasn't moving.

"He's gone!" he hissed in her ear.

She screamed angrily, mouth curling into a snarl. She looked nothing like the calm woman they'd just spoken to. It was like her god was taking her over—Borviet, that rabid human-boar, desperate for blood. Balen looked down at Thal, at the blood streaming from his neck. Dziove was covered in it.

"Leave him!" he screamed again, but she shook him off her. Balen fell back. Dziove stood to her full height and rolled her shoulders. She drew the two-handed sword from its straps. The tip of the heavy blade hit the dirt with a thud. Balen looked up at her from the ground, eyes wide. She threw her head back. This time the scream devolved into something brutish, the bright sounds of her scream corrupting; a monstrous growl took over her voice. She was going to launch forward. She was going to run blindly to the tree line and be struck full of arrows.

Balen raised the gauntlets and fired. At the same time behind him, Zavrius strummed a series of chords. Zavrius's attack was quick, shooting over Balen's head. Their arcane power melted together into a wall of near-transparent blue. The arrows met it and burst apart, their energy crackling out.

Balen grabbed Dziove's arm. Her eyes dropped to the gauntlets and went wide.

"We're not retreating," he said slowly, knowing what fighting honor meant to the empire. "We're regrouping."

Dziove scanned his face and nodded once. Dziove hefted her sword high as they ran back together, Zavrius hurling another chordal attack over their heads as they took cover behind the gedrok's thick ribs.

Balen bit back a curse. The arcanists had penetrated the palace. Where were the rest of the Paladins? There should be at least a dozen in the exterior garden alone.

"Velmuk!" Dziove said as she skidded to the ground. She whacked her head against the gedrok's rib. "Chy velmuk! Let Borviet fucking eat you!" She turned to spit into the dirt. Then she snapped back to Balen.

Zavrius studied her carefully. "Just so you know, this isn't my order."

"So your crown is being taken?" Dziove made as if to move and peeked around the corner. A flash of uncomprehending sadness flooded her face when she saw the priest's body once again. She ducked back as another line of arrows shot toward her. Balen heard them thud against the gedrok's bones and cursed under his breath at the irreverence.

Dziove gestured to the king. "They kill you and blame us, yes? If I must die, I should die fighting instead of hiding here with you."

"That would be the end of peace," Zavrius said. "Call me selfish, but I hardly think your True Commander would take kindly to your death."

"You flatter me," she said under her breath, accent curling as she spoke. "I am just one tool of many for the emperor's use."

"It's not flattery," Balen said, before Zavrius had a chance. "You're a tool for King Zavrius, too."

Dziove looked between them.

Zavrius shrugged. "He's not wrong. I need you alive. I hardly think a note of apology would be sufficient if I were to send all three of you back as corpses."

"If you survive." That usual empire neutrality slipped back into Dziove's features. Battle seemed the only time emotion was relevant. She bowed her head slightly. "And I'm to believe, after this, you'll let me live?"

After this . . .

Balen looked between them. What would be worse? Having to explain the murder of the diplomatic entourage, or letting the ambassador return with the knowledge the dynasty was struggling with infighting? A flash of that possible future filled Balen's mind: the empire advancing, safe in the knowledge the dynasty would fall.

But what was stopping them now? He'd been so confident when he'd told Zavrius the empire didn't want a war. And strategically, Balen knew they'd had every chance.

Zavrius opened his mouth.

Another volley of arrows rapped against the ribs, slipping through to thump into the ground. None of them were actual physical shafts—the arrows were arcane power focused into deadly bolts.

The amount of power that took made Balen's skin crawl.

The Paladin moved to a crouch. "Shall we focus on living, first?"

Dziove gave a slight nod, hand tightening around the hilt of her sword. She looked to Zavrius and tilted her head toward the arrows. "They have the exanimate's gift, don't they?"

She meant arcane power. Balen was reminded again how little the empire knew about the gedroks.

Dziove said, "We believed they only gifted the royal line and your protectors."

Zavrius glanced to Balen before he leaned into her assumption. "That is usually the case."

"They've favored others." A small gasp escaped Dziove's lips. "Is there a war among your gods?"

Balen was starting to feel sick. At some point the enemy would stop shooting at a distance. "We only have the gedroks—the exanimates. Not a pantheon like you."

Dziove frowned at that. "But the Heir Ascendant—your brother," she said, turning to Zavrius with a nod. "We were under the impression he had undergone evikreloz."

Zavrius frowned, trying to parse the word. "Apotheosis? I don't—" He shook his head. "Theo did not become a god."

Something ran screaming toward them. Balen looked up at Dziove, saw shock resolve into a focus. They stood together, backs pressed firmly against the ribs. The screaming arcanist burst forward, the force of the run making her stumble awkwardly into the clearing. At the end of the rib cage, she shuddered to a stop. Something about her was familiar, but Balen focused on what he could see: her youth, curly chestnut hair and bronze skin, covered in freckles. She wore trousers and a one-shoulder tunic over a blouse embroidered with a symbol Balen couldn't quite pick out.

She panted. The Paladin watched her tensely as she stood there, still, like she was gathering momentum. Then, animalistic, sensing where they were, her head snapped toward them. When she turned, she brought a thin rapier into view.

The arcanist kicked off the ground. Balen sank down onto his knees, watching her. She moved with speed—unnatural, quick, feet kicking up grass and flowers as she ran. The rapier drew Balen's gaze. It crackled, spitting blue energy across the metal. He steeled himself, ready to defend Zavrius, but Dziove peeled off the rib to face her. The ambassador bellowed, heaving her greatsword overhead to crack it down on the arcanist. That would end things fast. Dziove was strong and solid. Not even arcane power could protect against the force of that downward blow. But cat-quick and nimble, the arcanist moved so her rapier met Dziove's greatsword with a clang. The thin sword didn't shatter—all the crackling energy along the blade discharged in a blinding blast. Balen shielded his eyes. Dziove howled. Her body flew back into the gedrok's ribs, blue electricity still dancing on her cuirass. Zavrius was on his knees, cheek blackened from the blast. The arcanist didn't stop. She cut the air at her side and swung—for the king. She ignored Balen completely. The arcanist sliced down towards the king. Zavrius made a desperate off-tune chord; a half-formed scythe sliced across her cheek just as Balen parried, flicking the rapier out of Zavrius's path.

Balen put himself between them.

There was heat in his belly. A spark of arcane power pooled in him. His left hand twitched, power building in the cradle of his palm. This was controlled; the arcanist kept her arcane power flowing endlessly. She came at him again, aiming for his neck. Balen raised his arm to block. She was stronger than she looked; Balen's foot skidded back in the dirt. They were locked together, the girl madly grinning, eyes blue with arcane overload—angry. Balen's arm shuddered with the pressure. Their blades clinked together, both hilts interlocked.

A twang and hiss sounded; a force hit him in the heart. He looked down, surprised. An arcane arrow quivered there, then dissipated.

The arcanist got to her feet. Her blouse had burned, searing the skin beneath. Balen readied himself for another flurry of attacks. Zavrius began to play. It wasn't the usual rushed chords he used in battle, but a melody. A slow, droning song, an ebb and flow that felt like the ocean tide. Balen felt his skin prickle beneath his armor, felt the Paladin armor respond with a strange buzzing. Balen swung around to him.

"What are you doing?"

"Acting on a hunch," Zavrius said.

Balen bit his tongue at that, frustrated by the non-answer. Zavrius was concentrating hard, expression severe and focused on the arcanist. Balen could see the air around the lute-harp twist. It reminded him of waves of heat bending off hot ground.

Balen froze, suddenly aware that too many seconds had passed without an arrow being shot at him. He turned with his arm raised to block any attack. None came. From behind his arm, Balen watched the arcanist sway, locked in some trance.

Zavrius strummed and she rocked with the sound, like her bodies felt the ripples of his music.

Zavrius's power seeped into Balen's armor, making it hum unnaturally. His mind felt heavy. Before his mind could cloud, he swallowed hard and grabbed Dziove. The two of them backed themselves closer to the gedrok's ribs, out of Zavrius's firing line.

Dziove hissed, "What—"

"The king has his own methods of fighting," Balen said. "We need to get you out of here. Get you a horse . . . get you to safety."

Dziove scanned his face like she was looking for the lie. She came to some conclusion and nodded firmly at him.

Zavrius didn't stop playing. A fine mist of sweat covered his face. Balen laid a hand on his back to steady him. "How long can you keep this up for?"

Zavrius shook his head. "Don't know. It's—" He looked like he wanted to explain but couldn't.

"Don't speak," Balen whispered. "Just focus. Can you do that?"

Zavrius visibly swallowed, blinking sweat away from his eyes. "I can try."

Balen's hand slipped to the small of his back. He pushed lightly. Zavrius took a step forward. The arcanist did not respond.

"You're comfortable leaving her here?" Zavrius said. His voice cracked as he spoke. Balen glanced up at the gedrok skeleton. This wasn't the glade—there was no ichor left for them to take. And besides, these attackers were already oozing arcane power.

"Just focus on getting us out of here," he murmured. Zavrius nodded once.

They moved as one unit. Whether intentionally or not, Dziove and Balen matched every step Zavrius took. Huddled together, they walked closer to the arcanist. Balen had a vision of her breaking out of Zavrius's spell, lashing out quick enough to gut the king. But her eyes were glossy. She was focused on the lute-harp. Up close, Balen had that sense of knowing her—of feeling like he should know her.

"Balen." Zavrius's voice was a wheeze. Balen looked over and realized he'd stopped moving. He gave a final glance to the woman and moved back to Zavrius's side. Dziove's eyes were on her fallen priests. Thal was in the center of the garden. The other priest was sprawled close to the path. Dziove let go a small whimper as they stepped over him. Balen caught a glimpse of dead eyes half rolled back into his head, blood dripping from his open lips. He glanced away.

Zavrius turned slowly as they walked up the path. Balen chanced a look back as well; for the first time he saw the hidden ranged arcanists stumble out of the bushes. Two of them, well away and rendered useless without their ranged attacks, but looking at them made Balen's stomach twist. So many noble children coming to destroy the king.

The arcanists were ever-so-slowly moving toward the sound of the lute-harp. They were stiff-legged, moving in jagged bouts—not quite quick enough to stay close to the sound. Balen watched the trance begin to lift. The arcanists blinked rapidly, put their hands to their heads.

"This won't work," Balen murmured.

"No. And then they'll kill me," Zavrius grunted.

Balen knew he was right. This was an organized group intent on killing the king.

There was no doubt about it. Balen couldn't let any of them live.

Balen leaped forward towards the closest arcanist, who still had her rapier in hand. He slammed into her, shoving her backward. Her lithe body sprawled on the ground. Turning to the other, blade out and buzzing with the arcane, Balen spun and sliced across one archer's neck, then down the other's torso. Both collapsed, dead. Balen turned again to the woman sprawled on the ground. With his sword raised in both hands, Balen saw the magic disperse from the arcanist's eyes as they came into focus, growing wide. Balen stabbed the sword into her chest. A spritz of blood burst from her lips. She wheezed, gave three gasping breaths before her lungs stopped working. Balen ripped the sword from her chest, panting.

Then something flashed in his mind. Her eyes, the shape of her face.

Balen swallowed. "Polverc."

Zavrius shifted a little, grunting. "What?"

"Polverc's niece," Balen said, nodding at her body. The little knot in his mind unraveled—By the bones, that was it. All the Polvercs had that long straight nose and cutting glance. "She's Polverc's missing niece."

When he spun, Zavrius was staring at him, frowning. He stopped playing and let his quivering fingers rest against the strings. Dziove stood next to him, beaming like Balen was a long-lost son.

"Impressive," she said, looking between Zavrius and him.

Zavrius ignored the revelation. He blinked rapidly, frowning with this new knowledge.

Balen wiped the blood from the blade and sheathed it. "Come on."

≈≈≈

They were halfway down the colonnade when Balen knew that this was no mere assassination attempt, but a full insurrection.

Balen couldn't see a single Paladin. He looked up, hoping to spot a palace guard or Paladin somewhere on the roof. A body was sprawled facedown at an angle, weapons cast aside.

"Come on." Balen grabbed Zavrius's hand again and began to jog slowly through the palace halls. Dziove jogged behind them, sword on her back.

It was eerily quiet. They rushed past a dozen shut doors and rooms without a single soul inside. But as they got closer to the front palace steps, it was evident there had been fighting. At first it was only furniture strewn about, or pictures knocked from their place on the wall. Then it was bodies: a serving girl bleeding from the neck, a twitching stranger with a fire stoker in his gut. They stepped over them cautiously.

Balen sparked his gauntlets with power.

The sounds of fighting grew closer. Balen rushed to a window and pressed his face against it. The window looked out to the front of the palace, a porticoed landing with steep steps that led to various levels of the hill. He craned at an angle. Most of the view was obscured by the round base of one of the needle-point towers, but he could see something iridescent and shining, Paladin armor in a fight. He peeled his face back to look at Zavrius.

"We can't go out the front. We'll take the tunnels, make a hard line to the stables, and get the ambassador on a horse. Then—"

"No."

Balen blinked. "What? "

Zavrius hefted the lute-harp high. "I can save them."

"You're the king," Balen said with a shake of his head. "That's not your job—it's theirs."

"They didn't sign up for me," Zavrius said. "I know it's your job to protect me but saving their lives might secure my throne a little longer." He got close to Balen, so close Balen could feel Zavrius's breath against his throat. "At the very least I need the Paladins on my side. It can't just be us against the world."

Balen looked at him, really looked at him. He placed a hand on each of Zavrius's shoulders.

"But that's the truth right now. As far as we know, it is just us against the world. Don't waste yourself saving people who are not asking to be rescued." Balen cleared his throat.

Zavrius blinked and rocked back on his heels, disappointed.

"I don't want you to go out there. But you know I'll follow you anywhere," Balen said. "So make your decision."

Zavrius's eyes softened. "You don't have to—"

Dziove's laugh sounded through the silence.

"Your majesty, you are so sweet," Dziove whispered. "Honorable. More honorable than I expected. Someday you might be a good king. But today your sentimentality makes you stupid. You cannot protect the man sworn to protect you. He will follow you. So. Fighting is the way, no?" She glanced to Balen, who nodded an affirmation. She took the greatsword off her back.

Zavrius cocked his head. "You're not allowed to die in my care, ambassador."

"Ah, with all these dynasty secrets, I cannot afford to die." She smiled at them like it was a joke, but Balen's stomach twisted. Dziove nodded to the door. "I will fight my way to a horse."

Zavrius shrugged out of Balen's grip and flexed his hand. "Well, if all goes well, you won't have to fight at all."

Balen positioned himself by the door, pooling power in his gauntlets. "I'll give you cover."

Zavrius closed his eyes. Balen shoved the door open. It swung wide to reveal a porticoed landing with steep steps down a terraced hill that eventually led down to the front gate. The stables were near the bottom. A blast of power shot across his field of vision. Balen blinked and jerked back defensively.

Outside, the battle line was clear. Before them a line of Paladins held back dozens of arcanists. Bolts of arcane power flashed through the air, wild and endless from the attacking arcanists. They seemed to all be fighting as individuals, devoid of any unified tactic. Balen could identify no one captaining their assault.

From his vantage point atop the stairs, Balen fired a line of energy straight forward from his gauntlets. The bolts flew over the heads of his fellow Paladins, crushing the combatants at the center of the enemy force and allowing the Paladins to move their center line forward, splitting the invading force in two.

As Balen prepared another blast, Zavrius had begun to play.

It was that same humming drone, only now it built steadily, a wind-like force emanating from Zavrius's hands.

The air pulsed. Balen watched the trance fall upon the arcanists. A few Paladins disengaged, stepping back in surprise when their foes did nothing more than rock on their feet.

"Take them alive if you can!" Balen ordered.

Beside him, Zavrius groaned. There were so many of them—dozens of noble youths come to try their hand at regicide. Paladins began to bring them to the ground.

Zavrius had struggled in the garden. This was overwhelming.

"They're all . . . different," he managed. "There are so many. Everywhere."

Balen wrapped a hand around his waist to steady him. He wanted to ask what Zavrius meant, but speaking was too distracting. Zavrius needed to concentrate if they were making it out of this alive.

He heard Zavrius constantly changing the tune, or the speed, tweaking as they walked down the steps. Then he saw why: several arcanists would blink rapidly like they were coming back to themselves, and Zavrius would shift, reattune himself to the arcane power they were emanating, and rein it back under his control. For a single source of arcane power, it might have been easy. But there were ten on the ground. He was sure more were hidden on the roof.

"Dziove," Balen hissed.

She was a soldier, too, at heart—she knew what was needed. She put her back to him, sword at the ready. Balen turned to his Paladins and hissed, "Fall in," as if speaking loudly would disrupt the magic of Zavrius's music.

A few Paladins hesitated, their eyes still locked on the remaining arcanists. Some of the Paladins looked suddenly unsure, but one by one the Paladins fell back to defend the king.

Balen saw the look in his compatriots' eyes: confusion, and something else. Bright hope. Relief. They were coming together, for the first time fulfilling their purpose to the king.

They moved down the steps together. Balen chanced a look behind them. Over the helmeted heads of the Paladins, he watched arcanists appear on the roof, swaying and turning to the sound of the lute-harp. They stumbled forward, locked in the trance. Balen scanned them. They were archers.

"Watch them," he told the few Paladins who used shields. Whatever the range on Zavrius's magic, he wanted to be ready for when the spell broke.

"What's happening?" someone murmured next to him. Frenyur, he assumed, by the gruffness of the voice. A few Paladins craned their necks at the sound of the question. Balen kept his gaze shifting.

"Assassins," he said. "But not—not trained."

"But they're arcanists," someone else hissed.

"Yes," Balen said. He pressed his hand more firmly against Zavrius's back. "Somehow they are. Where is Lestr?"

"Rallying Paladins to head to the glade."

"Go with him," Balen told Dziove.

Zavrius made a low noise beside him. Balen snapped his head down, saw blood. He darted in front of Zavrius. One of the king's fingers had started to bleed.

Balen grabbed his arm and squeezed. "How much longer can you keep this up?"

"As long as it takes," Zavrius said with a nod.

Lying again, Balen thought.

"We to take at least some alive to question them." The sweat on Zavrius's forehead was obvious now, no longer a slight sheen but forming droplets. It was like he had a fever; his body started shaking as if from the cold. The notes coming from the lute-harp became muddied and distorted.

The king was still playing, desperately. Balen put his hand on Zavrius's. Abruptly, the music stopped, and with it the buzzing in Balen's chest.

For a moment, nothing happened. Then Zavrius looked up at Balen. His brows knotted together over teary eyes. He was shaking, clearly exhausted. In the corner of his eye, Balen saw movement.

"Paladins!" he managed to scream, just as the arcanists came back to themselves, blinking away the stupor Zavrius had cast over them. The Paladins backed against the king, swords and shields raised, except Frenyur, who tried to tackle an arcanist to take alive. Balen snapped his head to the archers. They stood and drew. Balen cast haphazardly, shoving Zavrius to the ground beneath him. Their unit started to disband as the Paladins fought. Balen glanced down the steps, considering bolting. He couldn't. He couldn't risk exposing the king.

Balen looked to Dziove, and the same knot of calculation was on her face, the same realization they couldn't make it down the stairs.

But there was another way.

Frenyur failed to contain the arcanist and was forced to fell him. The Paladin looked up and caught Balen's eye. There would be no taking these attackers alive. They had to flee. Frenyur glanced between him and the king and then nodded his understanding. Balen grabbed the exhausted Zavrius and backed up the stairs, past the fallen bodies of Paladins and arcanists.

"Protect the forge!" Balen called out as he retreated.

Zavrius slumped against him, but there was resistance in his step. He didn't want to leave; still, in this moment, he was worried about appearing weak.

Balen turned and walked backward, pressing Zavrius to his back and casting where he could to help the Paladins. Then, all of a sudden, they were back at the open doors to the palace.

Balen cast a glance at the fight. Chaos came from the roof in a rain of arrows. He watched them glance uselessly off the Paladin armor, but somewhere down the hill he heard a scream. Balen's gut clenched. Leaving felt like an awful weight, a terrible thing to ask, but this is what they'd trained for. This was the life of a Paladin.

Balen called out: "Paladins! You were each chosen for the order based on merit. You are not only worthy, but chosen! Defend the palace. I entrust it to you."

There was no cheer, no scream of triumph. But it bolstered them, made them stand taller, firmer. They came together: four shields raised at the front, the other armored bodies at the back, pushing back up toward the palace.

Then Lok yelled, "For the king!" and the echo of his voice made Balen shiver with relief.

He spun on his heel, draped his arm around Zavrius, and moved.

"We have to take the ambassador and leave here," Balen said to Zavrius as they pushed back through the palace.

"You'd have me abandon my seat?" The king looked up at him, mildly defensive. But he was in no state to do anything more than slightly raise his voice. He leaned against Balen, full weight pushing through his hand on the Paladin's shoulder.

"I'd have you live," Balen said.

Zavrius said nothing to that, but Balen felt his weight shift against him. The smallest of concessions, but he'd run with it.

He pushed them into the Great Hall with his gauntlets raised, half expecting to see the place thick with arcanist insurgents.

The long tables stretched out empty—the room had gone unused since the ball. Balen ushered them in and barred the doors but made Zavrius and Dziove stay put while he searched the long stretch of room. Zavrius slumped over a table with his hands splayed.

Dziove looked disappointed. She spat over her shoulder. "You hide us?"

Balen gritted his teeth at the echo of her voice. He thought he heard something in a corner and jerked toward the noise, gauntlets raised. Nothing.

Zavrius made a low noise beside him. Balen glanced at him, then over to the ambassador.

His eyes lingered on Dziove. There was a feeling in him like tar, a heavy guilt for what he was doing—saving an enemy at the expense of his own people.

Balen drew Zavrius's arm around his own neck. They hobbled the length of the hall and slowly climbed the dais.

"Shall I die on the throne, then?" Zavrius asked. He leaned heavily against his family's throne, a stale, pained look clear in his eyes. Outside, they heard a strangled scream. Zavrius grimaced and looked away.

"You won't die." Balen moved to the back of the throne. He ignored the piercing stare of the ambassador as he yanked the panel free. Zavrius grunted at the sound, eyes wide. Balen looked between them and caught the king stamping down an expression of surprise. Balen couldn't tell if Zavrius was angry at him and tried not to care either way. He was getting him out. He sent Dziove down into the dark first before Zavrius limped after her. Balen reached and pulled the panel shut behind them, hearing the clang of metal ring outside one last time before he plunged them all into darkness.

"Balen?" Zavrius whispered.

Balen went to him and helped him walk.

Even in the low light, Dziove's eyes were fiercely bright with interest. Balen thought she'd ask, but she stayed unnervingly quiet, surveying the tunnel for every detail. Balen grimaced and tried to ignore her.

But if they ever made it back to the palace, this tunnel would only be a liability.

"Come on," he said.

It was instantly cooler than the humid hall above. Balen blinked away spots in the darkness before he sparked his gauntlets with firelight and held his hand aloft. It barely helped. Save for the fire flickering in his palm, the darkness was dense.

He let Dziove take the lead. When there was enough space between them, he looked down at Zavrius.

"Are you all right?" Balen asked. The fire cast long shadows on the walls, illuminating a few patches of damp stone. Once he saw it, he could smell the musk of stale air.

Zavrius grunted, not bothering to look up at him. "Why don't I know about this place?"

Part of Balen was glad he hadn't known. That was one less secret Zavrius had kept from him all this time. But the Paladin who had sworn to protect the king's life wished he'd been aware of it—without the brothers' help. Without them, where would he be now?

Softly, not fully committed to answering the question, Balen said, "I wish I'd known about it earlier myself."

They both lapsed into silence after that, and apart from an oddly cheerful humming from Dziove, nothing more was said.

The tunnel had a slight tilt to it that told Balen they were heading downhill. When it ended abruptly, Balen extinguished the fire and pushed a massive boulder aside. It revealed the grate he'd seen Mallet open. They walked out, blinking into the bright light. Balen made them stay low. Dziove darted forward into the stables.

Sounds of fighting filled the air. Balen ignored them, reminding himself his duty was to the king.

Balen carefully positioned Zavrius near the stable's entrance, low to the ground and hopefully out of sight. Before he entered the stable himself, he glanced back to see the fight on the steps coming to an end. He thought he saw more Paladins standing than fallen, but he couldn't be sure.

Then, faintly, he heard voices—harsh, like an argument. He charged his gauntlets instinctively, went running with them raised.

Zavrius looked up. "What—"

Balen ignored him and rounded the corner.

Dziove was in the middle of an argument, yanking a horse forward. Two men were loudly complaining about her taking it—two men Balen recognized.

He dropped his hands with a sigh. "Mallet. Lance."

The two men turned to him in surprise. They were helmetless, which told Balen they'd been caught unaware.

"Balo?" Lance said, coming around the horse.

"Balen," Mallet corrected, hands firmly on the reins. "Sir. Tell her she can't take our horses."

Lance waved him down and clasped Balen's shoulders. "It is good to see you. So good. We were—we have no idea what's going on. No idea. And, uh . . . there are lunatics attacking everyone."

Balen pretended not to notice the redness of his eyes. "Are you deserting?"

"Would you blame us?" Lance said, gesturing toward the commotion outside.

"Teum Bett is looking mighty fine right now," Mallet said. He was staring at Dziove. "Is she from the empire?"

Balen didn't know what to think. A surge of anger went through him. Still, they were barely trained—how could he blame them? But then Lance said, "Look. We're not running. Not exactly. We're saddling horses. Just in case we did need them."

Lance was red eyed, grinning like a fool.

"Let her take the horse," Balen murmured through gritted teeth. Mallet let go of the reins immediately, putting both of his hands up. "What are you doing?"

"Nothing," Mallet said, hands still up. "We saw the Paladins were fighting. We're just . . . we don't have that level of skill."

"You want to leave," Balen said.

"We want to live," Lance finished. "And what are you doing?"

"I am escorting the king and a high-ranking foreign dignitary," Balen replied. He glanced back at Zavrius, who was propped up against a beam, looking pallid. He swung back to the brothers. Only two of the horses were saddled. "We'll need three more saddled—quickly."

"Two," Dziove said. "Bareback is nothing."

Mallet and Lance grimaced, but when Balen pointed them to another saddle, they jumped to work.

Dziove led one of the unsaddled horses outside. Balen followed, then leaned against the frame.

She mounted the mare with ease. It trotted in place, waiting.

"You coming with us to Teum Bett?" Lance called from the stable.

Zavrius peeled off the post and stumbled to the stable entry. "You're not going to Teum Bett."

The brothers stopped working. Mallet looked over to Zavrius carefully. "Your Highness?" And then, at the sight of him, "Sire, are you all right?"

"We're going to Westgar," Zavrius said, "and you're coming with us."

Lance cocked his head. "Are we?'

"We'll need you for the road," Zavrius said, in a way that sounded like an order, like there was no way for them to say no. "And if protecting your king is not enough incentive, gold can also be involved."

The brothers looked at each other. Balen wondered what they were thinking, whether or not they were embarrassed at being caught: two fighting men ready to run. Balen stood stiff-lipped and waiting, racking his mind for a way to convince them if they refused. But they looked away from one another without a word and went right back to saddling the horses.

Balen watched them and felt an ugly mix of emotion. The adrenaline from the fight was still in him, but it was slowly being eaten by another, darker feeling. Balen jolted when he recognized it. Disappointment. Was this how Lestr had felt, looking at him after Balen had disobeyed him?

He clenched his jaw, trying to keep his face impassive. He hated cowardice. It was a luxury he'd never been able to indulge. This feeling in him now was bitter, upsetting, all-consuming. The knowledge that these men—men he had trusted, men he had defended—would desert at the first sign of trouble stung. Balen was bound by his duty. They were fleeing theirs. It was a betrayal Balen was struggling to stomach.

They were different men than him.

"Is that a yes?" Balen asked, standing straight.

Lance only grinned to himself, continuing to work.

Mallet looked up at Balen, then slid his eyes to the king. He nodded. "I don't want you to think we aren't grateful. That we're just cutting and running, saving our own asses."

"I couldn't blame you if you were," Zavrius said.

Mallet smiled at him. "Well, you're a brave little bard, aren't you?" Then he paled, dropped to his knees in abject horror. "Your Highness, I—"

But Zavrius only laughed, a harsh wheeze that caught in his throat. "Oh, get up. We need to move fast."

Mallet and Lance went back to work.

Zavrius turned to him with a soft smile, but his eyes were dark and worried. "Westgar it is."

CHAPTER THIRTEEN

They rode out of the city at full speed. The district closest to the palace, the patrician quarter, was full of screams and panicked nobles. There were fires, but they were small and contained—superficial, Balen thought, meant for distraction. He felt bad thinking that. People were scared. Cres Stros should have been in shambles and under full attack. But the closer they got to the gates, the more he realized he was right. Nothing else had been hit. This was about dethroning Zavrius.

But replacing him with who?

On the road, Balen's mind circled around this subject until he closed it off.

Zavrius spent the first three hours of their journey slumped forward on his horse's neck, face in the gelding's mane, sweating profusely, as if his body was fighting fever. Maybe he was—Balen had never seen anything like the magic Zavrius had performed in the garden.

"What are you staring at?" Zavrius had wheezed, turning his head against the horse's neck. Balen flushed, realizing he'd been caught. Zavrius scoffed, glint in his eye. "Am I that pretty?"

Balen had snorted. Whatever that magic had done to him, he was still Zavrius at heart. The brothers shared one of their usual, silent looks in Balen's periphery. Balen tried to ignore why Zavrius's comment had prompted that, but Dziove made it difficult. She stared directly at Balen with an unrelenting look of pity. Dziove only did him the service of averting her gaze when Balen spluttered out, "What?"

Balen had them stop at a roadside merchant, which took some convincing given only Lance and Mallet had any coin on them. Balen thought that a kind of justice after their cowardice but kept that to himself. Once he'd bartered with the merchant for lower prices, the brothers paid for dried meats and bread, a saddle for Dziove, a set of plain tunics, and five cloaks made from the drabbest wool he could find. He made Zavrius swap his beautiful tunic for a boring beige one and made sure everyone was bundled up in their dull cloaks before they set out again. They went off-road for the night and ate their meal in relative silence, still shaken from what had happened in Cres Stros. Then they slept fitfully in shifts, save for Zavrius, who fell into a deep but fevered sleep the moment he was horizontal. Balen slept two, maybe three hours. Then he made them get on the road again.

Riding through the provinces west of Cres Stros, a gradient landscape emerged. Where Cres Stros was warmer and more arable, Westgar was full of mountains and streams, with dense forests in the far north. The Royal Highway took them through the southern part of Shoi Prya, the province sandwiched between Cres Stros and Westgar. The north of Shoi Prya was dominated by mountains, but the south was full of major plains—an open wound of a province, exposed to an unforgiving sun in the summer and dry and cold in the winter.

To enter Westgar they had to pass over the Duro River, which spanned across Usleth from Lake Bron Skea to the Prauv Ocean. The bridge that crossed the river was a double arch, supported by a large natural stone that split the water. It was beautiful, made from tightly packed pale stone, and old enough to bear Queen Rostaiva's stamp. Riding over it made Balen breathe deep. A transitory act, stepping over the threshold into his home province—something felt significant about it. A dark homecoming.

After that, it took just over a week of travel to reach Westgar. It was cold, with long stretches of mountains, plateaus and evergreen trees. When it started to rain one late afternoon, they stopped early for the day, setting up camp under a rocky overhang at the base of a cliff.

Balen was still being short with Mallet and Lance. Looking at them had started to anger him, perhaps disproportionately. He found himself feeling spiteful every time they talked to him. Eventually he stopped speaking to them at all. He knew he was being unreasonable, and the silence didn't help the hurt the way he thought it would, but their near desertion was a slap in his face. He couldn't reconcile his own devotion to duty with their willingness to abandon it all.

So when the brothers approached him that afternoon in Westgar, Balen walked away.

"Sir!" Mallet ran to catch up. "Sir, please."

"Let us explain, Balo," Lance said. "We're not idiots. We know how you look at us, and we know we disappointed you."

Lance sounded so defeated it halted Balen completely. He was out of the rock shelter and in the rain now, but he didn't care; he stood with his head half turned so the brothers were to his left and the cold, wet landscape of Westgar to his right. There was something about knowing he was in his home province that made this confrontation worse. This is where everything had changed for him. Pledging himself to the Paladins had spurred Balen to life. All he was now had come from that oath, from the decision he made daily to honor his word. He stood still, unable to turn around and face them. Some logical part of his mind told him he was being ridiculous. Righteous. But he couldn't help it.

"I thought you were good men," he said. He cursed himself for that harshness and shook his head, trying to amend it. "I wanted to imagine you and I were the same. And maybe that was wrong of me. But you made a commitment as a palace guard, and you were more than willing to desert the instant it became dangerous."

Lance wrung his hands together before he hefted his spear from off his back. "We're not fighters, Balo."

The Paladin spun around to face him, incredulous. "You can't pretend—"

"He means it!" Mallet cut him off. The big man ran his hands down his face. "We're showmen, sir. Just actors. Magdol runs the fight pit and we're the champions of the play weapons. But the real things?" Mallet held up the iron hammer the palace had supplied him. "We had no chance of winning against you in Teum Bett. We can't actually fight."

Lance looked sheepish. "We're sorry. But staying would have killed us."

Balen gritted his teeth. Blood was in his ears, this loud anger that he knew was unhelpful but was too powerful to stop. He choked out, "You made an oath."

It was all he said. They couldn't fight—but they'd gone to Cres Stros with the hope of making the city guard. They have made the oath to protect the king there as well. To him, that felt more important than any truth of their capability. Balen turned away and faced the blue misted hills. He squinted against the rain in his eyes, keeping his fists balled at his side, and when he heard the hesitant footfalls of the brothers leaving, he sighed and slumped forward. The anxiety over-whelmed him and he punched the air, shadowboxing with his frustration.

He only had a moment to himself. The footfalls returned. A burst of anger filled him up.

Balen turned, fuming. "I said—"

"Why are you being a baby?" Ambassador Dziove stretched her arms over her head, sighing against the pull of her muscles. She sniffed and rinsed her face in the rain. The crusted week-old war paint began to run. She wiped it off, then fixed Balen with a look. "I said you're being a baby."

"I—" Balen began, but he gave up quickly. He dropped his hands to his side. "What do you want me to say to that, Ambassador? They made an oath, and they broke it."

"You are Prime," she said. "Strong warrior. The best, apparently. And they don't know how to fight."

"They know the basics," Balen said, recalling their spar in Teum Bett.

"No. They were scared. There is no honor in humiliation. They abandoned the battle because they don't know how to fight," Dziove said, ignoring him. "They are your men. Good men. So why aren't you teaching them?"

Balen frowned. She raised an eyebrow and slapped him heartily on the back. Dziove hummed as she walked away, leaving Balen in the rain. He watched her go, still frowning.

It occurred to Balen, then, how poor a leader he was shaping up to be. He'd trained his whole life for the honor of Prime, and now that he had it, all he was doing with it was judging two men who put value in their lives. But Dziove? She looked at them and knew they were assets. Mallet and Lance were loyal, at least to Zavrius. Compared to the talk among the Paladins—who, despite their oath to the king, still questioned him—the brothers had never underestimated Zavrius's ability to rule. And what was Balen doing with them?

Balen turned back to the overhang. Dziove had taken her greatsword and wandered off down the hill. Balen watched Mallet and Lance struggling to build a fire from slightly damp kindling. He took a deep breath, deep enough to keep his pride from mounting an attack on his goodwill, and walked forward.

Zavrius grinned as he approached and stepped away to the back of the overhang to practice with the lute-harp. The brothers jolted at the sound of Balen's approach and tried their best to avoid his eyes.

"Here." Balen crouched. A ball of fire burst to life in his gauntlets. There was enough heat in the summoned casting to light the wet wood. The fire roared to life.

Mallet nodded at him. "Thank you, sir."

Balen tried to smile at him, but the air was so tense between them he had to glance away.

Balen could feel the ichor sparking in his belly, a reaction to how tensely he was holding himself. He forced himself to breathe and cleared his throat. "I know the king has forgiven you, and perhaps that just means he's a better man than me. But I can't ignore the reason for your desertion."

Both brothers grimaced and looked away. Lance wrenched tufts of grass from the ground. Balen wrapped a hand around his shoulder. Lance went rigid.

"You say you don't know how to fight," Balen said, nodding at him. "So let me teach you."

"What?" Mallet murmured.

"You both have the makings of guards. Of true defenders. You're creative. You have the loyalty. I need men like you I can trust and call upon to protect the king. But if you don't know how to fight, then you need to be trained." Balen stood and gestured for them to pick up their weapons.

A smile crossed Lance's lips and then Mallet's. The two brothers laughed and sprang up, gripping each other and rushing Balen, happy, and Balen laughed too as he was flooded with relief.

He spent the rest of the afternoon training them. They worked on their stances, on drills. They sparred and Balen critiqued them. He corrected their form, explained their openings and what they were doing that would get them killed. It felt good—not only because he was training men he could rely on, but because he was among friends.

They stopped when Dziove stumbled back with a boar around her shoulders, dripping wet with blood smeared all over her cuirass.

"Borviet demands we feast!" she howled. She dumped the carcass on the ground.

The brothers helped her prepare it. They all ate, and sang when Zavrius played, and sleep overcame them one by one.

～～～

Balen took the first watch. He sat with his knees propped up to his chest, listening to the sound of the rain on the hill. The smell of moss and wet earth calmed him, like a balm made from childhood memories. He sat like that for an hour or so. The night was peaceful. But when a twig snapped to his left, he instantly charged the gauntlets with red hot fire.

"Hm," Zavrius hummed, flashing a wolfish grin. "Did I frighten you?"

Balen put his hand down and leaned back on it. "You should be asleep."

"Should be," Zavrius said as he sat. "Unfortunately, my royal spine is finding this entirely unpleasant."

"Shall I procure a pillow for you?" Balen said with a laugh.

"Well, are you offering?" Zavrius grinned. "Last I remember, you had quite the pillowy bosom."

Balen snorted. He thought about flirting, then wondered if that's what Zavrius was doing at all. It was just Zavrius being Zavrius, he told himself. Nothing to be looked at too closely.

Zavrius sniffled and tucked his right leg up. He wrapped his arms around it. "You know, I remember the first time I saw you in your armor. My uncle had made the cuirass a little big, like he was encouraging you to eat. It swallowed you. I thought you looked ridiculous in all those peacock colors, and when I met your face, when I saw your eyes, I thought: what a sad sod."

Balen smiled a little. Couldn't help it. Zavrius smiled doubly wide at the sight of it.

"I mean it. You looked as miserable as Theo always was. Very serious. Then I saw you stifle a laugh when Theo botched some swordplay demonstration, and suddenly you became very interesting. You looked up at me. We both knew . . ." The smile faltered. "I miss that. The way you used to look at me."

Balen met his eyes.

"I wanted to thank you." Zavrius seemed like he was going to continue, but he fell quiet. He made a small noise and tried to smile.

They hadn't spoken about what happened in Cres Stros. Balen wrestled with the words, but the fear of speaking what happened aloud was too much. Instead, he asked, "How are you feeling?"

Zavrius smiled sadly. "Not tonight," he said. "I don't want to talk about that tonight."

Balen nodded, turning back to the dark landscape. "What do you want to talk about?"

"I don't want to say a word."

"Then what—"

Zavrius reached out and gently turned Balen's jaw toward him. Balen tensed. His heart raced, urgent, as Zavrius leaned over and kissed him on the mouth.

Balen inhaled against him. He closed his eyes, reached out to pull Zavrius close for a second kiss. It didn't matter that this made no sense. Up until now, Zavrius had made it clear that Balen's past dedication to the Paladins had bungled any chance of this happening again. But here he was, kissing him, like no time had passed between them. Balen kissed him hard.

Zavrius pushed him away.

Balen flinched, still smiling. He didn't comprehend what was happening until Zavrius didn't return his smile.

Balen's own smile faded. "Why did you do that?"

"Because I wanted to," Zavrius said. He rocked back on his haunches, shrugging. "Because you're a good man, or because you saved my life. Because of the way the firelight sharpens your cheekbones. Any of those reasons."

Balen's eyes softened when he looked at Zavrius. He couldn't look at the king harshly, even when it felt like Zavrius was playing him. "What does this . . . mean for us?"

Zavrius stopped abruptly. "You're my Prime," he said sullenly. "The role you wanted more than me."

Balen started. "Zav—"

Zavrius stood with a small smile. Before he left, he leaned down over Balen, his long braided hair sliding over Balen's neck. He kissed Balen's head. "Don't read into it, Balen. It's just a kiss."

But it was all Balen could think about for the rest of the journey.

CHAPTER FOURTEEN

They crested a hill and were greeted with the sight of Briym Plait lit by midafternoon sun. A cold wind cut across Balen's face and forced the exhaustion out of him. Adrenaline came with the end of the journey, a kind of relief that woke him up. He sat straighter in his saddle and made sure his bulky Paladin armor remained hidden beneath the cloak.

Usleth was a peninsula, and the Westgar province sprawled around Lake Bron Skea. Two isthmuses at the north and south of the province connected it to the mainland and the Rezwyn empire. Thenlass was the provincial lord of Shoi Prya, but he still had his fingers in Westgar; he was the one to spearhead the trade efforts with the empire that had made the whole province invaluable. Their destination was Briym Plait, a port city on the southern isthmus, built near the long Chela River. It reeked of spice, tar and urine. A sprawling network of buildings and high roofs, the distant lines of fishermen on the wharf, speckled by the sun. Too many houses were flying Theo's banner. Balen counted twenty before he made himself stop.

Balen turned to Dziove. She was staring past Briym Plait, to the mountains of the empire. To Balen's right, the king was sitting a little straighter in his saddle, a healthy amount of color in his cheeks. Balen considered himself, and the glinting Paladin armor he was trying to hide. He wrapped the cloak around his front and held it tightly. The province was cold enough they wouldn't look out of place bundled up, but he still felt exposed.

Soon they would complete their task of delivering Dziove back to the safety of her own countrymen. But they had to make it past their own countrymen first.

"I have to get out of this armor before we approach the border," Balen said. "There are too many Paladins there for them to mistake me for anything but the Prime."

Zavrius nodded. "Yes, you do."

The inn they found was small and shabby. Its only merit was the small stable attached to it, where the inn's stable hands led their horses to rest.

Inside, he asked for two rooms, and then had to turn to Lance and Mallet sheepishly to pay.

"You'll be compensated," he promised.

"Oh, it's fine," Mallet said, scratching his head as he pulled the coin from a purse. Lance couldn't keep his dismay from his face. He paled with every coin that was handed over.

"You really will be paid back," Balen told him, and Lance made a small noise in the back of his throat that might have been acknowledgment, or a strangled cry of pain at the sight of Mallet parting with the gold.

After everything that had happened, Balen refused to let Zavrius sleep alone. The king made no argument against that, which made Balen nervous. Zavrius started up the stairs. Once the king had turned away, the brothers exchanged one of their annoying, silent looks. Balen shot his own dark glare toward them right as Dziove laughed, once—a short bark that was the equivalent of amused disbelief. Balen was trapped between the three of them, jaw clenched so tightly he thought he might shatter his own teeth. Balen tried in vain to stop his face flushing. All three of them grinned.

"Wait for us here," he told the brothers seriously, frowning at the absurd width of their smirks.

"How long are you planning to be?" Lance asked with a grin. Balen started, flushing further, then forced a Paladin calm over himself. The bait was obvious, and he was still gladly walking into the trap.

"Stop it," he said, warning finger in Lance's face. The other man suppressed his smile. Dziove waited downstairs with her arms folded, massive greatsword strapped to her back. Balen was sure she was smiling too.

Balen followed Zavrius upstairs. The room was small and nearly empty. There was only the bed, the chamber pot shoved beneath it, a mirror and a small table with an oil lamp in its corner.

Zavrius sat on the bed with a sigh, and Balen kept his distance. Now that they had privacy, all his earlier worries flooded him.

"What . . . happened back there?"

Zavrius looked up with a disappointed frown. *Don't read into it, Balen. It's just a kiss.*

Loudly, Balen barked out, "At Cres Stros. Magic-wise."

Zavrius tugged at the strap around his chest, pulling the lute-harp to his front until it rested in his lap. He frowned a little, not looking Balen's way. "Truthfully, I'm not entirely sure."

"But you must know what you did."

"Must I?" Zavrius said, sounding annoyed. He sighed again, as if his quick temper frustrated even him. "You know what I can do with the lute-harp. My music can affect people's moods, if I want it to. But that's surface level. Like a . . . like a balm over the top of their personalities. Those people, if they can be called that, they're leaking arcane power all the time. It's like a stench. You can feel it too, right?"

Balen nodded once and pretended to inspect his hands. "I wouldn't even know where to begin. I don't think the gauntlets could do anything like that."

"Probably a lute-harp specialty," Zavrius said with a smile, stroking the instrument beside him. "But I doubt it would work if they had a greater grip on their minds."

Balen stared at the lute-harp. It had to be something to do with the material—gedrokbone and plate reflecting the arcane, containing it. But it made him deeply uncomfortable in a way he couldn't quite articulate. He didn't want to tell Zavrius that, not when the king had saved his life. But that type of control unsettled him almost as much as the thought of the ichor burning away his sanity.

They stayed silent for a moment. Zavrius turned to the window. "Do you think . . . ," he started.

"What?"

Zavrius shook his head and sighed, craning his neck back to stare at the ceiling. "Do you think Petra made it out alive?"

The question caught Balen off guard. Zavrius had seemed generally averse to speaking about what had happened in Cres Stros. Balen had been trying not to think about who might have been lost. Losing the palace was one thing, but losing Petra? She was some of the only family Zavrius had left.

"Of course she did." Balen made sure to keep any tremors from his voice. "That woman could withstand anything. Besides, she knows the palace's secrets better than anyone. She's fine, Zav."

"Hm," Zavrius said, smiling. "I hope you're right."

Balen turned away for a moment, pretending to inspect his armor for any dents. Zavrius's question had flooded his mind.

Was Lestr alive?

As soon as the thought crystallized, time seemed to slow. Balen imagined Lestr fighting, growing tired as he led the Paladins' attack, fatigue shooting through his muscles as his mind screamed to keep his sword up. Balen squeezed his eyes shut. Enough of that.

Lestr was his master. Even when Balen's mind had been filled with thoughts of his possible treachery, it didn't change what Lestr meant to him. Balen had to believe he was alive.

The Paladin cleared his throat and started to remove his armor. He could see Zavrius in his periphery, staring as he slid the gauntlets from his hands. The king's attention was a welcome distraction. Balen placed the gauntlets delicately on the bed. "Interested?"

Zavrius raised a brow. "In?"

"The armor," Balen said quickly. "Not a strip show."

"Shame," Zavrius said. He smiled and settled back onto his hands. He nodded toward Balen's cuirass. "Show me."

Balen pooled a small amount of arcane power in his palm and brought it to his left shoulder. He flexed his hand and the power sparked; the invisible seam unfused suddenly and snapped apart. He did the same to his right shoulder, then at his flanks. The cuirass popped open like the shell of a nut. Balen took both pieces and laid them on the bed.

"So if I were to tune this to match your arcane energy," Zavrius said as he patted the lute-harp, "I could strip you with a song?"

Balen exhaled, mouth open in a half smile. "It's taken less before."

Zavrius smiled briefly. Then something flickered in his eyes and he looked away. "Continue," he said with a small wave. This time, he did not watch.

Balen set his jaw and unfused the rest of his armor without another word. In the mirror, he could see the results of the last few weeks on his body. Streaks of grime spread over his chest and shoulders. Balen rolled them back, glad to stretch without the heavy plate. He caught Zavrius staring in the reflection, but the instant he locked eyes, the king glanced away. Suppressing a smile, Balen kept inspecting himself. There was a mottled bruise on his back. It had been healing, but taking multiple arcane arrows in the garden had turned it purple again. Blood had dried and crusted beneath his gambeson so that his skin was flecked with ichor. He raised one arm: there was chafing on his lats from a week of continuous wear. More than that, he stank.

A basin full of water sat next to the mirror. He turned back to Zavrius and inclined his head toward it. "I'm going to bathe," Balen said.

Zavrius shrugged. "All right."

"I only meant . . . if you wanted to leave . . ."

Zavrius leaned back on the bed. "And why would I want to do that?"

Balen decided it was better not to argue when he saw that very particular smirk on the king's face. He put his hands up to concede and got to work washing the grime off his body. At first, he could tell Zavrius was watching him, so he closed his eyes and let himself revel in feeling clean for the first time in a week. The water was cool but felt good. But at some point during Balen's washing, Zavrius stood and left the room. Balen didn't notice him stand; only heard the click of the door. When he opened his eyes, the king was gone.

Balen hid his armor and quickly changed into a dark blue tunic that he covered once more with the wool cloak. Being out of his armor made him feel small, without power: a regular man. This was different from how he felt in Teum Bett. There he'd been running on adrenaline from the attack on the road. But now, after abandoning the palace and taking off his armor, it unnerved him. And being back in his home province didn't help. He was hit with a sense of disconnect. He could imagine the kind of life he'd have led if he never went to the Paladins. But Balen told himself that was a good thing. He wanted to blend in, to look the part of hardworking fisherman. A regular man.

After he was done, they collected their horses from the stable, briefly refreshed from their long journey. They set out again, heading to the dynasty encampment that kept guard at the border of the Rezwyn Empire.

As a border town and sea port, Briym Plait was a melting pot of ethnicities. The majority were Westgar fair, but Balen saw the dark skin of Shoi Prya, Cres Strosian fawn, weathered faces from the Ashmon Range. A few wandered through with the oddly pale empire tones, and though many stared at them, their presence wasn't exactly novel this close to the border. Balen was glad for it; Dziove stood out far less here than she had in Cres Stros.

The streets were wide enough that four horses could ride abreast. Balen led the way as the brothers and Dziove brought up the rear. But Zavrius came up beside him and watched him in silence, mouth a thin hard line.

Balen reached out his hand. Zavrius looked down at it, confused, but slipped his own hand into Balen's palm.

"Are you all right?" Balen asked, squeezing once. The question felt lacking, but he couldn't figure out a better thing to say.

"I will be," Zavrius said. He fixed Balen with a stunned glare, brows pinched together.

Behind them, Lance said something indistinct. Zavrius took back his hand, turned away like he was embarrassed. Balen kept his hand hovering for a moment in the space between their horses, a half-finished bridge, before he drew it back to his side.

The street opened up to a much larger stretch of rocky field. Smaller merchant stalls were scattered across the field, widely spaced around winding dirt paths. Many of them were empire merchants, hawking their goods to soldiers. Two bored Paladins walked the length of the field, scanning the stalls as they passed. Balen kept his head down.

In the distance, a massive wooden fort filled the horizon. A wall of wooden spikes stretched the length of the isthmus. The fort gates were open; a sign of peace. Through the gates, an open path cut through to the empire. It was boxed on either side by wooden walls preventing travelers from wandering through the fort. A few people walked through without issue.

"You should go," Balen said to Dziove. "No point in you sticking around any longer than you have to."

Dziove looked at him and nodded. She stuck out her hand. Balen grabbed her forearm as she did the same. They held each other across their horses, eye to eye for a tense moment.

"Thank you," Balen said.

A wide grin broke across her face. "Words I should be saying."

"What will you tell the emperor?" Zavrius said.

"The truth," Dziove said. Then, after a moment, "And that you saved my life."

Zavrius looked at her for a long while, his gaze dark, calculating. Balen thought he might ask for something, request a favor of Nio Beumeut. Please don't kick us when we're down. Please don't annex us just because you can.

But Zavrius only nodded at her. "Don't you dare die."

"I'll do my best not to, Your Highness." Dziove bowed as best she could atop a horse. Then she pushed against its flank and urged it to a gallop. They watched her ride through the gates.

CHAPTER
FIFTEEN

Mallet cleared his throat. "What now?"

"Eventually to Thenlass, I think. He holds the most vital seat outside of Cres Stros, and he's well liked by most nobles. If I can get him on our side, I should be able to reclaim the palace. I hope that it's possible. But . . . I don't know." Zavrius snorted softly once the silence became too much for him. "Dziove said something interesting. Back in the garden, I mean. The way she was talking about Theo— she thought he'd been made a god."

Balen frowned. "What do you mean?"

Zavrius gestured vaguely. "The empire . . . their gods aren't static. They can change. They have their main pantheon. Borviet is their most worshipped, since he's the war god—Dziove followed him—but plenty of their generals have been deified. She thought that's what we had done to Theo."

"Your brother?" Mallet asked, voice rising. "A god?"

"She thought that," Zavrius said, cutting him off, "because too many people are still mourning him. They're still waving his banner."

Balen didn't know what to say to that. The thought of it unnerved him, upset him.

Zavrius set his jaw and looked back to Balen, stare firm.

"There. That's my brother's banner." Zavrius told Mallet and Lance.

"But why? He's . . . he's dead," Lance said.

"Not dead enough," Zavrius hissed. He turned his head away from them. As he did, Balen caught the pained look in his eye, a hint of rising panic. "It's clear there are many people here willing to end the Dued Vuuthrik line to be rid of me."

Balen's breath seized. Zavrius was out of his mind. Allowing Zavrius to come here had been stupid. "If someone recognizes you—"

"No one will recognize me," Zavrius said with a laugh. "They are not expecting me here."

Balen had to hope he was right. Terrifyingly, Zavrius urged them closer to the fort.

"What are we doing?" Balen asked, but as usual, Zavrius was silent.

As they got closer to the fort, Balen could see more flags waving in the gentle breeze: dynasty colors, for the most part, but many had patterns painted on them. Here and there he'd spy a burgundy field featuring a sword thrust upward through a crown. Theo's banner. One house sported Zavrius's banner: a geometric lute-harp on a warm purple background. There were echoes of Queen Arasne in the floral border.

"Oh, I have a fan," Zavrius murmured as they passed.

"I don't understand it," Lance muttered, nodding toward the majority of houses supporting the wrong man. "Who are they hoping to follow?"

But Zavrius had the right of it: for the most part, a king was an idea. Theo had been unhinged—but still a soldier. Someone to champion early dynasty values, whereas Zavrius was seen as an antiexpansionist dandy.

"They want a war," Balen said aloud. "Theo would have given them that."

"War?" Mallet swallowed. "Who in their right mind would want war?"

Balen considered the arcanists that had been attacking them. Patricians, noblemen sick of the ruling family and desperate to make a name for themselves. All of them contenders, if Zavrius were to die. He'd thought them mad, but that arcanist in the garden had been more lucid. Her intent to kill Zavrius had been just as strong.

"There's enormous profit in war if you're in the right position," Balen said.

Mallet's nostrils flared like he was smelling shit. "No way they're regular folk."

"Bastards," Lance muttered. "I swear nobles are a different breed."

"But they're not royal." Mallet looked puzzled. "How'd they . . ." He pulled his hands apart in a gesture, then scratched his head. "Get the ichor?"

Zavrius only shrugged. "Oh, how I wish I knew."

Balen had his own suspicions. Lestr had taken Paladins away from the palace to protect the glade. Sure, he'd been defensive about it when Balen returned from Teum Bett—vocal about the suggestion he'd been lax in his duty and let someone steal from the gedrok. But if he was in on it? If he had orchestrated the whole thing? Lestr had spent his whole life in Arasne's shadow. Maybe he would have accepted Theo—but Zavrius was guarded and cryptic and perhaps more dangerous than his warmongering brother would have been. A wash of fear came over Balen as he sat there, thinking of his master. He imagined him in the glade now, carving plate from the gedrok.

But that made no sense. There was no way Lestr would forget the importance of the Paladin armor. He was one of its greatest advocates, always shutting down any idiot that believed it was ceremonial propaganda. Unless, of course, Lestr had wanted them to go mad.

Balen didn't have time to consider the implications of that. He could feel his grip on his emotions slipping a little. He wouldn't let that happen. Not while Zavrius was alive and king.

But Zavrius needed to tell him what they were doing here, if he had any hope of doing his job.

Balen nodded toward the fort. "What are you hoping to find here?"

"Nothing," Zavrius said. Balen thought he was being reticent again, but when he turned, Balen saw his eyes. They were wide, glistening, his eyebrows set in a frown. Balen knew he was serious. Zavrius said again, "Nothing at all. I only hoped to escort the ambassador back home. I didn't mean to discover this, but I hope it's only a really gentle type of treason." He laughed a little. "Just people mourning the future my brother's reign would have given them. Something I'd be happy to turn a blind eye to."

"And if it's more than that?" Balen demanded.

He looked at Balen for a while, like he'd heard the correction in Balen's mind saying when. When they found something more, what would Zavrius do?

Zavrius visibly swallowed. "If I want to keep my throne, I can't be the king they think I am."

Balen took a deep breath. He wanted to pick that apart, scrutinize every intonation. The nobles thought him soft. What would Zavrius do to show them he wasn't?

"You're a good king," Lance said. He looked between them, nodding with conviction. "Or you have been so far."

Lance reached out like he was going to slap Zavrius heartily on the back. Mallet swatted him away.

"Look, my brother's right. Your father gave us war. For a town like Teum Bett, well. War effort couldn't find a good use for artisan woodwork. Arasne's treaty saved us. I swear you could scrape by in the common folk's good graces by doing nothing but keeping that treaty."

For a moment, Zavrius looked so sad. Then his smile pushed through the gloom on his face.

"I want to do more than that," he said. "I want more than rocky peace with the empire. We could give each other so much."

By now the sun was sitting low in the sky. The field took on a deep-orange hue, like hearth fire. Balen squinted at the horizon. If they didn't move soon, they were going to lose the light. But the fort was guarded, and even dressing down wouldn't disguise Zavrius for very long.

"We can't just ride in," Balen said.

"No." Zavrius nodded to their left, where a dirt path began to arc up a slope. Balen followed the short ridge with his eyes. It boxed the fort on one side, forcing the palisade to curve around it and continue until it met water. But that small hill would be enough vantage to peer inside.

Balen frowned. "You think there's more than just banners here, don't you?"

"I wouldn't have dragged you out here for fabric alone," he said, trying for humor. His voice lacked all conviction, making him sound tired, flat. "No. Petra's spies reported some activity. Something I hope isn't true, and something I'd have loved to ignore. But if she's right . . . I can't. I have to . . ." He left it unsaid.

They had to be here.

The king clicked his horse into a trot and the three of them followed him up the hill. It was covered in long grass, shrubs and small trees, none of which would give them excellent cover, but would surely help if anyone in the fort happened to look up. Moving closer to the fort made Balen realize how big it was. It was decades old now, made for war. He could see portable spiked logs—anticavalry measures— at the base of the fort. It had two towers on either side of it. The sloped roof of the nearest tower was the same height as the hill. Concerned about being seen and questioned, Balen told them to dismount fifty paces from the edge. Balen drove stakes into the ground and threaded the horses' reins through rings, leaving them to graze in the long grass. They ducked low as they got closer. Balen looked over at Zavrius, his duty rising bright in his mind. This was too dangerous. They shouldn't be here at all.

"Your Highness," he said. "Zavrius."

Zavrius turned to him, lips pursed. He said nothing. No doubt Zavrius knew what was happening in Balen's mind.

The brothers seemed to understand too.

"We can do this for you, Your Highness," Mallet said softly. "If you like. You could stay here, just in case. Lance and I'll take a look. Tell you what we see."

Zavrius smiled up at them. "You don't know what you're looking for," he said. Then, when Mallet's face hardened like he'd been kicked, "I don't mean that harshly. Only . . . I need to see for myself."

Balen frowned a little. He put his hand on Zavrius's forearm. "Why risk it?"

Zavrius's voice was hard. "We are spying from above. It's not like I'm walking in, announcing all my titles."

Balen thought he could hear the other thing, the desperation underneath the rest: Zavrius asking to let him have this.

He squeezed Zavrius's forearm. "I can't lose you."

Zavrius looked up at him. His lips parted. Softly, he asked, "As a king?"

Balen opened his mouth, but he couldn't say it.

Zavrius briefly closed his eyes and gently lifted Balen's hand from his arm.

"You know," he said as he turned toward the fort, "this is so close to where Theo died."

Mallet sucked in a breath. He glanced between them and pulled Lance back a bit, as if repelled by the vulnerability of the king. Zavrius crawled forward through the long grass and made them follow.

"Is that what this is about?" Balen asked when he caught up.

Zavrius shook his head. "There's nothing that can convince people I didn't have a hand in the assassinations that made me king."

"But you won't even try," Balen said. He could feel himself getting annoyed. Zavrius was too calm about those rumors. Maybe if he'd been firmer, if he'd found the source and rooted them out, the nobles wouldn't have been brave enough to try killing him. And that was it, Balen thought—the rumors had been the perfect backdrop to act against the king.

Maybe Zavrius was still mourning, or maybe he was caught up on a role he'd never wanted. Whatever the case, it would kill his rule, long before he had a chance to prove himself.

Balen gritted his teeth. He focused on crawling forward. The sun lit up the fort from behind, a beautiful honey glaze that softened the awful sharpness of the structure.

When they moved to the edge of the hill, Zavrius said, "What's the use?"

That ticked Balen off even more.

Zavrius continued, "The people who oppose me aren't looking for justice. They have their outrage, their own ambition. I'd be fighting them anyway. And maybe it would be better if they believed I am ruthless enough to have my family murdered."

And then, to prove his point, he gestured down toward the fort. Balen turned. Gathered beneath another of Theo's banners, Balen saw five or so people bent in supplication. Someone stood before them to speak, and a mass of others crowded around the kneeling few, standing with their heads bowed and arms raised.

"What in the . . . fucking bullshit is that?" Mallet muttered before Balen shushed him. He craned forward, hoping for a better view. The sunset made it difficult to pick out details. The speaker removed something from inside their cloak. Balen squinted. The movement revealed the armor underneath: a glinting, pearlescent shine that made Balen's heart seize. Paladin armor. A horrifying, dizzying feeling filled him.

Was that . . . Lestr?

When the speaker moved their hands, sunlight sparked and blinded Balen. He grunted and held a hand up to shield his eyes.

"Glass," he said. "Or metal. It's not prismatic like gedrokbone."

The speaker moved his hands and the light shifted. Suddenly, Balen could see more of his face and his build. It was a man, but he was tall, taller than Balen's stout master. A wash of relief ran over him before it turned his blood cold.

Zavrius was breathing heavily. "What is it?"

Balen took a breath. "Thenlass," he whispered.

"What?" Zavrius hissed. The king twisted to see for himself. Zavrius beat the earth once, struggling to contain himself. "That damn traitor. That vile, good-for-nothing . . . what is he doing?"

Balen looked again even though he knew. He'd drank his ichor from the very same sort of flask. He saw the glass-and-silver decanter glint in the speaker's hands and laid his chin down in the long grass. Everything was hopeless for an overwhelming minute. Balen reeled away from the edge and yanked Zavrius down with him. Their backs slammed against the hill. Mallet and Lance followed suit and lay down on either side of them. Both of them turned to look at Balen, hoping for answers. Balen stared up at the darkening sky, his heart racing. Then he composed himself and peered over the edge.

Lord Thenlass uncapped the decanter. The kneeling nobles opened their mouths. Drops of ichor fell down their throats. Afterward, they crawled forward and fell before Theo's banner, like supplicants, like the empire before their gods. Balen frowned. Their bodies twitched as arcane power bloomed through them. Thenlass wore the armor as a symbol—he only wore the cuirass. There wasn't a single piece of gedrok worn by the nobles. Ichor would burn through them. It was a perversion of his own ceremony, only instead of dedicating themselves to the dynasty, they were dedicating themselves to treason.

Zavrius's head snapped toward him. Firmly, he demanded, "What is it?"

"It's ichor," Balen said finally. "Those decanters are in the forge, once the ichor's extracted." He took a breath, was surprised at how difficult it was to breathe. "I think we've found the arcanist's base. They're doing it here at the border, in your brother's name."

Zavrius's eyes grew wet. He flipped onto his knees and started to stand like his plan was to dive into the fort and stab every arcanist himself. Balen grabbed his ankle and pulled him back down. Zavrius fell to one knee. He flashed him a scathing look.

Balen tugged him forward. "What's your plan?"

"I don't have a damned plan!" Zavrius hissed, voice pitching too loud before he reined himself in. He slammed his fist into the grass. He looked embarrassed after that and smoothed down his tunic.

"But wait—what did you ever do to them?" Lance asked.

He was thinking, Balen thought, like townsfolk might. You might hold a grudge if your neighbor broke your daughter's heart or stole your cattle. He wanted justification.

Zavrius laughed brightly. "Nothing. And I think that's the problem. The Dued Vuuthriks have been so obsessed with the empire for years that all we've brought the noble class are dead heirs and calls for monetary assistance. They are sick of it. They want power and they are united on two fronts: they want a new king, and they want an end to cooperation with the Rezwyns."

When no one said anything, Zavrius's eyes rolled toward Balen. "Thenlass wants the throne for himself, I think."

Balen nodded. "It looks that way."

"Then we get rid of him," Zavrius said.

"You want us to help you kill a noble?" Mallet asked, balking.

"A traitor," Zavrius corrected.

"Unless they win," Lance said. "Your Majesty."

"So what? Now you're the traitor refusing the orders of your king?" Mallet slapped him on the back of the head. "That was from father from beyond the grave."

Balen got onto his knees and peered out into the fort again. "Thenlass doesn't know we know."

Zavrius grunted, sliding farther down the hill. "But he'd be a fool not to suspect. If he launched the attack on the palace, he'd know by now I wasn't killed."

"If we don't confront him, then what?" Balen asked.

"Don't you have allies?" Mallet asked.

Zavrius raised a brow, looking him up and down. "Even the puppeteers in your little town of Teum Bett had something to say against me. Everyone I'm supposed to be friends with is still waving Theo's banner."

Balen swallowed. He hated himself for asking, but he said, "What about the merchant?"

Zavrius's face crumpled in confusion. "What?"

"The merchant." Balen sighed heavily, gestured vaguely toward the south of Westgar. "You know. Radek. The one you visited and . . . played for. You're close, isn't that right?"

Zavrius's face twisted in a show of hurt. He opened his mouth, closed it again. Then he turned away. "That's just a rumor."

Balen's chest twisted. "He's handsome. If we . . . if it means we have an ally—"

Zavrius snapped his head back toward him. "No, I mean . . ." He wet his lips. "I never . . . I played one song. I left by lunchtime. He was . . ." Zavrius pulled his hands apart, gesturing over his chest, clearly embarrassed.

Lance and Mallet moved away a little.

Zavrius visibly swallowed and kept his voice soft. "He didn't want to hear me play. I should have realized that's why he wanted me there, but I—I thought . . . I just wanted to perform."

Balen felt his heart unwind, and with the release of tension came a deep dread that hit him like an ice bath. "Did he touch you?"

"No." Zavrius gave him a half smile. "But even if he had, I had the lute-harp. It would've been easy to . . . change his mind."

Balen nodded slowly. He'd never been more grateful for the lute-harp's ability to charm people. He reached out and wrapped Zavrius's hand in both of his.

"We could kill him too, if you like," Balen murmured, only half joking. "Thenlass and this ass. We'll just politically collapse the whole west of Usleth."

Zavrius snorted. There was a glint in his eyes. "Radek has nothing on Thenlass. He's not bad. Just not for me."

"You're the great bard Zircus," Lance said with a grin. "As if he didn't want to hear you play." Zavrius laughed again at that.

"Come on." Balen tugged Zavrius's hand. "We can't stay here."

They had no plan, no real place to go. They gathered their horses in the twilight and rode back to the inn.

CHAPTER
SIXTEEN

"You know," said Lance, slamming a piece of parchment onto the table, "I think this whole place is fucked."

They were three drinks in now, at a corner table in the inn's tavern. A fire was going, which made the cramped interior warm and cozily lit. The tables were practically stacked on top of one another, all made from a dark wood. The walls were covered in niches filled with bottles. Rope ladders clung to the walls, ready for the barmen to climb. It gave Balen the sense of being at sea.

Balen had his back to the wall so he could face the door. He'd only had one drink, but he longed to be tipsy. Zavrius was slumped forward next to him, staring into his flagon, but he looked up with interest when Lance sat down.

"Forgive my brother's foul mouth, Zircus," Mallet said.

Lance balked. "Oh, shit."

Zavrius ignored them and leaned forward, eyes on Lance's hands. "What is it?"

Lance shoved the parchment toward them. "Found it at the bar, being passed around."

Both Balen and Zavrius bent toward it. It was a slightly prolix manifesto; not quite a call-to-arms, but a lengthy criticism of King Zavrius and the past Dued Vuuthriks. Save Zavrius's siblings, of course. The whole thing sang Theo's praises, its corner inked with a poor replica of the symbol on Theo's banner.

Mallet spat over his shoulder. "They're not trying that shit with regular folk, are they?"

"And use their precious ichor on lowly commoners?" Zavrius scoffed and held the manifesto above his head, inspecting it.

"No," Balen murmured with a sigh. "They're just planting the seed. Briym Plait's close enough to the empire that war still feels like a threat here. Easier for the rest of the dynasty to forget."

"Which might mean everyone here is well aware of what's brewing in the fort and support it." Zavrius put the manifesto down and glanced at his lute-harp. "Ah . . . I think I need to play."

Zavrius seemed paranoid, definitely unsettled. He kept craning his neck and running his hands through his hair. Balen frowned as he watched him.

Mallet cleared his throat. "Forgive me, Zircus, but that . . . doesn't make sense. Maybe that's how the soldiers feel, but everyone else?" He sniffed and drank, shaking his head. "Trade with the empire would be a boon for this province."

Mallet was right. Westgar had the least to gain from war and the most to gain from empire trade. Some of Westgar's nobility clearly thought otherwise, but Polverc's niece and the other Westgar arcanists had been young. Easier to sway. Balen nodded. "Shoi Prya was essential in the war. It'd benefit from another one. With the right amount of pressure and agitation, Thenlass could have stirred up Shoi Prya and just enough of Westgar to gather this army."

"Hm," Zavrius said after a moment, leg bouncing.

He stood abruptly, kicking back his chair with more force than was necessary. "Who wants to hear a song?" he called to the tavern. A raucous, pitchy cheer went up among the tavern's patrons, and for a moment it didn't matter the place was half empty. Balen kept an eye on the customers, wondering if they'd recognize the pearlescent shine of the lute-harp for gedrokbone. But no one seemed to bat any eye as Zavrius wandered up to the small stage. The king played like a bard whose living depended on performance. It was all filth and sex, but the bawdy songs were popular. Balen watched him striking poses, leaning backward until he was singing upside down. Lance and Mallet began to sing along. Balen smiled for a time until he watched Zavrius too closely and saw him slip. His eyes were far away. Balen wondered how much of this act was for him—or was it for Zavrius himself?

Balen cleared his throat to break the spell. "Lance." The singing faltered.

"Uh-huh? I mean. Your Primeness. Yes."

Balen suppressed another snort. Primeness was a name that was sticking, apparently. "It's Prime. Just Prime. But, uh… maybe stick with Balo for now." He circled the air with his finger, hoping to remind them where they were. Then he waved for their attention. "What happened with Polverc's chair?"

It took Lance a moment to remember. Then his eyes snapped wide. "Oh, loved it. Sang our praises and all that."

"I think she forgot who she commissioned," Mallet said. "But a bit of praise from a noble's a rare enough thing."

Lance grunted his agreement. "We drank it up."

Balen clicked his tongue. "Her sister was from Westgar, wasn't she?" Balen knew the Polvercs were a prominent Westgar family, and asked it anyway.

"Her sister?" Lance asked.

"Szargrid said she was commissioned for a condolence gift. Polverc wanted it for her sister?"

"Oh, right. Westgar. The niece went missing from Westgar."

Like too many others.

Balen saw the image of her in his mind, dead in the garden. He wondered if she had been sent from this fort, reborn an arcanist. If she'd been with the army, drinking ichor, accepting madness for a chance to dethrone the king. Strange things were happening in Westgar and Shoi Prya.

On the tiny stage, Zavrius plopped down again, lute-harp hefted above his head in a celebratory wave. When the applause stopped, he returned to the table and drank deep from his flagon.

Zavrius scrunched up his face as he sat, glancing between them all. "Why are you talking about the Polverc girl again?"

"She's another one from Westgar. At least we know there aren't a dozen factions littered across the dynasty." Balen tapped the table. "The main force seems to be located here."

Zavrius didn't look happy about that. He grunted again and tried to sit upright, squeezing his eyes shut as he did. "I suppose."

Balen pulled a face at his tone. "You're unbothered."

"On the contrary," he said, stretching, "I'm really quite put out by the whole thing." He turned to Balen with a lazy smile, but he dropped it quickly. Balen couldn't help but frown. Zavrius slumped. "Don't look at me like that. It's been a hard week."

Balen rolled his eyes.

There was a firm thump as the flagon met the table. Zavrius sneered. "Oh, what?"

"Nothing," Balen said. Everything. He really was getting sick of this pretend nonchalance. At least he hoped it was pretend.

If Zavrius was truly this apathetic, Balen thought he might go mad.

He was different before. But that was only half true. When they'd been closer—before Balen had pulled away and Zavrius decided it meant they'd never be that close again—Zavrius had been more open. Perhaps the crack in the door had been barely the width of a knuckle, but at least the door had been open. Now it felt like Balen was prying off the hinges with bleeding fingernails. Zavrius's reticence was getting to him.

"Right," Zavrius said. "Nothing. Of course." He downed the rest of his drink and wiped his mouth with the back of his hand. "If you don't mind, I'll call it a night."

No one said anything. Zavrius stood again, his chair scraping loudly along the floor. Balen watched him stalk through the tavern and up the stairs. He heard the muffled thud as the door was slammed shut.

"All right?" Mallet said, leaning closer.

"Fine," Balen replied.

Mallet clicked his tongue. He had something to say but was clearly holding back. Balen missed the honesty, the camaraderie they'd had before they were on the run. Candor—the real, bared truth he craved—was in short supply.

Balen watched the brothers in his periphery as they turned to one another. Their silence ticked him off. "What is it?"

Both brothers snapped their eyes away.

"Well?" Balen tried to keep the impatience from his voice but failed.

Lance cleared his throat. "We mean no disrespect . . ."

"I preferred your disrespect," Balen said, snapping. He shut his eyes. "Imagine I really am Balo and he is the same smart-mouthed bard you met at the market, and tell me."

Mallet tightened his jaw and sat straighter in his chair. He wasn't going to say anything. Balen turned to Lance, saw the man fidget under Balen's stare. He kept glancing at him, then back at the fire in the hearth. Balen kept his stare firm.

Lance threw his head back and sighed. "Gedroks, the tension hurts."

Balen glanced between the brothers, not comprehending. "What?"

"Lance," Mallet cautioned.

Lance threw his arms out. "What? Come on—you're thinking it, too. It's exhausting." Lance turned fully to Balen and knocked the table. "You need to get laid."

Balen flushed. "I—"

Mallet said, loudly, "You can't—" He looked wild, scared. "You can't just—that's a . . . that's a damn dangerous thing to be saying."

"No, what's dangerous is heading straight for the province spewing out assassins specifically after you, but what do I know? Listen." He put his hand on Balen's forearm. "Maybe you think it'll make you fight harder for him, or it'll give you the strength to protect him. Something dumb like that. But I can tell you this: nothing ever gets done right when you're horny."

Balen's throat felt like it was closing up. Deep heat filled his face. He opened his mouth, emitted a surprised laugh, and shut it again.

Lance patted his arm with an awkward, knowing smile.

Mallet blew out his breath and clapped Balen's back. "Well . . . what my brother lacks in subtlety, he makes up for in—"

Balen shot him a dark look.

"Oh, Balen, come on. There's obviously a lick of truth in it."

Balen knew he should be saying something—anything—to keep a shred of the dignity the brothers were yanking out of him. He couldn't. His teeth were clenched so hard his jaw was starting to ache. Instead, he groaned.

Lance chuckled. "Look, if all you're thinking about is dicking him down, you're—"

"Would you stop saying it like that?" Balen hissed. "And be quieter."

Lance gestured to the stairs Zavrius had stalked up. "He's clearly wound so tight you can piss him off with a stare!"

"That doesn't mean it's—" The words died in his throat. Balen wet his lips, opened his hands in an empty gesture.

"What's stopping you?" Mallet asked. Disbelieving, Balen swung toward him with a frown. Mallet shrugged. "Something's stopping you."

Balen swung his arm out and gestured to the chair Zavrius had been in, and the path he'd carved through the inn, open-palmed. What was stopping him? Have you seen him, he wanted to say. He's the king. He's untouchable.

But was that really it?

Zavrius's fingers were etched into his mind. Slender, gentle against his cheek, then firm, pressing desperately into his back. And his eyes—Balen always thought there was something in his eyes, something that was only there when Zavrius was naked and beneath him: a smile nothing like his cat's grin, a truth he always hid. It wasn't just his body Balen wanted. But Zavrius was too far away. Too distant.

He thought all that and said, "I don't know."

The brothers said nothing for a while. Lance glanced over at Mallet, then looked away, mulling something over. When he spoke next it was quiet. Apologetic, in a way. "Is there truth to the rumors?"

Balen didn't have to ask what rumors they were.

He swallowed. "You really think he had his family killed? Wiped out his siblings for a throne he doesn't even want?"

Lance kept his mouth shut. He looked briefly frightened.

Balen turned away. On the hill by the fort, Zavrius had said that he only played one song for the handsome aristocratic merchant before he left. One song. Gone by lunchtime. He'd wandered back into the camp by evening, and by then his siblings had been dead.

All those hours unaccounted for.

He looked up. Mallet and Lance were looking at him, waiting. Balen sat up straighter.

"No, I don't think Zavrius is a fucking murderer." He pushed his chair back and followed Zavrius upstairs.

Balen opened the door to the soft glow of the oil lamp. The flame flickered faintly at the edge of the open terra cotta bowl, sending a long shadow toward Balen's feet. Zavrius leaned on the windowsill, his whole body hunched over the spread of his hands. Even with his back toward the door, Balen knew. Zavrius was so rarely like this, never so obvious with it, that his mood wafted toward Balen like an acrid stench. Balen stood in the threshold. He'd taken the stairs in twos, body alive with anger and outrage, and now he stood there buzzing with panicked adrenaline, staring at Zavrius's back, unable to speak. He didn't want to think about the rumors. He didn't want to think about where Zavrius had been for all those hours when his siblings had died. He wanted the Zavrius of his youth, wanted to lose himself in Zavrius beneath him.

"Don't just stand there," Zavrius spat. "What do you want?"

Balen looked down at his hands. The sweet Zavrius he let occupy his dreams was long gone, if he ever existed at all. This was Zavrius the king.

Clearly annoyed by his silence, Zavrius spun on his heel to stare at him. "If you have nothing to say, then—"

"I am sick of this," Balen said.

Zavrius shut his mouth. Balen stepped into the room and latched the door behind him.

"Sick of it?" he asked. His voice was a whisper. "Sick of what?"

"Of you!" It slipped out with an edge to it. Balen stepped forward with his hands raised. He stabbed one finger toward the door. "What is it with you and this jaded act? You think it makes you look stoic?"

Zavrius's laugh was breathy. He turned all the way to face Balen. "That's what you're sick of? I thought it would be serious. So what do you want, exactly? You want to hold my hand? Talk about how I'm feeling?"

"Do you even know how you're feeling?" Balen was in the center of the room now. Zavrius visibly swallowed, hugging his arms closer to his chest. Balen sucked in a breath, hoping it would calm the adrenaline-shake in his hands. "I want you to be open with me. Honest. I want—"

"You left me," he said.

Balen shut up.

Zavrius's arms unraveled from around him, and with that motion the fury in him became something softer. Much sadder. He opened his hands in a shrug. "You left me."

They were silent. Balen could hear his own breathing: a raspy, rapid sound clawing over the lump in his throat. His mind was blank. What could he say to that?

"This isn't . . . about that."

Zavrius's eyes snapped up to him. He was furious. "No? Then what?"

Balen scoffed. Was he serious? "People are trying to murder you. The palace is lost. The forge might have fallen into the hands of the corrupt—Gedroks, you keep everything from me until the last minute and wonder why it goes shit every time."

"You want to know me?" Zavrius stalked forward, palm flat against his chest. "Huh? You want to be privy to all the titillating details before they're relevant? Well, I'm sorry, Balen, but you lost that fucking privilege when you decided you were sick of me."

"What are you—" Balen rubbed his temples. "You know that's not what happened."

"Oh—your Paladin training came first. How could I forget?"

"Yes, because being fucking Prime is not a birthright! I had to earn it!" Balen stepped closer, jabbed a finger into Zavrius's chest. "But I have never wanted Theo. I only wanted you."

"You left me," Zavrius said, grabbing onto Balen's tunic, "to be his attack dog!"

Balen shoved Zavrius against the wall, arm pressed across his collarbones. Zavrius grunted at the force. "Well, Theo's dead, so now I'm your bitch. Happy?"

Zavrius was silent again. Breathing in, breathing out, eye contact firm and unshakable. His mouth was clamped shut, nostrils flaring wide. He didn't try to move Balen's arm away. He just stared up, wide eyes glistening. Then, with a sharp intake of breath, he pushed himself forward. Balen went still. Zavrius moved and kissed him. The Paladin watched the king's eyes flutter, closing for a half moment before Balen jerked himself away. Zavrius pulled back. His lips were still slightly parted in the motion of the kiss. He looked surprised with himself, then angry. Balen felt his cheeks begin to burn; he wanted to press himself into Zavrius, ignore everything but that kiss. He didn't.

Balen kept him firmly against the wall. Shame flooded Balen—not for the kiss, but for the feeling he'd let Zavrius sit in for years. "Look at me. I'm sorry I hurt you. I want to try and make that right."

"It's not that," Zavrius whispered, lip curling. It was like he was giving up his earlier anger for some other weight on his chest. "Something terrible happened."

Balen flinched, surprised by the change. He lifted some of the pressure from Zavrius's chest. "What? What aren't you telling me?"

Zavrius shook his head; shook it over and over. Very suddenly, his eyes filled. Then, voice creaking like a ship at sea, the sound curling over his tears: "I did it. I killed them all. I killed Avidia, Lysio. I killed Gideonus." His movement halting and fearful, Zavrius made himself meet Balen's eyes. He opened his mouth. Whispered, "And Theo too."

Suddenly Zavrius was heaving sobs. His legs couldn't hold him. They buckled. He slid down the wall. Balen watched him with his heart pounding. There was a rupture at the edge of Balen's mind. Everything he'd sequestered away flooded him at once, every thought he'd had about Theo's death, about the rumors circulating Zavrius—Balen sank to his knees.

He couldn't say anything; his disbelief was making him mute.

Zavrius heaved sobs for a minute. Balen just sat there, watching, unable to comfort him but also unable to withdraw. Eventually, Zavrius hiccuped over his tears. When he could manage it, he began to speak.

"They attacked me all at once." Zavrius tried to smile, but his expression quickly buckled at whatever memory ran through his mind "They tried to murder me. And I didn't know why. They knew before I did. The dispatch must have come days before. We had a camp on the border of Shoi Prya and Westgar. Thenlass was staying with us. They always talked, him and Theo, sometimes for hours. Theo made Thenlass lots of promises. And some letter came from Arasne—I didn't think anything of it. She was on her death bed, sending Theo messages. That all made sense when he was going to be king. But looking back, I think that letter changed everything."

Balen frowned, still reeling. "What do you mean?"

"My mother made me heir," Zavrius said. "Officially. In her last act as queen."

Balen's breath stopped short. If that were true, the rumors about Zavrius's ambition were void. He'd have no need to murder his siblings for the throne. It had been given to him.

Zavrius looked down at his hands and continued. "I didn't see the letter until after. They were all . . . so terrible to be around. Father took a Rezwyn halberd in the neck a decade ago and our mother made her peace with it, but my brothers and sister were on some mission for vengeance that would've sent us to war. I just wanted to disappear. I'd met Radek, the merchant, a year or two earlier. He praised me after a performance. I knew he was in Westgar, close to the border—I wanted a damn break from them."

"So you went to play for him. Alone?"

"Well, Lestr wasn't there to stop me." He tried for a smile, but it faded fast. "I only played one song for him. I had a whole performance planned. But he got up, clapping.

Came over to me. Put a hand on my thigh." Zavrius gestured, face scrunched up like he was ill. "Getting me out of awful situations—that's the lute-harp's specialty. He didn't push his luck, but I left shaking, like he'd gotten what he wanted. I went immediately to ride back to camp. And then I saw them on the horizon. Silhouetted riders. I counted the heads. Avidia, Gideonus, Lysio, Theo." Zavrius bobbed his head in time with each name. His mouth tightened. "Four soldier-arcanists against me. Their little weakling of a brother. I couldn't fight that. I didn't even try. I ran straight for the empire border. They followed. Relentless." He balled his hand into a fist. "At first, I thought maybe Arasne had died. But all four of them riding me down . . . I knew what they were coming for, even if I didn't know why. Staying still would've killed me, and I didn't think . . . I didn't want to attack them outright. So I ran. Turned the horse and rode it hard to the border, passed bloody Briym Plait, passed the fort. Suddenly I was in the hinterland, freezing. If I kept riding, Beumeut's soldiers would've seen us all."

There were tears in his eyes again. He stared off distantly, teeth running over his lip. He gave a small shake of his head.

"I pulled back on the reins. Dismounted. If they were going to kill me, I'd die standing. When I sent the horse back to the fort, they didn't touch it." He looked down at his hands. "I waited until I was sure, Balen, until Avidia raised her bow. I don't think they expected me to fight back. They certainly didn't expect me to be any good." He wasn't looking at Balen now, was doing everything to keep his stare firm and fixed. "I strummed the lute-harp. Sent a wave cutting toward them, made them split apart. It shocked them. But everyone except Avidia needed to get close to me. So, while they were scrambling, I played. I tried to calm them at first, but they were too angry. Charming them wasn't working; they felt righteous. Gideonus and Lysio rode toward me, flanking. Theo just rode forward, dead-eyed stare, like it was his duty to slay me. Like it was my duty to die." His eyes drifted back to Balen. "So I killed them. Tried for their necks. Tried to make it quick. As soon as Gideonus fell, I was running back to the border. I saw Lysio, his belly . . ." He gestured in a way that made Balen envision the great wet mess of a man's insides toppling out. "I kept playing, and running—but at some point I couldn't see anything more than my own tears. It was a mess. Next thing I knew I was heaving, on my knees at the base of the fort. And when I turned, I saw the red heap. Their bodies, just . . ."

Zavrius squeezed his eyes shut like he could burn the image from his mind with enough effort. Balen breathed deep—he was trained to ignore shock. Still, he felt like he'd run for miles. He told himself this was Zavrius. This man in a near grovel, guilt-laden, craving retribution and absolution equally—Zavrius had carried this alone for too long. He had the pressure of the dynasty on his back, its future marked in the blood of his family. And even if Balen had never expected Zavrius could be capable of any of those things, there was a ring of truth in the words.

An odd, roiling skirmish brewed in Balen's belly: a pang of pity, an strange admiration. He felt the youth in him recoil, the buried dream of being Theo's Prime disintegrating with each word from Zavrius's lips. This was what it was to be Zavrius's Prime.

Balen reached out and took his hand. "I'm sorry you had to fight them alone."

"You don't even question me." Zavrius sounded abnormally angry. He got onto his knees. "Why don't you question me?"

Balen thought for a moment. He considered Theo; considered some reality where Theo had become king. The war that would have followed, the blood that would have drenched Theo's hands—Balen wouldn't have stopped it. His duty was to the king. Even when the king's actions threatened the stability of the dynasty, the Prime was always meant to defend the king.

Zavrius was king now. And their country was better for it.

Balen met Zavrius's eyes. "My duty is to defend you, not to question your morality."

"I want you to question my morality," Zavrius said, crawling forward. "Someone has to. Just because I'm king—someone has to. People have to know the truth."

Wide eyed, Balen grabbed his shoulders. He had to stop Zavrius from unraveling. Balen shook him, once. "Apart from me, do you know who needs to hear this story?"

Zavrius scanned his eyes. Tears gathered again. "Who?"

"No one." Balen gripped Zavrius's shoulders hard. "No one ever needs to hear you speak those words again. And you should forget them, too. No one benefits from knowing the truth of what happened in your family."

"So what? I should blame it on the empire?" Zavrius's lip curled into a sneer.

"Not unless you want Theo's war after all."

But that answer didn't satisfy Zavrius. He shook his head. "The people should know the truth."

"And then what?" Balen hissed. The morality of it didn't matter; he knew what would happen. "The people find out and come for you. I'd die defending you, they declare you a tyrant, behead you. Our country would be leaderless."

"Why would you die defending me?"

Balen frowned. "I would do my duty." He scanned Zavrius's eyes. "Have you decided to die? Do you hate your kingly duties so much you'd lie down and let the mob kill you?"

Zavrius's lips were pressed firmly together. Then they split apart, just wide enough for a stilted whisper to slip out. "Is it only duty that drives you?"

Balen closed his mouth. What was Zavrius trying to say?

Zavrius glanced away for a moment, eyes glinting. Then he forced himself to turn back and meet Balen's eye. "Are you speaking as my Prime, or as my . . ."

"As your what?"

Zavrius only shook his head.

Balen said, "Say it."

"Gedroks, I hate you." Zavrius reeled away.

"Do you?" Balen said, breathy. Zavrius turned. Balen tilted, felt like he was falling forward. He put one hand on Zavrius's shoulder. "Because I love you."

Zavrius laughed quietly. He turned his head, averted his gaze. "You love the king. It's only luck that man is me."

"I do my duty to the king," Balen said. He cupped Zavrius's cheek. At the touch, Zavrius's eyes fluttered up to meet his. Balen smiled. "But you are the man I love."

Zavrius stared at him.

Balen said, "Zav, it was not your fault."

Zavrius looked caught between breaths. Impossibly still, crease between his brows, he looked like he was trying to understand what Balen had just said. Zavrius sat up from his slumped position on the ground, perching himself on his knees. Then he moved abruptly. He sprang forward, heaving Balen off-balance. Balen's back hit the wall, legs splayed as Zavrius crawled between them. Balen had no choice but to grab his waist and pull him close, his broad hands encircling him, and that touch made this all seem so familiar that Balen really had no choice but to kiss him.

Balen sucked in a breath as their lips met. His fingers gripped the back of Zavrius's neck to pull him closer.

They broke apart. Zavrius scanned his eyes. "Are you sure?"

"Sure of what?" Balen said, stroking Zavrius's hair.

"Sure of me," Zavrius murmured. "Sure of who I am. After—"

"If Arasne named you heir then that only legitimizes your position more," Balen cut him off.

Zavrius's lip wavered. "That's not what I mean."

"It's your right to defend yourself, regardless of who you are." Balen scanned his eyes and saw, finally, the Zavrius he had been missing. The raw honesty, the vulnerability—the fear he always hid.

Zavrius's face crumpled for a moment. He knocked his forehead against Balen's. He was shaking. "I was so tired of lying to you."

Something shifted in Zavrius's gaze. The fear ebbed away; some age-old want replaced it. Zavrius dipped his eyes to Balen's lips.

Balen closed his eyes and kissed him, slow and intimate. It was one long kiss: a chance to re-learn Zavrius, to remember just how he liked it. After that, the kisses were urgent, graceless. Balen used the wall for support, his head and back braced against it as he dragged Zavrius further into his lap. Zavrius sat with his knees on either side of Balen's legs. His hands quickly tangled up in Balen's hair. The king's was already a wispy mess and Balen took a moment to undo the braid. The hair fell across his shoulders, and Zavrius seemed more eager now, like the braid had been yet another formal restraint. With more force, Balen grabbed his waist and grinded up. Zavrius moaned against his lips, gave one desperate thrust against Balen's stomach.

"Zav," Balen murmured, breathing heavy against Zavrius's cheek.

The king peeled his mouth away, eyes heavy-lidded, faintly streaked with tears and days-old kohl. Then Zavrius turned his head and exposed the length of his neck. Balen leaned into it, burying his face against the pulse of his heart, kissing, teeth bared and grazing across Zavrius's skin.

He hissed. His grip in Balen's hair tightened. Balen rocked forward with one arm around Zavrius's waist and he dragged them both to standing. The king, mussed up and beautiful, stumbled against him. His messy kiss was misaimed and only caught the edge of Balen's mouth. He walked them back to the bed, hands working on Zavrius's tunic as he moved. Zavrius let Balen pull the tunic over his head before he closed the space between them again, his fingers trying to undo Balen's laces; but he was distracted with desire and kept fumbling. Balen smirked, removing the king's hand to make quick work of his own tunic, shucking the thing like it was burning his skin. They were both breathing heavy, trying and failing to keep themselves restrained.

They'd always been passionate. But years of build-up made the tension unbearable. Zavrius's eyes dropped over him. He sighed like he was relieved, like the sight of Balen's bare torso was a comfort. He walked forward to press a palm against Balen's chest. It sparked something, a twofold memory: The first time Zavrius laid a palm against his bare skin, rising on the tips of his toes to kiss him. The last time Zavrius had touched his chest, weeks ago in his quarters, with the sun haloing him. Balen came back to himself. He looked down at the king now and saw restraint melting off him.

Zavrius tilted his face up. "I want—"

Balen cut him off with a kiss. He knew what Zavrius wanted. Balen spun them both around and pushed the king onto the bed. He landed almost shyly, hunching his shoulders with a timid smile. Zavrius propped himself on his elbows. He dragged one leg up, hitching his hip, a tease that kept most of his body hidden, but exposed the curve of his hip and the length of his thigh. How had Balen survived years without this? Impossible.

Balen kicked off his boots and climbed onto the bed. Sucked in a breath at this new angle, at the sight of Zavrius beneath him again. Finally.

Balen dropped his eyes over the king's collarbones, the lean muscle and quick rise-and-fall of Zavrius's chest. He ran his palm over him and Zavrius shivered as Balen settled his hands into the dip of his hips.

"I missed this," Balen whispered. "You."

Zavrius's hand grazed up Balen's arm. He sat up, leaning over to settle his nose against Balen's shoulder. He kissed the muscle there. There was a shake to his hands. Balen shifted his weight so he could lace their fingers together. "What is it?"

Zavrius's eyes were wide, brows pinched above them. "I . . . spent years wanting you to miss me. To hear you say that . . ." He trailed off.

Balen kissed his forehead. "Let me prove it."

By way of answer, Zavrius pulled him down for another kiss.

Balen squeezed the little curve of Zavrius's hip, vividly aware of his own arousal. He settled over him, kissed his chest, the hard rise of his ribs, his stomach. Zavrius was breathing hard, firm grip on Balen's head, pushing him down. He slid his legs apart, brought one leg to rest high on Balen's shoulder. Balen saw the crotch of Zavrius's trousers straining, tented high, and turned his head to kiss the draped leg. He pulled off the king's boot and threw it behind him. Zavrius raised his other leg obediently for the same treatment. Balen leaned down and kissed Zavrius's stomach again, one hand sliding up his chest as the other held one of the king's legs open. He let it fall to the bed, moved his hand to hook a finger under the waistband of Zavrius's trousers. Teasingly, Balen rubbed at the skin beneath, finger gliding back and forth. Zavrius's groan was frustrated, half swallowed. Balen sat up onto his knees and took off his own pants, prompting the king to prop himself up. Zavrius inspected him, eyes hazy and fixed in a way that made Balen suddenly dizzy. With a lusty sigh, Balen crawled forward and kissed him again, couldn't stop touching him. His hand found Zavrius's trousers once more, and Balen stopped being content with this hesitancy: he needed it, needed Zavrius to need him. He tugged the trousers down and off. Zavrius sprawled and stretched. It thrilled Balen to see him like this: naked, twitching.

"You're so fucking beautiful," he murmured as he ran a hand up Zavrius's thigh. Zavrius arched at the touch, reacting with a repressed grunt. When Balen kissed the fine skin at the top of Zavrius's thigh, the king tugged at his hair, desperate. Balen took him in his mouth. Zavrius responded with a soft, high moan. He rolled his hips up and distractedly loosened his grip. Balen moaned at Zavrius's response, at every slight shift beneath him. But the way Zavrius was writhing told the Paladin his mouth wouldn't be enough. Zavrius grabbed his hair and pulled him up. Balen drew his lips away, thumbing the head of the king's cock as he met hooded eyes. Some tangible thing passed between them, an acknowledgment that Balen couldn't take control until he was allowed it. Balen went still, half-forgotten arousal aching as it pressed into the sheets.

He waited for the king to say it.

Softly, panting, Zavrius opened his mouth. He whined, "Fuck me."

Balen dropped his head, breath rushing out in a woozy exhale. Zavrius dragged him into a messy, aggressive kiss, his limbs unfolding beneath Balen. Urgently, the king flipped himself onto his stomach. He tilted his hips, and the Paladin was caught by the sight of the curve of his lower back as his thighs slid apart. Balen pressed against him, bringing his head down to kiss the base of the king's neck.

The sweetness of it seemed to only frustrate Zavrius. He rolled his hips. His long hair shifted with the movement, so it spilled off his back and hung, a dark backdrop for his eager expression. Balen felt his cock jump, knew there was deep flush to his cheeks. It was so hard to breathe when Zavrius was looking at him like that. Balen squeezed him, peeled away to reach for the open basin of the oil lamp. He covered his fingers, brought them back to Zavrius's body. Zavrius watched him over his shoulder, involuntarily noise edging out of him as he brought himself into an arch. Balen pressed a finger against him and slid it inside. Zavrius exhaled, head dropping slightly. Balen groaned at the sight of him, at the unsteady, hitching breaths as he added another. He was moving, eyes fixed on the fractional frown on Zavrius's face, the heavy, openmouthed breathing, soft noises—he was the one making the king feel like this. Zavrius's movements were small at first, helpless reactions to the slide of Balen's finger. Then more eager: the king writhing back on his fingers, and when Balen angled them just right and ghosted over his prostate, Zavrius gasped and rocked his body to the side and pulled him up. Balen moved to kiss him. Slow, deep. Zavrius's arm slung over his neck. Balen could feel as Zavrius's body began to open.

"Fuck me," Zavrius said again. This time the sound was raw, more demanding. Balen's eyes fluttered closed as a moan rolled out of him, his cock twitching with a sudden rush of new heat. Balen's fingers were slick and warm as he slid them out. Zavrius repositioned himself eagerly and the Paladin splayed one hand on his back, felt an eager rush flood him as he pressed slowly forward into Zavrius.

Zavrius cried out, the sound curling into a high, airy moan.

Balen's mind swelled with a series of impressions—all the times he had done this before—but the added tension of years of wanting made it impossible to hold on to any solid thought. He was left with the feeling of warmth and oil, all restraint melting when Zavrius bucked against the slow drag of Balen's thrusts. Then he couldn't help but push deeper. He drove against Zavrius's hips, and Zavrius's head fell into the pillow with a loud, sweet sound that only urged Balen on. Zavrius's hands twisted in the sweat-covered sheets, moans high and inarticulate save for the occasional desperate urging that Balen not stop.

"Zav," he said, by way of answer. He couldn't stop. He drove himself into Zavrius, the heat, the free noises the king made into this pillow, all of it drawing Balen deeper. They moved together hungrily. There was a tremor in both their bodies, a cresting pulse.

"I—I'm—" Zavrius's hand splayed against the headboard and his body jerked.

He came, moans fracturing with the shudder of release, and Balen's own body filled with sudden urgency, building until the pleasure shattered him and he came inside.

Balen shuddered, a swell of pleasure rumbling through him as he rolled off Zavrius to lie beside him.

They lay panting for a while. The king turned his head to face him. There was a stillness in Balen's mind that Zavrius's expression reflected, a sense of quiet that trickled into the space between them. Not exactly peace. It was the eye of the storm, a moment in chaos the pair of them had carved out for one another. But it felt like cresting a hill only to have the view obscured by fog.

Balen pressed their foreheads together. The fog could be faced together. Zavrius's eyes closed, and very quickly he was asleep. Balen brushed his lips against the king's forehead. Then he, too, closed his eyes to dream.

CHAPTER SEVENTEEN

When Balen woke he found Zavrius still curled into his arms. His hands were tucked up by his face, thick hair draping across his shoulder, cupping his own cheek. This beautiful, still moment felt age-old and brand-new, something to hold on to, to remember. In the predawn darkness, sometimes Zavrius would shift and Balen would think him waking, but each time he'd nestle back against Balen's arm, and Balen's heart would ache. Balen watched him. Found he couldn't look away. When the sunlight arced across the room and hit the curve of Zavrius's cheek and back, his eyelids like a bronzed sky—when Balen saw he was a king in his nakedness, then a surety rose up in him. He loved the entirety of Zavrius. He loved the king and the man.

Balen looked down at Zavrius pressed against him and felt the ease of waking vanish. The king looked calm when he was sleeping, but exhaustion seemed to cling to him. Months of it, months of holding on to a terrible, terrifying thing—the king had endured that dread in his body. This sleep seemed heavy. Long awaited. Balen stroked Zavrius's head. He imagined the betrayal Zavrius had endured, fleeing from the brothers and sister he grew up with, knowing with all certainty that they were there to kill him. How had Zavrius kept his mind? How had he woken every day since and ruled without it breaking him completely?

By the bones, Balen needed to keep Zavrius alive. Keep him safe. And with Thenlass amassing a force to kill the king, it would be harder than ever. Balen shifted his gaze to the ceiling. The Paladin instinct took over. He took stock of their assets: the four of them, the remaining Paladins provinces away in Cres Stros . . . If Zavrius was to secure his throne, he first needed to eliminate all threats. Thenlass had to go. But the extent of Thenlass's army meant their odds of success were . . . minimal. The thought came to him that their best course of action would be to appeal to the Rezwyn empire, but convincing Zavrius of that would be impossible.

He felt Zavrius stir beneath him. Zavrius rolled and blinked up at Balen, squinting at the morning light. His smile was tentative, but warm. Half sleepy, he reached for the side of Balen's head, stroking his hair.

"Good morning," he mumbled.

Balen smiled. Meeting Zavrius's gaze made him woozy with the memory of the previous night; he felt a wash of heat rush to his groin and dispelled it with another tender kiss.

"Good morning."

He lay back into the pillows. The bed smelled of the two of them, of sex and dried sweat, but Balen reveled in it. They lay there looking at one another for a long while, hands slipping together. Balen stroked the soft skin of Zavrius's palm and watched the play of light on Zavrius's skin.

Something passed over Zavrius's face, a flicker in his eyes, tense lock of his jaw. He gently pulled away his hand. If he'd been wearing a tunic, he'd be smoothing it down by now, trying for his usual nonchalance. Instead, he averted his gaze.

"You regret it," he murmured, lips pursing. He nodded once to himself as if accepting this new reality. "All right. It didn't have to—"

Balen shook his head. "Don't be ridiculous."

Zavrius kept his stare distant, but every part of him was rigid: he ground his jaw, kept his shoulders high. He looked terrified by the possibility of rejection, devoured by the thought Balen would leave. Which made no sense. But perhaps Zavrius thought there were two of him, king and man, and Balen's love couldn't possibly pass between them.

Balen guided Zavrius's face toward him. Zavrius turned to him then, reluctantly, hand unconsciously clenched in a fist around the sheets.

"I love you."

"Do you?" Zavrius squeezed his eyes shut. "I haven't had terribly good luck with love before."

Balen leaned back. "Loved often, have you?"

"No," Zavrius said quickly. They faced each other. The king's stare was calculating. Balen watched the movement of his jaw, imagined sharp canines applied to the soft flesh of Zavrius's tongue, rolling over it, mulling. Zavrius said finally, "And you?"

Balen smiled and took Zavrius's hand again. "Just the once."

The king blinked rapidly and looked away—looked oddly in the grip of nausea or fear, or a competing disbelief. "I think you're a fool for loving me."

"All right."

"I mean it." Zavrius shot his eyes toward him. Balen saw it, saw the strange anger in his eyes. A part of him ached at Zavrius's disbelief. Did he wish that Balen hated him? Did he want Balen to treat him like the monster he thought himself to be?

Balen wet his lips. "Do you want to go back to how it was? Pretend nothing happened last night?"

Zavrius's sudden laugh was high and bright. He made a noise that sounded at once like a small defeat and gladness, a sigh that he unraveled with. He unclenched his fist. His shoulders dropped.

"I'll let you decide that," he said, voice low. His tongue curved around the edge of his canine, side-smile teasing.

Balen felt a range of overlapping emotions, most fervently a kind of desperate, protective desire. He pulled Zavrius into a hard embrace. Zavrius resisted at first, then curled into him, nuzzling into his chest. Balen breathed in his hair, hoping to preserve the moment. When they left this room, he knew Zavrius would be different. Not wholly his. Not quite.

A bang sounded on the door with sudden, intense force.

The pair of them jolted apart. Zavrius sat up with panicked speed, as if he were ashamed to be caught like this, but then he sat there like he was contemplating the danger of sitting still. He was king, after all.

And really, assuming they hadn't been spotted and recognized, there were only two people that would bother checking on them.

"All right?" The voice was muffled through the door, but undoubtedly belonged to Lance. "Your Hi—I mean. Zircus. Balo. Is that—am I doing this right?"

There was no soft thud or otherwise correcting voice. Lance had clearly come alone to wake them.

"We're awake," Zavrius called back calmly. "Go and eat. We'll be there shortly."

Lance accepted this with a muffled affirmation. They heard him shuffle off.

Balen glanced at Zavrius, strangely caught on him answering for the both of them. He liked it, liked they were a couple, at least in language.

As if hearing Balen's mind, Zavrius turned to him. As he did, he moved his hair to drape down one shoulder. His expression was reserved, and Balen understood this was what he should expect when they were in public. This was the kingly facade resettling over his face now desire had been dealt with. He kissed Balen lightly and got up. Balen turned to see the jutting curve of his shoulder blades as he rose from the rough bedclothes. He waited there seemingly transfixed, before he shook himself out of the haze and dressed himself.

The Paladin armor glinted with the warm glow of the sun. Balen eyed it for a moment, thinking how odd it looked piled on the floor like this. How irreverent. Then the ache in his body consumed that quiet speculation. In the past few weeks, Balen had spent a handful of days out of armor and suffered. He needed it. His body felt raw without it. He put the gauntlets on and worked to fuse the joints together.

Wearing it again after days felt like coming home. Out of the corner of his eye, he saw Zavrius watching him. He knew he'd be iridescent in the sun, knew he'd look a Paladin again. When he was done with the cuirass, he realized how anxious he'd been without it—exposed, unprotected. Even without looking, Balen knew Zavrius still had his eye on him. Part of Balen worried when they left this room, there would be some separation between them, a greater expanse than Zavrius's kingly reserve. But when he turned and met his eye, Zavrius's smile cracked across his face. Balen's body filled with an overwhelming relief. Zavrius strode across the room and draped the cloak over Balen's back. Then he gently took Balen's hand.

"Shall we face the world, Prime?"

Balen smiled. "Whatever Your Highness desires."

They met Lance downstairs. He was seated at the same corner table they'd taken the night before, biting into meat and bread and swishing it all down with ale. He was eating fast, like he was famished. When he spotted them approaching, he dropped his fistful of food and stood, still chewing. He wiped his hands on his pants. Wiped his mouth again.

"G'morning," he said, wide eyed. Lance gestured for them to sit.

Balen raised a brow. "What's going on with you?"

Lance glanced at him, then snapped his head aside. The way Balen had left things the night before, storming off, unbidden and indignant as he said: no, I don't think Zavrius is a fucking murderer—it all came back to him. Balen was filled with a layered, embarrassing feeling. Zavrius had killed his attackers. In doing so, he had preserved himself as the rightful heir to Usleth. But some nagging thought that was more obligation than truth told Balen he should feel shame at what Zavrius had done. He didn't. He couldn't. Zavrius had no choice—and more than that, even without their weapons at his neck, perhaps he would have been right to do so.

The silence stretched. Zavrius was standing in an overly straight-backed stance, inspecting his fingernails. He was, perhaps, remembering the way he'd stormed to bed. Or he could have been thinking that he needed a nail file. Had Zavrius ever been in the position to cut his own nails, Balen wondered?

Balen took a seat and shifted forward across the table, hoping he could avoid Zavrius hearing this.

"Sit," he told Lance. The man shifted and plopped himself down on the opposite bench. Balen rested his arms on the table, trying to gesture an explanation. "The way I acted last night . . . I'm sorry for it."

Lance swallowed his mouthful of food. "Oh," he said, slightly shaking his head. "No, I . . ." He waved over his head. "It's forgotten."

"Is it?" Balen dipped his head.

Lance nodded. His posture didn't change, but there was a well-hidden wariness that looked odd on him.

But Zavrius's interest was piqued. He dropped his hand and turned to them. "Forgotten what?"

"Nothing," they said together, with overlapping urgency.

Zavrius gave a small "Hm" but left it alone.

They sat in that silence for a while. Lance nodded toward Balen's armor beneath his cloak. "A Paladin again, I see."

"We're riding out," Balen said. He tugged the cloak a little tighter around his body, glancing around the inn in case any wandering eyes had spotted the gedrokbone shine. He wanted the attention away from himself, so he gestured back to Lance. "What is it then?"

Lance was wide eyed. "What's what?"

"This." Balen gestured at him. "Your mood."

"Not in a mood," Lance said. He was speaking oddly fast. He looked between Balen and Zavrius and gave a small nod. "Just . . . it's good."

Balen felt a new tension creeping into him. "What's good?"

"You seem"—Lance nodded at him, quirking a brow— "like you've had a good night."

Balen felt himself flush. He tightened his jaw; by the bones, he didn't want to have this conversation again. Especially since Lance had really been right. He opened his mouth to say something, but Zavrius leaned forward instead.

"Are you insinuating he bent me?" he asked Lance.

Lance flinched. "Oh, by the bones, Zircus. No. No, I was—"

Zavrius raised a hand to stay him. "No need to explain what you weren't doing, then."

Zavrius turned his attention to picking at the food. Both Lance and Balen sat there in silence, their gazes fixed on each other, as still as their bodies would let them be. Then Balen broke the tension with a wink and a small nod and Lance's smile corresponding smile was so big it devoured his whole face.

When Zavrius snapped up to look at him, Lance shoved more food into his mouth.

They ate in silence for a while then Balen gestured at the empty seat. "Where's your brother?"

Lance took a breath, seemingly glad for the change of conversation. "Reconnaissance."

Balen frowned at that.

Zavrius turned, gaze firm. He said, "Not the fort."

Lance shrugged a little. "It's all he said to me."

Underneath the table, Balen patted Zavrius's thigh. Zavrius froze at the touch, so unnaturally stiff Balen pulled his hand away immediately. That was too intimate for a setting without a door, apparently.

Balen cleared his throat. "Mallet is smart. It's not like he'd walk straight into the fort."

"But being close is still a risk," Zavrius hissed. He was still frowning, obviously concerned by whatever he was imagining Mallet was doing. "He shouldn't have—" He broke off, then straightened, voice solidifying to say, "He shouldn't have gone. I give the orders."

Lance balked a little. He was especially nervous around Zavrius this morning—Balen worried they'd never recover their camaraderie again.

"It'll be fine," Balen tried to say. He turned to Lance. "He said nothing else?"

"I—"

There were footsteps behind them.

"I'm back."

Balen turned as Mallet came around quickly, shoving himself into the seat with an urgency that unnerved Balen.

"Your Highness, I apologize," Mallet whispered, eyes wide and nodding in Zavrius's direction.

Zavrius's lips were pursed. He shook his head a fraction, eyes dropping over Mallet. "You're nervous." His voice was quiet, stripped back. "What have you seen?"

Mallet's eyes scanned him for a moment. There was a glint in them, a true fear gilded with something like an apology. It was as if he was sorry for whatever he'd seen. Sorry he'd seen it at all.

Zavrius turned to face him fully. "Tell me."

"We have to go," Mallet said. "Today. Now."

Balen rocked back on the bench. He wanted to curse. "Thenlass?"

Mallet shot him a look. He nodded. "I asked around. A Paladin fitting Lord Thenlass's description was seen riding out of Briym Plait last night. No idea why he's leaving. From what I could see, the army isn't mobilizing. "

"They're not mobilizing?" Zavrius clarified. He looked between them like he'd missed the crux of an excellent joke. "So where does Thenlass mean to send them?"

Mallet swallowed. "Your Highness?"

Zavrius looked vaguely nauseous. "They know I've fled the palace. They clearly don't know I'm here, or we'd be dead. So, either Thenlass is keeping them here to invade the empire, or he's waiting for me to show my pretty head. But why has he abandoned them here?"

Zavrius looked to Balen. "Tell me what you think."

He knew the king was right. Those were the only two reasons Thenlass had this army, and neither were reasons Balen liked.

"All right. We can't determine where he means to send the army. The most important thing is finding Thenlass. He summoned them, so he means to lead them," Balen said. "But he's already left Briym Plait. If it were me, and I was trying to remove the king, I'd want more soldiers."

Zavrius considered that. "You've said it before. Shoi Prya serves to benefit from a war, far more than Westgar does. Do you think he's returned to his stronghold?"

"I don't see where else he would go. But if he wants more soldiers, he needs more ichor. And the ichor . . ." Balen trailed off. How many gedroks were left? Who had access to them? He ignored the sick twist in his stomach and met Zavrius's eye. "Someone in Cres Stros has betrayed you."

Zavrius's lips twisted in an ugly grimace, like he had known but wanted to forget. "I'd really hoped you were going to say literally anything else."

Balen turned to Zavrius. As steadily as he could manage, he said, "Right now we only have two real options: we can either fight or flee."

"Fight how?" Lance demanded.

Zavrius's lip curled. "And flee where?"

"Fight Thenlass in single combat as Prime Paladin, or flee to the Rezwyn Empire and ask for sanctuary," Balen said.

Zavrius cocked his head. At first he seemed angry; Balen knew he was suggesting letting Thenlass's army ravage Usleth. But then something passed over his face and he seemed torn. Balen could tell he was unhappy. When they'd discussed going to Thenlass, he had been their method for taking back control. But the man was a traitor. He'd written his own fate—though he was such a prominent figure in Shoi Prya that Balen feared murdering him outright would only be more polarizing for the kingdom. If so many of the nobles supported him, they might just make his death another mark against Zavrius's name. And without their commander, what would happen to the arcanist army he had amassed? It might splinter into factions, subgroups intent on Zavrius's death, but Balen doubted it could remain organized.

"What about hiding?" Lance demanded. "Hiding is also a thing that we could do."

"True. The other two sound like suicide," Mallet agreed.

Balen managed a smile. There was something about the brothers wanting them to flee together that felt significant. Somehow in a matter of weeks, the four of them had formed a friendship worth preserving. Worth going into exile for.

But hiding wasn't an option.

Zavrius shook his head. "Where? On whose lands? Is there a single noble I can trust?" He put both hands on the table and stretched, craning his neck to the ceiling. Balen felt a pang watching him; they'd worked the tension out of his body together the previous night, and here it was again, more potent than before. "Either way, I would release you and your brother from my service. No one knows you've helped me. You should be safe from retribution."

Mallet frowned, keeping quiet, but Lance's jaw opened like Zavrius had slighted him. Zavrius turned to his Prime. Balen wanted to comfort him with a touch, but knew it was unwelcome in public.

"I agree with you." Zavrius nodded to Balen. "Thenlass is too dangerous to keep alive."

Balen looked at him and thought, strangely, of Zavrius's reaction to the arcanists that had accosted them on the road. That initial attack had thrown them, but Zavrius had done the kind thing and kept their identities, and the cause of their death, hidden from the kingdom. Had that earned the respect of their parents, or their contempt?

Balen drummed his fingers on the wood. "The rest of the insurgency might break ranks if they know he's dead," Balen said, despite being already convinced how unlikely that was. "You could give them a chance."

Zavrius turned to look at him. His expression communicated silently what he thought about that idea; it was a pipe dream. Balen knew it too. None of it would matter if these noble pups pretending to be arcanists kept casting, wild and free with their power. They're already driven by emotion, Balen thought, remembering the hate he'd seen in their eyes. He knew it would get worse. If their minds succumbed to the corrosive force of the arcane, intense emotion would overtake logic. Their attacks would become indiscriminate and ferocious. No one would be safe.

"Do you truly want to fight Thenlass in a duel to the death?" Zavrius asked.

"Duel or not, he needs to die. Besides, it's the best option available to us. If we withdraw to Rezwyn territory—and this is assuming we make it past the army, let alone the emperor, who might just kill us on the spot—it would mean giving up the throne and living in exile . . . wherever we're allowed," Balen said.

"Is that so bad?" Lance asked. "Couldn't we ask to travel through the empire to Veprak or Myrtrana and live there? Both are warmer than frigid Doskor, at least."

"I've heard Veprak has pretty women," Mallet commented.

"You've heard everywhere has pretty women," Balen muttered.

"Everywhere probably does." Mallet shrugged. "That's the best reason to travel."

"It's not about us," Balen said. "It's about stopping Thenlass from starting a needless war of aggression."

"It's more than that," Zavrius said. He rubbed his face and sat back in his chair. "How am I supposed to navigate being king of Usleth if I'm in exile in a foreign country with no support? I'll be eaten alive. Besides, the longer I'm away from Usleth, the longer someone else has a chance to seed themselves as ruler. The minute I cross that border, I lose what little hold I have here. I will never sit on the throne again. Unless, for whatever reason, the emperor has me marry one his daughters—which would be a sad fate for the lot of us." He gestured between himself, Balen and the empty air meant to signify Zavrius's future disgruntled bride. "Really, taking Thenlass on is my only hope."

"No pressure," Balen murmured.

"Of course not." Zavrius flashed him that cat grin, tongue perched on his canines. "We're only talking about my life, my crown and my family legacy." After a silent beat, Zavrius added, more solemnly, "You'll win, won't you?"

The question stopped Balen short. A few weeks ago, it would have been an unequivocal yes. He'd still had enough of an unbruised ego to believe that, too. Now he could only say, "I have a better than average chance."

"And what shall we do if you win and the insurgents attack anyway?" Zavrius drummed his fingers slowly on the tabletop.

"Play them a song?" Balen answered easily. "No one can resist the dulcet tones of Zircus."

He was only half joking. The lute-harp had a power in it, a power Zavrius could use. But whether it would overcome the king like it had after the attack on the palace was another thing altogether.

"All right," Zavrius said, lips curled upward. "But you best have some idea of what we'll do when they inevitably attack. Surely knowing their Thenlass is dead will only make them hate me more."

Balen felt he could argue the nuance of it for hours, without fully knowing where he stood. Thenlass needed to die. It was what would happen after that irked him.

Mallet was looking antsy. Balen took a breath and made to stand.

Zavrius stopped him, hand firm on his arm. Balen hesitated, watching Zavrius stand in his stead. The king's expression was pinched, gaze locked on the seated brothers.

"I think it's time we part ways," Zavrius murmured.

There was a silence. Lance and Mallet made no move, but their faces slowly shifted, the realization unraveling their quiet contemplation. Their jaws were clenched. A pained, wounded glint flashed in Lance's eyes.

"Why?" he asked.

Zavrius's nostrils flared. He breathed deep and glanced away. The pressure changed on Balen's arm as Zavrius adjusted his grip. "I told you. It's not safe. You've done a lot for me. But I can't ask you to—"

"So don't ask," said Lance.

Zavrius closed his mouth.

Mallet nodded and stood, dragging his brother up. "It's not a thing you'd have to ask. And unless you order us to flee, we're staying."

Lance nodded. "Even if you order us—"

"Pretty sure we have to obey that, actually," Mallet cautioned.

Zavrius face remained neutral, but his relief showed through the hardness of his eyes. The intense pressure on Balen's arm relented. Balen gave a pained smile as he pried the king's hand off him.

Balen squeezed Zavrius's hand. "We can talk details on the road."

Mallet gave a grateful sigh. Zavrius nodded, swaying slightly like the bough of a tree with root rot—anxiety had its grip on him.

Balen moved nearer to him. Voice low, hand on his shoulder, he asked, "Are you all right?"

"Quite fine," Zavrius said quickly. Then he sighed low, a slight chuckle behind it. He looked at Balen, gaze filled with warmth. "Not at all. Not even slightly." He squeezed Balen's raised arm. "Save for you."

Balen felt the brothers staring and boldly turned to hold their gaze. He raised a brow. Both of them jumped away.

Balen smirked and peeled away from Zavrius. He knew Mallet was concerned and did his best to placate him. "With the size of that army, getting them across the country won't be an easy feat. We'll have time."

Mallet nodded. "All right. But time to do what? Prime."

Balen took him by the shoulder. "It's Balo," he said. "If you find it uncomfortable to call me your friend, I'm at least your comrade in all this."

"Good enough for me," Mallet said.

"Let's get on the road." Zavrius said, slinging the lute-harp over his back.

They left the inn and collected their horses. Leaving Briym Plait, Balen turned at the top of the slope and looked past the city to the wooden fort. The gates were slung open. The people inside looked like ants. But there were hundreds of them: dots milling about, practicing forming into the squared formations in which they'd march into dynasty lands. Balen's horse moved beneath him, fidgeting.

He turned to find Zavrius staring at him. The king's brows were furrowed; he'd been watching the fort with the same fervor, a despondent, anxious look about him. But some part of meeting Balen's gaze made his expression harden. He sat straighter in his saddle, looked more like the king Balen was sworn to protect. And when he gave Balen a firm nod, Balen found himself nodding back.

It felt like a contract of sorts, a covenant they'd consummated the night before and would sign again in Thenlass's blood. Balen thought: I'll never leave you, and knew he meant it.

CHAPTER
EIGHTEEN

During Balen's Paladin training he had extensively stud-ied Usleth's geography and townships. He knew Cres Stros well—all the places that had the best ale, food, lodgings and boys he made sure to commit to memory. Anything beyond Cres Stros's provincial borders was given a less intimate treatment. He knew names, a detail or two that might help if he needed to visit it.

Shoi Prya was a long, narrow province. Its summers were drawn out: humid, hot stretches of time broken up by sharply cold winters. Muggy rain fell all year round. Jammed as it was between Westgar and Cres Stros, a mountainous coastline contoured the northern part of the province, but much of it was woodland and grassy plains. For Balen, it had always been an intermediary place—a liminal space that never felt fully its own.

They traveled a few days without incident. Then when they were a day or so out from reaching Thenlass's strong-hold, Balen called them to a halt.

Piron was a hamlet tucked near the Haestek River that originated high in Westgar's mountains. Though small, it had long ago been established as a waypoint for Paladins and other travelers, and its entire trade had been built around respite for those passing through. Long ago, it would have had its own Paladin for protection. But like Teum Bett, after the ancient Queen Rostaiva pulled all Pal-adins back to Cres Stros, its human protector had since been replaced with a Paladin statue.

When Balen had left Westgar that first time, the last time he had ever been just a boy, Piron had been the place Lestr made them rest.

"You'll learn all this in time," Lestr had told him. "Exactly how these smaller settlements are good for a Paladin. We're forgettable here. Part of the rabble. Piron makes its trade off travelers, so people are always moving through."

Over a decade later and Balen hoped the turnover was still high, so their strange troupe wouldn't stand out. Even so, he was tense. Balen ground his teeth together until his jaw began to ache. It wasn't their location making him like this. Thinking about his master was dangerous.

The mere thought of this town and the memories they'd formed here had forced Lestr into his mind. With it came a barreling force of emotion: years of Lestr's teachings, his discipline, and in some moments the type of gentle care Balen longed for. But it felt odd to be thinking of his master, now more than ever. Someone had been feeding Thenlass's army ichor—and very little happened in the Paladin order without Lestr's knowing.

Balen yearned for this to be one of them.

He led Zavrius and the brothers to a roadside inn to eat. They kept their heads low. Balen made sure to keep his cloak bundled tight, and Zavrius's lute-harp was given the same treatment. Gedrokbone would be too much like a beacon here.

And as they were eating, they heard the news of Zavrius's death.

"I'm telling you, he's dead," a woman hissed nearby. "Palace's breached and he's missing—what else are we to think?"

Zavrius visibly tensed. Balen gripped his forearm and tried to turn covertly, scoping out their right. Three people sat bunched together at the table next to them, two women and a man. They were a mix of the ruddy brown skin common in Shoi Prya and the paler tones of Westgar locals. Not soldiers or mercenaries, by the look of them, which took the edge off Balen. Though clearly news of Cres Stros's attack had spread.

"We're to think only that he's missing," one of the other women said with a shake of her head. "Missing doesn't mean dead."

"Town crier said the attack was violent. Unknown attackers, a breach in the palace. . . don't be a fool, El."

"King Zavrius isn't a soldier," a stout man said in agreement. His tone was enough to convey his meaning: how could one such as Zavrius have survived that attack?

The one dissenting woman offered nothing else, and the conversation shifted.

Balen and the brothers all stared unmoving at the king. A silent beat passed. Then Zavrius dropped his wooden spoon into his stew, laughing. "It's nice to know I'm popular enough to grace the conversations of the masses. Though I'm glad they stopped talking. I thought they might start placing bets."

Balen squeezed his forearm. "Zav."

Zavrius slackened and briefly closed his eyes. He fixed Balen with a smile. "It's just talk. I'm alive. But if we cannot stop Thenlass, then all this speculation will be true. I'll be the dead dandy king with nothing to show for it all."

"Then let's make sure that doesn't happen," Balen murmured, eyeing Zavrius and the brothers, who gave him a stiff nod of approval.

Whatever happened, whatever terrible thing Thenlass was planning, Balen wouldn't let Zavrius die.

They rode for another day.

Once he spied the speck of Thenlass's hold on the horizon, Balen guided them off the traveled path and into the grass. It was a practical decision; the thoroughfare had too many people, and Balen was tense enough to suspect every traveler was Thenlass's eyes. That kind of paranoia would keep him cautious, but he couldn't afford to be delusional.

Off-road, they were alone. The grasslands felt unnatural, like remnants of the war were lingering in the soil. The pale, tufted blades skimmed over his boots and pressed high on the horse's flank: a hundred brittle fingers reaching for him. He shivered. Told himself he was paranoid. Still, he couldn't help but imagine a dozen bodies lying in the grass, idle arcanist killers waiting for them to get within range. He expected Thenlass to have surrounded himself with them—Balen certainly would have, if he were the lord of Shoi Prya.

But of course, Balen was not.

Though dizzyingly, in another life, he could have been.

Both he and Thenlass had been simple Paladins at one point. Both close to royals who were obsessed with war. It was Thenlass's assault that had forced the empire to relinquish their hold on Shoi Prya. That assault had given the Dued Vuuthriks the much-needed push to rid the country of Emperor Nio Beumeut's presence entirely. Thenlass had fought in the skirmishes that had pushed them out of Westgar and back into Rezwyn territory. He'd fought side by side with Zavrius's father, Sirellius. Thenlass had been with the old king when the halberd took him through the neck, had killed the men responsible and dragged their bodies back to Cres Stros behind Sirellius's royal pallet. He had been the man to recount the death before Queen Arasne, who through her tears had thanked him for his service and awarded him the land and the seat to be lord of Shoi Prya.

Balen grimaced, uncomfortable at the similarities. He wondered how easily that could've been him.

But all that seemed to mark Thenlass a patriot, not a traitor. A soldier-Paladin, and war hungry, but not so hungry he would do this. What had possessed him to commit treason? It made no sense.

"Be careful," Zavrius said ahead of him.

The wind picked up as he spoke, a lukewarm breeze that stole his voice. Zavrius turned to look back at him. His hair was like fine whips around his face. Mallet and Lance shared a glance, exchanging some silent message Balen couldn't parse. He ignored it, eyes fixed ahead. Seeing the speck of Thenlass's hold in the distance made Balen grimace. Nothing about this felt good.

Thenlass's holding was a stretch of gray stone. Half of it was still in ruins. From this vantage, it looked like a dried fruit pit: a puckered, rounded mass on the horizon, shot through with holes. Only the main keep had been rebuilt, making it one of the smallest noble holdings across the dynasty. Before Thenlass had claimed his seat, when he was still but a Paladin, the structure had been occupied by empire forces. Thenlass's seat had been built from the pockmarked ruin. Why it still showed marks of empire occupation was undoubtedly down to who Huez Thenlass was as a person. It was Thenlass's own decision to display the ruins alongside his hold. Balen knew then thinking of him as a patriot was dangerous. He was a soldier, as Theo had been. As all Zavrius's siblings had been. And just like Zavrius's siblings, Thenlass was dangerous.

Balen raised his chin. "You're expecting traps."

"Aren't you?" Zavrius lifted a brow. "I keep thinking I spot flesh between the blades of grass."

"I thought the same," Balen said quickly. He fell silent. A gust of wind blew through them.

"You better be fucking wrong," Lance whispered under his breath. His voice was strained as his eyes darted around his horse, watching as if a mass of arcanist nobles would spring up from the beast's hooves.

"Lance," Mallet spat. He batted ineffectually toward his brother, jabbing a finger in Zavrius's direction. "Have some bloody manners."

"In this instance, I have no quarrel with being wrong," Zavrius said. He didn't snort, as he normally would when the brothers acted this way. That odd calm of his made Balen nervous. He watched as Zavrius's horse shifted, grunting. Zavrius patted its neck. "But we'll keep an eye out all the same."

"And your plan for issuing the combat challenge?" Balen called back.

Days ago, Zavrius would have ridden off without answer. Now he turned back, brows quirked in a strange, overwhelmed way. With a little laugh he said, "Balen, I haven't the faintest."

Balen was used to having no plan from Zavrius. Part of him knew he should worry—usually there was at least a delicate, ready-to-fall-apart skeleton of a plan—but Zavrius's candor was refreshing. Gratifying, even.

"Not even the faintest?" Lance asked, voice high. "Your Highness?"

Balen glanced around at the open expanse. He spent some time scanning the horizons, looking for a growing mass of dots that would make up an army. But there was nothing. He turned back to Zavrius with a frown. "Where are the soldiers?"

"All in Westgar, I expect," Zavrius said, "still waiting for the moment to invade the Rezwyn Empire."

"What?" Lance asked.

"The army of arcanists cannot have been created to overthrow me—it was already in place before I was king," Zavrius said. "It must be the vanguard of the invasion force Theo would have needed. Whatever reason Thenlass has to return here, he brought no army to support him. So it's simple. All we need to do is walk in and issue the challenge. Then you win and we ride back and take control of the army in Westgar."

"Zav." Balen's voice flatlined, eyes locked in a dead stare. "This plan is shit. We should make some effort at reconnaissance. We don't even know that Thenlass has really arrived."

Lance and Mallet exchanged a look. Lance clicked his tongue and slung an arm around his brother's neck. "I think this calls for our expertise."

Mallet nodded. "Exactly."

"Smoking ogir moss isn't going to solve any problem we have right now," Balen said.

"You're funny, Balo," Mallet said. "He means acting."

"Right. We go in, say we've been guarding the king and that he's hidden in a safe place. We just have to see how he reacts," Lance said.

"And if he reacts poorly? How are you supposed to get back out to us?" Balen asked.

"We'll bring a message back to you that it's safe to come." Lance spoke as if this was the next logical step.

Mallet nodded. "I suppose if he wants the king captured, he'll let you walk in the front door without issue."

"He'll be on guard," Balen said, shaking his head. "Zavrius is missing and suspected dead, but he shows up here completely unharmed? Anyone with a lick of sense would find that suspicious."

Zavrius rolled back his shoulders. "So I don't show up completely unharmed."

Balen's gut clenched. "What did you say?"

Zavrius chuckled and gestured over toward the keep. "Well, you're right, Paladin, aren't you? Thenlass is cagey. He's left his treasonous arcanist army at the border and returned here. We don't know why. We're at a disadvantage. If he sees me skipping happily over his threshold, he'll likely strike me down before you have a chance to demand the challenge."

"So what, Zav?" Balen asked, incredulous. "You want me to hobble you?"

"Certainly not," Zavrius said. "Just a light stabbing."

Balen balked, but the brothers spoke his panic for him.

"Wh—"

"Sire, you can't—"

Zavrius stopped their protests with a raised hand. "I promise you I'm not insane! I can even give the wound to myself. So here it is: you go in and distract them, I've been accosted on the road, and I very dramatically react to a tiny wound—"

"—and Thenlass drops his guard because the king he underestimates is having a tantrum." Balen finished.

"I like it," Zavrius pronounced.

"It's only slightly less shit than your original plan," Balen remarked.

"I know that," he said, before he leaned across his horse and whispered, "but since it has you using nicknames over epithets, I'm sticking with it."

"What?" Balen said with a laugh, watching Zavrius push his horse into a trot.

Zavrius turned in the saddle, slight tinge of insanity on his face. "I quite like it when you call me Zav."

Balen sat stunned on his horse. Then he let slip a smile, even as his face flushed red.

Lance brought his horse alongside Balen. "Does the ichor make your cock magic, too?"

Balen choked. Spluttering, he turned to Lance. "Does it what?"

"Well, I'd say it's a decent question to be asking," Mallet said, nodding in Zavrius's direction. "He's a different man since that morning, and the only thing that might have changed him is—"

"All right, thank you!" Balen said, throwing up his hands. He started his horse into a trot. Half laughing, he turned in his saddle to jab a finger at the brothers. "I swear, you two have no respect."

Lance shrugged. "If I recall correctly, it was our disrespect you wanted."

Mallet nodded. "And you've earned it."

Balen shook his head with a slight snort and turned to follow Zavrius.

The setting sun backlit the king, obscuring his face with dark shadows. Balen was suddenly consumed with the absurd thought that he was never going to see Zavrius again. It was nonsense. It was pure, unaltered fear. He stamped it down and drew his horse alongside the king's. Balen reached out and took Zavrius's hand in his own. With the light behind them, Balen fixed his eyes on every part of Zavrius's face and tried to hold the image of him there.

"Nightfall won't be long," Zavrius said, squeezing Balen's hand. He slipped it free to undo the braid, then shook out his head. Thick wafts of hair fell over his face. "A handful of minutes, maybe."

The brothers trotted past them, positioning themselves ahead to wait for Zavrius's signal. In his heart of hearts, Balen wasn't sure how strongly he believed this would work. At the very least, Mallet and Lance could get an idea of the level of fortification in Thenlass's hold. Zavrius's part in this plan was a risk—but one they had to take.

"Do you think they can do this?" Zavrius asked.

Balen told him yes. Emphatically. There was no reason to decrease morale any further when the plan was as shaky as this.

"It's you I'm worried for," Balen said. "If I die fighting Thenlass, what will you do?"

Zavrius turned to him, the final streaks of sunlight resting atop his cheekbones.

"You're not going to die," Zavrius said with a roll of his eyes, voice slightly mocking. But Balen sat tense, tense enough that he couldn't keep it from his face. Zavrius shook his head, expression serious now. "And neither am I."

Balen let his eyes close, drew in a deep breath. He nodded. Then settled back into a silence.

Balen's armor refracted with the setting sun, splitting the twilight glow from his cuirass. Rays of sunlight sparkled on the armor like corridors of fading color. Zavrius watched him for a time, and Balen turned back to face him. The light faded, seemed to run like sweat off Zavrius's face. Balen heard him sigh. Zavrius slung the lute-harp into his lap and played softly: none of it music, but more an ambient, anxious movement of his hands. As the dark grew around them and Balen lost sight of him, he was comforted by the sound.

"Am I different to you now?" Zavrius said suddenly. Balen shifted, looked over at the shadow of him, wondering if he'd waited for a time the dark would hide him before he would speak.

"In what way?"

"I'm a murderer now," he said. Quickly he added, "It's news to you, if not to me."

Balen smiled a little, reached out in the dark to find Zavrius's hand. "You're cute when you're like this."

"Am I?" He was defensively embarrassed; Balen heard the slip in his tone, a giddy sound. "Cute. What about murder is cute?"

"That you forget who you're talking to," Balen said. "I've also felled enemies in battle."

Zavrius said nothing to that. He might have hated the comparison. Maybe he thought the two things incomparable.

Balen squeezed his hand. "Think about it like this. Your brother would have started a war. Reveled in it. I would have killed so many to protect him. More than I've already killed to protect you. By my very training—perhaps my very nature—I am meant to take lives."

"That's different."

"Is it?" Balen rubbed his thumb across Zavrius's, wishing he could see his face. "Because you struck down family? Blood is not the strong bond people think it is."

Zavrius didn't answer.

"Do you feel guilt for the act itself, or because it's what you're supposed to feel?" he asked.

He felt Zavrius tense in his hand. "I do not know."

It was a better answer than Balen had expected. More honest, less evasive. Zavrius had spent years building up his own myth: the weakest of his family, the eccentric one. Any honesty must have scared him.

"I think what I feel is fear," Zavrius whispered. "Fear they died for nothing. Fear I'll . . ."

Balen removed his hand to touch Zavrius's thigh. He knew the fear. He'd seen it in Zavrius his whole life. This thing he had never wanted but had killed for. It was not greed that had brought Zavrius here, nor ambition, not even his own survival. Theo had wanted him dead because Zavrius would not be him.

Balen murmured, "You will be a good king."

"How can you be so sure?"

"Because you're scared, Zav." He squeezed Zavrius's thigh. It was a poor substitute for holding him. "Scared you won't be enough. No one with a lick of power-hungry ego would give a single shit about anything but their own throne. You will be a good king."

"And I have you," Zavrius whispered.

"Always."

They waited a little longer, and when the firelight appeared in the windows of the hold, Zavrius slung the lute-harp over his back and dismounted shakily.

"Stake the horses," he told Mallet. "And run. Be desperate. You have to sell it."

Mallet gave a smirk. "Your Highness, prepare to be amazed."

Mallet moved to do as he was told. As he walked, he seemed to shift. Mallet was a big man, but the way he held himself often made Balen forget his true size. Now, Mallet expanded. He straightened himself, puffed out his chest, seemed to take up more space than he physically occupied. The careful man Balen knew him to be slipped away as Mallet buried his hand in the ground and smeared his stubbled face with dirt. He seemed brutish and strong. It didn't take much to make him one of the king's retinue, a man ready to die defending the throne.

Balen nodded at him and breathed deep. For the first time in nearly a week, Balen pooled his power into his palms. This was no large casting, but a tiny, controlled trickle of the arcane; his fingers twinged, urging Balen to be loose with his power, almost like the magic in him craved released. Balen ignored the feeling. There would be plenty of time for unbridled power later, with Thenlass on his knees. This time, all he did was cast enough to light the end of a torch. He handed it to Mallet for him to see by. Mallet nodded his thanks, but his eyes were distantly fixed on his brother. Balen turned. Lance hovered with his arms crossed, staring out into the dark field.

Balen patted Mallet on the shoulder and went to him. "What is it?"

"Nothing," Lance said, and in the same breath, "I know I came up with this plan, but if we die, I'm gonna be so pissed with you."

"That's fair," Balen said. "I'll let you haunt me."

"You believe in that empire shit?" Lance said with an intrigued smile. His lips quirked. "All right. Gods and ghosts. So be it. If I die because of this and the empire was right all along, then my ghost will spend eternity annoying the shit out of you."

"Deal."

"And you know Mallet's ghost won't hesitate to help my ghost out."

"I know."

"So that's two ghosts you've got haunting you. Not a moment of peace. When you're sleeping, eating, fuck-ing—I'm gonna be there reminding you I can't do any of those damn things because I'm dead."

"Lance." Balen cast his eyes high and grabbed the man by the shoulders. "You don't have to do any of this."

"I know! That's why I'm pissed!" Lance said, throwing his hands up. "Mallet and I are doing it 'cause . . ." He ges-tured to Zavrius. "The two of you. I don't know . . . By the bones, Balen. It just feels like you and him might actually try to rule well."

Balen's brows came together, a bright, surprised smile pressing through the grimace. He thought how odd it was to have friends—not friends you were bound to with oaths, or who felt nothing but jealousy for you. This was something genuine. And another feeling welled in him at that: a fear that pummeled him over the head so suddenly he staggered at the realization of it. He who had craved glory for years, the honor that came with public adoration, was now standing in a field preparing to fight his own countrymen. That loud ache for recognition had fallen away without him knowing. Now, Zavrius loved him, the brothers were his friends. Even with the dynasty on the edge of chaos, there was a calmness inside Balen he did not want to lose.

"All right?" Mallet said, coming up behind him. The torch lit up Mallet's frown, so scrunched and searching as he tried to read Balen's expression.

Balen exhaled and grabbed him, drew Mallet and Lance against him. They fell into his chest surprised, both their faces pressed against his hulking pauldrons. Balen didn't care. He squeezed until the two of them groaned, and then pushed them back, a hand on each of their shoulders.

"If it gets bad, you run," he told them. "If he sees through you, if you have even the smallest inkling—or if you see him move to draw his sword—"

"Balen." Mallet touched his shoulder. "We'll be fine."

Balen rolled his tongue over his teeth. "Among the Gifted Paladins of legend, he's a legend himself." Balen paused, looked Mallet in the eye, made sure he understood the gravity of it. "There's no shame in running from that."

"Do you even know us?" Lance said with a laugh. "Besides a real lack in my personal ability to feel shame, we usually run at the first sign of trouble."

"You clearly magicked us," Mallet said. "No other reason I'm volunteering for this shit."

Half turning, he saw Zavrius in his periphery. Balen sucked in a breath.

"I think it's time," he murmured to the brothers. "Run."

"Good luck," Lance told him quietly. Balen nodded at them. Found he couldn't speak. He watched for a time as the brothers backed away into the dark, the light from the torch bobbing in a pulsing ring across the long grass.

When they were far enough away and he had mustered his courage again, he turned.

Zavrius had moved beside him. It took Balen some time before his eyes adjusted to the dark. Faintly, he could tell Zavrius was staring down at the stiletto, breathing heavily.

Balen's stomach dropped. A selfish panic replaced it, a desperation that crawled its way into a body well oiled for the rejection of this plan. Balen spun and grabbed him. "We can do something else. Anything. You said we only needed to buy a little time, and a story—"

"It needs to be believable," Zavrius murmured. He barely reacted to the pressure Balen was placing on his shoulders. "And we've already sent them off. But I . . . I think I was wrong before."

"In what way?"

"I don't think I can do it myself." Now he looked up. Balen couldn't see his eyes, but when Zavrius took his hand softly and placed the cold hilt of a dagger in his palm, Balen knew Zavrius's eyes held an apology.

As soon as the stiletto registered in his hand, his throat closed. Stiffly he said, "No."

"Only a graze," Zavrius said. "Nothing so deep I'll be useless in a fight. Just below the naval, here." He pressed Balen's other hand against the lower left side of his belly. "Really, just a graze."

"You think I'll press harder than I have to?" Balen whispered. He knocked his forehead against Zavrius's, slipped the hand from the front of his belly to around his waist.

"This is the privilege of knowing my mind," Zavrius said, his laugh quiet and half dead. He slung his arms around Balen's neck. "You should be grateful for the honor."

Balen kissed Zavrius's forehead. He pushed a hand against the back of his neck, and pressed the stiletto at an angle through his tunic and his flesh.

Zavrius gasped violently and pulled at Balen's hair. Balen gritted his teeth. He was grateful for the dark but scrunched up his eyes anyway, not wanting a single moment of Zavrius's pain to register.

"Are you all right?" he said, gently pulling the dagger free. He pressed his hand against the wound, felt the blood pool. "Are you all right?"

"Oh no." Zavrius reeled back, pressed both his hands against the gash.

"Zav?" Balen stumbled forward after him, palm over both of Zavrius's hands. He'd pressed too hard. He'd cut him too deep. Balen's heart struck the walls of his chest, incensed—he'd fucking killed the man he loved.

Zavrius peeled away. "Balen," he murmured, looking down at the wound. "Was the sex really that bad?"

And Balen's exhale was furious and relieved and full of adrenaline. "You bastard," he said. "You son of a bitch."

"Your Highness! Exalted Zavrius!"

The cries echoed out across the field. Mallet, Lance—along with voices he didn't recognize.

"Here!" Balen bellowed. He made his voice crack high. "He's here! Help me!"

There was a sudden flurry of bodies, torches bobbing up and down as their bearers ran. Then Mallet and Lance were upon them, well ahead of Thenlass's staff.

"Oh, gedroks." His desperation and shock sounded real. Lance's hands hovered near Zavrius's palms, his face a shocked, washed-out brown. Mallet took Zavrius's other arm and pressed his left hand against the wound. They dragged him forward, Zavrius grunting weakly as they moved.

Zavrius gave his command: "Tell me."

"It's odd, sir," Mallet murmured. Balen barely caught his words. "Nearly empty. Skeleton staff. Most of them are armed."

Lance whispered too. "Five or six in total. That's a guess, though. Couldn't see the kitchen. And one more thing, Your Highness."

"What is it?" Zavrius hissed. Thenlass's staff drew closer.

"The chancellor is here."

Balen's breath stopped. He watched Zavrius's whole body react: lean muscles growing taut, then slackening. A momentary relief encased him. Then, just as Thenlass's servants came to collect them, Balen spotted the quiver in Zavrius's brow. The king shot a look over his shoulder, eyes popping wide with more than surprise.

Balen knew, instinctively, intrinsically, what that look meant. Petra was here, of all places. Petra, who knew everything about the palace, and much about Usleth.

Whose side was she on?

"Quickly," one of the servants said. She was the housekeeper, Balen supposed; an older, rounder woman with a stern face and Shoi Pryian tones. She was accompanied by two armed guards in livery embroidered with Thenlass's decanter-and-pine symbol. It had seemed an innocuous symbol when Thenlass had worn it at the ball, but after witnessing his use of the decanter in the fort, Balen struggled not to balk. There was bold and then there was fearless, and Thenlass seemed to have neither the shame nor the sense to know the difference. Embedding the tool of his treason in his personal symbol marked Thenlass as different. He wasn't a simple traitor. He was calculative, deliberate—and happy to play under the crown's nose.

Balen took a breath and centered himself. He focused his attention on the structure.

Much of the original fortification wall was still in ruins, spanning most of the wider grasslands that made up Thenlass's seat. Up close, the unfixed ruins meant it was hard not to imagine the war. A visual marker of the empire's presence, and all Thenlass had done to rid Usleth of their impact.

The smaller main keep that Thenlass occupied had empty battlements. All the trappings of fortification were there, but if the brothers were right, Thenlass was severely underprotected. Balen couldn't fathom it. This was a military man, with decades more experience than him, and the real lived experience of war. What was he thinking leaving himself so unguarded?

The only way it made sense was if he'd truly not been expecting them.

Was this Petra's doing? The chancellor's presence unnerved Balen completely. He tried to make sense of it. If Thenlass had returned to meet with her, he wouldn't have expected to stay long.

But what could the two of them have to talk about in secret? Balen cursed himself. He had to know why Petra was truly here, and if she had sided with Thenlass over Zavrius, before he went and issued a challenge. The memory of her interrogating the traitor at the coronation ball filled Balen's mind. The way she'd question Balen's choice of friends, the critiques she had for Zavrius's treatment of the empire—all of it made Balen nervous. The woman could be ruthless. Petra was a serious player, well connected and uniquely positioned to destroy Zavrius completely. He couldn't attack Thenlass without knowing where she stood. But that left him and Zavrius right in the enemy's lair with little plausible reason to leave. After this, he swore, he would never let Zavrius enact another shit plan again.

"Come." Thenlass's servants brought the light close

as they moved. They entered the massive, carpeted foyer, avoided the wide-set stairs that would have made Zavrius bleed more, and instead took a hard right. Balen had never been here, could barely register any details beyond its size and grandeur. A small palace filled with art, glinting things on pedestals—Balen guided Zavrius's weaving, bloody form through it all until they reached something like a sitting room. It was lit up with a dozen lamps. A low fire flickered in the hearth. The room was so warm it felt like summer in Cres Stros, the heavy heat before a storm.

"I see the weeks have been kind to you, Your Highness."

Balen shuddered and looked up. Lord Huez Thenlass, dynasty savior, was at least two decades Balen's senior. He walked with a limp now. It made him stiff as he approached. Short-cut hair, a wiry beard and thick brows, all salt-and-pepper—intimidating, more intimidating than Balen remembered from Zavrius's ball. But at that point he'd thought that maybe Thenlass had been his ally.

Balen scanned for Petra. The hold had seemed close to empty as he'd dragged the king through it. He hadn't spotted her out there, and this room was similarly devoid of her presence. Balen wasn't sure what he wanted. If she was sitting pretty, sipping Thenlass's tea, he'd have had a fit. Yet how was it any better if she was lurking in the shadows? He recalled the way she'd run to grab Zavrius when they'd returned from Teum Bett. The fear in her, the relief at Zavrius's homecoming—perhaps Lance and Mallet had been mistaken and hadn't seen her here at all.

Balen blinked as Zavrius's weight changed. The king was slumped between Mallet and Balen, a very real tension holding him rigid against the pain. Balen stood with his armor polished and shining. He caught Thenlass staring at it before the older man nodded.

"Lay him out," he said gruffly, pointing vaguely to the opposite end of the room. "On the cloth, preferably. It's a damn good table."

Balen didn't turn but was instead tugged by Mallet toward a stretch of table laid with a white tablecloth. He slipped the lute-harp from Zavrius's shoulders and slung it over his own shoulder. With his palms pressed against Zavrius's back, Balen tried to lay him down gently.

"Fuck," Zavrius said anyway, bloody fingers clenching around his stomach. Balen rested his head against the table. Couldn't help but stroke a line of hair away from his face.

"Now move," Thenlass said. Balen shifted away, his eyes on Zavrius's pained face. He saw the ex-Paladin in his periphery and felt the youth in him quake.

Thenlass's Paladin helmet was mounted above the hearth like a hunting trophy. It flickered iridescently, flames reflecting on its surface. Balen stared at, an uneasy feeling rising up in him at the sight. A Paladin head, forged from the body of a gedrok. It felt righteous in a way. It felt like Thenlass had slain the Paladin he once was.

"Your Highness." Thenlass bowed slightly as he approached the table. His voice had the same summer quality as the heat in the room: warm and polite but with an edge to it, like sand was lodged in his throat.

"Lord Thenlass." Zavrius's voice was quiet and wisp-like. His eyes peeled open slightly. "There was an attack at Cres Stros. I fled. But there were bandits on the road. . . I'm afraid I must ask for your hospitality."

"My hospitality," Thenlass said. He sounded oddly amused. "Let me take a look."

Gently, he peeled Zavrius's hands away. Zavrius let out a panicked cry—Balen jolted at the sound of it, his heart pounding.

"Now, now," Thenlass cooed, seemingly at the both of them. "You're quite all right."

"I'm dying," Zavrius whimpered. A few tears fell before he shuddered. "I've been killed."

For the life of him, Balen couldn't believe anyone else bought this act. But this was the king they imagined

Zavrius to be: dramatic and pathetic, unfit for his role. Cautiously, Balen glanced over at Mallet and Lance. Their openmouthed stares were deeply convincing. Past them, Thenlass's servants hovered in the door.

There was one door into this room and it was filled with Thenlass's people.

"Clear the room!" Balen bellowed. His voice shook. "Give the king space!"

He waved the servants out and pushed Mallet and Lance out with them. At the threshold he dropped his voice to a whisper. "Talk to them. Find out what you can, what they know. And by the bones, if you spot an arcanist anywhere in this hold, tell me at once."

Neither one acknowledged him with anything more than a slight nod. He closed the door, glanced over to see Thenlass looking at him.

Balen's stomach knotted.

"Will he be all right?" Balen asked.

"You're a soldier, Balen of the Gifted Paladins. It's barely more than a surface-level wound. You should know he'll be fine."

Balen held his breath and blinked, trying not to feel like Thenlass had been expecting this. Balen reminded himself it wasn't possible. Thenlass had laid no traps for them, had been sitting happily and unaware at his fire before Mallet and Lance had burst through his door. Balen gripped the lute-harp's strap tightly and quickly returned to Zavrius's side.

"Don't look so concerned." Thenlass patted him soundly on the back. It reverberated through the armor. "He's a Dued Vuuthrik. They're a resilient lot. Or were. You've done your duty by bringing him here."

Thenlass eyed him with a bright smile entirely wrong for the situation. Balen stayed still, put his whole energy into not flinching or moving away. Thenlass moved away first. He took his time rolling up his sleeves, enough time that Zavrius's eyes flickered open and caught on something in Balen's, on the concern there. They held each other's stares, and Balen tried to hear whatever Zavrius was telling him. Was it placation or warning in his eyes? Was he calm or biting back his panic? Balen moved to the edge of the table and carefully began to undo Zavrius's tunic. There was no quip from Zavrius's lips—there couldn't be, not in front of Thenlass—but it made Balen feel distinctly nervous.

"We should withdraw to my study. You can clean up the wound there," Thenlass said. "But then you must tell me how you've survived. Quite frankly, King Zavrius, half the country thought you dead."

"I'll tell you," Zavrius said, "but first I must thank you for your loyalty."

"Please don't thank me, Your Highness. It's my pleasure to serve your family." And Thenlass's smile was so pitying and smug Balen thought he was going to be ill.

CHAPTER
NINETEEN

Thenlass's servant brought bandages and Zavrius settled on a green velvet chaise longue near the window. He gave a single moan and fell into a fairly convincing faint.

Lance and Mallet stood on opposite sides of the door.

Thenlass gave them one somewhat disparaging glance, then sat in a wingback chair near the hearth, watching Balen.

"You're quite familiar with him. Our king," Thenlass remarked.

Balen didn't answer.

He gently laid the lute-harp on the floor within Zavrius's reach and approached Thenlass. He didn't take the chair. Standing felt safer, somehow, like he was further out of Thenlass's reach.

"Sit," Thenlass said, pleasantly enough. Balen sat. Thenlass handed him a glass, considering him for a long moment before his eyes fell away to some distant point on the floor. He sipped his drink in the silence. Then, when he'd settled on something, he took a deep breath and nodded.

"You love him," Thenlass murmured.

Balen's breath stopped. He cleared his throat, tried for an easiness he did not feel.

"Of course," he said, bringing the glass to his lips. The drink was sharp in his throat, but welcome. "He's the king."

"He's the king," Thenlass repeated, like it was a lie for appeasing idiot children. Balen blinked, rapidly aware of some feeling in him—Thenlass was at once his senior, his equal, his underling, a man who might have been Prime, who would have fought Balen for the honor if he thought the king worthy. Zavrius had not been worthy. Thenlass hadn't even tried. He felt his uneasiness grow.

Balen pretended not to hear the bitter note in Thenlass's tone.

Thenlass leaned back in his chair, firelight softly pulsing on his cheek. He rested his chin on his hand, considering the two of them with a look Balen suspected was far more calculating than it seemed.

"Tell me. Where did you go after the palace was lost?"

"The road," Balen said, knowing it was vague. "Staying in one spot wasn't an option and seeking out nobles proved to be . . . impossible. The arcanists," Balen said slowly, like he was revealing some great mystery to Thenlass, "are of noble birth."

Thenlass shrugged a little. "Naturally. They're quite upset by the visionless future our king seems to be setting."

Far too casual with that talk, Balen thought. Far too confident; like Lestr that day of Zavrius's ceremony, only more twisted.

"And how were you so certain I was not a transformed, mad fanatic myself?" At this Thenlass moved his hands about his head, gesturing insanity. Insanity—like the minds of arcanists rotting from arcane use. Something he couldn't have known without knowing the arcanists more intimately than he was letting on. Did Thenlass realize what he'd just confirmed?

Balen cleared his throat. "He was injured. He knew you would take him in. For Theo's sake."

"For Theo's sake," Thenlass repeated, so softly the sounds of the popping fire smothered half his words. In the silence that followed, Balen had to look away. When he glanced over at Zavrius, he had his eyes open. Thenlass noticed, too.

"Ah, Your Highness," he said. "Back in the land of the living? You came so close to death."

He gently pushed himself up to sitting, his hair curled and frizzed from the heat. "Do not mock me," Zavrius said, voice low.

"Why ever not?" Thenlass's voice was bright. He gave a wheezing laugh, the hearth spitting beside him. "You've already made a mockery of this country. Don't"—he sat forward with his hands raised, trying to calm the outrage on Zavrius's face—"take it too harshly, my king. I say it only out of respect to your brother, and the future he had planned."

Balen bristled. Two conflicting forces filled him up, the first belonging to the little boy he had been long ago, dreaming of the Paladins, hearing of the triumph of Huez Thenlass and craving that same honor. But the second force was born from Zavrius, from his love for Zavrius, as both his Prime and his man, and it was not a quiet thing. All respect he had for Thenlass, any mark of doubt at his involvement, shed itself like rotting skin sloughing from a carcass.

He couldn't help himself. Ignoring the confidence Thenlass had slathered over his words, Balen clasped his hands and leaned forward.

"How dare you. You know nothing of King Zavrius's vision."

"And whose fault is that?" Thenlass said lightly. "If you think the Dued Vuuthrik name will survive you, sire, it will not. Clearly your noble brethren feel the same way."

"You would align yourself so openly with traitors?" Balen spoke like he was spitting venom from between his teeth.

"It's all right," Zavrius said softly. He shifted and sat up, pushed midlength curls across one shoulder. "He's not my Prime, Balen. He has every reason to question me." He turned to Thenlass with an appeasing nod. "I'll admit I've kept my plans for our great country close to my heart. I see now it was a mistake."

Thenlass's face shifted. Contemplative, with an edge of sadness to it—but how much of that was truth?

Thenlass uncrossed his legs and put his glass on the floor. "Of course, Your Highness. You bear a great burden for our dynasty. Not only your siblings, for whom the entire country grieves, but for your mother." At this, he nodded down at the lute-harp in Zavrius's lap, and made to reach for it. Zavrius lifted it from the floor before he could get near. He drew it closer to his body, his calm expression buckling slightly. Thenlass paused and raised a brow. "I always found it very sweet, how you took Arasne's art over Sirellius's."

"Art? Fighting, you mean? I suppose you could call making war an art," Zavrius said, looking down at his nails. "But not an art I was ever particularly adept in."

"Well, no." Thenlass gestured to the instrument again. "Which is why you were your mother's."

Zavrius pursed his lips. He smiled. But it was not a happy smile. His cheeks rose and squeezed against his eye, his eyebrows a flat plane against which his eyes sank—he couldn't keep the scorn from his face. Softly he said, "You pity me, don't you?"

Thenlass shrugged. "A little."

"War will not save this country. It will, at best, stagnate it," Zavrius said.

"You're wrong, sire," a voice said at the door. "Usleth will thrive."

Balen hadn't even heard the door open. He flinched, surprised, swinging toward it. The bottom of his stomach dropped.

Petra stood with her hands clasped together, a serene, neutral expression on her face. From the look of her, she was not surprised to see Zavrius. If anything, she looked bored. Balen shot a look to the king. He managed to keep it from his face, but Balen knew his body. Tension strapped him, a marionette with all its strings pulled taut. A flicker of something—heartache, despair—shot across his eyes. Then he raised chin.

"Ah," Zavrius said. "You know, I was rather hoping you weren't here."

"I hate to disappoint you," she said, "yet I must do what's best for Usleth."

"And to think I've spent days worrying over your well being," Zavrius spat. "I should have been begging the empire gods to strike you down." After a moment Zavrius asked, "Did you open the palace doors to the arcanists?"

Petra stayed silent. Balen wanted to launch into an interrogation, draw out all the reasons she had betrayed them, determine exactly why she was here in Thenlass's hold. His mind was racing with memories of the coronation ball. Petra had done everything to sniff out Mariel Kus. Had that all been a ploy? Or had her loyalties shifted in the aftermath? Balen shut down the running thoughts. All those questions could be answered later. First, Thenlass had to die.

Balen watched as Zavrius silently worked his jaw. No doubt he had a lot to say to Petra. Yet something was stopping him from opening his mouth. Zavrius had accepted the treason of a few noble youths as necessary, expected. But this was a betrayal on a personal level. Balen could feel the hurt wafting off him.

Petra stepped over the threshold. She positioned herself near Thenlass's chair. Behind her, another person came into view: Adzura Polverc, with her head held high and a polite smile on her lips. She drifted into the room without sparing Zavrius a glance. Thenlass rose to meet her. She kissed both of his cheeks and embraced him with a laugh, this strange giddy sound that made Balen think of drunken revelry, something joyous and fun. Balen and Zavrius both sat tensely watching this. It felt as if they were intruding on something personal.

Zavrius raised his head and smiled at Polverc when she turned to him.

"Zavrius," she said with a nod.

"Adzura," he replied with a tense grin. "How upsetting, but not entirely surprising, to see you."

Polverc gave a half-hearted curtsy and took the other side of Thenlass's chair. Now Balen had his back to the door, a close means of escape. If things got bad, he could throw Zavrius from the room and keep these traitors occupied.

"Well, here we are," Zavrius sighed. Exhaustion crept into his features as he gestured at the three of them. "Huez Thenlass gathers an army at the border of Westgar. My own aunt, chancellor to the throne, supports him over the rightful king. Even one of the oldest families in Usleth betrays me as well. Where does that leave me, except in a place where I cannot let this slight go unchecked?"

"And what will you do, Your Highness?" Thenlass said, sinking back into his wingback chair. He opened his hands in a wide shrug. "Find some way to have us killed? Half the country tells me you're rather good at that. So greedy for the throne you'd have your siblings murdered in cold blood. Not only that, but doing so on empire territory to force a conversation with the enemy. So what will it be?"

"Do you have nothing else but your rumors?" Balen spat.

Thenlass turned to him like he was seeing him for the first time. He dropped his gaze over Balen's armor and tilted his head to the side. "Your attack dog has a loud bark," Thenlass said, glancing back to Zavrius. "We all know these aren't rumors."

Zavrius said nothing. Somehow, he was keeping his breathing even. He turned to Petra. Some of his usual chaos came back to him, likely sparked by anger. He cocked his head. "And what do you have to say on this, aunt?"

Petra was a statue, unmoving. She looked over at Zavrius calmly. "You accuse Thenlass of sedition, and he accuses you of taking the crown by force. Neither of these are news to me—and both of them are true."

"You know of the army?" Zavrius asked, skipping over Petra's knowledge of what he had done. Finally, real hurt broke through into his voice. "You know what he plans, and you still stand here beside him? How can you support him? Your love for my father should not have made you this blind. You know what will happen! You know—"

Zavrius clamped his mouth shut. He was flushed, his skin was sweaty. The heartbreak was palpable; Balen's chest seized at the pain in Zavrius's voice. Seeing Zavrius like this set a fire in Balen's belly. Ichor boiled his blood with his rage, red hot and scorching. He flexed his hands. He would kill them. The three of them with their smug faces, with their righteous, conceited convictions. Balen would raise his gauntlets and burn holes through all their traitorous stone hearts.

Thenlass sighed like he was sick of Zavrius's drama. "Petra has done what her heart told her to, Zavrius. How could you expect her to support you after you killed for the throne? But not I. I do as the king wills."

Balen scoffed, frowning. "I don't understand. You're vying for the throne? You think you can lead this country?"

"You mistake me. I'm not talking about myself," Thenlass said, eyeing Balen up and down.

"Then who?" Balen asked.

Thenlass smiled. It was like he'd been waiting for this question for a very long time. "Theo."

A long moment of silence passed. Balen spoke. "Theo is dead."

Thenlass only smiled. "Is he?"

"Yes," Zavrius said firmly.

Thenlass raised his chin. "And why are you so sure? You, who wasn't there. You, who had nothing to do with the strange deaths of your siblings." Thenlass gritted his teeth and chuckled. "Ah—unless that's just the lie you've decided to tell yourself. You can't bear it, can you? The truth of what you are."

Zavrius went stiff. His hands moved until his fists were clenched around his swordbreaker. "Theo," he said, strained, "is dead."

Thenlass seemed to break. He launched out of his chair and rushed forward, eyes popping madly.

"You think I worship a dead man? You think I would debase myself by groveling to a grave? No. It is not grave dirt I sink my hands into, but blood—empire blood that will be drained from the source by the true king of the Dued Vuuthrik Dynasty. The last of Sirellius's dream for our future. Don't you see, Zavrius, you fucking cur?" He drove a finger toward Zavrius's eyes. "Theo is alive."

The room went still. Polverc finally gasped shrilly. Balen saw Petra in his periphery, hand clutching her heart. They hadn't known. How hadn't Petra known? All of them were caught on this reeling sensation; the words took an age to register, for the full weight of their meaning to crash down over Balen's mind.

"That's right," Thenlass said, sounding pleased. He nodded at Zavrius with a sneer. "You weren't even good enough to finish the job."

Zavrius turned to look at Balen. For a moment there was this conflicting, layered reaction: hope and regret and fear piling on top of one another. Relief, a chance at self-forgiveness, this sudden clinging desire to not be the killer he thought himself to be. Then some greater wave in him breached that dream. Hopelessness flooded his eyes.

Balen could feel the nerves in Zavrius's body. He reached for him; was pleasantly surprised when Zavrius let himself be held.

Zavrius gripped his pauldron and walked in front of Balen. He was blinking back tears. "My brother truly lives?"

Thenlass raised his chin. His lips were twisting with the hint of a smile. "He does. Theo will crush you first, then finally destroy the empire. The Dued Vuuthrik Dynasty will expand to the far reaches of this world."

Some resolve came back to Zavrius. He wiped the tears away. "Even if that's true, Arasne named me heir." Zavrius reached into the bowl of the lute-harp and drew out a piece of parchment. "I have the edict here."

Polverc shifted. Balen flashed a look to Petra and saw the slightest crease appear in her brow. Another thing she hadn't known.

"That matters not," Thenlass said, eerily calm. He dismissed Arasne's edict with a wave of his hand.

Balen took a breath. Thenlass had too much invested in this. Theo was the last connection Thenlass had to Sirellius; an eidolon of the man he'd gone to war for. Nothing more could be done to convince him.

In three quick strides, Balen was beside him.

"Huez Thenlass," he said. "I challenge you to a duel. Paladin against Paladin, for the fate of Theo's army."

Thenlass jerked suddenly, like he'd lost all control of his body.

Polverc made a strangled noise, and Petra turned her gaze to Zavrius, as if deciphering whether this was his plan. Thenlass ignored the commotion. He glanced at Balen with a horrible smile on his face. "It won't matter if you kill me. That army is mine and Theo's. They won't listen to you. They're too far gone for any of that."

Balen held his breath. Thenlass wasn't wrong; ichor was corrosive. Without their sense intact, these people were being driven by the vapors of their fanaticism, the very thing that had made them drink the ichor in the first place. If they knew Theo was alive, there would be no amount of gold or pardons or promises that could change their ichor-addled minds. Even Thenlass couldn't stop them. But letting this man go unpunished was not an option either.

"Fight me," Balen said. "To the death."

At this, Zavrius visibly stiffened. Perhaps he hadn't realized exactly what the challenge would entail, or perhaps it had new impact now that Balen was saying it aloud, the weight of what could happen burrowing into Zavrius's mind. Balen only knew that he couldn't die. He couldn't. Zavrius and he were on the cusp of something; their intimacy a dream Balen had been nurturing for years, and now it was becoming his reality. Together, he knew they could rule Usleth well.

So, death wasn't an option.

Balen wanted to live.

Thenlass looked over at Balen and cocked his head. A shiver slithered down Balen's back, and he held himself tense, coming alert. The precise feeling of observation, of being assessed, pricked at Balen's mind. Thenlass was looking at him truly for the first time. Balen held himself still, feeling caught in the sight of a predator. Then after some indeterminable thing had satisfied him, Thenlass straightened.

A leering smile split his lips apart. "I accept."

He sees my youth, Balen thought. But it was more than that. Thenlass also saw Zavrius; like a miasma, Balen's association with the underestimated king meant Thenlass was miscalculating Balen, too.

Thenlass was the stuff of legends, but even legends could be broken. Balen rolled back his shoulders and gestured to the mounted Paladin helmet.

"No need," Thenlass said, not even bothering to turn. "I don't need it."

Balen bit his tongue. Like him, Thenlass was a Paladin. He had the same burning ichor in his blood. Why anyone would let it scorch their insides and turn them mad, Balen didn't know—but his reasons did not matter. If Thenlass had no filter for his power, he would be doubly hard to take down. Balen pursed his lips.

Thenlass caught the motion and raised his head. "You want to ask me why. I'll answer. Theo has transcended death. I have transcended the limitations of our order. The power in the blood of a Paladin is not to be cowed. My army shows that, and I'm a man who stands by my convictions."

Balen had no answer to this, and Thenlass didn't wait for one. He strode past him with an easy grace and flung open the door.

"Ladies," he said, holding it wide for Polverc and Petra to slip out. Petra glanced back at Zavrius, just for a moment, before she followed Polverc out. The door swung shut, leaving Zavrius and Balen alone.

In an instant, Zavrius was on his feet. He drummed his fingers on the lute-harp. "We need a signal. The very moment it gets bad, you shout it, and I'll—"

"—do nothing." Balen put a steadying hand over the king's frantic fingers. "You know this must be done properly. We have witnesses, Zav. At least one person here knows the power you have with that instrument. If there's even a chance Thenlass was slain unlawfully, it will be another mark against your name."

Zavrius shook himself away from Balen's touch. "No. Polverc and Petra have turned," he said hurriedly. "It won't matter what we do. We need to take him down."

Balen stopped him. "Not at the cost of your credibility."

Zavrius stared at him. It wasn't rage pulsing in his eyes, but a fear with the same fire. His grip on the lute-harp tightened. Balen knew he was taking something from Zavrius: stripping him of the comfort of a weapon, the security that came with his gift of charm. But Balen knew, too, that he was right.

"You will be a great king. You will. But only if you're given the chance to rule. So put your faith in me, Zav. Let me do my duty and save you in this way."

Zavrius said nothing. Saying anything would be too much: the tension and fear in the air around Zavrius was a brewing storm. Zavrius dispelled it by standing on his feet and kissing Balen on the cheek.

"Save me, then," he whispered. "And rid Usleth of this stain of a man while you're at it."

Thenlass's voice called through from the entrance hall. "Are you two praying to the empire's crude little gods?"

Balen ignored the goading slight and took Zavrius's hand. He didn't care what that might say about him, and he refused to let go until they were standing in the open expanse of the keep's entrance.

They arrived in time to see two of the armed servants lugging decorative pedestals to the side of the room to clear the center for the challenge. Thenlass had shucked his overcoat and was carefully rolling up the sleeves on his white undershirt, exposing a raised brown scar along his left arm. Balen wondered if he'd once blocked an attack with it.

Petra and Polverc had positioned themselves by the far-left stairs. Balen was glad to see Mallet and Lance stationed near the opposite corridor. A big man he assumed was the cook stood behind them, cleaver in his hand. The brothers looked stricken. Balen gestured them over and they gratefully bounded across the hall to stand alongside Zavrius.

Balen turned to Zavrius and kissed his hand. Thenlass ignored this display.

"Protect the king," Balen told the brothers. The three of them moved in the direction of the keep's great doors, and no one moved to stop them.

"Whatever happens here is law," Thenlass called. A servant carried his sword forward. After inspecting it, he made a show of pointing it from his servants to Polverc and Petra in the corner. "You are my witnesses. You will not let news of what happened here be warped or distorted. The outcome of a Paladin challenge is to be honored. This means no retribution will be taken if I am killed. If the Prime is killed, the king is free to leave." At this, Thenlass turned and fixed Zavrius with a savage smile. "His death will come later. There is someone else who has missed him fiercely."

Balen remembered standing in the makeshift pen at Teum Bett in a much simpler challenge. This time, the weapons were real, and there would be no adjudicator. They both knew the rules. All Paladins learned them.

In a challenge like this, there was only one.

Do not die.

They faced each other on the floor. The room was silent. Balen knew Thenlass was expecting him to attack. He was the cocky young Prime who had never been in a real battle. He would show all his hands in the first few moments of the fight and grow tired quickly.

That was the man Thenlass expected, and at first, that was the man he would get. He drew only Zavrius's stiletto.

With ichor pooling in his belly, Balen attacked. He rushed forward, gave a wide slash that was easily countered. Thenlass stepped out of the way. Balen barely felt the impact of the other man's blade flicking his aside. Thenlass parried lightly, slipping back to center before Balen could stop his own motion. Balen threw himself forward again: another blundering move. He heard the light scoff escape Thenlass's lips, the old Paladin's grating assessment in his mind. Thenlass had sized him up.

Now Thenlass attacked. Balen retreated, rushing to pull his dagger up in an awkward defense. It clattered against Thenlass's steel. Thenlass leered at him through the cross of their blades, manic and unhinged, eerily familiar. Balen kicked him away and gathered his power in his empty palm. Then, through the gauntlet he pushed a prismatic beam of searing light toward Thenlass's face.

Thenlass made a low noise and dodged. The old Paladin raised his hand.

Balen saw nothing, but he felt it: a raw and vicious maelstrom of energy that threw him backward and crushed the breath out of him. Gasping for air, Balen floundered with the gauntlets. His fingers twitched as he tried to heave his arm upward. The invisible pressure made him groan. But then he focused on feeling for the edge of the attack.

Balen at last found the strength to repel the overwhelming pressure of Thenlass's arcane force long enough to raise his hand and cast.

Flashpoint sparks of fire burst along Thenlass's body. He cursed, forced to drop his attack entirely to pat them out. When the weight lifted, Balen keeled forward. He staggered. Made himself stand, refused to fall. Thenlass's focus was split—but not for long.

Balen rushed him. He sliced upward with his stiletto. Thenlass lurched away, countering with a sloppy jab Balen easily evaded. Thenlass gave a fierce, angry howl and came at Balen with renewed speed. Balen let him come, weathering a barrage of attacks, each one ripping pain down his arm. The old Paladin was starting to pant. Balen could see his injury now, the limp in his leg flaring up. But then Thenlass's blade sparked with rabid energy, bolts curving off the blade.

He was charging the weapon for a full attack.

Balen barely had time to react. Thenlass raised his blade and brought it down toward Balen's chest. Balen threw himself to the floor and rolled, narrowly avoiding another three attacks that ruptured the floor. Shards of tile scraped over his face.

When Thenlass came close, Balen kicked the other man's knee, driving it backward with a sickening snap. Thenlass bellowed in agony. Balen swung and sliced across Thenlass's thigh. Speckled blood sprayed out of the wound, but it wasn't deep enough to be fatal. Balen scrambled to his feet. Thenlass staggered to the table, leaning heavily on it. His leg was badly wounded, possibly crippled.

"Had enough?" Thenlass grinned at him. "You have no chance. You can't stop me. You can't beat me. Theo is king."

Balen's jaw was tight. He would not fail. Zavrius was king. Not Theo. Not anyone else.

Through clenched teeth, Balen said, "Wrong. The king is . . . who I . . . protect."

Balen howled. It ripped out of him, a burst of overflowing arcane power that made Thenlass waver. Roaring, Balen pulled himself to his full height and put all his arcane power into that small stiletto.

Thenlass's face buckled. He tried to raise a hand. "Wai—"

Balen didn't wait. With one fluid motion he sank the dagger in the other man's throat. Thenlass choked once, then fell with a thud.

Balen turned to Petra and Polverc, bloody dagger still gripped in his hand. "Do you accept this judgment?"

Petra gave a silent nod. Polverc stood staring, transfixed by the sight of the dying man in front of her as he choked, struggled, then finally stilled. She made some calculation. Whatever she decided made her turn to Zavrius and drop into a deep curtsy.

 CHAPTER
TWENTY

They left Thenlass's hold a bloody wreck. Zavrius
shoved outside ahead of them and raised his head to the
sky. In his wake, the oak door swung open to blue dawn
light. The air was crisp and stagnant, night loosening its
grip on the world. Zavrius stalked into the long grass. Balen
and the brothers followed at his heels, silent, caught up in
Thenlass's death. It was quiet enough that it felt like a waking dream, like watching the king marching through a field
in the heartland toward his own demise. Balen had a vision
of Theo crawling his way out of his own grave, a revenant
come to be his brother's undoing.

They couldn't just flee into the fragile morning like this.

Balen rushed up to Zavrius and met his strides. "Wait."

"There's no time," Zavrius said. His gaze was fixed on
the horses, pace just short of a run until he reached his gelding's side. He pressed his hand against its flank, preparing
to mount. Balen grabbed his wrist and spun him, dragging
him close by the waist.

"Listen to me."

"What are you—" Zavrius hissed, flushing. His eyes
darted over Balen's shoulder, no doubt to the brothers coming up behind them.

"Theo is alive," Balen said slowly.

Zavrius tried to wrench himself free. "I fucking know
that!"

"Hey. Hey!" Balen let go of Zavrius's wrist and cupped
his cheek. Zavrius's whole body was tense, a man on the
edge of collapse. "You need to calm down."

Zavrius shoved at his chest. "Don't you—dare tell me to
fucking—"

Balen wrapped his arms around him. Smothered
Zavrius in an embrace, bundled him close against his

armor and held him there until Zavrius stopped struggling and the tension seeped out of him. Zavrius took a shaky breath and knocked his head against the hard plane of Balen's breastplate.

Balen reached across and kissed his forehead.

"Do you want to run?" he asked, seriously.

Zavrius went still against him. In his periphery, the brothers turned their heads away, pretending not to listen. Zavrius looked up at him, lips together, frowning. "What?"

"If you want to run, I will run with you."

"You would abandon this country? Your title, everything you worked for?"

In a heartbeat. Without question. If Zavrius wanted him to run, he would do it, even if it meant the rest of his days were spent in moral turmoil. Whatever that said about him and his principles, Balen didn't care. He loved Zavrius. He wanted him to live. And, after all this, if anything happened, anything irreversible, anything that hurt him, Balen would go insane.

He didn't say any of that. Instead, he repeated himself, one last time, one last offering: "Do you want to run?"

Zavrius's eyes shifted, like he fell into an understanding. What was being offered, what saying yes would give or take away. He looked at Balen's lips, and perhaps in that moment he imagined their life together, as people, without the mantle of leader, without the burden of a country. Balen wondered what he saw, what kind of life. He wanted to know what ultimately led Zavrius to shake his head no.

"We stay here in Shoi Prya and fight," Zavrius whispered to him. It sounded mournful, almost, the way he whispered it. He patted Balen's chest like he was a child with a lovely dream and nothing more.

Balen had expected this. Of course he'd expected this. Zavrius was a good man, and he would be a better king. He had killed kin for this burden. He would not leave it, not even for love. Still, Balen felt a mild ache at his firm tone.

At his surety. The certainty of where they were going and what they would be doing ended in this decision. The distant dream of their lives together became a hazy blur Balen suddenly couldn't see. And still he took Zavrius's hands and kissed his fingers and said, "Okay," with a smile.

He was Prime Paladin and Zavrius was his king. If they died together defending the country, they'd only be following an archetype long ago written for their stations. Zavrius turned back to the hold. The sun was cresting behind them. Golden light dragged over the ruined structure, splitting when it met broken stone.

Zavrius brushed his hand against Balen's, hooking their pinkies together. "Shoi Prya is essential. You just killed for it. And Cres Stros is a mess, Balen. It's my father's seat. A dusty relic full of spies, alliances, memories . . . I can't make anything new there." He looked up at the sky. "Shoi Prya is the most important province."

Balen turned to him. "You want to move the whole capital?"

Zavrius hesitated. He unlaced their fingers and ran a hand over his loose hair. "Well, the capital is wherever I am," he said, grinning. "And I plan to stay here."

Balen knocked their heads together, a quick stolen moment. With his cheek still pressed against Zavrius's forehead, Balen turned to the hold. "What do you want to do?"

"What do I want to do?" Zavrius scoffed. "It's a mess in there. I want very much not to deal with any of it. I'd much rather a hot bath and something sweet to eat."

Balen sighed. "Zav."

"Give me the stiletto." Zavrius's tone shifted suddenly, losing all of its charming flavor. Balen flinched. He bent down and wiped the bloody thing on the grass before he flipped it in his hand and gave Zavrius the hilt. The king took it with a flourish, whipping it around his fingers and holding it up to the sun. Light refracted off the metal.

Zavrius bumped the hilt against his head, face scrunched horribly. Then he straightened, impassive, and walked toward the hold.

Balen unstaked the horses and gave their reins to the brothers.

"Are you all right?" Mallet asked softly.

"Fine, I'm fine," Balen said. He was distracted, watching Zavrius stalk back toward the open oak doors.

Lance cocked his head toward the king's retreating figure. "What about him? Is he all right?"

Balen grimaced. "Remains to be seen."

They followed him back to the hold. The brothers staked the horses near the entrance and Balen stood with them watching Zavrius's back. The king stared unmoving just beyond the open doors, grip firm on the dagger. Then he raised his head and walked inside. Balen followed.

Thenlass lay in a heap, blood a stagnant pool around his neck. Balen met his glassy stare. He felt nothing. All the fear he'd had at their parallels was dispelled by this sight. Balen dragged his eyes away.

Petra and Polverc were whispering to one another near the stairs where they'd left them, but the rest of the hall had been abandoned. The tiny audience that had gathered to watch their master fight the Prime had vanished. Balen didn't mind that; he wanted every mark of Thenlass wiped from the world. Out of sight felt just as good for now.

When they approached, the two women fell silent. Petra raised her chin, not with defiance but with a calm acceptance of what was to follow. Her eyes flickered over Zavrius's body. Balen saw her quiver when she spotted the knife.

Polverc began, "Your Highness—"

"Don't." Zavrius raised the stiletto. He was shaking, his whole arm wavering like it was reflecting the state of his will. The woman quieted and Zavrius dropped his arm. It was a heavy thing, that anger. Balen could tell. If Zavrius didn't keep it in check, he would start to drown.

"The hall is empty," Zavrius said. "Have Thenlass's men accepted the outcome?"

"They've fled," Petra said. Her voice was perfectly even. "There are three servants in the kitchen, but those are mine from Cres Stros."

Zavrius said nothing aloud, but his eyes held an epic. Balen tried to decipher the details. He could see the shape of Zavrius's turmoil, the desperate, fearful anger behind his eyes. The king was trying hard to keep it from his face, but Petra's stare was shaking him.

"Why?" he whispered.

Petra opened her mouth. Her breath caught in her throat—silence.

"Never mind." Zavrius's grip on the knife tightened. Woodenly, he raised it up to her. "Tell me why you deserve to live. Tell me why I should not just kill you now."

It was not a demand. His voice was polluted by fury and despair; he was pleading with her. Begging for a reason to keep her alive.

Petra exhaled shakily. "Zavrius—"

"King Zavrius," he snapped. He swung wide with the dagger, slicing the air. "King. Your betrayal does not change the truth of what I am. Whether you want me or not, I am Arasne's heir."

Petra's calm facade split apart like the skin of a rotten fruit. "And if I had known, I would never have done it!"

Zavrius didn't waver. He frowned at her, shaking his head. "I can't believe a thing you're saying."

"Then make her tell the truth," Balen said.

Zavrius flinched at the sound of Balen's voice. He glanced back over his shoulder, nodded once and threw the dagger to the side. It skidded with a clatter. Zavrius tugged the strap and the lute-harp slipped into his arms. Without hesitating, he began to play.

His fingers conjured a variation of what he'd played the night Balen was made his Prime. Polverc made a soft sound of recognition and crossed her arms across her chest. Petra stood watching him. Neither were resisting. Zavrius shifted the music. The mournful elegy was now stripped of Arasne's arcane arrangements and replaced with something new. The melody was drawn out, in a way languorous, but a staccato rhythm pushed up beneath it and stabbed its way through each beat.

Balen's heartbeat slowed. He grunted to himself, blinking as his body adjusted; the tension and ache of the fight with Thenlass ebbed out of his body. It took a moment for him to realize what was wrong—even if nothing felt wrong. Zavrius's fingers plucked casually at the strings. His face was still and peaceful. The music was a balm for sores Balen hadn't even realized he had.

But Balen knew enough about intoxication to recognize the signs, and he'd spent years affected by Zavrius in more ways than one.

Even when he felt helpless to stop the feeling, even when he could barely muster the want to pull away, Balen forced himself to shake his head. An immediate chill washed over him. He shivered. Very suddenly, he was without Zavrius's influence.

He stepped back toward Mallet and Lance and shook them back into awareness.

Zavrius raised his head, still playing. "Why did you betray me?"

"I thought it was you committing treason, not us," Petra said. "I thought you'd killed for the throne."

A twang sounded: Zavrius's fingers slipping from the strings and distorting the melody. He recovered, let the music swell until another wash of honeyed calm settled over Petra and Polverc.

Zavrius hissed, "Did you think I took this throne because I wanted to?"

"Queen Arasne was less forthcoming than you might imagine. You were always in opposition to your siblings, from the moment my brother drew that line between you. If you were filled with resentment and wanted the crown, it wouldn't have surprised me."

Where Zavrius was attuned to some personal frequency of Petra and Polverc, Balen was focused on him. He saw every slight crook of the king's brow, every tensing of his shoulders. This barely contained rage moving like a gnat under Zavrius's skin. Balen could see flickers of that man Zavrius had told a story about. The killer of his own kin. Zavrius was standing here, and at the same time he was in a field specked with his family's blood.

Zavrius scoffed. "Did you think I killed them for the fun of it?" Then, as if he didn't want her to answer that, he asked, "Are you loyal to the madness that is my brother?"

Petra hesitated. Balen got the sense she was not fighting his influence, but searching, digging for the truth in herself. She looked up at him. Tears glistened unshed in her eyes. It was the most emotion Balen had ever seen from her.

She spoke: "King Zavrius, you are my nephew. You are my blood. But more than that, you are the legacy of the Dued Vuuthriks, the legitimate heir to the crown. An hour ago, I did not know this. Like your Prime, I am loyal to the crown, the rightful ruler of Usleth. Everything in me thought that was Theo until the edict proved otherwise."

Zavrius swallowed. "You thought I'd committed treason?"

"Yes."

"And you convinced Polverc to join you and your so-called just cause?"

"Yes," both Polverc and Petra answered together.

It was quiet for a time. Zavrius played, a melodic canon that repeated often, as if his mind was caught in a loop. He stared down at the tiles, thinking. When he spoke next it was sharp and whispered: "Do you have any love for me?"

Immediate, wholehearted, Petra said, "So much."

Balen could tell he wanted to go to her, to embrace her, but he kept that urge at bay and did not move.

Petra continued, "But I was worried that you wouldn't be able to be a king."

"Why?" Zavrius took a shaky breath. That infallible truth seemed to strike him. So much of Zavrius's family had hated him. Balen could tell he didn't know what to do with his aunt's declaration, or her honesty.

"Because the truth is that leadership is not something that is conferred. It's a responsibility, and you've never demonstrated the capacity for it, much less the ambition. Usleth cannot survive an absent, disinterested ruler." A tear trickled down Petra's cheek and she scrubbed it away. "But I see now that you want it enough to do your best for all of us."

"I want Usleth to thrive," Zavrius murmured. "I want to avoid war. If that means wearing a crown, then that is what I'll do."

Zavrius pushed on with his next question. "And Lestr?" His voice cracked slightly. He cleared his throat. "Did he betray me?"

Balen went rigid. He'd forgotten about that possibility. The muscles in his neck and shoulders went tense as a defensive adrenaline surged through him. Breathe, he told himself, trust your master.

"Not once," Petra said. She smiled sadly, perhaps wishing she could say the same thing about herself.

The rush of near panic lifted, a whiplash effect that left his mind buzzing, filled with the bliss of that revelation. Lestr was not a traitor. This man who had raised him was still to be trusted; Balen's instincts about him were still true. He took a slow, steadying breath.

Zavrius nodded, less fazed. "Good," he said. "Why did he melt the weapons?"

To protect you, Balen realized, just as Petra echoed his thoughts.

"Whether you'd killed your siblings or not, he would have stood by your side," Petra whispered.

The king drew in a deep, gasping breath. He stopped playing. The silence spread, enveloping Zavrius, amplifying his melancholy. Then something shifted in him, a masklike deference consuming this tired, emotional version of him. Balen knew it was that kingly persona again, stepping into place. Swinging to Polverc as he replaced the lute-harp, Zavrius only had to gesture to bring her forward.

"I'm sorry about your niece," he said.

Balen saw a flash of the palace garden in his mind, the body of a woman lying prone as blood dripped from his blade. He glanced up. Polverc's chest expanded briefly, a sharp intake of air she quickly controlled.

"She made her choice," she murmured, dipping her head to Zavrius in deference.

The king scanned her eyes. "Prove your loyalty. Write a list of coconspirators. Mark anyone who will follow Theo not because they believed him heir, but because they share his vision of war."

"My lap desk is upstairs. I'll retrieve it, Your Highness." Polverc curtsied again. Her eyes cut to Balen as she walked past him up the stairs. He had a chance to think how different she was now from the guarded, dangerous woman he knew her to be. Embarrassment had softened her. All it had taken was the edict. A piece of paper with the queen's official seal.

"One more thing," Zavrius called. Polverc stopped her ascent. Zavrius glanced between her and Petra, but he didn't reach for the lute-harp; a test, Balen guessed, of their loyalty. "Where did Thenlass get the ichor?"

Petra and Polverc turned to one another. Whatever passed between them made Petra give a curt nod. Polverc looked down at Zavrius, lips pursed firmly. Balen watched her pale hand grow whiter from the strain of her grip.

"From Shoi Prya," she said finally. Polverc twisted to face them. She laced her fingers together, trying for elegance but displaying only fear. "From here."

Balen felt himself grow cold. His body was stupefied, but his mind scrambled ahead, trying to outrun the heavy fog that came with shock. But the revelation was fast. He couldn't get ahead. Out of reflex he mumbled, "That's not possible."

In the corner of his eye, he saw Zavrius's body sway. The king made a low, crude noise in his throat, before he laughed sharply. He pinched the bridge of his nose and flung his head back with a sigh.

"You're telling me," Zavrius muttered, "that you've discovered another gedrok?"

Not possible, Balen's mind chimed instantly. It couldn't be. The Paladin order—his order—was intricately bound up in gedroks. The search across Usleth had not been a light one. Even during Balen's early childhood, digs, expeditions and entire crews dedicated to unearthing another body had set out and returned unsuccessfully. When the search was abandoned, it had not been an easy decision. If there was another gedrok, he should have been feeling relief.

Balen took a breath. Ichor filled his belly and centered him, calming his nerves. He often fancied he could sense the gedroks; that by wearing their scales and bone he was an extension of the creatures, and with the ichor in his blood, it was a more intimate connection than most could ever reach. But with the palace gedrok nearly stripped completely, and the sanctity of the glade gedrok breached by the Paladins' need, the order desperately needed this find.

Petra spoke with a cutting edge: "Why do you think Thenlass asked for Shoi Prya in the first place?"

Balen turned to Zavrius. He expected to find the king tense, calculating, but instead Zavrius was staring intently at Thenlass's corpse. Zavrius walked to it and crouched. No malice or annoyance tainted his face, only a calm nothingness.

"Very smart," Zavrius told the corpse, then, "Polverc, write me that letter."

"Right away," she said.

Zavrius snapped his gaze back to Petra. "Show me the gedrok."

Petra gave a slight dip of her head. She shifted toward the grand oak doors. "Follow me, Your Highness."

Outside, the morning chill had yet to vanish. Zavrius shivered, making Balen wish he had something to cover him with. But even slinging an arm around him would be unwelcome now. Zavrius was tense.

Petra turned left and waded through the long grass. The sky above her was a wash of blues and the orange of the fleeting sunrise. They followed the outer wall of the reconstructed stronghold until it fell away into ruins. Petra made her way through the toppled archways and crumbling pillars.

"Balen," Mallet hissed beside him. "What's going on?"

"A gedrok?" Lance asked, coming up on Balen's right. The brothers knocked both shoulders against him, somehow avoiding the metal points on his pauldrons.

"Weren't you paying attention?" Balen kept his eyes on Zavrius.

"But if there's another gedrok," Lance said, ignoring Balen's question, "isn't that a good thing?"

Balen gritted his teeth. He didn't know, and he hated not knowing. It could mean great things for the Paladins—but with Theo at the helm, it could be their end.

He could only say, "Depends if someone's gotten to it first—what state it's in."

Lance and Mallet let him catch up to Zavrius, who acknowledged him only with a worried grimace he quickly refixed on Petra.

Petra stopped walking. She had led them to a semi-enclosed section of the ruins. Grass, moss and ivy had burrowed into the stone. The long grass was dewy; Balen breathed in the morning air and the pervading scent of dampness invaded his nose. He paused and turned toward the scent, squinting against the rising sun. To the left, backed up near the intact hold, stood a towering wall with a curved, half-domed roof. A fresco adorned the upper part of the wall, a discolored Paladin combat scene that he glossed over then dismissed. The lower half of the wall was filled by an open archway leading into darkness. The whole thing was out of place somehow; the wall, the archway—the stone was different. This had been built more recently. Sure enough, he spotted Thenlass's symbol stamped into the stone.

"The gedrok is here?" Balen prompted, pointing toward the open dark pit beneath it.

Petra nodded. "It was uncovered during the war." She peeled back thick strands of ivy and led them through the archway and down. Steps had been built, which gave Balen the false impression that this entire underground tunnel had been carved out. But then the slope evened out and the naturalness of the rocky cave became clear. Iridescent mushrooms and crystals glowed, pulsing soft light throughout the corridor. It was tight and cramped. Petra walked forward until she was swallowed by the shadows of a much larger space.

Zavrius slowed his steps and held his hand. Balen took it and squeezed. They walked forward together.

The corridor opened.

"By the bones," Zavrius murmured.

The cavern was an open expanse, a dizzying stretch of darkness punctuated by the intermittent luminescence of thousands of glowworms flickering throughout the cavern. Balen hadn't realized how steep the entrance was, but the hold must have been directly above them. On the cavern floor, crystals protruded from the stone in clusters, mushrooms and underground plants bubbled out of cracks, and the smell of dampness was suffused throughout. A still pool of water filled in the center of the cavern. Half submerged within that was the gedrok.

It lay curled around the edge of the pool. Save for its left flank, which had been peeled back to expose its rib cage, it was untouched. Balen had never seen one so perfectly preserved. Its scales had faded to white. A few crystals ran up its arms. In the light, it refracted all the luminescence of the cavern. Balen watched a wash of color coruscating over the walls. The cave roof seemed to stretch forever above the creature's head.

Lance rounded the corner. A choked noise of surprise fell from his lips.

"Beautiful," Mallet murmured.

After that, no one spoke. Balen could see a puncture wound in the exposed bone, from which the ichor had been tapped. A brief surge of rage flooded him—this ancient thing, this creature whose ichor was mingling with his blood—had been defiled. But no more. They had captured another gedrok from the enemy. He stood taller, telling himself this was a victory. The future of the Paladins was secure. And more than that: the primordial majesty of the gedrok was safe.

No one would degrade it again. Not if he could help it. With his gut twisting, full of tension, Balen made that promise to himself.

He would protect it at any cost.

Balen walked forward, heart thrumming. The gedrok's glassy eye stared at him. He thought, momentarily, that something flashed in it: a spark of life, a glint of recognition. He drew a shaky breath. His armor seemed to hum, like this gedrok's brethren was calling to it. Up close, he could see the peeled-back plane of scale was short and sawn through. The bone was exposed beneath. Some of it was missing.

"By the bones," he spat.

Zavrius stepped forward. "What is it?"

Balen didn't answer right away. He scanned the rest of the gedrok's form, searching—and hissed when he spotted a chunk of bone missing, carved away near the site of the ichor tapping. That rage roiled in him again.

"They've taken more than ichor," he said, casting a glance back at Zavrius, whose face twisted at the sight of Balen's rage. "They've taken scale. Bone. I've never—the disrespect of it—"

"What for?" Zavrius asked, a mounting fear in his voice.

"It's obvious," Balen spat, swinging back to the gedrok. "They're forging arcane weapons."

Saying it aloud made him shiver, but the look on Petra's face confirmed it. Whatever they created from the stolen material would be derivative of the very armor he wore. A mockery of everything he stood for. The sanctity of the gedroks to the Paladin order, the reverence with which they were meant to hold them—it suddenly felt foolish. To know there were people out there willing and ready to trample on everything he believed in infuriated him.

Balen waded into the still pool, ignoring the rush of water in his greaves and sabatons. The iridescent light pulsed as he moved. When he was close, he bowed his head. No matter what Theo thought: the gedrok deserved respect. The creature wasn't dead, not in any meaningful way. Its ichor, its life force flowed through those mad arcanists the way the life force from the gedrok in the glade in Cres Stros flowed through Balen. Its body on his body, its power his power.

"I'm sorry," he whispered to it. He reached out and put his gauntlets against its flank. "I'm sorry for what has been taken from you, for the disrespect with which it was done."

Balen shivered. He opened his eyes. The gedrok's body was quivering, a hum that was echoed in Balen's gauntlets. His hands buzzed, every nerve in them tense and shivering, and Balen found he couldn't pull away.

"Balen?" Zavrius called, voice cracking. "What's happening?"

"Stay there!" he called back. "It's fine! I'm fine."

Forcing panic away, he centered himself. With his eyes closed it was easier to feel the swirl of ichor in his body. Then: a rush of ichor in his hands. The gauntlets thrummed with it, a whirring drone that built and echoed in the cave. The crystals on the gedrok's body flared with brilliant, prismatic light, and suddenly the cavern was filled with it, refracting and splitting the iridescence. Blinded, Balen squeezed his eyes shut. Ichor pooled into his belly of its own accord, and Balen grunted as his head spun with it, a new and buzzing power. The whirring softened. Just as quickly, the cavern was silent again.

Balen panted and snapped his eyes open. He stumbled back from the gedrok, half falling into the water. Arms looped under his own to drag him from the pool; Mallet and Lance fumbled over him, asking him questions he barely heard.

Zavrius shoved between them and pushed them away. The king swung down to kneel beside to Balen, patting him down, searching for injury. Tears sprang to his wide, terrified eyes. Balen's heart jolted. He reached out and put a hand on Zavrius's cheek.

"Zav," he told him, "I'm all right."

Zavrius slowed. He took a shuddering breath and nodded. But when his eyes fell on Balen's gauntlets, he froze. Balen looked down with him.

Tiny crystals had blossomed across the surface of the gauntlets.

Balen's heart raced. All at once, he was hit with a strange, disconcerted tension. The triptych emblazoned on his palace chambers, the mythical power of that dead Paladin . . . Balen clenched his right fist and carefully thumbed one of the crystals. It was lodged in place, not embedded but like it had sprung from the very bone from which the gauntlets had been forged.

Balen tried to pool ichor into them. It came easily, but if he felt different than his usual casting, it was buried beneath the buzz of adrenaline. Slowly, he looked back at the gedrok.

"What happened?" Zavrius asked. "What was that?"

"Wait," Mallet murmured, pointing at them. "That's—"

Balen shook his head. It had been one thing to discuss crystal gauntlets when they'd been nothing more than paint on his chamber wall. Mythical attacks, gedrok-given power . . . With an army no doubt advancing, they needed something like this. But if all of it was myth, if these crystals were little more than pretty ornaments, he didn't want to give false hope.

Mallet seemed to understand and fell quiet. No one said anything for a long time. Shivering, the Paladin focused his gaze on the gedrok. Whatever had passed between them, Balen wasn't sure. But he stood staring, hoping something more could be communicated, some knowledge shared.

Dirt crunched behind him. Petra came and gently lifted Balen's hand up. She inspected the gauntlets with a gentle, near reverent touch. Balen was grateful for that.

The Paladin watched her intently, like the furrows in her brow could tell him what she saw. Eventually Petra breathed deep and looked up at him. "A gift."

Cautiously, Balen drew his hand back. He looked down at the crystals, twisting his hand in the light. "A gift," he repeated, eyes locked on the colors splitting across his hands.

Zavrius turned back to the gedrok. He stood staring at it for a long time. Then, without warning, he spun on his heel and exited the cavern.

Balen rushed to catch up with him. Had he been overcome by emotion? Despair? Fury? But by the time Balen had made it back to the hold, Zavrius had regained his regal demeanor.

Polverc was propped near a table, finishing up her letter.

"Are you done?" Zavrius sidled next to her and whipped the quill from her hand. "Get the horses ready, Balen. And the brothers. I'll meet you outside."

Balen did as he was told and ensured the horses were prepared for whatever Zavrius had planned. The brothers shifted uneasily beside him. Petra lingered by the doorway, watching the three of them.

Zavrius hurried out. Two letters were clutched in his hand.

"What is that?" Balen pointed to the letter. Zavrius hefted both high. "On my left, Polverc's list of traitors. On my right, a letter to Oren Radek."

Balen gritted his teeth, preparing to ask a question he didn't want to. "What about Theo?"

That name halted Zavrius for a moment. He looked down at his feet. "I can't kill him."

"Zav—" Balen spoke firmly, with as much kindness as he could manage. "I'm sorry, but if Theo won't acknowledge you, then he must die."

Zavrius looked down for a moment. When he glanced up again, his eyelashes held his tears, morning dew in the misty morning.

"That's not what I meant," he said, his voice hoarse. He swallowed and held his head high, nodding. "My blood, the blood of my family, walks around and hates me; has a beating heart to hate me with. He has a voice to lead armies with, enough of a mind and a will to turn people against me. I've known my brother all my life. I know what must happen to him. Still, it almost feels good to know I didn't slaughter all of them. Maybe some part of me wanted him to live."

Balen said nothing. He didn't know what to say. He settled instead for what he hoped was a comforting squeeze, but Zavrius's eyes closed with a tired nod; he'd seen some finality in Balen's touch, not the solace he'd intended.

"So I know," Zavrius murmured. "I know Theo must die. But it can't be me. It wouldn't matter that it was self-defense," Zavrius murmured as he pulled away. "It wouldn't matter if there were no witnesses, or a hundred people saw it. If just one person decided I struck him down for the throne—"

"The rumors alone would end you," Balen finished for him. The common people of Usleth had no honor tied to witnesses, not in the same way Paladins did.

Zavrius grimaced and stepped away with a nod.

"We could do it," Mallet said. He slid beside Balen as if he'd only just come upon them, but he wrung his hands apologetically.

Zavrius half turned toward him, brow firm. "What?"

"You wouldn't have to touch him," Lance said. "Not a mark on your name, but on ours. And we're nobodies. It won't matter."

"It will matter," Zavrius said sharply.

"Not in the same way," said Mallet.

"Death always matters. And you are not no one," Zavrius said. Both brothers fell silent. "And if you want it on paper, then I'll make it so. If you want land—by the bones, if you want a title, you shall have it. I want nothing in exchange except for the both of you to live."

Mallet's face crumpled up. "Your Highness . . ." He sounded tense, uncomfortable, like Zavrius had asked him to die. He shook his hand and clapped Lance on the back. "That isn't why we're still here. Not that I wouldn't fancy a nice house."

Lance rolled his eyes and gave his brother a shove. "What will we do then, sirs?"

Zavrius said it for him. "I want you to go to Awha Stad. It's a town near Briym Plait. You'll need to find Oren Radek, the merchant. He has a private militia that helps guard his caravan routes. With them you two will destroy the bridge over the Duro River. It will only slow Theo's army a few days, but that's more than nothing. I know it's dangerous, but I have no one else I can trust."

Lance beamed, and Mallet clapped his hands together, grinning with pride.

"Whatever you say, Your Highness," Lance said, at the same time his brother nearly fell over himself in a bow.

"A great honor," Mallet said, hand over his chest.

"Theo is coming," Zavrius said firmly. "You need to be quick. Balen will accompany you as far as Piron."

The smiles slipped from both their faces. "He will?"

Balen knew instantly why. "I need to activate the Paladin statue at Piron. It will call the Gifted Paladins to us here."

"Of course, Your Highness," Mallet said. He turned sharply to Lance. "Let's go."

They took the letter out of Zavrius's hands and mounted the horses. Balen lingered just long enough to lean down and kiss Zavrius, breathing in the scent of him.

"I'll be back soon," he murmured.

"You better be," Zavrius said.

Balen mounted his own horse and nodded down at the king. Then he nudged his horse into a canter and rode.

The three of them reached Piron in a day. The Paladin statue was treated as little more than decoration. No one stopped him as he got close.

"What do you have to do?" Lance prompted.

Balen glanced at him. He'd only ever studied this; Lestr had lectured them about it, and he'd read books about the call to aid the statues could invoke. Briym Plait's invasion by the empire had been the last time they'd been activated.

"I'll show you," Balen said. At the statue's base was a glyph, a carved symbol that marked this statue as the Paladin for Piron. Every Paladin statue had its own unique symbol. He'd memorized them all as part of his training but had never needed that knowledge—until now.

Balen laid the palm of the gauntlets against the glyph on the base. He centered himself and closed his eyes. His fingers pulsed; the altered gauntlets seemed to shiver when he touched the statue, like they could feel the piece of gedrok lodged within its form. Ichor thrummed through him. He edged it out, letting it leak into the stone. Intent mattered: he let all his frustration and fear and need leave him. Balen looked up and held his breath.

Nothing.

He set his jaw, scanning the statue for any sign of change. He didn't pull the gauntlets away, waiting, hoping for it to ignite.

Mallet looked at him. "Sorry, sir. But what exactly is meant to—"

The statue rumbled. Light erupted from it, a column of pure prismatic light that blasted into the sky. Balen staggered back from it as townsfolk yelled and pointed in awe and fear. He craned his head, watching as the sky filled with light in the shape of the Piron glyph. Then, more murmurs; Balen swung to see another pillar in the distance, shuddering to life as another shot up. The glyph of Piron blared in the sky. In both directions, from Cres Stros to the border, Piron called the Gifted Paladins.

"Incredible," Mallet exclaimed with a laugh, clapping Lance across the back. He spun his head between the two paths of light. "But won't this trigger the Paladin in Briym Plait, too?"

"Theo will know where we are," Lance whispered, happy expression wilting with the realization. He took a shuddering breath. "He'll know what's happened to Thenlass. Your Primeness—"

"I know," Balen told them. He turned and placed a hand on both their shoulders. "It's a challenge as much as a call to action. We fight Theo on our terms, at the place we just killed for."

They nodded at him, both of them plainly trying to stamp down their fear. Balen squeezed each of their shoulders; neither of them were willing to run now. Balen pulled them in for a brief hug.

"What's going on?" a woman called from a growing crowd. She shivered when she saw him. "You're a Paladin. Is it war?"

Many of the villagers were gathering near the statue. Balen saw panic on their faces, a memory of war and invasion filling up the sky. He pushed in front of the brothers and raised his hands.

"This is not to warn of the empire," he bellowed, "but to warn of a threat from within. An army has been raised to usurp King Zavrius, rightful heir to the Dued Vuuthrik Dynasty, as named in an edict by the late Queen Arasne. I have called on the Gifted Paladins to aid in this fight, and now I call on you. Will you bear arms against the usurpers and defend your king?"

He was met by silence. Balen stood with his teeth clenched, scanning the gathered villagers for any sign of movement, any banners of Theo hanging from nearby houses. Then: a man shouldered his way out of the crowd.

"I will!" he yelled.

It was enough to rouse a few others. A brief but wonderful chorus of agreement sounded: ten, eleven people stepped forward, brave and willing to fight for King Zavrius. Balen's heart swelled. He couldn't stop his grin.

To the remaining villagers, Balen bade them send any Paladin to the stronghold. With his new conscripts, Balen prepared for his return. It was here that he'd leave Mallet and Lance to reach Awha Stad and Radek with the letter.

It wasn't lost on him that Oren Radek was to be instrumental to their success—but he could reckon with that later. Radek had defended Zavrius in front of Polverc and Sorbetka, risking the advancement of his station for a man he barely knew.

Balen was grateful for that now.

The brothers readied themselves. Once in their saddles, they turned back to Balen.

"It's been an honor, your Primeness," Mallet said, in a way that was too close to goodbye.

"We'll be back," Lance said. "Promise."

They nudged the horses into a canter. Balen watched until the horizon swallowed them.

 CHAPTER
TWENTY-ONE

Balen didn't return to the hold until nightfall. After settling his new conscripts, he went searching for Zavrius.

Upstairs was a long stretch of what used to be a hallway, but the roof had long since collapsed. Massive arched windows still stood in the stone wall, but the sky above was an obsidian sea. Balen walked the length of the hall. He tugged open creaky doors, hoping for Zavrius. Most of them were out of commission. The few with intact roofs were dusty and decrepit.

A sudden light flared out from beneath the door of a room at the end of the hall, streaking the stone floor with blocky brightness. Balen went to it and pushed the door open.

It was the master bedroom. The suite was enormous, just slightly smaller than Zavrius's Royal Apartments at the palace. A grand four-poster bed with a canopy lay to the left, both the wood and the curtains a deep blue-black. The curtains swelled over the bed, thick and luscious, faintly glinting silver with embroidery. Arched shelving nooks lined the far wall, interposed with geometric leadlight windows. A heap of books and knickknacks was piled on the floor, along with several of Thenlass's robes—Zavrius had started clearing his things out, and clearly gotten bored and stopped. A thick, pale red carpet covered the stone floor. To the right, the room dipped; a two-step drop led to a fireplace. Near it, the lute-harp had been rested atop a pile of neatly folded clothes. In front of the fire was a claw-foot tub, in which Zavrius reclined.

The tub was positioned in front of the fireplace and gilded gold. Zavrius looked more than royal sitting in it; he was something else, an arcane creature radiating beauty.

The fire crackled behind him. Its warm ebb sent light pulsing along his exposed neck. His hair was up in a messy bun. Curled strands ran over his ears, and wisps wound at the base of his neck. Balen took a long, slow breath at the sight of him, forced himself to ignore the heated twitch that shot down from his belly.

"I take it from your expression that the Paladin statue ignited?"

"It did." Balen drew himself up proudly. "And I've conscripted a few dozen workers from Piron to help build fortifications."

"Impressive, Paladin. But don't let your victory allow you to forget your station. Don't you know you should announce yourself in the presence of the king?" Zavrius purred.

Balen walked to him, clenching every muscle in his body. Zavrius had his legs up on the edge of the bath. He uncrossed them as Balen drew closer, smiling when Balen's gaze drifted.

Balen cleared his throat. "Forgive me, Your Highness, for the lapse in protocol. Only trying to get my bearings. I didn't realize I'd be so lucky."

"Lucky?" Zavrius prompted. Balen raised a brow and gestured down to Zavrius's naked form. That earned a laugh. Zavrius stretched with a happy sigh. "I suppose you are. In any case, you can rely on my bearings." He grinned at Balen. "This is not the first time I've visited Thenlass's stronghold."

Balen cast a furtive look back at the bed. "Hopefully the first time you've visited his room."

Zavrius snorted and pressed a flexed hand over his heart. With his usual dramatic flair he proclaimed, "What are you talking about? Clearly, he was just my type."

Balen raised a brow. This good mood felt intoxicating. All the nervousness of what was to come, all the pressure that had been bearing down on him that day—it all started to ebb away in Zavrius's presence. Zavrius had the two-fold power of riling him up and calming him down. Balen breathed deep. "Just your type?" he prompted. "What's that? Old?"

"That's right." Zavrius gestured to Balen's forehead. "You only have a year on me, and you're as lined as plowed land."

Balen fought the urge to reply with something filthy. Whatever passed over his face gave him away. Zavrius put his tongue on the edge of his canine, grinning, seemingly pleased with his reaction. He sat up suddenly.

"Bathe with me."

Balen exhaled. His hand shot up to his armor, ready to pop the arcane clasp, even as his mouth feigned protest with, "Can I fit?"

"Where?" Zavrius whispered. He twisted and leaned on the edge of the bath, nuzzling his chin against his arms. "In the tub, or in—"

Balen's cuirass clattered to the ground. Zavrius laughed, breathless. Balen stripped out of the rest of his armor and clothes and stood there, looking down at Zavrius and himself. Gold-flecked blood and grime covered his chest.

"Hm." Zavrius's eyes lingered low. He grunted, seemingly satisfied, and drew his legs up under his chin. With barely enough room to get in, Balen edged into the tub.

A layer of dirt lifted off his chest the instant he hit the water, which made Zavrius snort. He exhaled as the warmth covered his body, and sucked in a sharp breath as Zavrius's foot skimmed somewhere it shouldn't. Zavrius smiled and drew his foot away, using it to stroke the side of Balen's thigh. The coy look in Zavrius's eyes made Balen's stomach flip—he tried to expel his nerves with another exhale. He broke eye contact and spent some time washing, splashing his face with water. Their legs brushed against one another.

Balen's heart thudded. He loved this—but it was more than a little cramped.

"Zav," he began.

"I know," Zavrius laughed, shifting to give Balen the space to stretch his legs. Then Zavrius crawled onto him. He put all his weight on Balen's chest and leaned forward.

"Better?" he asked.

"Much."

Balen reached up, running a finger across Zavrius's cheek. The king knocked his head against him with a smile. Up close, he was more beautiful than ever. Balen's eyes lingered on the plump curve of Zavrius's lips, the way his eyelashes grazed his cheek, the freckle forming under his right eye. Maybe it was because Balen knew Zavrius was his, that the need he had for the other man was reciprocated. Or maybe this was just the first time in days he was seeing Zavrius without his kingly demeanor. In any case, Zavrius was beautiful: a sun Balen would gladly go blind to stare at.

"I love you," Balen murmured against Zavrius's forehead.

Zavrius splayed a hand against Balen's chest, nuzzling closer. "I love you, too."

His eyes glinted golden brown with the firelight. The look in them was so warm Balen felt an overwhelming prick of emotion at the corners of his eyes. Zavrius smiled, shifting to slip the top half of his body over the edge of the bath. When he drew back, he had a small decanter of red wine.

"I've been saving this, waiting for you. Letting it air," he whispered, taking a sip directly from the bottle, which was at least a quarter empty.

Balen raised a brow and motioned for it. "I'll pretend I believe you," he said, taking a sip. He took a few more for good measure. Phantom touches from the young king pricked along his skin, spurred on by Zavrius's familiar, heavy-lidded gaze.

Balen carefully placed the bottle outside of the tub. As soon as he settled again, Zavrius leaned down and pressed their lips together, nibbling at his bottom lip. Balen ran his hand into Zavrius's curls and firmly pulled him closer. They both ducked in for another kiss at the same time and their teeth collided in a clack that made Balen laugh, expelling all that giddy warmth stinging through him. Zavrius laughed too, knocking his forehead against Balen's softly, staring contentedly down at him.

"Didn't we do something like this once?" Zavrius asked. He widened his legs and straddled Balen properly. Water dripped from his shoulders as he slipped a hand over Balen's chest. He palmed the downy curve of muscle and firmly pressed along Balen's stomach. "Bathtub and all?"

Balen remembered with a low, lusty noise. The memory collided with this moment; Balen arched at the touch, body twitching as Zavrius's hand grazed the nearby skin.

"Remind me," he said anyway. Zavrius leaned in and kissed his throat, thumbing the head of Balen's cock. It throbbed beneath the touch. Balen breathed in, sharp, and dropped his head back against the bathtub's edge.

Zavrius continued to thumb him. He stroked the length of him, achingly slow with his movements, far too gentle. It was frustrating. Balen eagerly hitched his hips to encourage a quicker pace, hands gripping Zavrius's thighs.

"Be patient," Zavrius told him. And then, with unmistakable glee, he added, "That's an order."

Balen's breath caught. A raw sound choked out of him. Never before had Zavrius used his station like this, but Balen found himself unable to disobey; he fought himself and loosened his grip, tensing the muscles in his neck to keep from begging.

"Aren't you a good Paladin?" Zavrius purred, firelight gleaming on his canine.

"Zav," Balen sighed. He watched Zavrius work him through hooded lids, involuntarily rolling his hips toward Zavrius's hand. All this teasing was making Balen flush; the heat from the water flooded his head, and the pooling warmth in his belly was becoming a steadily growing pressure in his spine.

Zavrius pressed his own arousal against Balen's stomach, still moving at that maddeningly languid speed. Balen grunted, frustrated, and grabbed Zavrius, dragging his chin down for a kiss.

He felt himself twitch and quiver in Zavrius's hand when suddenly the pressure was released.

"What," he murmured. His eyes fluttered open in time to see Zavrius standing out of the bath. There was a rush of water falling off his body, and then he was out of the tub completely, bending forward to pick a towel off the floor. Balen pored over him, eyes catching on the inviting hollow of his lower back. Zavrius started to dry himself.

"What are you doing?" Balen said, edged frustration leaking into his words.

"Letting you ogle," Zavrius laughed. He considered Balen with a soft, teasing smile. "Let's make this place ours, Balen."

He flung the towel over one shoulder and reached up to undo his hair, moving toward the bed. Balen watched him wrench the pins free. Dark curls spilled over his shoulders. Indolently, Zavrius pushed his fingers into his hair, looking back at Balen with a sly glance. "Are you coming?"

It was only when Zavrius turned away again that Balen realized he was gripping the edge of the bath with white-knuckled fingers. Then, Balen was out of the water and drying himself with a towel he was trying not to trip over. His heart was on the run again as he followed Zavrius, still drying himself down. Before Zavrius reached the bed, he spun around and tore the towel out of Balen's grip. He thudded against him, pulling him down into a messy kiss, the palms of his hands poised on Balen's pelvis. He brushed their bodies together. A glimmer of arcane power mixed with his arousal; he felt the burst of ichor tingle through his body, eager and electric.

As Zavrius pulled away, Balen gave a woozy exhale. Zavrius grinned. Eagerly, he walked Balen back until his legs hit the bed. Balen let himself fall, precum smearing his belly when his cock toppled onto it. He glanced up in time to see Zavrius's body jolt at that sight, a little moan dripping out of him. Balen pushed himself farther up the bed, positioning himself among a set of lush pillows as Zavrius crawled onto him.

He dropped himself on Balen's chest and kissed him, lavishly, tongue dipping shallowly in his mouth. Balen grasped the back of his thighs and pulled him closer. The kisses were different from the ones they shared in the tub: more pressure behind them, a potent intention. Their bodies grazed together and Zavrius shuddered, a reaction that made Balen reach up and tug back Zavrius's hair, grip firm.

"Ah," Zavrius whimpered. His teeth skimmed across his lip, and Balen felt the slick head of his cock twitch at the sight.

Balen wanted him. No use in fighting that; he wanted him, felt a roiling urge in his body he was barely keeping at bay. He opened one eye and scanned the bedside table— audibly groaned when there was no oil lamp to steal from.

Zavrius laughed and reached into the pillows behind Balen's head. The movement pushed his shoulder into Balen's nose; Balen breathed him in, running his hands along Zavrius's back.

When Zavrius sat upright, he had a small crock of oil in his hand.

Balen froze, barely comprehending, then emitted a surprised laugh, half sitting up. "What?" he chuckled. "Where?"

"Pilfered from the kitchen," Zavrius said proudly. "I went for the wine, initially, but . . . then I thought . . ."

Balen swallowed, imagining exactly what Zavrius had been thinking about. Zavrius put the jar on the bedside table and unscrewed the lid.

"And it was such a bounty you had to hide it under a pillow?"

Zavrius smirked. "I didn't want to embarrass myself, in case you weren't in the mood."

"You didn't have to worry about that."

Zavrius's eyes raked over him, the fingers of his left hand curling around the head of Balen's cock. He slid themt gently over the slit, pressing the pad of his thumb against another welling bead of precum. "Oh, I can see that."

Balen snorted and threw his head back against the pillow. He turned to reach for the jar, but Zavrius slapped him away. Balen groaned when the pressure of his touch disappeared from around him. But then Zavrius reached over his body and scooped oil onto his own hand. Staring intently, he sat up, straddling Balen as he stroked the slick oil up and down his index and middle fingers, coating them fully. He reached down and covered Balen with gentle strokes that only made him hungrier.

"Oh," Balen gasped, enjoying the look on Zavrius's face at his vocalization.

Sinking his fingers in the oil again, Zavrius rolled back onto his knees. His smile was bright and tinged with longing—he knows, Balen thought, exactly what he's doing—and reached around himself. He tilted his head to the side. Balen couldn't see the specifics of what he was doing, but he saw the reaction; furrowed brows, a stilted gasp that transformed into a moan. Soft hitching sounds escaped him as Zavrius gradually tipped his head back, exposing the stretch of his neck.

"Do you like the view?" Zavrius asked. Before Balen could answer, Zavrius gave an eager, indulgent moan.

A feral desire shot through Balen's body. Balen's hands found their way to Zavrius's hips. He rocked them gently, an anticipatory motion, hands gripping and flexing as the heat of his own erection started to make him desperate. Balen slid himself over the hot skin of Zavrius's stomach. Then he couldn't take it anymore; he reached around and urged Zavrius's fingers out, replacing them with his own.

Two fingers slid in easily; Zavrius gasped, then relaxed, pliant and beautiful.

"Ah, Balen . . ."

Balen propped himself up and drew Zavrius forward hungrily. His fingers were slick and warm, pumping in and out. Zavrius thrusted back against his fingers, a muffled whine sounded over the wet noise of Balen's movement and heavy breaths.

Balen looked up. "Kiss me."

Zavrius moved with his eyes closed and made a sound against his lips, a breathless keening noise Balen caught in his mouth. Balen added another finger. Zavrius rolled forward with a sharp, loud whine, both hands collapsing onto the bed to stop his fall.

"Fuck," Balen said, because there was no other word for how overwhelmed he was by the sight of Zavrius like this.

Zavrius smiled, breathless, and put a hand on Balen's chest. Carefully, Balen slipped his fingers out. Above him like this, Balen dragged his eyes over Zavrius's body: the firm chest, slightly soft stomach, twitching erection—it was all too much.

"I want you," Balen growled. Zavrius's cock jumped at the sound; he bit his lower lip and laughed, swaying forward and positioning Balen's erection against him.

"Take me, then," he whispered. With great care, Zavrius lowered himself down.

They both moaned. Zavrius curled forward, both hands resting on Balen's chest. Balen clenched Zavrius's thighs, breathing unsteady as Zavrius's body enclosed him. A tight and welcome warmth; there was no resistance save for a slight tensing as Zavrius took the length of him. Zavrius's chest expanded with a deep breath. His head fell back, body clenching with a lusty sigh.

The sound drove Balen mad. He pulled Zavrius down into the cradle of his hips, firm and eager, eliciting a pleasured yelp. Zavrius's head fell forward, shoulders heaving, shuddering with pleasure.

"Patience," Zavrius said, one hand pushing firmly against Balen's chest as if to keep him still. Zavrius drew up on his knees and brought himself low, dragging himself along Balen's length with a slow and deliberate pace.

"Zav," Balen grunted, squeezing his eyes shut. He briefly tried to do as Zavrius bid him, keeping his grip firm and steady on the king's thighs. But it was as if Zavrius intended to send him insane with frustration—he drove his hips up, craving him, but was stopped by fingers digging down into his chest. Zavrius would make him endure that agonizing pace.

"You have no reserve, Paladin," Zavrius hummed. Balen caught the wide-eyed gleam of his grin; he knew he was being goaded. But he couldn't stop it. Balen wanted him desperately, needed him—and was finding fewer and fewer reasons not to beg for it. Then Zavrius teased him with a searing twist of a nipple. Balen hissed in surprise.

He flipped them: a fluid, strong turn that propelled Zavrius into the pillows with a slamming thrust.

"Oh, fuck!" Zavrius's moan was high-pitched, needy. With a wobbly gulp at the change of position, Zavrius wrapped his legs around the Paladin's waist. His fingertips dug into Balen's shoulder hard enough to bruise. Balen stared down at him, affectionately stroking his thigh, feeling his muscles clench around him eagerly.

"Well?" Zavrius challenged, low and impatient. He poised his fingers on Balen's shoulder. "Are you going to—"

The words clipped off at Balen's first heavy thrust. Zavrius's openmouthed moan pulled Balen forward; he rocked onto his hands and buried himself deep. Zavrius twitched and panted, bucking his hips.

"Fuck," he whined, and Balen pushed his fingers into Zavrius's hair for grip to drive into him. As he dropped his head low over Zavrius's chest, the room filled with the sound of their shaky pants and firm, wet thuds. His back and forehead were beading with sweat, but he kept moving, speed climbing so every impact into Zavrius earned a rapturous cry. He squeezed his thighs around Balen's waist, eyes rolling back as he stretched his arms over his head.

Balen moaned at the sight, reveling in Zavrius's shaking body. He loved Zavrius like this. He loved that he could make Zavrius feel like this. With a fervent moan, he slammed into him harder, sweat dripping from his hair as the pace mounted.

Zavrius's voice met the same cadence of Balen's motion. So vocal this time, so eager. "Oh, Balen. Balen."

Balen clenched his fist around the sheets, heart hammering against his chest to the time of his thrusts. He crushed their mouths together fiercely. Beneath him, the king shivered and clenched. Balen gazed down at his desperate, twitching length. Balen's groan was guttural. Flustered, he took Zavrius in his hand, thumbed over the leaking head.

Zavrius's head rolled back, jaw slack as he let himself drop into an intoxicated state. His prolonged moan wavered as Balen pounded into him. Balen's left arm ached with his entire weight as the right stroked Zavrius up and down. On the next thrust, Zavrius's head bobbed up. He was hazy with ecstasy, flushed. His brows crashed together as he stared up at Balen—that stare sent a rush of new heat down Balen's body.

He pulled his hand away and planted himself either side of Zavrius. He stopped thinking of anything else; he let go. Balen threw himself forward, hips surging with new speed. Zavrius's legs spread wider. The sound he made was guttural, and it wasn't long before he couldn't keep upright. He twisted, head bouncing back as Balen hammered into him. Zavrius took hold of his own length.

Balen watched him, smiling. He whispered, "Come for me, Zav."

"I," Zavrius panted, half sobbing, "I can't—I'm going to—"

"Yes," Balen told him, and Zavrius raked down Balen's back as he came, legs locked tightly around Balen's hips. Balen drove into him again and all at once he was coming, bucking and pulsing. Balen rocked forward with a groan, movements erratic as he kept dragging himself through the aftershocks.

Gasping, Balen stared down at Zavrius. He leaned forward for an exhausted kiss. Then Balen shifted. A soft noise left Zavrius as Balen pulled out, warm spill coursing onto the sheets. Zavrius wiggled backward, making room for Balen to crash into the bed beside him. Balen ran a hand through Zavrius's hair. He was watching every quiver of Zavrius's brow, the pleasured exhaustion and droplets of sweat running over his face.

Zavrius stretched, eyes fluttering closed. "I don't think I'll ever get sick of that," he murmured.

"Well, one can hope," Balen said, smiling.

Zavrius snorted and rolled, planting a firm kiss on Balen's forehead. He settled, breath slowing. Balen laced his arms around his waist, holding the king's head against his chest.

Balen clung to consciousness. He stroked the side of his finger along Zavrius's cheek, thinking to himself how beautiful he was, how lovely; that in that moment, there was no army on the horizon, no terrible battle to come.

There was only the two of them in the afterglow, the king and his Prime. Only them.

CHAPTER
TWENTY-TWO

The first Paladin arrived at sunrise the next morning.

Bright prismatic light cut through the leaded glass, splitting geometric patterns across the stone floor. Balen sat up and peered out the window, heart swelling at the dizzying sight of Paladin armor caught in the sun, walking the road toward them. The dreamlike quality to it made him sit there for a moment. But as he blinked away sleep, he knew it was real.

He nudged Zavrius awake. The king groaned against him, groggy.

"You see?" Balen murmured, pulling him close as Zavrius squinted outside. "A Paladin. The first of many. They will rally to you, Zav."

Zavrius looked at him and smiled. "To us," he said, like speaking it would scare the reality away. "The king and his Prime."

It took a week for the Paladins to converge. Very few Paladins were scattered across Usleth. Paladins were a band, and most of them had been stationed at Cres Stros before the battle at the palace. But the straggling way they appeared at the stronghold told Balen the order had been scattered.

That gave them the advantage. Smaller groups meant quicker travel than an army, but even with that advantage, he worried. Balen watched each Paladin walk in and wondered if this was the last. If everyone else had been killed.

He spent the week shoving this brewing fear to the back of his mind and focusing on fortifications. Thenlass's open wound of a hold needed repair—Balen worked with the amassing Paladins and village conscripts to reinforce walls and make defensive obstacles out of spikes, trying to give themselves as much advantage as they could manage.

The more they worked, the more word spread; villagers from Piron and other settlements continued to join. And for perhaps the first time Balen realized how much of this was a nobleman's battle; war would not benefit the peasantry. They craved peace as much as the king did.

When Olia, Lok and Frenyur arrived—Paladins from the very center of the palace battle, Paladins whose lives Balen had feared for—he ran to them on the road. As he grew closer, three bodies became four; shifting from shadows came a man propped up by the weight of the other three.

The man they carried was hefty, hunched forward on his knees. He seemed too exhausted to lift his head. He was still in his armor, but the stockiness of him was too familiar for Balen not to know. Balen's stomach flipped. An angry, insistent panic appeared in his chest.

It was Lestr.

"No," Balen called. He ran to him, helping the others lower him onto the grass. Flecked blood caked his face and neck, and Balen spotted the dents in his cuirass where he'd been pummeled.

"Stop your fawning," Lestr wheezed. "I'm alive."

Balen clenched his jaw. Seeing his master like this made his stomach twist. Every niggling doubt that had been in Balen's mind now disgusted him. How had he ever entertained the thought this man—this man—could be a traitor?

Balen swallowed. "What happened?"

"We went to protect the glade," Frenyur said. He spoke hoarsely, as if saying the words aloud was painful. "Sorbetka and Mordsson launched an attack on the gedrok."

"They were after the ichor," Lok whispered. He looked shaken, still: a green boy after his first battle.

Balen patted him on the shoulder. "How many did we lose?"

No one answered him. The silence grew, mildew in the space between them. It was enough to tell him they had lost too many.

Finally, Lestr said, "I took ten Paladins with me. We were the only ones to survive. But they died securing the glade. Good deaths. The traitors are dead."

Balen nodded. Putting away the brief surge of panic—they were so few that six deaths made Balen's head spin—he took Lestr's hand in his own. Something passed in his master's eye, an emotion Balen had often seen in a mirror. Lestr felt guilty. But this wasn't something to be acknowledged aloud. Balen couldn't imagine the enormity of his commander's shame, to be alive when so many of his men and women were dead.

"Did you take Alick with you?" Balen asked, shifting the focus from his master. Besides, as much as their friendship had been strained, he cared for his brethren. And the last he'd seen of Alick, the palace was under attack. He braced himself. Made himself ready to hear the other Paladin had died.

But Lestr shook his head. "We were separated in the battle at the palace. I only took those closest to me. I'm sorry, Balen. But I'm not sure of his fate."

Balen shook his head and looked out onto the horizon. He thought of Duart, of the others they had lost. Tried to tell himself Alick would be fine. "I'm sure he'll come."

Lestr's big hand patted Balen's. "You did well. You've done so well."

"It's not over yet," Balen said, struggling with the compliment. "Let's get you rested."

He helped the Paladins bring Lestr into the hold. Petra knew enough about wounds to patch him up. But when she heard what had happened, her face darkened. Was she thinking about the odds, Balen wondered? How few Paladins were left? He watched her eyes fall on Zavrius, standing hunched over a table strewn with maps. Whatever the king's strategy was, Balen hoped it relied on more than numbers.

Turning back to Petra, Balen chose to say nothing to her. Not because he wanted to leave her festering with worry, but because of his own fear. Giving voice to it, speaking aloud the dread of what was to come—even acknowledging the possibility felt like feeding it power.

There was no room for that fear in his heart.

Two days later, Mallet and Lance rode into the hold with Radek and his militia in tow.

Eighty people arrived, some on horseback, but most on foot. Mercenaries had been repurposed to protect Radek's shipment, all of them well dressed in doublets and fine tunics, like Radek was plying his wares as much as rallying to the king. Briefly, Balen worried they wouldn't be up to the task. But he knew Radek had carved a small empire for himself in lower Westgar, and he had a reputation for seeing goods arrive safely.

Whether he'd been driven here by loyalty or the yearnings of his heart—or cock—Balen decided he didn't mind. They needed Oren Radek.

The man in question was on horseback, a beautiful black stallion saddled with a decorated blanket in Zavrius's colors. He wore a beard now—which only made him more handsome, Balen noted sullenly—and a short half cape over a green velvet tunic.

Overdressed, Balen thought, and realizing only half a breath later he'd unconsciously stood straighter.

Zavrius came out to greet them. The king wore a sleeveless black kaftan, something of Thenlass's he'd altered to suit him. With his arms exposed, Balen turned his attention to the taut, sinewy muscle of his arms.

"Stop ogling," Zavrius ordered with a smile as he came to stand by the Paladin's side.

"You didn't mind it so much the other night," Balen teased. He let his finger graze the side of Zavrius's hand as they stood side by side, watching these troops amass to defend him. Balen breathed deep. It felt almost impossible, this moment; mere weeks ago they'd been running for their lives. Now they stood with Paladins and soldiers and villagers willing to fight for the king's rightful place on the throne.

Balen couldn't stop the swell of joy he felt when he saw Mallet and Lance at the head of that small army. But Zavrius felt tense beside him. No joy or relief relaxed his face.

He leaned over to Zavrius. "What are you feeling?"

"Too much," Zavrius murmured. "All kinds of fear and all kinds of pride. If you want to add yourself in that mix— the love, the desire—well. It's a wonder I'm not stark raving mad." He smiled, giving Balen a sly smirk, but it slipped a little as something in his mind dislodged the happiness. He frowned. "A lot of fear, Balen. I kept dreaming he was coming back from the dead, and now he is."

Balen gave the king's hand a covert squeeze. With his eyes trained on the approaching Radek he said, "Theo will not touch you. I promise you that."

Balen recalled the promise he made on the night he'd received the gauntlets, the way Zavrius had snubbed it. But this time when Balen made a pledge, Zavrius let him honor it.

"Your Highness."

They were interrupted by Mallet, who had his head bowed. Balen grinned at him, gripping his shoulder with happy relief.

"Well done," he whispered.

Zavrius nodded between the brothers. "Thank you. And the bridge?"

"A bit of rubble in the Duro River, as Your Highness ordered." Positioned between the brothers was Oren Radek.

He was ruggedly handsome, his dark skin glowing under the Shoi Prya sun. Hand over his heart, he bowed low.

Zavrius nodded. "Thank you, Radek. This won't go unrewarded."

Balen spied a twitch run through Radek; the man glanced up and met Balen's fierce gaze before he threw his head down again.

The king half rolled his eyes at Balen's jealousy. He mouthed the word "Unbecoming" at him and spun to the nearest Paladin to organize Radek's militia. Mallet and Lance took the horses to rest.

"Radek," Balen said with a nod, urging the other man to stand. He put out his hand. "Thank you for this."

Radek considered Balen's gesture as if he'd gone and poisoned his gauntlets. He glanced up at Balen, brow raised. "I thought you considered the likes of me touching your armor the height of rudeness."

"I've had time to reconsider my position," Balen said. When Radek didn't move, he said, "By the bones, just shake it, Oren."

Radek rocked forward and clapped his hand into Balen's. "All right, Paladin." And then, a beat later, scanning the stronghold's fortifications, he added, "We're going to win this one, right?"

Balen let go and turned to look at the stronghold. Zavrius's banner flew high; men and women walked the ramparts, watched from the parapets, worked on the final modes of defense they had planned.

From a crumbling laceration on the land to the beating heart of an army in less than a week, the stronghold now seemed alive. Balen breathed deep and felt some of that old confidence return to him.

"That's right, Radek. We're going to win."

≈≈≈

The sky was gray when Theo arrived, the sun threatening to sink behind the horizon.

The scouts rode back at midday, hollering about the approaching army, and everyone moved to ready themselves, tense and waiting as the usurpers approached.

Balen put the king on a parapet and ordered Lance and Mallet to guard him.

"I love him," Balen told them, "so make sure he keeps his pretty head."

Before the army had even come into view, Balen felt them. The crystals on his gauntlets buzzed, reacting to the arcane energy leaking into the air from the incoming horde. Balen stared at the crystals. A thrum of power burst through his hands. He flexed the gauntlets, feeling the strength in them.. Petra had called this a gift, and he was not about to waste it.

He joined the rest of the Paladins on the ground in front of the hold. After a quick glance back at Zavrius, safely stationed on the parapet above, he turned and watched Theo's army approach. They stopped a fair distance away, brazenly waving Theo's banner: a dark block on the earth.

Two men walked out from the army. The first was taller than Balen, broad shouldered with bulky muscle. He'd had curls before, the same thick hair that Zavrius had, but he'd since cut it short against his scalp. A steel crown sat on his head, sharp points glinting as rays of sun slipped through the clouds. Balen scanned him. He was dressed in a messy sleeveless tunic that looked like he'd ripped the arms off it himself. Something dark stained it in parts, turning it from green to a blotchy brown. Balen seethed. He knew the way a prince walked. He knew the kind of cultivated ego that allowed a man to stride so happily toward their waiting army. Still, there was clearly something under Theo's skin, puppeting him a little differently from his princely self. This man had tasted death and become incensed at the sight of his own blood. This man would destroy the country he claimed to love.

Theo Dued Vuuthrik stood before him, and he was very much alive.

The other man caught Balen's attention next. When he walked into the sun, he lit up; he was resplendent. Fractal colors spread in a starburst and made the grass glow. Balen saw the same thing behind him, dotted throughout Theo's army. His breath stopped.

Paladin armor did that. Paladin armor.

How many of his brethren had turned? Balen shuddered. Slowly, like he was fighting some resistance pressing against his neck, he strained forward for a better look. Deep down, he knew who it was. But he looked anyway, hoping against hope his mind was making connections from nothing.

It was Alick.

Balen's stomach twisted, ichor, rage and grief blazing in him. But when he spotted a glint from Alick's hands, all the anger left him.

Alick was wearing gauntlets.

"Bastard," he mumbled, clenching his fists. His gauntlets seemed to respond, the crystals in them sparking with arcane power. Part of Balen felt hollow: the gedrok beneath the stronghold calling out for the parts that had been stolen from it without ceremony. Alick wore the defiled creature on his hands.

Beside him, Lestr cursed. "Out of my way," he hissed, shouldering out of the ranks to the head of the army. He had a limp to his leg, and his belly was held together by stitches, but anger drove him. "Out of the bloody way."

Alick half froze when he saw his master, Lestr. His eyes were wide and wet, his jaw clamped tightly shut. Balen read his lips: Alick's mouth opened a fraction to whisper, "I'm sorry."

Lestr laughed, a sharp bark that cut across Alick's piti-ful tone. "Sorry?" he spat. "You're not bloody sorry, you traitor. No. You would've known exactly what you'd done the first time you saw the aberrant fucks this usurper calls arcanists."

Alick said nothing, so Lestr didn't stop. "Stealing ichor is one thing—a big thing, enough treachery to do my head in. And taking from a gedrok without ritual. How fucking dangerous . . ." Lestr shook his head and gestured back to Theo's army, to the masses wearing only steel and plate to wield their corrosive power.

"But no armor, Alick? You let Theo drive half our nobil-ity raving mad?"

"I—" Alick stared at him. He looked utterly lost. Theo came over and slapped him hard against the back. Alick jolted with the force then stepped back from Lestr.

"Now, now," Theo said. "Alick did exactly as he was told. Like a good Paladin would." He smiled and it looked like Zavrius's cat grin corrupted, a thousand times more mali-cious. Balen hated how he could see Zavrius in this man. So much hate was in his throat. He wanted them all dead.

Theo glided his hand across Alick's back and slung his arm over the Paladin's shoulder. "Calm down, uncle."

Lestr scanned his face, a frown slowly forming as he looked Alick over. Loudly he said, "Theo was not Arasne's heir."

Balen's breath hitched. His gaze darted to Alick. The other Paladin flinched, cocked his head. He half smiled. "What?"

Again, loud enough the open field echoed with his voice, Lestr proclaimed, "Arasne made Zavrius her heir."

Balen sought out the reaction, craning his neck to see the Paladins in Theo's army: iridescence dotting the land-scape next to dull armor, shifting uncomfortably with this revelation. He wanted them to step out, to renounce Theo and beg Zavrius's forgiveness. At least the Paladins still had their minds intact. But even when they only turned to one other, wide eyed, asking questions, Balen tried to take it as a victory.

Then someone burst out from the ranks: a woman, green, freshly confirmed at Balen's ceremony. She broke rank and began to shoulder her way toward their line, swayed by Lestr's declaration.

Theo flicked his wrist. An arcanist stepped out and punched forward with a halberd. Unnatural strength pushed the sharp edge through the Paladin's gorget. She stuttered to a stop. Blood ringed her neck and seeped down the patterned grooves of her cuirass.

The suddenness of it startled Balen so much he tilted forward, dizzy with shock. Balen stepped forward. A craving, vicious rage welled in him. Ichor streamed into his hands, called by Balen's impotent will to save her. But she crumpled to the ground, dead.

Balen's reserve came back to him with a shuddering breath, and he stood, rolled his shoulders back. No one else moved from Theo's ranks.

Balen looked to Lestr and saw his master seething.

"You cur," Lestr spat.

As Theo stalked forward across the grass, Balen recalled the righteousness Theo used to have in his youth. Conjuring some memory of Theo watching the Paladins train, Balen remembered how easily displeasure had crumpled the Heir Ascendant's fine features. Theo wasn't just hard to impress. He was easy to dissatisfy. For a noble, a prince's displeasure was little more than nerve-racking. But Theo would beat servants. Humiliate anyone he thought deserved it.

How Balen had ever considered serving him without question, he no longer knew.

"Cur?" Theo snarled. "Who are you, traitor, to stand before your king?"

Lestr didn't reply. But Balen saw a shameful rage overtake him, shoulders hunching forward; to be called a traitor was one thing, but to be called it by Theo—the irony was too much. Lestr was irate. He couldn't keep it from his eyes. Balen's master might have served Theo once, but not now.

Theo backhanded Lestr. A crack boomed as his hand smacked across Lestr's head, reverberated by the stronghold's wall. Lestr spat blood onto the grass.

Balen jolted into a run, gauntlets sparking—but Lestr flung out a hand to stop him. He shook his head. Balen swallowed the urge to disobey and stopped.

"Will you bow to me now?" Theo asked, almost sweetly. He cocked his head, raised his arm like he would tilt Lestr's chin to face him. Lestr shrugged off his touch, his cheeks stained with shame. Lestr's whole body tensed. It wasn't fear though, Balen thought, but a haunted, regretful sadness.

Theo must have seen it too.

"You won't bow to me," the usurper said again. This time, though, his tone was different. Certain. Theo raised an armored hand and slammed it down across Lestr's face. The man crumpled to the ground at his feet. Balen saw his hand twitch toward his stomach. The stitches had split.

Theo stood proud and sneering at Lestr slumped on his knees.

Balen wanted to move. He twitched in place, all the energy crowding into his limbs, urging him to thunder forward. But he made himself stay still. He stared at Lestr, waiting for a signal. He had the awful feeling his master wasn't going to give him one. That what he was watching now was deliberate: an injured man martyring himself to blemish Theo's image. A sacrifice. None of it would matter—not when these arcanists were little more than empty bodies.

In any case, Balen couldn't let it happen. He crept forward, just as Theo nudged Alick's sword toward Lestr's throat.

Balen sparked his gauntlets and readied them. Surely Alick wouldn't do it. Not Alick, not to Lestr. How could he?

The Paladins behind Balen felt the same. Frenyur and Lok appeared in his periphery, readying to run at Lestr's signal.

"Do the honors, Paladin," Theo said.

Balen raised his gauntlets.

Silver crescents surged over Balen's head and struck Theo. Howling, the usurper jolted back as sickle-thin cuts bloomed across his cheek. Balen swerved around. The king stood flush against the parapet's edge, lute-harp raised and furious expression knotted into his brows.

Theo laughed, a high and broken sound. Balen watched him smear a welling bead of blood across his cheek. "How ludicrous you are. A king defending a Paladin."

Zavrius's face twisted in a scowl. Balen heard him softly playing, a tune that carried his words easily to everyone assembled below. "You have it wrong, brother. I'm a nephew defending his uncle. It must be hard to hear, Theo, but I'd defend anyone and anything from you. Especially Usleth!"

Balen knew a signal when he heard one. He sent a prismatic beam hurtling toward Alick and screamed over the roar of the arcane, "Gifted Paladins—attack!"

Balen sprang forward ahead of the army. Both groups moved smoothly, ranks steady and even. The Paladins kept formation even as Theo's arcanists started to split, the zeal of their power overcoming order. Balen ignored them, focused on getting to Theo. Cutting off the head—that's all he could think about.

Before he could get to him, arcanists dashed forward. The battering crash threw Balen backward. He roared and raised his hands, firing a barrage of brilliant arcane shards as cover. He couldn't stop to fight them; Theo moved like nothing was happening. He whispered something to Alick, who nervously raised his sword. Balen shuddered—Lestr was still on his knees.

Driving forward, Balen barreled into the nearest arcanist and burned through him. Shoved the body aside, made space ahead in time to see Lestr raise his chin.

Theo wrapped his arms around Alick and thrust the sword forward into Lestr's belly.

Balen screamed. Prismatic light erupted through him: red hot, angry, searing—a stream of it burst from his hands. Theo saw it and spun, taking Alick with him. The iridescent flames rolled over the Paladin's plate, only faintly licking at Alick's chin. The man yelped and skidded back.

"Balen!" Theo shouted happily. "What a pleasure."

Balen ignored him. "Frenyur! Paladins!" he bellowed, calling for the aid of his brethren.

He cast at Theo, just as one of Zavrius's spinning missiles split Theo's upper arm. All around them, Zavrius's attacks whistled past, bombarding the enemy from his place above them. The usual dulcet tones of the lute-harp were twisted. Zavrius was furious. Zavrius was watching. Knowing this, Theo turned, trying to disappear in his ranks. Alick spun to follow; Balen shot after him, exploding the ground to cut off his escape.

"You're not going anywhere!" Balen yelled.

He risked a glance at Lestr; the man was bleeding, moaning. Paladin armor moved into view and dragged his master out of the battle. Balen shut it down, tried to forget the image and the rabid gust of fear that had nearly felled him. He looked at Alick, let the exhilaration of fury fill him up.

"Alick," Balen roared. "Fight me!"

Theo rolled his eyes. His arcanists moved around them, fighting, unbothered by their presence. "Jealousy is not your color, my friend. But I think you're well and truly my brother's toy now." He held Alick by the shoulder and shook him slightly. "Alick has been loyal from the start, you know. Never had to question who he'd support. Which makes you the ultimate disappointment, Balen." He purred, sounding very little like the serious man Balen had known him to be. "We would have been so good together."

Balen said nothing. In his periphery, he saw the arcanists' behavior change; a group moved to flank Theo.

Balen fought to keep his face blank. Theo ignored his lack of reaction. "Whatever you might think, Zavrius is wicked, Balen, he really is."

That was the extent of what he could take.

"Wicked or not, he is my king." Balen surged forward. The crystals vibrated; a beam of fractal light whizzed toward the arcanists—Alick blocked him, gedrokbone gauntlets deflecting the force of Balen's spell upward into the sky. Then Alick charged his own gauntlets. He fired.

Balen caught the attack in the palm of his gauntlets and sent it barreling back into Alick. The other Paladin dodged, but now they were engaged. Back and forth, the two Paladins exchanged arcane blows, fractal light bursting around them. Shots whizzed passed Balen's ears, wild and misaimed. Balen's head turned as a bolt scraped his cheek and thudded into the ground. He returned first with a carefully focused arrow. It split through Alick's defenses and lodged itself between his cuirass and pauldron.

A strangled cry split the air. The arrow dispersed. Wincing, Alick pulled Theo back to the safety of their line.

Balen cursed. Several arcanists pressed toward him. One, a boy, screamed his youthful rage as he charged forward.

Balen dodged, stepping easily to the side as the young man's sword cut down through the air. The force of the swing took the young man with it; he stumbled forward out of Balen's sight. Another filled the gap. The arcane spilled from the man like blood. He was exuding so much of it, Balen could almost smell it. He met the arcanist head-on. Knocking the other man's fist aside, Balen punched forward savagely, crushing half the man's face. The arcanist crumpled, sword flailing uselessly. Balen felt a crackle of arcane energy behind him—he ducked instinctively. A wide, horizontal swing whooshed over his head. Reactively, he glanced up. The blade above his head danced with a buzzing, electrical energy. A woman pulled back, teeth bared, and hurtled forward again. In the screaming field, Balen twisted, casting three bolts of arcane power toward her. She dodged the first one but couldn't pivot out of the way of the oncoming two, forcing her to settle for a messy backward dive. Too slow. One of Balen's bolts caught her arm. Blood flew out of the wound; she screamed and fell onto her back.

Balen got to his feet and turned just as the young boy came at him again, venting another boyish screech.

Balen didn't have time to think of the morals of it. This arcanist was out of control. But some guilty tug in the Paladin's mind forced him to pull back; he aimed to graze, maim, deter. The boy rushed him, making some chittering, high-pitched sound that sickened Balen. A crackling bolt shot from Balen's gauntlets and skimmed across the iron cuirass, somehow hewing into it. The boy staggered sideways and used the momentum to swing down. Gauntlets buzzing, Balen tried again, shots glancing across the boy's legs. Nothing felled him.

Balen cursed. When the next attack came, just as his opponent darted in, the Paladin raised his leg up and shoved the boy back with a forceful kick. His opponent stumbled onto his back. It gave Balen the time to assess: he drew in a quick impression of the battlefield, of the hundreds of wild arcanists ripping apart their army's formations, and he felt something in him shift.

There wasn't any way out of this that was pretty. And Zavrius was casting from the parapet, waiting for his Prime to secure the throne.

The crystal gedrok flashed in his mind.

His hand spasmed. All along his gauntlets, the crystalline edge glinted and hummed, a droning buzz that undercut his thoughts. The arcane had been a gift to him. Ichor, offered in ceremony as he knelt before a gedrok, now coursed through his veins. He'd had that power for years. But what he felt now, the sheer amount of strength he felt, was something more. Balen shuddered. His gauntlets had been changed. A gift, Petra had called it. A gift from a creature long dead to this world, but whose magic still pulsed all throughout Usleth. Balen took a breath. He felt like he could reach out and pull back the very air.

So he did.

The gauntlets began to whirr, energy sparking from his fingers.

"Fall back!" he called out to his fellow Paladins. "Return to the king!"

There was a brief halting moment of confusion. Zavrius's attacks still whizzed overhead, and the battle was raging, both sides still even. But when he caught Lok's eye staring at the gauntlets, the young Paladin nodded.

"Fall back!" he echoed Balen's order, slashing his way back to the stronghold. Paladins peeled away from their opponents and retreated. Arcane bursts spluttered out from their weapons. The sky brightened with half-abandoned arcane attacks, diverted upward as their casters ran.

Balen shut it all out. Even when a few arcanists broke rank and ran, he let it all pool in him: pure arcane, pure ichor, his crackling will meeting that of the desecrated gedrok in the crystal cave. Arcing branches of power split off from his hands. Balen dropped to the ground, gauntlets pressed into the earth.

Someone dove at him. In the back of his mind, a growing awareness told him it was Alick; raging, wide eyes welling with his gauntlets trained at Balen's neck—

Power flooded out of Balen and into the ground. At first it felt like any casting with the ichor: a force pushing from his belly, drawing on the source in his blood. But then it shifted. His veins felt like fire was coursing through them. Involuntarily, Balen howled. Something wet ran down his cheek. He ignored it, even as the crystals on the gauntlets glowed and cut through the beams of light, refracting the gauntlets into the earth tenfold. The field rumbled, breaking apart from the force Balen was sending through it. Then: screams. A prismatic surge erupted from the soil, a gigantic, consuming orb of light that covered the field. Blinded, Balen squeezed his eyes shut. The last thing he saw was Alick's open-mouth howl that echoed throughout Theo's army.

Balen collapsed. He wasn't breathing—his lungs felt heavy. Desperation clawed at his throat. He opened his mouth, sucked in the sweetest, deepest breath he could. The air felt like hot coals singeing him as it raked over his throat. Balen grunted, noting the shake in his hands. Every nerve in them felt stripped back and raw. Struggling, he dragged himself to his knees.

The field was razed. Everything was quiet. The shock of what had happened, of what Balen had managed, stilled the battle. Theo's army was split, the central forces dust in the upturned soil. Balen knelt there shaking and openmouthed as Theo's remaining forces fled.

He dropped his eyes to the lump in front of him. Half of Alick's body had turned to dust. Balen swallowed and forced himself to stand.

When he turned, he watched the still Paladins and Radek's militia track his stumbling return to the hold. A few let out a rancorous cheer, but Balen raised a gauntlet.

"We can't celebrate!" His voice was nothing but a harsh rasp. "Until we are sure the usurper has died, we cannot celebrate!"

Balen raised his chin, ready to kneel before Zavrius on the parapet. But it was unmanned. The king was gone.

Balen turned to scan for him, and stopped himself, focusing. He limped forward, leaning into a light jog. "Regroup," he told Olia when he got close. He turned to Frenyur. "See to the wounded."

"Sir," someone said, croakily. Lok stood beside him, shaking from the battle. Blood oozed from a cut on his forehead. The look on his face was haunted. Fearful. Lok gulped. "Sir. It's Lestr."

Balen went cold. His master—bloody, moaning on the ground, Alick's sword sticking out of his gut. He snapped toward the hold. "Show me."

A path cleared as they rushed into the hold.

Lestr was lying on a makeshift pallet. They'd left the armor on him, not even tried to tend to what Theo had done to him. Balen set his jaw and dashed forward, heart in his throat. He collapsed on his knees. Hands shaking, he hovered over his master's chest. Lestr was alive, but barely. He was wheezing, hand weakly clamped around the blade of Alick's sword.

"It's okay, it's okay." Balen heard himself speaking but was barely conscious of the words. He gathered Lestr up and tried to support his head. Every part of him ached at the sight of his master prostrate and dying.

Once Balen touched him, it was like Lestr knew he was there: perhaps Lestr's armor, or the ichor in his veins, or some goodness in him, some familiarity. Lestr shifted and opened his eyes. Made to wipe his mouth, like there was something improper about speaking with blood on his lips.

"Balen . . . by the bones, you look like shit."

Balen swallowed a sob. Failing, he felt warm tears down his cheek. Lestr reached up to brush them away. His fingers came away with blood. Balen jolted at the sight, scubbing at the bloody tears on his own face.

"Yeah," Balen laughed. "But a damn sight better than you."

Lestr grunted, laugh choking into a cough. "Mm. It's hardly difficult."

When he spoke, his voice was hoarse. Maybe it was caught somewhere between this world and death. Balen hated how it made Lestr sound: useless, empty. Nothing like how he really was. He grabbed Lestr's hand, squeezed.

"You'll be fine."

"Don't baby me," Lestr wheezed. His voice whistled so badly Balen couldn't pick his tone. "I've seen enough dying men to know."

"Prime, Sir!"

Balen twitched and turned toward the noise. He didn't want to be interrupted, but when he saw Mallet and Lance—without the king between them.

If Zavrius was hurt, if something had happened—

"Where is he?" Balen growled.

"We saw Theo flee the field," Lance gasped. "He headed for the gedrok's cavern long before you pulled that move."

"Well done," Mallet added. "But the king—"

"—followed him," Balen finished for them. He sank his head against Lestr, breathing heavily. Love and honor and a vow made under the moon pulled him to chase Zavrius, to protect him.

But Lestr was dying.

"Let me go." Lestr said it lightly and carefully peeled his palm from the sword in his belly. Balen firmly replaced it, adding the pressure of his own weight.

"You're not giving up."

"You can watch me die," he said, "or you can stop Theo from accessing the gedrok."

Balen stared, frozen, unable to speak.

"Draw your sword," Lestr murmured, nodding to the blade Balen had largely abandoned during the battle. "And protect the king."

Balen wanted his master to say more—say more about himself, about being Prime and his closeness to Zavrius. He wanted some acknowledgment that he had done something right. He wanted Lestr to be proud of him. It was a selfish, human feeling. Balen closed his eyes and squeezed out the brimming tears. When he opened them, he set his face like stone. He wiped the blood away. Then he stood and bowed to his commander for the last time.

CHAPTER
TWENTY-THREE

Balen rushed into the cavern, then pressed himself firmly against the wall.

He scanned the cave, noting the tightly packed crystals and rocks. His hands twitched, like the crystals could sense their siblings. Whatever force had changed his gauntlets was ripe here. Whether that was the gedrok or the cave, the knowledge settled on him. He couldn't cast in here, not in a place oozing arcane power like this. Minutes earlier, such power had razed the field. If he let loose, there was no telling what kind of damage he would do to the cave—or himself.

Balen flexed a hand around the hilt of his sword and carefully stepped inside. The cave was empty: quiet drips, the sound of water—and then the insidious, persistent tapping of something metal against the gedrok's plate. The sound of someone seeking ichor.

Balen rushed forward, scraping the sword from its hilt. "Stop!"

Theo halted, sending a wild glance back over his shoulder.

"Make me." He grinned. The cave echoed with the scraping release of sword from scabbard.

Balen waded into the water, eyes trained on the glitter of Theo's steel crown in the crystal light. Ice and frost crept up the usurper's blade and Theo's face twisted at the raw arcane power traveling through him. No armor to mellow the force. Potent and unstoppable; he would drive himself mad for this. Theo howled and swung down. Balen caught Theo's blade in the palm of his gauntlets. The impact drove him back until his arm was stock-straight and shaking.

Theo put his head back and laughed. "Oh, come on, then. We haven't sparred in some time. Let's see what Paladin training really did for you."

Balen dove forward before Theo finished speaking. Water splashed around them, glowworm lights sputtering out as the surface rippled. They traded blows, driving each other back and forth near the gedrok until they were well away from the head. Theo was fast. He slammed his head forward into Balen's face and lashed out with one foot, trying again to topple him. Balen staggered but didn't go down. Blood trickled from his nose.

"It doesn't matter if you kill me," Theo said, a manic tone overtaking his voice. "A king is always recognized as king; death won't change that."

In the shadows, a voice cut through. "You really have gone mad."

The voice seemed to echo a little, but not in a booming way. Zavrius's voice stuck to the gedrok like meat on its bones, lingering as a spell.

Theo spun and backed away at an angle. He held his sword in the space between Balen and Zavrius. When Zavrius stepped forward, Theo's lip curled back off his teeth. "Hello, you murderous little snake. You are not fit for this."

"Not fit for this?" Zavrius casually shifted the lute-harp into his hands. "Are you sure about that, brother? You should have stayed dead!"

It was a panicked thing to say. Sounded nothing like him.

"You should have stayed in your place!" Theo grimaced and lunged forward.

Zavrius played violently, losing that steadied calm he'd seemed to have. A series of short chords spun toward Theo but missed. Theo retreated farther into the cavern.

Zavrius cursed and readied himself to climb the gedrok. Balen ran up and stopped him. He spun him around and pushed him back against the gedrok's skull.

"Stop," Balen said.

Zavrius opened his mouth to protest, pointing toward Theo's disappearing form to explain himself.

Balen said, "Don't chase him. He has nowhere to go. He has to come back this way."

Zavrius's brow crinkled, but something shifted behind his eyes. "I know what to do," he murmured.

The king grabbed Balen's face and pulled him into a kiss.

"I love you," he said slowly. "So much."

"I love you, too."

They kissed again, then Zavrius pushed him away with force. Balen caught sight of him wiping at his eyes.

"You better not die," Zavrius whispered.

"Me? Please. I just destroyed half an army," Balen said. "But if you die, I'll fucking kill you."

Zavrius snorted and settled. Then he began to play.

The king must have felt the power of this place too. There was an added vigor in his playing, a potency. The compulsion was strong. The crystals resonated with the sound of Zavrius's melody, amplifying not only the volume but the force of it. Balen drew himself close to Zavrius without even realizing he'd moved. And where before he had been able to shake himself from Zavrius's power, now he struggled.

Balen turned himself as footsteps splashed through the water. Theo grunted, drawn forward unwillingly by his brother's playing.

The air moved around the usurper. Cuts appeared across his cheek. They seemed to come from nowhere. Zavrius's fingers made only light vibrations on the lute-harp's strings, a quivering, near-silent sound that droned and echoed. More controlled than Zavrius had ever been. The king struck again, played a quick melody that sent silver-lit scythes spinning toward him.

Theo bared his teeth. Ignoring his brother, he set his dangerous glare on Balen. "You really are the biggest disappointment of this whole affair," Theo muttered. "My brother's made himself your bitch, but what a weak-minded man you are for falling for it. And I'm sure you'll pay the price for that. As my siblings did."

"You never loved him," Balen said. He put a hand on Zavrius's shoulder and squeezed. "You think my love for him will destroy me."

Theo scoffed, breathing heavily. "Not just you. Everyone."

"You think he has no power. You think whatever happened to you out there in Briym Plait was pure luck. He is flamboyant and bright and useless with a sword—everything Sirellius trained out of you—and he's more brilliant than the lot of you combined. What more proof do you need, Theo? The rest of the Dued Vuuthriks are dead."

Theo's face shifted horribly, crumpling into a look of incensed horror. It was enough to break the compulsion. He writhed out of Zavrius's charm and charged.

Within moments, Theo was on top of Balen again. Balen hastily raised his sword. They parried back and forth, Theo tirelessly swinging his blade overhead. Each of his strikes felt unnatural, altered. Each gathered force too quickly, with a speed Balen's eyes could barely track—no doubt abetted by the arcane. And then the brutish tones of his cry were softened.

Music started in the water again.

The lute-harp, gentle, rich, expressive—Zavrius playing a melody somewhere between an elegy and a rally. Balen could sense no arcane flourish, but Theo reacted like he'd been stabbed in the chest. He flew back from Balen with a muffled groan, face twisted horribly.

Zavrius had tried to charm Theo before and failed. But he'd been up against his siblings, cornered and alone. Now, with Theo leaking his arcane, with the refracted power of the cave, the king could easily attune to him. The charm was tenfold.

Balen felt the energy of the gedrok, the resonance of Zavrius's music, and knew he was succumbing all the same. Theo fell shaking to his knees, trying to fight it.

"You're nothing," Theo said, voice straining. "The two of you are nothing. You will be the bitch at his heels while he runs this country to the ground. Destroys everything. Destroys our legacy."

"That's change. Change is destructive," Balen grunted. "But it's not always death."

Theo's brows crashed together.

Zavrius's melody shifted: a violent move to something haunting and mournful. A blatant funeral dirge. The king entombing his usurper brother in the sound.

Balen skidded back. Seeping through Theo's skin were liquid-like flames. They curled out of his skull like smoke, gentle at first, licking at the usurper's skin. Theo screamed and shook, desperate to wrench himself free from the heat, but Zavrius's charm was stronger. His body calmed itself; his eyes popped wide. Balen glanced away. He sucked in a breath. It shuddered in his throat as he looked up and saw—

Nothing.

All of Theo was ash.

It felt odd to acknowledge it, knowing what he had once been destined for. What Theo had once been to Balen. But what he had become, and what he'd planned for Zavrius? It felt fitting that Theo's resurrection should end in him being reduced to a nothingness.

Zavrius staggered to Balen. Together, they climbed out of the pool and leaned against the rocks.

For a time, they sat there in the darkness, hearing nothing but the sounds of their own labored breathing, the flitting beats of their worn-out hearts.

Balen pressed his lips into the back of Zavrius's head. He cradled him like that. Beyond grateful. Brimming with something that felt ancient, a long and steady love.

Then: footfalls in the dirt.

Balen stiffened.

"Do you hear that?"

Before he heard a reply, he heard something else. In the distance, a horn sounded. Paladin-made, carved from gedrokbone, it sung out to him.

It was the call of victory.

EPILOGUE

"I think," Zavrius said one summer morning after breakfast, "I'll go for a walk."

Balen went with him, happy for any stolen moment when Zavrius didn't have to be king. The air was crisp and sweet, filled with the scent of blossoms. They walked out of the hold and down the path toward the gedrok's cavern, nodding at the workers tending to flowers or deep in the construction of the new Paladin forge. Half a year after the battle, and Zavrius had transformed the crumbling stronghold into the bright, new capital of Usleth. It bustled with activity, a lively, growing center for the recovering country. Balen shielded his face from the sun as he stared up at it.

"You've really done so well," Balen murmured.

Zavrius hummed a little laugh. "Thank you. I'm quite adept at giving orders."

The focus had been on restoring the hold, so much of the space outside the gedrok's cavern was still in ruins. But Zavrius liked it there. Something about the beauty of the felled arches and upturned stones, or the arcane lingering in the air. In any case, it was a spot of quiet.

Balen accompanied him frequently. Every time Zavrius needed to escape, to have time away from the policies and dignitaries and all the complex administration that came with running a country, he would slip out with the king. And even though people wanted his attention, Balen could keep Zavrius uninterrupted with the menacing look of his armor and a dirty, stern expression sent to anyone hoping to trap the king in a conversation.

But usually these walks were desperate suggestions Zavrius threw out into the air in the afternoons, after particularly long weeks.

"It's a bit early for this, isn't it?" Balen asked, unable to keep the concern from his voice. One eye tracked the Paladins training up a collection of new recruits. Crystal Paladin armor shone in the morning sun.

Zavrius arched back to stare at the sky. "Oh, I don't know. It's never too early for a respite. Besides, the day is beautiful. Let me enjoy a bit of sun before I lock myself in the office."

"Is that an order?" Balen asked

A spark of something wild flashed in the king's eyes. He raised a brow. "I'm finding my orders are having quite a different effect on you these days."

Balen suppressed a snort, but he felt himself flush with a myriad of memories. "In my opinion, I'm only getting better at following them."

"Stop it," Zavrius warned, canines flashing in a grin. "I've only just finished breakfast."

They walked into the ruins. Zavrius propped himself up against one of the fallen stones and stretched, baking in the sun like a languid cat.

Shoi Prya looked good on Zavrius. The sun had browned him, made him glow with a genuine, internal warmth. Balen liked to think some of that was him, but he knew the place and the peace had helped Zavrius thrive.

Balen watched the king for a time, enjoying the look of him like this. The Paladin briefly closed his own eyes and enjoyed the warmth, but eventually he had to know. "What is it, Zav? You have something to tell me?"

"Not really," the king said. A moment later he rolled his head down low, eyes piercing up at Balen with a poorly hidden glee. "How strange is that? How wonderful? I don't have a thing to tell you. You know everything there is to know."

Balen smiled; by the bones, Zavrius was glorious. Sitting on the stone beside him, he brushed his fingers against

Zavrius's hand, hooking their pinkies together. The king looked down at that connection, eyes soft, smile warm.

Peace was odd to Balen—he'd never experienced the true thing. The threat of war had always been there, that creeping shadow in the corner of his eye. But Zavrius on the throne had quelled that brewing storm.

For six months, the king had rebuilt. He'd put the focus on roads: extended the Royal Highway to reach Shoi Prya and Westgar, and started construction on many smaller laneways to encourage travel between the provinces. Zavrius had improved irrigation, begun building out Piron. A makeshift wooden theater had been erected for entertainment.

And at Awha Stad, he'd built a harbor. Something to give a certain merchant lord an edge over Briym Plait as the main port for seafaring merchants.

Balen had clicked his tongue when he'd read the construction program. He'd tapped the paper against his hand and made sure the king was looking at him when he said, "Radek will be happy. You've made him a rich man, I suspect."

"I've made him a busy man," Zavrius had replied, laughing. "Give it a few years and he might want me dead."

It was slow work, the lot of it, but he was making sure Usleth would thrive. A process of unweaving and discarding old traditions: Zavrius had decided Usleth and the love for war could be unpicked, the energy refocused into better things.

He'd left Cres Stros to Petra, the only one with the mind to untangle the secrets and alliances that knit that province together. They had embraced, once, before she'd left. But something in her letters always made Zavrius smile, and Balen knew whatever hurt was there could be undone given time.

Staring into the hollow of the gedrok cavern, Balen leaned onto his thighs. Zavrius shifted and did the same, curling his back like the gedrok that lay inside. They stared into the darkness unmoving, breathing in the arcane that seeped from it.

Zavrius knocked his head against him, and Balen brought his head down, pressing his face against the king's curls. His hair smelled of sweet oil and the unnameable scent of him.

They stayed like that for a time, leaning against one another.

Zavrius shifted, curls falling over his beautiful face. He glanced up at Balen with a smile that turned devious. "Should we head to town?"

Balen frowned. "Why?"

Zavrius shrugged and stretched. "There are a few old friends I've been meaning to see."

Balen laughed and stood. "Oh, they'll love this."

Zavrius didn't disguise himself, but instead trumpeted his status. He wore a knee-length mustard-and-gray doublet with his circlet, hair loose and cascading over his shoulders. With Balen at his side and a trail of Paladins behind him, they headed to Piron.

The townsfolk who spotted him whispered and bowed politely, some stealing covert glances whenever they could. Zavrius just smiled, though Balen could tell he was still unused to this attention. He was attempting to seed a different culture, pulling the focus from war to Usleth's growth. But he had a nervousness about him when he met with the people whose lives he was affecting.

"Zav," Balen whispered. He squeezed the king's hand. "We can do this."

Zavrius looked at him. The Paladin hoped he saw everything he meant by that: the life he was going to spend with him, the mistakes they would make together.

"I know," the king said with a smile. "How lucky am I?"

At a two-story building, a wattle-and-daub stand-alone near an oak tree, they stopped and knocked.

A big man wrenched open the door. "Oh, shit, Your Highness. Is everything all right?"

Mallet clasped his hands together. In the distance they heard the muffled repetition, Your Highness? and the sound of Lance bounding down the stairs.

"Come in, come in!" Lance beckoned, dragging Zavrius over the threshold. Balen gave a nod to the Paladins and left them outside.

The brothers' house was filled with character: knick-knacks, papers—the marks of two people still trying to find their place in the world. Zavrius had given them the house and coin to do what they wanted, but for now they only knew they wanted to stay. And so they did.

"You should've given me some warning," Mallet hissed as Lance drew the king down the hallway. "Place is a mess."

"He's Zavrius," Balen said with a laugh. "He loves mess."

The kitchen smelled of bread and something sweet. They bundled up together at a tiny table and ate, talking, sharing stories. A moment for Zavrius to be human, for the lot of them to reminisce.

Zavrius laughed and made the Paladin turn; he hovered on the king's wide, joyful grin and thought to himself how he had never loved anything more.

Balen had put himself between Zavrius and the world. They'd caught each other in motion, stopped each other's fall.

And every day with him Balen heard that victory call, the gedrokbone horn like a whispered echo in his mind, reverberating and reminding him of all of it: every moment he'd had with Zavrius and every moment yet to come.

ACKNOWLEDGMENTS

Reforged began after I shelved a completely different novel. Given the opportunity to write something new, initially as a mentorship with Blind Eye Books, I was drawn to the things I love: Dungeons & Dragons, fanfiction, danmei and men. I wanted to write about love, to recognize that a genre so often looked down upon—primarily because it appeals to women and queer folk—is often packed with true human tenderness. I hope this book has shown that.

First and foremost, I owe it all to Nicole Kimberling, my incredibly dedicated and lovely editor. She has led me through the hardships of writing and offered immensely invaluable insight. Her belief in my work and her willingness to share her knowledge to grow me as an author is beyond belief. I will be eternally grateful to her and Blind Eye Books for seeing something in me.

I must thank Maeve Lysaght for passing my work on to Blind Eye Books and introducing me to Nicole Kimberling. Thank you for seeing something in that other manuscript and thank you for passing it on. That decision has helped my craft develop greatly.

To C. S. Pacat, who interrupted an anxious ramble to tell me that if I wanted to be a writer, I should simply write: thank you. To the friends I made during the Writers Victoria Fantasy Novel Intensive in 2017—namely Jake Corvus, Alex Dupriez and Tchan Cua—thank you. You have let me dart in and out of your lives for years with questions and always been so kind with your answers.

I must thank Pamela Freeman for her teachings and endless support. I've been very grateful for her advice and insight. Thank you to James Winestock and Amelia Wagg, my writing siblings. You always help me see the best in my work.

Thank you to dear friends: Chrissie Hague, Ellie Taylor, Ruby Rooke, Serena Hack, Jemima Gulliver, Madeline Roche, Evelyn Robson and Gemma Driscoll. You have listened to me wax poetic about this dream for years. Not once have you ever mocked me, doubted me, or done anything other than believe in me. How incredible is that? How unlikely? You are all true friends, and I'm so lucky to have you.

To my new friends Rebecca Deveaux and Bronte Marie: I can't believe I have to acknowledge TikTok, but what an incredible tool for finding friends. I'm excited to go on this journey with two such wonderful writers.

Jullie Dillon, thank you. Your work is the stuff of dreams and you make my heart swell with your depiction of Balen and Zavrius.

Daniel Wang—soul mate, chaotic gremlin love—I won't embarrass you too badly. You asked me why I would put you in my acknowledgments, which says a lot about the selfless person you are. I will say this: Thank you for helping me. You don't realize the extent of what you do.

To my parents, Martyn and Maria: Every friend of mine who has ever met you tells me I am lucky. They don't know the half of it. It is a rare thing to have parents who will support you so entirely no matter what. You trust in me, and you celebrate every step I make toward the dream, and you give so much to help me make it happen. Thank you eternally.

Finally, impossibly, I must thank Zavrius and Balen. I love you as much as you love each other. Thank you for being my firsts.

ABOUT THE AUTHOR

Seth Haddon is a queer Australian writer of fantasy. He is a video game designer and producer, has a degree in Ancient History, and previously worked with cats. He lives in Sydney with his partner and their two furry children. Some of his previous adventures include exploring Pompeii with a famous archaeologist and being chased through a train station by a nun.

CPSIA information can be obtained
at www.ICGtesting.com
Printed in the USA
BVHW040036100622
639357BV00003B/4

9 781956 422009